At Home by the Sea

PAM WEAVER

Published by AVON
A division of HarperCollins*Publishers* Ltd
1 London Bridge Street
London SE1 9GF

www.harpercollins.co.uk

HarperCollins*Publishers*
1st Floor, Watermarque Building, Ringsend Road
Dublin 4, Ireland

A Paperback Original 2021

First published in Great Britain by HarperCollins*Publishers* 2021

ISBN: 978-0-00-836621-6

Typeset in Minion by Palimpsest Book Production Limited, Falkirk, Stirlingshire
Printed and bound in UK by CPI Group (UK) Ltd, Croydon CR0 4YY

MIX
Paper from
responsible sources
FSC
www.fsc.org FSC® C007454

This book is produced from independently certified FSC™ paper
to ensure responsible forest management.

For more information visit: www.harpercollins.co.uk/green

... from birth, Pam Weaver trained as a nursery nurse
... in children's homes, premature baby units, day nur-
series and at one time she was a Hyde Park nanny. A member
of West Sussex Writers since 1987, her first novel, *A Mother's
Gift* (previously published as *There's Always Tomorrow*) was the
wi... in the Day for Writers' Novel Opening Competition
and was bought by HarperCollins Avon. Pam's novels are set
in ... ing during the war and the austerity years which
... Her inspiration comes from her love of people and
... ries and her passion for the town of Worthing. With
... n one side and the Downs on the other, Worthing has
... ring of small villages within its urban sprawl and in
... ses tightknit communities, making it an ideal setting
... nodern saga.

*The book is dedicated to the memory of
David Procter 1936-2020*

*A man of great faith who was a wonderful
example and a true friend.*

One

February 25th 1947

Izzie started and sat up in bed. What had woken her up so suddenly? The room was deathly quiet. She strained her ears but all she could hear was the sound of her sister's rhythmic breathing as it filled the chill night air. As her eyes scanned the darkness, she heard muffled voices coming from her parents' room across the small landing of their two up, two down cottage. Tossing back the covers, she shivered as she tip-toed towards the door and leaned her head against the wood, her short plaits falling over her shoulders. Her heart sank. They were arguing again and her mother sounded upset. She frowned crossly. Oh, why did he have to come back? Everything had been all right until *he'd* turned up again.

Everybody in the street had been so excited for them. 'One of the last of our brave boys to come home,' Miss Grey, her teacher, had said. 'You must be so proud of your dad.'

There had been parties and people calling by with their good wishes and gifts. Her mother seemed embarrassed by all the fuss but Izzie had been carried along by the euphoria of it all. The grocer had brought a box of food, the butcher had sent over a lamb chop and a couple of rabbits wrapped up in newspaper. For a week or so, it was a time of plenty, a time of fun and laughter, but as the days went on, it wasn't fun anymore.

Her father was almost a complete stranger to her. Izzie had been seven when he'd gone to war and her sister was just five. Izzie remembered him coming home on leave for a few days (Linda didn't) but when he went back they never heard from him at all. It was as if he'd vanished. Her mother said he was a POW but it was ages before Izzie understood what that meant – prisoner-of-war. A few months after he'd gone, they all moved to Worthing. 'A new start,' her mother had said, but Izzie had worried that Dad wouldn't know where they were when he came back from the war.

Izzie and Linda got on with life and it was just fine being the three of them. True, her mother had some funny ways. She didn't like her playing with some of the kids who lived near the shops, and she wouldn't let the girls join the Brownies, but apart from that, she and Linda were allowed to do pretty much what they wanted. The neighbours, apart from Mrs Sayers, who was also the Brown Owl, were friendly enough. They all pitched in and helped each other in the difficult times and the street party they'd put on when the war ended had been one of the best in Worthing. Everybody said so.

In her parents' bedroom, the voices grew louder, but Izzie couldn't quite make out what they were saying. She wrapped her arms around herself and sighed. It wasn't fair. Brian Turner said it was the best thing ever when his dad was demobbed in 1946 but when Izzie's father walked through the door with his suitcase, everything had changed. He was so strict; much more strict than Mummy. She'd lost count of the number of times he'd barked, 'Do as you're told,' and 'Don't answer back, young lady,' when she'd protested about something. Life had been so much more fun when it had just been her and Mum and Linda. They'd all been happy back then.

Her sister was still asleep. They got on quite well. In fact, Izzie owed her very name to Linda. When Linda was two, unable to get her little mouth around her sister's full name of Isobelle, she had called her big sister Izzie and it stuck.

Over the years, the wood on the bedroom door had warped and it no longer shut tightly, which was why Izzie could hear some of what her parents were saying but when they lowered their voices the sound was too muffled. She didn't want to miss anything so, praying that the hinges wouldn't creak and wake Linda, she pulled the door slightly open. The hall was in darkness. The only light came from under her parents' bedroom door. Izzie glanced back at Linda as she heard her mother's shrill voice saying, 'You're drunk again.'

'I am not drunk,' her father protested grumpily. 'One beer, that's all I've had.'

'How come you're so late home then?'

'What is this?' he said tetchily. 'What gives you the right to interrogate me?'

'Because I know you. You spend all your time in the pub,' her mother complained. 'You promised you were going out to get a decent job.'

'I'm trying, Doris,' he said. 'Good God woman, I spent the whole day traipsing around Worthing but there's nothing to be had. I reckon somebody's put the word about.' Izzie heard a 'plink, plink' as he tossed his cuff links into the little bowl on the dressing table.

It was cold standing barefoot on the linoleum. Izzie rubbed her feet on the backs of her legs to warm them up and shivered.

'I hope you're not thinking of going back to your old ways,' her mother said.

Her father scoffed. 'Don't be daft. I've learned me lesson.'

'I can't go through all that again, Bill.'

'You won't have to!' her father cried. 'It's just that I have to start from bloody scratch again, don't I. You never should have let go of the stall.'

'I had no choice!' her mother cried. 'When you went, you left us high and dry. What were we supposed to live on?'

Her parents' bed springs creaked and then she heard the 'thud, thud' as his boots hit the wooden floor. There was a moment of silence then her mother said, 'No, Bill.'

'Come on Doris.' Her father's voice was softer now.

'I don't want to. All this talk about the old days . . . it upsets me too much.'

'Then let me help you forget.' There was a short period of silence before her mother said 'Get off me! If I've told once, I've told you again and again, I can't. I just can't.'

Disturbed by the rising voices, Linda rolled over in bed. Izzie pushed the door shut and held her breath but as luck would have it, her younger sister didn't wake up. Good job. Linda would have sat up and made a great big fuss which would have got them both into trouble. She turned her attention back to what her parents were saying.

'But you're my wife!' Her father sounded agitated. 'It's been nearly six years, Doris. How much longer do you expect me to go on waiting?'

'I don't know.' They had been talking in heated whispers but her mother's voice rose. 'You don't seem to understand. All this worry . . .'

'For God sake!' her father shouted. 'I've given you the rent money haven't I?'

'Yes, but where did it come from?'

Izzie's heart was beginning to thud in her chest. She'd heard this conversation before and it usually ended up with her father stomping downstairs to sleep in the sitting room. Tonight it sounded more desperate. She felt a tear sting the back of her

4

eye. This wasn't the idyllic homecoming her mother had talked about through all those years of the war, when she'd tucked them up at bedtime. 'When your daddy comes home,' she'd said with such conviction that Izzie had believed every word, 'we'll have such fun. We'll go for long drives in the country; we'll pack our bags and go on holiday; we'll catch the train to London and maybe we'll see the King himself . . .' Well, Dad had been home for two whole months now and they hadn't 'done' any of that, and what was even more alarming, her parents' arguments were getting worse.

'Doris, this is tearing me apart.'

'No!'

Everybody said her father was a decent sort of chap but to Izzie's way of thinking, her mother seemed a bit wary of him. She wouldn't let him kiss her and pulled away from him, saying she was busy or she was tired if he tried to hug her. Her father and Linda got on very well but that was because he spoiled her. Everyone said Linda was a lovely looking child whereas Izzie was only 'nice'. Linda had fair curly hair like Shirley Temple and Mummy gave her a ribbon at the side. Izzie's hair was mousy brown and hardly had a kink in it let alone a curl so she wore it in plaits with an elastic band on each end. Their father played chase with Linda and he'd push her ever so high on the old tyre swing under the apple tree. At first Izzie was desperate to be included but she never was. 'Don't be so rough, Izzie,' he'd said one day when she'd pushed in front of Linda so that he could tickle her too. 'You're nearly thirteen. You're too old for baby games.' After that, Izzie decided that she didn't like him very much.

'Doris . . .' He was coaxing her now. 'I understand how difficult it's been but it's all water under the bridge now. It's time we got on with our lives.'

'Got on with our lives!' she retorted in a hissy whisper. 'Oh that's easy enough for you to say. I take it that you haven't bumped into Brenda Sayers since you came back?'

'I can't for the life of me understand why she came to live here,' her father muttered.

'Her uncle left her the shop. I already told you that.'

'Yes, but why come here? She must have known you were just around the corner.'

'Of course she did!' her mother exclaimed. 'She doesn't want me to forget, does she! The last six years have been an absolute torment for me. You have no idea . . .'

'Bloody hell, woman,' he snapped. 'Don't start lecturing me again about life being so hard. What do you know about hardship? You didn't spend the last six years locked up in a prison.'

'I may as well have done,' she hissed. 'I wish I'd never done it now. I didn't realise it was so bad. I thought you'd just get a ticking off.'

'You what?'

A voice right behind Izzie made her jump. 'What are you doing?'

She spun around. Linda was sitting up in bed and rubbing her eyes.

'Shh,' Izzie said crossly, 'or they'll hear us.'

On the other side of the door, her father shouted in an angry whisper. 'What are you telling me, you stupid bitch?'

'Stay over that side of the bed,' her mother was saying. 'Don't touch me.'

There followed a scuffling sound, and her mother's voice, shrill again, burst out. 'No. Bill stop it. Leave me alone.'

'Then tell me,' he snarled. 'What did you do?'

'Why's Mummy shouting?' Linda said in a voice that was far too loud. 'I want Mummy.'

Izzie closed the door quickly. 'Oh shut-up, will you?'

'But what are they doing?'

6

Izzie scrambled back into her bed and pulled the covers up. 'Nothing,' she said tersely. 'Grown-up stuff. You wouldn't understand.'

They both lay in the dark in silence listening to the scuffling across the little landing. Izzie didn't understand herself but it was making her feel scared. At one point they heard a heavy object fall to the floor with a loud thud and Linda cried out in alarm. Izzie thought it might be a book or something but then they heard the sound of the alarm clock drumming against the wooden floorboards.

'I don't like it,' Linda whispered plaintively.

'That's because you're only a baby,' said Izzie in a superior tone. There was no way she was going to admit to her little sister that she felt just the same. If she and Linda argued and fought the way their mother and father did, they'd have got a smacked bottom.

'I'm not a baby,' Linda cried indignantly. 'I'm eleven next birthday and—'

She was cut off by a terrific bump followed by a masculine howl of pain then their father shouted, 'You bitch! You bloody bitch.'

Linda took in her breath noisily. Izzie lay perfectly still, eyes wide open, her heart pounding in her chest. The room seemed suddenly very dark and scary. What on earth was going on in there?

It was with some sense of relief when she heard the door of her parents' room opening, allowing more light in their room, but then someone rushed down the stairs.

'Who was that?' Linda whimpered.

'I don't know,' said Izzie, her own voice quavering with fear.

A few moments later, they heard the front door open and then it was slammed shut. Izzie shuddered. Maybe that thud meant that one of them had had a bad fall and the other person was running down the road to the telephone box on the corner to get help. She climbed out of bed cautiously and crept towards the door. Linda made to follow her.

'Stay there and be quiet,' Izzie said sternly.

Lifting the latch carefully she allowed the door to open just a little way. Her father was coming out of his bedroom, one hand on his face. She saw a trickle of blood seeping between his fingers from a cut on his cheek. His face was as white as paper.

'What happened?'

'Nothing,' he said gruffly. He leaned against the wall to steady himself. 'Go back to bed.'

'But I heard Mummy going outside.'

'She's just gone to the toilet, that's all.'

Izzie hesitated. She knew that wasn't true. He was lying. If her mother was going to the lavvy, she'd have gone out through the kitchen. 'But she went out of the *front* door,' Izzie protested.

'Get back into bed!' her father bellowed.

Izzie blinked in shocked surprise and promptly shut the bedroom door. The two girls stared at each other through the gloom with worried expressions. A few seconds later, the front door opened again and they heard him calling their mother's name out in the street. 'Doris . . . Doris.'

Miserably, Izzie climbed into bed and lay on her back, still listening. She could feel the tears pricking her eyes and her chin was wobbling. Her mother had run away and it was all *his* fault. Her heart began to thud again. She hated him. Hated him.

'Izzie,' Linda whispered. 'Where's Mummy gone?'

'Shh,' Izzie said savagely. She heard her sister gulp back a tear and immediately regretted the way she had snapped. 'They just had a fight, that's all. Grown-ups do it all the time. She'll be back in a minute.'

Now that her eyes were accustomed to the lack of light, Izzie stared at the long crack on the ceiling. It was funny how it turned from a friendly spider into an angry octopus depending on the mood she was in. Right now, with her heart banging away in her chest, it seemed as terrifying as the ghostly grey hand she'd seen on the poster outside the Odeon cinema for that horrible looking film – what was it called? *I Walked With a Zombie.*

The front door closed again. Izzie strained her ears to hear voices but there was only silence. After a few agonising minutes she got out of bed again and opened the bedroom door just a crack to peep out to the landing. Her father was sitting at the bottom of the stairs with his back to her as he leaned forward with his head in his hands. She waited for him to turn around but he didn't and then, to her shocked surprise, she suddenly realised that he was crying. As quiet as a mouse, she closed the door again and padded back to her bed.

Linda had begun to cry. 'I'm scared, Izzie.'

'Come on then,' she whispered, and as Izzie lifted the bedclothes her little sister, trembling like a leaf, dived in beside her and snuggled up close. Linda soon went to sleep but it took her big sister a little longer. Izzie didn't finally relax until she heard the front door open and close again and she heard the sound of a woman's voice in the hallway.

*

Izzie woke up warm and snug under the bedclothes but with a very cold nose. It was going to take all the courage she could muster to jump out of bed and go downstairs for a wash. The only room her parents heated was the kitchen. There was a fireplace in the sitting room but that was only lit when they had 'company', something which had only happened once or twice to Izzie's recollection. Her mother had a roaring fire the year Granny and Grandad Baxter came for Christmas and she lit the fire in that room when Linda was poorly a couple of years ago. Her sister had lain on the sofa until she was well again. Normally, in winter, everybody huddled together in the kitchen, so it seemed sensible to use their meagre coal ration where it was needed most. In the morning, her mother would hang their school clothes over the clothes horse to warm in front of the fire while they had a strip wash in the small scullery next to the kitchen. Once the girls were dressed, they had breakfast; usually bread and jam or toast and dripping and maybe if they were very lucky, an egg.

The smell of toast encouraged the two of them to get up and run downstairs. The kitchen was bathed in a haze of blue smoke but it wasn't their mother who stood beside the grill. It was Mrs Marshall, their next-door neighbour. The shock of seeing her made Izzie stop dead and Linda crashed into the back of her.

'Hello girls. I expect you'll be wanting your wash,' said Mrs Marshall. Lifting the kettle, she poured some warm water into a bowl on the table. They watched her carry it into the scullery. 'You can both share can't you?' Pushing a bar of soap and two flannels beside it, she added, 'I'll leave you to it.'

'Where's my mummy?' Linda asked.

Mrs Marshall didn't look round. 'She just popped out for a moment ducks. She'll be back soon. Now hurry up with your wash and then you can eat your breakfast.' The scullery door closed leaving the two girls alone.

The children were used to Mrs Marshall coming in. When their father was away in the war, Mrs Marshall would sometimes look after Izzie and Linda while their mother went shopping or to see the doctor. Sometimes it took all day and when she got home, Mummy was very tired. Mrs Marshall was a pleasant woman but very old, at least fifty, so she couldn't run around and play games or anything, but they liked her well enough.

Linda looked as if she was about to burst into tears again.

'You go first,' Izzie said firmly.

'But I want Mummy,' Linda said, her voice choked with emotion.

Izzie gave her sister a little push towards the bowl. 'Go on,' she coaxed. 'It'll be all right. You'll see.'

*

They were sitting at the kitchen table eating their breakfast when their father came in. Izzie saw him and Mrs Marshall exchange an odd look and then her father shook his head. He sat down wearily at the table and Mrs Marshall poured him a cup of tea from the tea pot she'd hidden under the old tea cosy Izzie's mother never used.

'Where's Mummy?' Linda asked again.

Her father stared down at the oil table cloth. 'She's gone to see a friend.'

'She's run away, hasn't she?' Izzie said coldly.

Her father sighed deeply before sipping some of his tea.

'Now, now, Izzie,' Mrs Marshall said firmly. 'Get on and eat your breakfast or you'll be late for school.'

Izzie sprang to her feet, her chair scraping the floor. 'You hit her, didn't you, and now she's run away!'

Linda burst into tears.

'Izzie!' Mrs Marshall said in a shocked tone of voice. 'You shouldn't say such things.'

'But it's true,' Izzie blurted out. 'He's been horrible to Mummy. She kept saying no and then he shouted at her. And now she's run away and he doesn't even care!'

Mrs Marshall's mouth had dropped open. There was an

awkward silence before Izzie's father rose to his feet. 'Thanks for looking after the girls, Mrs Marshall,' he said, totally ignoring Izzie's outburst. 'Could you take Linda to school for me? I'll settle up with you later.'

'No need for that Bill,' Mrs Marshall said with a dismissive wave of her hand.

Bill Baxter sighed. 'I think I'll have a bit of a lie down before I go back out again.' His voice was sad.

'Good idea,' said Mrs Marshall. 'You look worn out.'

They watched him shuffle towards the door at the bottom of the stairs and they heard his slow and weary footsteps going up to the bedroom. As the door swung closed again, Izzie muttered, 'I hate him.'

'That's not a very nice thing to say about your father, young lady,' Mrs Marshall scolded. 'And as for saying that he doesn't care, let me tell you, he's been out there all night looking for your mother. Now get your coat on. You'll miss the bus if you don't get a move on.'

Izzie gaped in surprise. Her father had been up all night? A shiver of fear passed through her body. So where was her mother?

Linda was still crying as Mrs Marshall helped her into her coat. 'Now be a good girl and don't you worry,' she said brightly. 'There's plenty of people out there helping to look for your mummy now. They'll soon find her.'

Pulling on her own coat, Izzie said nothing but she wasn't so sure. Mrs Marshall sounded confident but if her father had been looking for Mum all night, why hadn't he found her? Where on earth could she be?

As the three of them opened the front door and walked onto the street, Linda was still stifling a sob and Izzie was trembling inside. This was going to be a memorable day for all the wrong reasons. She had never felt so miserable. She was upset about her mother and she was upset because not one person had remembered. Of course she knew they all had far more pressing things to think about but all the same, it hurt.

The day was cold and crisp. There had been a frost overnight because the gate post and the low wall in the front of the house glistened white. It was the sort of day when you looked for a frozen puddle to have a quick slide, but Izzie didn't feel like it today. She felt too sorry for herself. Stuffing her gloved hands into her pockets, she hurried towards the bus stop. Nobody else was waiting but she hadn't missed the bus. She could see it coming in the distance. She shouldn't be thinking about herself, she told herself crossly, but it would have been nice if just one of them had said something. They'd all forgotten, hadn't they? Understandable of course, but couldn't just one of them have remembered that today was February 26th and her thirteenth birthday?

*

Brenda Sayers stiffened. Inside the Woolly Lamb, her little wool and haberdashery shop, she had been filling the shelves with a new stock. There were no customers as yet but she was confident that once their housework was done, the place would be buzzing.

She gave the young constable, who looked as if he should still be in school, a puzzled frown. 'What do you mean, Doris Baxter has gone missing?'

'She appears to have been very disturbed when she ran off late last night,' he said. 'We're asking everyone around here to look in their sheds and outhouses to see if she's there.'

'Why all the fuss?' Brenda said. 'She's a grown woman.'

'As far as we know,' said the constable. 'When she ran off, she was only in her nightdress.'

Brenda raised an eyebrow. 'More fool her,' Brenda said tetchily. 'Well, she's hardly likely to find her way into *my* shed now is she?'

The constable flushed, suddenly realising his mistake. 'Yes, yes,' he flustered. 'I'm sorry. It's just that I was asked to visit all the shops here on the Goring Road in case she was hiding out back.' He raised his forefinger to the edge of his helmet in a form of salute and fled the shop.

The bell jangled madly. Brenda stared at the closing door for a second or two then stepped through the beaded curtain that divided the shop and her little kitchen cum rest area. She was shaking. She glanced across to where in the photograph on the shelf – her son, Gary, holding a minnow in a jam jar – smiled down at her. How chuffed he'd been to catch it. Only six years old, she thought to herself. He would have been eleven now. There was another boy standing next to him in the photograph, his cousin Raymond, but his face was hidden by a carefully draped handkerchief. Raymond was slightly older than Gary, nearly seven, but when she looked at the whole picture, the look of envy on Raymond's face was clear for all to see. Sometimes it pleased her, but at other times it made her upset because she couldn't forget that seconds after the photograph was taken the little tyke had tried to snatch Gary's jam jar and it broke. They couldn't save the fish and Gary had been devastated. She sighed. Life was so unfair. Raymond was always getting into trouble; in fact, he'd been a trial to his mother since the day he'd been born. She didn't wish him ill of course, but she often wondered why her perfect little boy had been the one whose life had been so tragically cut short. She sighed. Like they say, only the good die young.

She turned her head towards the window and the storage shed beyond. She wouldn't bother to go out to see if that woman was in there. She could see from where she was standing that the stout padlock on the door handle was untouched. The shed was empty in the winter; too damp to keep her stock in it. No, the wool she was putting on the shelves right now had been delivered to her own home. She'd pushed it here in the old pram. The pram she had used when Gary was a baby. Brenda choked back a sob. There were no more children nor were there likely to be. Gary was her only son, her lucky surprise at a time when she'd thought she was too old for mother-hood. She and Doris may have been friends once upon a time, but she made up her mind that she wouldn't feel sorry for her.

Not after what that family had done to Gary.

Two

February 29th 1949

'Happy birthday to you,
Happy birthday to you,
Happy birthday dear Isobelle,
Happy birthday to you.'

Izzie looked up as her grandmother placed a birthday cake in front of her and a small gasp of appreciation escaped her lips. It was absolutely perfect with pretty pink and white icing and a little china bust of a Victorian lady on the top. The cake itself was her dress and behind her head were fifteen candles; a veritable forest of flame. Her relatives and friends sitting round the table clapped as Izzie blew them out.

Her grandmother leaned over her and kissed the top of Izzie's head. 'Happy birthday, my all grown-up granddaughter.'

Izzie wriggled with a warm glow of pride. Yes, she was all grown-up now, wasn't she. Fifteen years old and wearing her first ever pair of stockings with a suspender belt. Gone were the hair ribbons and plaits, she now had her hair cut a little shorter and styled in the way of the Hollywood star Susan Hayward. Her clothes were more grown-up too. No more school gymslips, Izzie was wearing a red, three-quarter

16

length sleeved jumper under a plaid pinafore dress in blue and grey.

She and her sister Linda had been living with their grandparents in Dial Post, a small hamlet twelve miles from Worthing ever since their mother had run off in 1947. Their grandfather worked on one of the farms on the Knepp Estate.

'Well, go on then,' Grandad said, his breathing laboured, 'open your presents.'

While her grandmother gathered the cake and took it out to the kitchen to cut, Linda put the beautifully wrapped birthday presents onto the table in front of her. Birthdays were bittersweet for Izzie. She had never forgotten the misery she'd experienced when she was thirteen. It was three days before her father discovered the birthday presents her mother had hidden in the bottom of the wardrobe. He'd apologised profusely and tried to make it up to her but Izzie knew that his heart wasn't in it. She had opened them in front of Mrs Marshall and her sister, and although they were nice things, it wasn't the same without her mother.

The night Doris Baxter had run off had been bitterly cold and because she was only in her nightie, some old boots and a thin overcoat when she left, everybody expected the worst. Friends and neighbours around Elm Grove, where they had lived, had spent the whole day searching for her. Her father had contacted everyone he could think of, but it was well known that since that dreadful summer of 1941 when Izzie's father went away, Doris had kept herself to herself. In the end, some children on their way home from school told their mother that they'd heard funny noises coming from the shed near the Working Man's Club House on the corner of Bruce Avenue. Convinced an animal was trapped inside, their mother had persuaded their father to investigate when he got home from work. The animal turned out to be Izzie and Linda's mother.

Delirious and in spite of the cold, burning up with fever, they rushed her to hospital while the local bobby came to fetch Izzie's father. Everyone was thrilled that she'd been found but it wasn't a completely happy ending. Although she had survived the ordeal, Doris was far from well. 'The doc reckons she's not right in the head,' Izzie heard her father telling Mrs Marshall a day or two later. 'He says she won't be coming home any time soon.'

And once again the same dark thoughts had filled Izzie's head.

It's all your fault.

'Can we go and see her?' Izzie had asked some time later, but her father had shaken his head.

'I'm afraid she's too ill at the moment,' he'd said. 'As soon as she's feeling up to it, I'll take you both.'

But he never did.

At the time, Izzie didn't really understand what was going on but she knew when grown-ups were hiding something. How could she fail to notice her father giving Mrs Marshall a funny look when she'd asked which hospital her mother was in. Her father wouldn't say anything in front of her and Linda but she'd heard them whispering in the scullery. But even though Izzie pressed her, Mrs Marshall wouldn't say anything. It was very frustrating. Izzie wrote letters and Linda drew pictures for their father to post. They disappeared from the mantelpiece all right, but had he actually given them to their mother? They never had a reply, so Izzie had her doubts. Night after night, she and Linda silently cried themselves to sleep while their father became more morose and sullen. After a month or two, and without any discussion, she and Linda had been shipped off to Dial Post to live with their grandparents. They were promised that it was only a temporary measure but here they were, two years on, and still living in Dial Post.

The first present Izzie opened, a tin of talcum powder, was

from one of her school friends who had come to her little tea party. Izzie thanked her friend as she turned the top and a delicious smell of lily of the valley filled the room. When she opened her other presents they were just as nice; a tin of Sharp's toffees and a box of handkerchiefs. Izzie was thrilled with them all.

'Open the long one,' Linda coaxed, but Izzie had decided to leave that one until last. The next present she opened turned out to be a lovely knitted cardigan. She was surprised to see that it was from her grandmother because it was very fashionable and delicate. Knitted in cream 3ply wool it had embroidered red and blue flowers down the front, just like the one worn by the model in her grandmother's *Woman* magazine. Granny had added some pretty pearl buttons and Izzie heard her friends gasp with admiration as she shook it from the tissue paper wrapping.

'Oh Granny, it's lovely!' she cried.

Her next present was a book from Grandad. He knew her love of reading so he had bought her a brand new book called *The Franchise Affair* by Josephine Tey. Izzie turned it over in her hands and stroked the dust jacket lovingly. 'Thank you.' She rose to her feet and planted a kiss on her grandfather's papery cheek.

'Aah, go on with you,' he said with a chuckle.

'I've never owned a brand new book before,' she said.

'The man in the bookshop said it was very popular,' her grandmother called from the kitchen where she was arranging the sliced pieces of cake onto a plate.

Izzie smiled. She could hardly wait to get started. Most of her reading was done with County Library Service books housed in St Mark's Church hall, Horsham or occasionally, when she could afford it, one of the few books in the shilling lending library at the back of the grocery van which came around isolated areas once a week. Up until now, she'd only read children's books but this one looked like the sort of thing an adult would read.

'Don't forget the long one,' Linda reminded her as she sat back down at the table.

The long present was from her father. Izzie always had such mixed feelings about her father. She'd hardly looked at him since he'd arrived and even now she kept her head bowed as she picked up the box. She was glad that he had come but she still hadn't forgiven him. It had taken her almost a year to find out that the day her mother was found in the club house shed, she had been 'committed'. At the time she hadn't a clue what that meant, but judging by the hushed tones the adults used when talking about it, she'd understood it wasn't good. When she finally prised it out of Granny, it had come as a terrible shock to discover that her mother was in a mental hospital; and what was even worse, she was *locked up* all day and every day. The frustrated anger she'd felt towards her father came roaring to the surface again.

'But it was all his fault,' she'd ranted.

'I don't think so, darling,' her grandmother had said gently. She was busy rolling pastry on the drop down work surface on the tall cupboard.

'Oh yes it was,' Izzie insisted. 'I heard her. Mummy said she didn't want to but he made her and then she ran away.'

Her grandmother's eyes had almost popped out of her head. 'Didn't want to what?'

'I don't know,' said Izzie. She took a deep breath. 'First of all Daddy said, "*You're my wife*," and Mummy said, "*Get off me*." Then Daddy said, "*You should never have let the sock go*."'

'Let the sock go?' her grandmother had said incredulously. She laid the rolling pin down and turned the pastry clockwise. 'What on earth does that mean?'

Frustrated, Izzie cried, 'I don't know, but then Mummy said, "*Stay over that side.*" And Daddy said, "*It's time we got on with it,*" and Mummy said, "*No, Bill, it upsets me too much. Stop it. Leave me alone.*"'

'Izzie!' Her grandmother had gone very pink. She picked up the pin again and began to roll the pastry with a vengeance. 'I think you've made a mistake.'

'No I haven't!' Izzie insisted angrily. 'I heard her say that.'

'Child, you're talking about things you don't understand,' Granny had said firmly. 'I don't think we should discuss this anymore.'

'But why not?' Izzie had demanded.

Her grandmother had banged the rolling pin down. 'Because I said so!'

It was plain that the subject was closed. Izzie had been annoyed at the time, but what could she do? Her grandmother always stuck up for Izzie's father but then she would, wouldn't she. He was her only son and in Granny's eyes he could do no wrong.

As she tore the paper from the gift, Izzie was very aware that her father was watching her over the rim of his cup of tea. He didn't visit that often but he did make sure he was around for family occasions. Her grandfather said it was because he was a businessman now – he had an emporium, whatever that meant.

Once the wrapping paper was gone, Izzie found a long black box. Before she actually reached for his present she'd planned to be polite but put it down in favour of another, yet when she opened the plush padded jeweller's box with a silk lining, it was impossible to hide her delight. Slim and elegant with a thin leather strap, it was her first real watch.

'Here,' her father said, 'let me put it on for you.'

'I can do it myself,' said Izzie, pulling her arm away from him.

'All right, Independent Annie,' he said with a chuckle, and everyone admired Izzie's watch.

A moment later, her grandmother passed the cake around and then they played a few parlour games like Charades and Consequences.

It wasn't long before people wanted to go home. With the exception of Izzie's father, they all lived within walking distance but it was already dark and it was very cold outside. The weather forecast on the radio had said it was going to freeze so everybody wanted to be back in their own homes before the bad weather set in.

'Before you both go up to bed,' her father said when the last of their visitors had gone, 'I've got a surprise for you.'

'Ooh, what is it?' said Linda as she quickly perched herself on the arm of the chair where their father was sitting.

Bill Baxter smiled. 'You're coming home,' he said.

'What? You mean we're going to live with you and Mummy again?' Linda cried.

Izzie's heart soared. They hadn't seen their mother for two years and now at last they were going to be together again. This had to be the most perfect birthday present of all. But then she saw her father and grandmother share an odd look.

'Not with your mum, I'm afraid,' her father said quietly. 'She's still too ill.'

Linda pouted. 'Oh.'

'Sorry, sweetheart,' their father said. 'But look on the bright side. Things are going well with the business and I want my girlies back home. I miss you.'

Izzie frowned. 'Why?' she said coldly. 'This is our home.'

'No,' her father said patiently. 'This is your grandparents' home. Your home is with me.'

Linda threw her arms around her father's neck. 'Oh Daddy, when can we come? Can we come tonight?'

Their father shook his head with a chuckle. 'I was going to bring the lorry round in a couple of weeks' time to collect your things but everything's gone so well, I reckon I could make it by Saturday.'

'Why?' Izzie complained. 'In a few weeks' time would be better.'

'We may as well start as we mean to go on,' he said. 'It still gives you time to get used to the idea and gives me enough time to get the new house ready.'

'You mean we won't be living in the house at Elm Grove anymore?' said Izzie.

'No,' said her father. 'We're moving right into the heart of the town, to Chandos Road.'

'But I liked the house in Elm Grove,' Izzie protested. 'All my friends are there.'

'This is a brand new start,' her father said firmly. 'Your mum never actually wanted to stay in Elm Grove, not after . . .' his voice drifted. 'Anyway, she would be happier somewhere else so I've found us a little house at the back of Montague Street.'

'So Mummy *is* coming back,' Linda cried.

Their father hesitated. 'Maybe.' He glanced at their grand-mother, adding, 'and I think she might be happier in the town.'

Izzie frowned. 'I hope the house is near my old school,' she said crossly. 'I want to go back to my old school.'

'You won't be going back to school though, will you,' her father said. 'You leave school at fifteen.'

The realisation hit Izzie like a ton of bricks. Of course she knew she would be leaving school this year and she'd looked forward to it . . . until now.

'I leave at Easter,' she said tartly.

'You can leave now,' her father insisted.

Her father sighed impatiently. The atmosphere had suddenly become frosty. Izzie's grandfather rose to his feet. 'Well, I think I'll turn in, mother,' he said to his wife. 'It's been a long day.'

'Yes, and I think it's time for you to come upstairs, Linda,' their grandmother said. 'Give your daddy a kiss.'

Linda looked up at the clock. 'But it's only a quarter to eight,' she protested.

After Linda was persuaded to say her goodbyes, Izzie and her father sat in silence. They could still hear her grandad coughing and Linda's shrill excited voice as she decided what things she was going to pack into her suitcase.

'I don't want to come back with you,' Izzie said crossly.

'Well, you're going to have to,' her father said.

'Linda can go but I'm staying here.'

Her father leaned forward. 'For once in your life, Izzie, will you do as you're told? You have to come back home with me.'

Izzie jumped to her feet, her cheeks flaring with anger. 'I don't have to do anything,' she retorted. 'Granny likes me being here. If I ask her, she'll let me stay, you wait and see.'

'Are you really so blind?' her father hissed. 'This is your grandmother's idea.'

Izzie stared at him in disbelief. 'You're lying. She wouldn't just turf us out. She wouldn't!'

Bill Baxter sighed. 'Izzie, your grandfather is ill. You've heard the way he coughs; you can see the way he can't always get his breath. He's got Farmer's Lung. He needs looking after and Granny can't cope with having the two of you in the house as well.'

Izzie's mouth had dropped open. Grandad ill? She lowered herself back down onto the chair. Of course she'd realised he wasn't his normal self and that he'd slowed up. She'd even noticed that he was often breathless, but it never really dawned on her that he was seriously ill. 'What's Farmer's Lung?' she said quietly.

'You get it from breathing in the mould on hay and animal

24

feed,' her father said. 'When it's really bad, you can't breathe properly and you cough all the time.'

'And Grandad has all the symptoms.'

Her father nodded. Izzie's eyes stung with unshed tears. 'Then I should stay here and help Granny,' she insisted. 'Oh please let me stay.'

'Izzie,' her father said, 'his time has come and they just want some time to themselves.'

'But I . . .' Izzie began again.

'I, I, I,' said her father. 'It's not all about what you want.'

Izzie bit back her tears. 'Do you die from Farmer's Lung?'

Her father looked at her steadily. 'Probably, yes.' There was a short pause then he added, 'Izzie I'm sorry, but you can see now why you both have to come back to Worthing.' He stood up wearily and opened his arms but she stepped away from him.

'Please yourself, but I shall be coming back with the lorry on Saturday,' he said firmly, 'and you're coming back to Worthing with me whether you like it or not.'

Three

It had been a terrible wrench to leave Dial Post and it took some time for Izzie to settle down in Worthing. After the silence of the countryside, the town seemed very noisy. It amused her to recall that when they had first arrived in Dial Post to live with their grandparents, she had taken just as long to get used to life on the farm. Back then, she had complained about the peace and quiet. Her grandfather had laughed.

'The countryside is full of noise,' he'd said. 'You just need to harken.'

He'd been right of course and it hadn't taken long for her ear to become attuned to the sounds of the farm. Apart from the obvious like the cows mooing, the chickens clucking and the crow of the cockerel, she heard nightingales, turtle doves and the cuckoo. In high summer the weald was alive with the sounds of crickets and bees as she watched the tranquil paddling of dainty little blue damsel-flies on the stream. She soon learned to recognise different species of butterflies like the Purple Emperor, the Brown Argus and the Chalkhill Blue. In autumn, she learned to identify the difference between the tweet of the Tawny Owl and the shriek of the Barn Owl. In the spring, the cooing of the woodpigeon heralded the mating season and at night a vixen called her mate; things she'd never heard before she'd moved to the country. On the other hand,

Linda was the exact opposite. She had been very excited about the move back to town because she had always complained that life in the country was boring and that there was nothing to do.

They had set off in their father's lorry on Saturday with the smiles and waves from their friends and neighbours and their cries of 'good luck' ringing in their ears. Izzie had apologised to Granny as she'd left.

'I'm sorry if I didn't help you enough,' she'd said tearfully.

Her grandmother had enfolded her in her arms. 'Don't you ever worry about that my dear.' She smelled of warm wool and lavender.

'You'm been a good girl,' said Gran, giving her another hug, 'and I shall miss you both. Try and get on with your dad, won't you?'

Izzie grimaced. 'I'll try,' she said grudgingly, 'but he's always cross with me.'

'He doesn't mean it,' said Gran. 'He never was much good with women and you're the spitting image of your mother.'

Izzie blinked in surprise.

Her grandfather leaned over the garden gate as the lorry trundled down the road. Now that she knew about his illness, it was obvious how much weight he'd lost. How come she had never noticed before? Even though she feared the worse, Izzie hoped that now that her grandmother only had him to care for, he might make an improvement.

When they arrived in Chandos Road there was no-one to greet them. The street ran parallel to Montague Street and was no thoroughfare. At one end, the houses backed onto Buckingham Road. At the other end, on the north side, was Walter Gardiner's photographic studio and on the opposite side of the road was Fred Allen and Sons, fruiterers. Izzie's new home was part of a terrace with no front garden and a front door which opened out onto the pavement. But for all that, the houses looked substantial.

'Can I go to the pictures?' Linda asked almost as soon as they had arrived.

'Not today.' Their father had chuckled. 'Let's get you settled in first.'

Inside their new home, it smelled musty and damp. There were a few bits of mis-matched furniture. The two girls raced around the house and upstairs to choose their bedrooms.

'Bagsie the front room,' said Linda.

'Oh no you don't,' said their father, coming up behind them. 'That one's mine.'

Before he'd closed the door, Izzie had caught a glimpse of a double bed in the room and she caught her breath. Perhaps her mother might be coming back after all.

The two back rooms were of equal size so Izzie told Linda she didn't mind which one she had. The bathroom was downstairs off the kitchen, which did mean they would have to come all the way downstairs at night, but at least the lavvy was indoors and it had a flushing cistern. No more having to put on a big coat and wellington boots in the middle of winter and no more smashing the ice on the top of the bucket with a stick before you could have a wee.

In the kitchen, the china and other utensils were spartan, so that night they ate fish and chips from the chip shop for their supper, and in the conversation around the table, Izzie discovered that their father had given up their old house in Elm Grove some time before. Until he'd moved into Chandos Road, he had been sleeping 'on the job', as he laughingly called it, in the emporium.

'What is an emporium?' Linda wanted to know.

'I sell everything from kitchen tables to army surplus,' her father explained. 'I do have a few antiques but I also stock new

28

things.' He paused before adding, 'I shall never rival Warnes by the station, but I do make a decent living.'

'Where is the shop?' Izzie asked.

'Teville Gate,' he had said. 'The bus goes right by it so I get plenty of custom. Only trouble is,' he added with a note of caution, 'the council plan to redevelop the area, so I may have a compulsory purchase order slapped on me before long.'

'What does that mean, Daddy?' asked Linda.

'They will force me to sell them the shop.'

'But that's not fair!' cried Linda. 'Why should they? It's *your* shop.'

Her father chuckled and rubbed her hand. 'That's the way it is I'm afraid sweetheart.'

Izzie watched them, her sister simpering, her father gazing lovingly at her, and she inwardly curled her lip. You might forget what he did to our mother, she thought acidly, but I never will.

He suddenly glanced up at her. 'You all right Izzie? You're very quiet.'

'I'm fine,' Izzie sniffed. Standing, she collected the dirty dishes.

Her father made no attempt to tell Linda to help her with the washing up, so sullenly and with a bad grace, Izzie did it herself.

'Izzie, I've made arrangements for you to go to work for the green grocer on the corner,' her father had said as she dried the plates. 'Mr Allen seems a very nice man and he says you can start straight away.'

'You've got a job for me already?' said Izzie. How dare he do that without even asking her? 'I think I'd prefer to look for my own job. Maybe I don't want to work in a green grocer's.'

'Tough,' said her father.

Izzie spun round and glared at him. 'You can't make me.'

'I can't but if you won't work, you don't eat,' said her father. 'You can't sit around here all day doing nothing. You need a job.'

Izzie's face flushed with anger. 'Who's Mr Allen anyway?'

'He owns the shop,' her father went on. 'It's right on the doorstep and you start first thing on Monday morning.'

With an angry glare, Izzie returned to the dishes.

'Where will I go to school, Daddy?' Linda chirped.

'Davidson's School for Girls,' her father had said. 'It's where Izzie used to go, you remember, just past Worthing Tabernacle and opposite the new Town Hall. Don't worry about finding it, I'll take you there myself.'

Of course you will, Izzie thought grumpily, as she put the washed plates onto the dresser.

*

In time, Izzie looked back on that moment with a little discomfort. Yes, she'd been jealous of Linda and angry with her father but it was hard to keep it up. Sometimes during her lunch hour, especially during the school holidays, Izzie met up with Linda. They would share an ice cream or just stroll along Marine Parade or in the shops. Once, the street photographer on the prom spotted them arm-in-arm and took a picture. Izzie went back to the booth the next day and bought a copy. Their father had promised to look out for a photo frame and now it had pride of place on her dressing table. Funny how she and her sister got on well at times and yet at other times they were at each other's throats.

They hadn't been back in Worthing long when Izzie wrote to a couple of old school friends. Susan's letter came back with 'not known at this address' scrawled on the envelope but Patsy had replied. She told Izzie she was training to be a typist at the local college. They arranged to meet on Izzie's half day off and paid thruppence to walk along the pier. The gaping hole the authorities had blown through the middle of the pier at the start of the war in 1939 had been repaired. It was supposed to be a safety precaution to prevent the pier from being used for enemy disembarkation in the event of an invasion. The fact that the waters along Worthing were too shallow for troop ships seemed to be lost on the powers-that-be but now, at last, the pier was back open for business.

The two girls linked arms and shared their news. Patsy was doing well with her training and hoped to get a job soon. She was slightly smaller than Izzie, with dark curly hair and dimples on each cheek. She was wearing a pink top with a blue and white checked skirt. Izzie was wearing the outfit she'd worn on her birthday.

'The college has a good reputation for placing girls,' Patsy said confidently.

'Do you like it?' Izzie asked. 'Typing, I mean?'

Patsy shrugged. 'Not much but I don't care. I'll get married before long.'

'Are you courting then?' asked Izzie.

Patsy shook her head. 'Not exactly but I go to the dances at the Assembly Hall every Saturday and there are some good looking boys there. You should come.'

Izzie laughed. 'My dad would have a fit.'

Patsy squeezed her arm. 'I missed you when you went away.'

'I missed you too.'

'It must be nice having your mum back home again.'

Izzie stopped walking and looked at her friend. 'She's not.'

Patsy seemed embarrassed. 'Oh! Sorry. I thought she was.' She paused then added, 'When we heard she'd been discharged from hospital, I just assumed . . .' Her voice trailed. 'Sorry.'

'Who told you my mother had been discharged?'

31

'My mum.'

'Does she know where my mother is?'

Patsy frowned. 'Don't you?'

Izzie shook her head.

'That's all I know,' Patsy said with a shrug. 'But I'll ask her if you like.'

'Yes please,' said Izzie as they started walking again.

When they reached the arcade, Patsy said, 'Fancy having a go on the slot machines? I've got about ten pence to spare.'

Izzie grinned. 'And I've got a bob. Okay, you're on.'

*

As expected, Linda did well at school. She made new friends and was soon top of her form. Their father had bought her a bike and Linda spent most Saturdays out and about with her friends. As soon as she'd reached thirteen, she got a paper round at Millward's Tobacconist and Newsagent's. She was allowed to keep all of her earnings, which meant she was able to go to the pictures or on the bus to Brighton with her friends. All was well until the morning her employer called her into the back room. Linda was hugging her coat closely to her body.

'Stomach ache?' Mrs Millward asked.

'Monthlies,' said Linda. She grimaced with the pain.

'I don't think so,' Mrs Millward said coldly. 'You told my husband you had your monthlies less than ten days ago. What have you got inside your coat?'

Linda's face flushed. 'I don't know what you mean,' she said indignantly.

'You can either give it back to me now,' Mrs Millward went on, 'or I tell your father and we telephone the police.'

Reluctantly, Linda opened her school coat and a *Picturegoer* magazine fell to the floor.

Mrs Millward glared. 'I shan't be requiring your services anymore.'

'Oh please,' Linda said, bursting into tears. 'I've never done anything like this before.'

'Don't come the water-works with me, Linda Baxter. You've been pinching stuff ever since you came here.'

'I promise I won't do it again,' Linda begged.

'Too late, my girl. You've been caught out and I don't employ thieves.'

Linda stopped crying and gave Mrs Millward a filthy look. 'Who wants your poxy job anyway?' she snapped as she flounced out of the shop.

Mrs Millward was right. She had been pinching the magazines for a few months. She'd hidden them under the mattress in her bedroom, only reading them when she was sure to be alone. Undaunted by the sack, Linda found another newsagent not far away and started a paper round with them. But she'd learned her lesson. She'd be a lot more careful next time.

Four

Izzie became very popular at the green grocer's, so much so that at Christmas she'd been delightedly surprised when several of the customers popped into the shop with a 'Christmas box' for her. She'd ended up with a couple of small tins of sweets from Woolworth's and Hubbard's department store and the odd home-made mince pie. She also had a few Christmas cards containing a bob or two here and half a crown there. Mr Allen was a fair employer and Izzie enjoyed the work.

Market day in the town was on Wednesday and one day she heard a voice behind her. 'You don't remember me, do you?'

Izzie had been weighing out potatoes and putting them into folded pieces of newspaper she had fashioned into carriers ready for the rush. She looked up. The woman standing in front of her was tall and wearing a brown coat. The bit of her hair which was visible under her brown felt hat was grey and curly. Probably permed, Izzie thought. She looked about fifty, but she could have been younger. Her face was lined and she had sad grey eyes. Izzie shook her head. 'I'm sorry Madam,' she said politely, 'I'm afraid I don't.'

'I knew your mother,' the woman said coldly.

Izzie's eyes widened with surprise. 'My mother?'

Mr Allen began hovering nearby as if he was expecting trouble.

Izzie stood. 'Can I get you something?'

'A pound of carrots and a cabbage.'

Izzie weighed the carrots and tipped them into the woman's bag. Her customer gave her a long hard stare. 'You're Bill Baxter's girl aren't you?'

'Yes, yes I am,' Izzie said as she handed her a cabbage. 'That will be eleven pence please.'

The woman gave her a shilling and Izzie handed her a penny change. 'May I ask, do you know where my mother is?'

The woman shook her head.

'I don't know if you are aware of it but she went missing,' Izzie went on, all the old feelings of loss and longing resurfacing again. 'It's coming up for three years now. They found her but she had to go to hospital and that was the last we heard of her. Someone told me she had been discharged but I still don't know where she is.'

The woman had remained still, as though she was mulling something over in her own mind. 'I'm sorry young lady,' she said eventually. 'I can't help you.'

'Could you get some more apples from the store room, Izzie?' Mr Allen said, interrupting them.

Izzie hurried outside and when she came back, the woman had left the shop.

'What was that customer's name, Mr Allen?' she asked her employer.

'Mrs Sayers.'

Izzie nodded her thanks. As far as she knew, she had never seen the woman before so why was that name vaguely familiar?

*

Izzie woke up. She could hear her sister crying. Pulling on a cardigan, she padded to Linda's bedroom.

'Linda,' she whispered. 'I'm coming in.'

It was early morning. The street lights were off and the pale grey light of a new day filtered through the curtains. Walking into Linda's bedroom, Izzie sat on the edge of her bed. 'What is it? What's wrong?'

Linda sat up. 'Oh Izzie,' Linda said brokenly. 'Why didn't Mum come back?'

'I don't know,' said Izzie, 'but I'm sure she must have had her reasons.' She changed her position so that she could put her arm over Linda's shoulder. 'When I asked Granny, she just said Mum was too ill.'

Linda blew her nose. 'I remember making her pictures and stuff, but she never wrote back or anything.'

Izzie pressed her lips together. She didn't want to voice her own suspicion that their father had never even sent the things they'd made.

'Do you miss her?' Linda asked.

'Yes I do.'

They sat for a while, each lost in her own thoughts.

'Maybe I should talk to Dad?' said Linda.

'I tried that,' said Izzie. 'He got angry with me. I don't think he wants to talk about it.'

Linda began to cry again. 'There must be somebody who knows where she is.'

Izzie sighed. Now she too was beginning to feel teary.

'I got top marks in science last week,' said Linda. 'Miss Leigh gave me a commendation.'

'Oh Linda, that's wonderful.'

'But I wanted to tell Mum.'

Izzie squeezed her sister closer. 'You could have shown me. Can I see it?

Linda blew her nose again. 'You can . . . but it's not the same.'

'I know, I know.'

There had been a few times when Izzie had helped out at the emporium, usually when she had the odd day off or half a day.

The building was more like a warehouse than anything else. It was stuffed full of everything from wardrobes to books, from lamp shades to second-hand clothing and almost at once, Izzie could see the whole place was a shambles. Her father and his driver-cum-helper Mick Osborne, a rather greasy looking individual who always looked as if he was badly in need of a proper wash and shave, brought stuff in by the lorry load but there was no organisation when it came to storing it. As a result, everything was thrown inside higgledy-piggledy, which meant that half the time Izzie couldn't even reach something the customer wanted to look at. Her father didn't like it much when she mentioned it to him and they ended up having an argument.

'Stop telling me what to do, Izzie!' he'd shouted.

'But can't you see, you're losing customers?'

'Don't talk such Tommy rot.'

'But Dad,' she said, pointing to a large stack of chairs precariously balanced, 'that lady really wanted to buy that small table up there, but I couldn't get at it.'

Bill walked away with an irritated scoff and shut himself in his office. Izzie could have screamed.

It wasn't until someone tried to pull a suitcase from under a pile of carpet pieces and almost caused the catastrophic collapse of another precarious stack, that he finally agreed to let her try and sort it out.

It was jolly hard work but before long, Izzie had managed to achieve some semblance of order. Books were in one corner, arranged on bookcases which could be easily off loaded if someone wanted to buy one, china and ornaments were displayed in an attractive way in another corner, army surplus had its own area, garden tools another – the list went on and on. With Izzie's intervention, a visit to Bill's emporium had become a pleasure and was no longer a serious risk to public health. Izzie was pleased with what she had done, but she wasn't tempted to work for her father full time.

Life at home wasn't so easy. Linda kept herself to herself. When their mother first went, Linda cried a lot and wanted Izzie to cuddle her but she was past all that now. She didn't even want to talk about Doris anymore, something which Izzie found hard to bear. Izzie was anxious to keep the memory of her mother alive, but as time went on it was becoming more and more difficult. There was nothing of hers in Chandos Road – not so much as a picture or a hair brush. As well as all that, the work load in the house fell mostly on Izzie's shoulders. They sent the heavy stuff like the sheets, pillow cases and table cloths to the laundry – their father's shirts went there too – but everything else had to be done by the girls. Linda did as little as possible and their father regarded anything to do with the house as 'women's work'. Izzie would complain, she'd asked Linda to help, she'd written rotas and given explicit instructions about how a thing should be done so that there was no confusion but it was all to no avail.

By the time her sixteenth birthday came around in 1950, Izzie was still working in the green grocer's shop but she knew it wouldn't last. Right from the start, Mr Allen had made it clear that as soon as his son left school, he wanted to establish him in the family business, so Izzie would have to find something else. Even though she had lived frugally, Izzie didn't have much in the way of savings but at the back of her mind, she knew she wanted to leave home. She had been putting what she could into a small tin she kept at the back of her drawer but because her father took so much of her money for her keep, it was slow going. What she needed was a better paid job but they were hard to come by. It therefore came as a bit of a surprise when Mr Allen called her into his office at lunch time one Friday.

'I know you are looking for another job, Izzie,' he said, regarding her over the rim of his spectacles, and indicating that she should sit, 'so I wondered if you would consider working for one of my customers.'

Izzie lowered herself into the chair in front of his desk.

'Mrs Shilling is looking for a young person to help her mother-in-law. The post doesn't involve any nursing care for the old lady, but they would like someone to amuse her during the day.'

Izzie frowned. Entertaining some old duffer? It sounded rather boring. 'I'm not sure—' she began.

'The pay is good,' Mr Allen interrupted, 'better than the usual rate, and old Mrs Shilling is a very nice person, or I should say, was. Unfortunately, she's recently had a stroke.'

She was probably gaga as well, Izzie thought. Apart from the pay, the more he told her the less appealing the job became.

Not wishing to appear rude, Izzie chewed her bottom lip. 'Well . . .' she began again.

'I would be happy to give you a recommendation.'

Izzie hesitated.

'Look,' Mr Allen said quickly as he picked up the telephone, 'why not take the afternoon off and go round there to meet them? I'll give them a ring to say you are on your way.'

Izzie walked to her appointment. She felt sure she would hate the job but she couldn't break her promise to Mr Allen after he'd gone to all the trouble of ringing *young* Mrs Shilling, as he'd called her, to say she was on her way. As she waited to cross Richmond Road, a bus heading towards the town went past. A face at the window brought her up with a jolt. The woman seemed surprised to see Izzie too. They stared at each other for several seconds before the bus moved out of sight. It was Mrs Sayers. What was it about that woman that made her feel so uncomfortable?

Five

The White Lodge was a big Victorian house on the corner of Victoria Road and Richmond Road. The maid who opened the door to her seemed pleasant enough, but Izzie's first impression of young Mrs Shilling, who was standing in the hallway in front of the mirror, wasn't so good. The maid left. Izzie waited.

The woman might have been known as *young* Mrs Shilling, but she wasn't that young and she seemed a bit snobby. She had smiled briefly when Izzie explained who she was, but after that, she'd hardly looked at her. She was obviously getting ready to go out. Izzie couldn't help admiring her elegant suit with a new look length skirt in a stunning royal blue, but Mrs Shilling made a point of saying that she couldn't stay long, making Izzie feel that she was a bit of a nuisance even being there.

'I'm meeting friends for afternoon tea,' she explained as Izzie watched her tightening the little black belt over the top of her jacket to emphasize her dainty waist. 'Mr Allen tells me you're a hard worker,' Mrs Shilling went on, 'but I must say you're very young. What experience do you have?'

Izzie's account of her working life was very brief.

Mrs Shilling leaned forward in front of the mirror on the hallstand and patted her hair before putting her hat on. 'How long have you worked in the green grocer's?'

'Since I left school, Madam.'

Mrs Shilling raised an eyebrow. 'And why are you leaving now?'

'Mr Allen wants his son to learn the family business,' Izzie said.

Having taken her gloves from the drawer on the front of the hallstand, Mrs Shilling opened her handbag and found her lipstick, which she applied to her already brightly covered mouth. 'Mr Allen can give me your references?' she added before rubbing her lips together.

'Yes, Madam.'

They were interrupted by the sound of a car horn on the road outside. 'Good,' said Mrs Shilling as she gathered her things. 'Then you'd better go and see mother-in-law.' She breezed past Izzie with hardly a backward glance and opened the front door to wave at someone outside. Before closing the door again, she leaned back into the hallway and, waving her hand irritably said, 'Off you go then. Along the corridor, third door on the right.' The front door banged and, with that, Izzie was left alone in the hallway.

Annoyed by Mrs Shilling's attitude, it was only the thought of having to tell Mr Allen that she hadn't actually met old Mrs Shilling that prevented Izzie from walking out herself. She made up her mind that if the old lady was gaga, or as rude as her daughter-in-law, she definitely wouldn't be staying.

Izzie set off down the hall and knocked on the third door. A surprisingly strong voice called, 'Come in.'

The old lady was sitting in a big leather chair which was pulled up to a table in front of the window. The table itself was covered with boxes and what looked like some very unusual pieces of pottery.

'Who are you, dear?'

'My name is Isobelle Baxter but everybody calls me Izzie.

I've come about the post.' And at the old lady's behest, she went through her résumé once again.

Mrs Shilling listened attentively and then smiled. 'Well, you seem like a very capable girl,' she began, 'so let me tell you a bit about myself.' She indicated that she should sit down so Izzie perched on the nearest chair.

'My husband and I were archaeologists,' the old lady went on. 'We worked mainly in South America. He died just before the war and I came back to this country. I spent the war years working as an archivist. With the threat of invasion hanging over our heads, we had to do all we could to protect the nation's heritage.' Mrs Shilling went on to explain that after her retirement, she had spent her latter years writing reports and papers on the work she and her husband had done. She was so fascinating that Izzie found herself relaxing; making herself more comfortable as she listened to the story.

They were both in a lovely room overlooking the garden. The walls were lined with books and there were some interesting and intriguing things on display.

'I planned to write a book about our experiences but my health has let me down,' Mrs Shilling continued. 'Still, I am luckier than most. My stroke has left me with a weak arm and my leg isn't too clever but fortunately I haven't lost my marbles . . . yet.'

Izzie chuckled. As she sat listening to her, it didn't take long to realise that working for someone like Mrs Shilling would be very interesting indeed.

'Tea?' the old lady asked.

Izzie nodded. 'Yes please.'

Mrs Shilling rang the bell on the table next to her and a little while later the girl who had opened the front door to Izzie came into the room. 'Could you bring us some tea please, Esther?'

'What I want is someone to help me put everything down in black and white,' Mrs Shilling said as Esther closed the door again. 'Can you type?'

With a sinking feeling, Izzie shook her head.

'Not to worry,' old Mrs Shilling said brightly. 'I shall dictate everything slowly so that you can write it in long hand and even if you can only type it up with one finger, it will be good practice for you. So what do you say? Can I tempt you to come and work for me?'

The tea tray arrived with crumpets, home-made jam and cake.

As Esther set the tray on the table in front of them, Izzie smiled and found herself saying 'Yes.'

*

Later that evening, old Mrs Shilling's nurse had helped her to wash and put on her nightdress. Her long hair had been brushed and the old lady hummed to herself as she massaged some cream onto her hands.

'You should make it part of your night-time routine, Madam,' the nurse had said. 'I know it's hard but you should try and keep as active as possible.'

The old lady was sitting up in bed when her daughter-in-law breezed into her bedroom. 'Hubert has just told me that you've decided to employ that young girl,' she blurted out without preamble.

'Yes I did Muriel,' said old Mrs Shilling. 'Such a delightful person.'

Muriel Shilling glanced at the nurse. 'That will be all, nurse,' she said curtly.

'I was just going to . . .' the nurse began.

'I said, that will be all,' Muriel snapped.

As soon as the nurse, her face bright red with anger, had left the room, Muriel Shilling rounded on her mother-in-law. 'Hubert tells me you're going to pay her four pounds a week. That's far too much. A young girl like that would be grateful for half the wage.'

'Don't you think that's up to me, dear?' said old Mrs Shilling.

'It's a third more than I pay Esther,' her daughter-in-law snapped.

'That's as may be,' the old lady said, 'but Izzie and I have decided four pounds will be her wage.'

'I only wondered if you fully understood what you'd said,' Muriel said, flustered.

'I understood perfectly, dear.'

Muriel was flabbergasted. 'Well I think you should have discussed it with Hubert,' she snapped. 'The amount you are proposing to pay her is, in my humble opinion, quite ridiculous.'

'Point taken.' Her mother-in-law smiled sweetly. 'But it's my money.'

*

'I've got another job.'

Izzie was standing in the doorway of the scullery while her father was shaving in front of the cracked mirror hanging over the sink. Her father had turned towards her but showed no reaction when she told him about Mrs Shilling. Turning back to the mirror he drew his Gillette super speed razor down his soapy jaw and then shook it in the bowl of warm water in the sink before commencing the same move on the other side of his face. 'Good money?'

Izzie nodded. 'Four pounds a week.'

'Good,' he said, wiping his face clean of the little shaving soap that was left. 'From now on, you can pay two pounds ten shilling for your keep.'

Izzie frowned angrily. 'Dad!'

'Don't complain about it,' he said. 'Everybody has to . . .'

'Pay their way,' she chorused with him.

He turned his head and their eyes met but he said no more.

Izzie hesitated. 'Dad, do we know a Mrs Sayers?'

Her father was twisting the handle of his razor to get the blade out. As the butterfly doors on the top opened he froze. 'Why?' he said coldly. 'What's she been saying to you?'

'Nothing,' said Izzie. 'It's just that she came into Mr Allen's shop a while ago and asked if I knew her.'

Her father's face had clouded. 'Did she ask about me?'

'No.'

'Did you tell her where I live?'

Izzie was startled. 'Of course not. Why should I?'

Her father took the razor blade out of his shaver and patted it dry on his towel. 'You stay away from her.'

Izzie frowned. 'Why? What's she done?'

'Just stay away from her!' He was angry. 'That woman is nothing but trouble, do you hear?'

Izzie was surprised by his venom but it was obvious her father wasn't going to say any more about Mrs Sayers. All the same, Izzie couldn't resist one more try about the subject which troubled her most. 'Dad . . . about Mum . . .?'

He spun round, his face like thunder. Barging past her, he headed for the stairs. 'Leave it out Izzie. Just shut-up about her, will you.'

Linda came into the kitchen and put her satchel on the table. 'What's up with him?'

Izzie sighed. 'I asked him about Mum.'

Linda pulled a face. 'I asked him the other day,' she confessed. 'He went bananas.'

Izzie frowned. 'Why?'

Linda shrugged. 'I dunno.' She turned towards the stair door. 'I still miss her.'

'You and me both,' said Izzie.

*

Izzie enjoyed her work with old Mrs Shilling almost immediately. It was difficult to say exactly how old her employer was but her hair was steely grey and she had rheumy eyes. Although she looked fairly robust, Mrs Shilling tired easily and the nurse asked Izzie to make sure she didn't overdo it. Izzie arrived at the house each day by nine-thirty and stayed until four, which gave her the opportunity to do some of the household chores at home before she left for work in the morning. Linda still did very little to help.

'Linda would you—'

'I would if I could but I haven't got time right now,' Linda said airily as she pin-curled her hair. Izzie had asked her to peel some potatoes. 'I've got homework to do.'

'Oh Linda!'

'Don't keep on at me!'

'I'm not,' Izzie protested, 'but I get fed up doing everything.'

'I took the bin out last night,' Linda protested, 'and you didn't even notice.'

'Oh, pardon me,' cried Izzie. 'Next time, remind me and I'll give you a medal.'

Her sister walked out of the room, slamming the door.

*

The house was much more of a home now, even though everything they had was second hand or hand-me-down. Izzie had no intention of staying at home anyway. She was convinced that life was passing her by and she was becoming old before her time. If her job with Mrs Shilling hadn't been so fascinating, she would have been tempted to clear off altogether, like Mum, and leave them to it.

According to the policy makers, things were finally beginning to look up as far as the country was concerned. What they had called The Great Depression after the war was coming to an end and small signs that things were going to get better began to emerge. In March the previous year, the clothing rationing had ended so Izzie was able to wander around the shops knowing that only lack of money prevented her from buying something new. Her father still demanded that she hand over two pounds, ten shillings of her four pounds wage for her keep. She had protested of course and tried to bargain with him but he was adamant. What a chump she'd been telling him the truth. She should have said she was only getting three pounds ten shillings.

In fact, everything seemed to be conspiring against her. The new National Health Service, which had begun in 1948, meant that Izzie also had to pay her National Insurance stamp and her taxes as well. That didn't leave a lot for her to spend or save. She and Patsy went to the pictures sometimes and occasionally Linda would tag along as well, but thankfully their father always paid for Linda's ticket.

Izzie tried going to the dances at the Assembly Hall but they were noisy crowded affairs where she got too hot and couldn't afford the soft drinks so she didn't enjoy them very much. The prevailing fashion was for up-beat music like jazz but Izzie preferred the more romantic ballads like 'Some Enchanted Evening' or jolly songs like 'Powder Your Face with Sunshine', the sort of music they played on *Family Favourites* on the BBC Light programme. Hosted by Jean Metcalfe in London and Cliff

Michelmore in Germany, the broadcast was aimed at families who were separated; husbands in Germany as part of the British Forces Overseas, and the wives and children who were left at home. Izzie particularly liked the programme because the thought of people who loved each other aching because they were apart was something close to her own heart. Even after all this time, she still ached for her mother.

Linda wanted to go dancing too but their father deemed her too young. For that, he said, she would have to be sixteen. There were a few rows about it but for once Linda didn't get her way.

Six

After the heatwave in 1949, which turned out to be one of the hottest years on record, the summer months in 1950 looked as if they would be much more moderate. All the same, old Mrs Shilling decamped to the summer house in the garden and the pair of them plodded on with her book. Izzie loved it there. It felt like a tiny taste of Dial Post and she was often distracted by a blackbird bathing in the bird bath or a pair of quarrelsome pigeons fighting over what was left on the bird table. Throughout the summer they trained a squirrel to come ever closer to the doorway after Mrs Shilling had thrown some of her tea time scone in his direction.

As well as helping old Mrs Shilling with her memoirs, Izzie would occasionally push her employer in her wheelchair for a stroll along the promenade and on to a tea room in the town in the afternoons. Mrs Shilling's all-time favourite had been Mabel's in South Street, near Lawley's the china shop, but it had closed down.

'Worthing has changed so much since the war,' Mrs Shilling complained sadly as Izzie pushed her past the boarded up shop. They crossed the road and headed towards Hubbard's or Marine Parade and The Dome Tea Rooms. 'It's just not the same; pleasant but not the same.'

Just by the bus stop, someone running for the bus dashed in front of the wheelchair.

'Watch what you're doing,' said an angry voice. The woman turned to glare at her as she boarded the bus and Izzie took in a breath. It was that Mrs Sayers again.

'I'm sorry, Mrs Sayers,' Izzie apologised, though it was hardly her fault.

'Are you all right, dear?' asked Mrs Shilling.

Izzie nodded. 'I keep bumping into that woman and she's always so angry with me.'

'Why?'

Izzie shrugged. 'I haven't the foggiest.'

*

The rest of the Shilling household had little to do with Izzie. Young Mrs Shilling (Muriel) had a very busy social calendar so she only popped her head around the door to say goodbye. Izzie sensed a tension between them but the two women kept up the pretence of polite concern for each other. Mr Shilling was usually gone to work before Izzie arrived. He was a bank manager somewhere in Brighton. She had seen him a couple of times when he came home early to get ready for some function or to entertain a client for dinner. A nondescript man in a grey suit, balding and with deep set eyes under very thick and bushy eyebrows. He would smile affably at Izzie and say something like, 'Mrs Shilling keeping you busy, eh?' as he planted a kiss on his mother's cheek.

Esther, the maid, kept them both well furbished with tea or cold drinks throughout the day and while the two Mrs Shillings ate their lunch together in the dining room on the days when she was at home, Izzie sat with the other members of staff at the kitchen table. It was opportunity to chat with Mrs Dore the cook and Esther in between her duties serving at table. Mrs Dore, a plump woman with a florid complexion had worked for the Shillings for ten years or more. She liked old Mrs Shilling and her son but her opinion of Muriel Shilling, she declared with a pinched expression, was best left unsaid. Izzie could easily guess why.

'How am I expected to stretch that squitty bit of meat between the seven of us?' she heard Mrs Dore say on more than one occasion. 'There's hardly enough there to feed the cat! Oh, she can spend money like there's no tomorrow on clothes, but she's as tight as a dog's bottom when it comes to the house-keeping.'

Her outburst gave Izzie a shrewd idea that Mrs Dore was expected to manage the household on a rather meagre budget. Certainly the meal portions in the servant's kitchen were very small although Izzie didn't mind too much. It helped her to get a trimmer figure.

She and Esther soon struck up a friendship and on the odd occasion when their off duty times coincided, Esther joined Patsy and Izzie at the pictures.

By the end of July, the first draft of the memoir was finished and old Mrs Shilling finally admitted that she was exhausted.

'I'm going to take a break,' she announced. 'I shall go down to Bournemouth to see my sister.'

Izzie nodded sagely. So this was it. Her nice little job was at an end. 'Would you like me to come back when you return to Worthing?' she asked without much hope of a favourable reply.

'I should like you to come with me,' Mrs Shilling declared stoutly. 'Do you think your father would let you?'

Izzie couldn't hide her delight and excitement. 'I'd like to see him try and stop me!'

Later that day, as Izzie came back from her lunch, the dining room door was still open and she heard the two Mrs Shillings having a heated discussion.

'Have you any idea how much all this is going to cost?'

'Not really, dear.'

'A chauffeur driving all the way to Bournemouth, the two of you staying in the Royal Bath, and that's not cheap; a nurse to come in twice a day . . . Good God mother, you could go to New York on the *Queen Mary* for the same price.'

'Muriel,' old Mrs Shilling said firmly, 'I don't care. Why shouldn't I have a little pleasure in my old age?'

Izzie didn't hear any more. The dining room door suddenly closed, leaving only the sound of angry muffled voices.

*

Little did Mrs Shilling know but Izzie faced the same kind of reaction from her father. He did his best to put his foot down when she told him but when she said if she gave in her notice she would earn a lot less in a shop and would probably only be able to give him half as much money for her keep, he relented. 'Well, I suppose it's only for a week,' he said grudgingly.

Linda was green with envy. 'It's not fair,' she said, stamping her foot and glaring at her sister with a pouty mouth. 'You'll be leaving me to do everything.'

As she picked up the dirty dishes to put them in the sink, Izzie allowed herself a small smile. Just like you leave me to do everything the rest of the year, she thought acidly. Now you'll find out just what it's like.

'Don't you worry sweetheart,' she heard their father say as he put his arm comfortingly around Linda's shoulders. 'We'll eat at Mick's fish and chip shop during the week and just for a treat, I'll take you out somewhere nice on Friday.'

Gripping the edge of the sink, Izzie felt her face flush with the unfairness of it all.

*

They set off a week later. When they arrived a couple of hours later, Izzie's first impression of Bournemouth was wonderful. As they motored down from The Lansdowne, the leafy tree lined streets led them down a hill and she could see the sea glistening on the horizon. The weather was good and to Izzie's delight and amazement, their chauffeur driven car pulled up outside a posh hotel only a few minutes' walk from the beach. A bevy of porters descended upon the car to carry their suitcases and unload the wheelchair and her own private nurse was on hand to help Mrs Shilling freshen up in her room. On the way down, Mrs Shilling had explained that Izzie's duties were to be quite light, mainly to push her around the town and down to the beach in her wheelchair. The old lady had also decided to replenish her wardrobe so their first day was spent walking around some amazing shops like Bobby's, Plummer's and Beales. The assistants had been pre-warned that they were coming so they were more than helpful. Most of what Mrs Shilling looked at was old fashioned but while she was busy in the changing rooms, Izzie got a chance to catch a glimpse of some fantastically modern clothes on the other rails. The shop assistant at her elbow pulled some out to show her but although Izzie admired them, she shook her head. Everything was way beyond her price range.

Her employer was a gregarious woman so it wasn't long before she'd got into conversation with the other guests and invariably they'd invite her to join them in a rubber of bridge or a game of whist. Izzie kept a weather eye on her but she also took the opportunity to take a turn around the garden behind the hotel or to browse the magazines on a table near the entrance. A couple of times, a young man would try to engage her in conversation, until he found out that she wasn't some lonely heiress looking for Mr Right.

Their evenings were spent mainly in the hotel dining room and lounge where Izzie was sometimes asked to keep Mrs Shilling company. At the dinner table, Izzie enjoyed some of the most amazing meals she'd ever had and tasted wine for the very first time.

'You won't tell my daughter-in-law what we've been up to, will you?' Mrs Shilling said on the second evening when they'd just tucked into roast pheasant, pommes rissole and Brussels sprouts followed by sherry trifle (heavy on the sherry and with lashings of cream) and coffee.

Izzie grinned. 'Your secret is safe with me Mrs Shilling.'

On Wednesday, Izzie had a day to herself when Mrs Shilling took a taxi to visit her sister. She walked through Bournemouth Gardens, admiring the formal flower beds before setting off for the shops. Avoiding the more expensive stores, Izzie headed along Commercial Road towards The Triangle and the more affordable shops. After an hour or so trying on different things, she treated herself to an adorable white blouse with short kimono sleeves and an imitation artist's bow at the front. She bought it just in time as Wednesday was half closing.

At lunch time she ate a sandwich and had a cup of tea in a small café near the pavilion but the highlight of her day, if not her whole time in Bournemouth, was her afternoon trip to the Pier Approach Baths. Here she splashed out for a ticket to see the aqua-show where swimmers and divers showed off their skills in a mixture of comic routine and dazzling displays of skill. Back in the hotel that night, she sent a postcard to her father and Linda.

Having a wonderful time. Went to the Aqua show. I saw Roy Fransen the European champion diving from the top of the board. He was amazing.

'Tell me a bit about yourself,' the old lady asked her on their last but one morning as they drank coffee on the balcony of Mrs Shilling's room. 'Where did you grow up? What do your parents do?'

And although she hadn't meant to, Izzie found herself pouring her heart out. She spoke of the night her mother left home, of the desperate search to find her and finally being told that she was in hospital. She talked about grandparents and their house in Dial Post. 'My grandfather died about six months after we'd left Dial Post,' she went on, 'but I still keep in touch with Granny.'

'Do you see her very often?' Mrs Shilling asked.

'Not as much as I would like to,' Izzie admitted.

'You must miss her.'

'I miss my mother more.' Izzie had blurted it out without thinking. Embarrassed by her outburst, she kept her head down so that her employer wouldn't see the tears standing in her eyes.

'I'm so sorry my dear,' Mrs Shilling said. 'It must have been awful for you.' She leaned forward to pat Izzie's hand. 'Well,' she went on, 'I don't know about you but I fancy a little drive out into the countryside. Fetch my things, will you dear, and ask the desk to call the chauffeur service.'

That afternoon, they enjoyed a glorious ride around the area; the chauffeur taking them to Ringwood, a small market town on the Hampshire–Dorset border. From there they motored back to Wimborne with its ancient minster and on to Poole where Mrs Shilling bought an expensive carafe in the Poole pottery shop. It was made by Head of Design Claude Smale, who was busy working on some pieces that he'd first made for the Festival of Britain, which was held in London. It was late afternoon before their chauffeur drove them back to Bournemouth. He was a cheeky man who kept winking at Izzie in the rear-view mirror and he flirted shamelessly with her when Mrs Shilling stopped for a comfort break in Wimborne. Izzie did nothing to encourage him and why would she? He was thirty years old if he was a day.

'You know my dear, I've been thinking. It shouldn't be too difficult to find out what happened to your mother,' Mrs Shilling said kindly as Izzie escorted her back to her room. 'Have you talked to your father about it?'

'I did when I was younger,' Izzie admitted, 'but he used to get cross. Besides, he was always sparing with the detail so I suppose I pushed it to the back of my mind and gave up.'

'Perhaps he thought you were too young to understand,' said Mrs Shilling. 'Why not try again? Surely he can see you are very mature for your age.'

'I don't know,' said Izzie cautiously. 'I get the feeling my father has closed that chapter of his life.'

Mrs Shilling nodded sagely. 'Just as you wish my dear, but remember, if you need to talk or I can help in any way, you only have to ask.'

Seven

Bill Baxter was feeling tempted. Business was slow. He'd found a few good items in his last house clearance but because he was still paying off a loan, money was tight. In order to kick start the business, he had borrowed money at an extortionate rate of interest and it was imperative to keep up the payments. What he needed was some quick cash.

It had been a good move getting the girls back. Izzie paid her way and now that she'd got a better paid job, he'd persuaded her to put enough money in the kitty to cover a little of Linda's keep as well. Of course, Izzie grumbled and complained, but he'd told her in no uncertain terms, 'that's life'. You never do get something for nothing. She did the cooking and cleaning, which meant he didn't have to employ a housekeeper. The house wasn't as clean and tidy as it was when he was married to Doris, but it didn't matter that much. He was hardly at home anyway and so long as he had his tea and a clean shirt, he'd get by. Good times were just around the corner because he had met someone. He wasn't about to get serious but if he was to keep her happy, he needed money. He arranged three antique snuff boxes on a piece of green velvet. They were pretty stunning. Years ago, he'd promised Doris he would never go back to his old ways but when you're desperate for some ready cash, what can you do? Should he

58

take a risk? If he was careful, he told himself, it should be all right.

He reached for his loupe and looked over a William IV sterling silver table box with a beautifully executed floral design, a slightly smaller box, round, with impressed dark blue enamel panels and an Edwardian oval silver box with a hardstone lid. All were clearly hallmarked and all were stolen. Bill glanced up at the man in front of him. He'd probably hit hard times himself. Bill took a deep breath. This was too good an opportunity to miss.

'I can't offer you more than seventy quid for the lot.'

The man's face paled. He may be well dressed in a striped suit and camel coat, but Bill could tell a shady character when he saw one. 'What? Good God man, they're worth four hundred on the open market.'

'But we're not talking about the open market are we,' Bill said levelly. 'And I shall have to wait a long time for my return.'

The man scowled. 'All right damn you. I'll take seventy, no questions asked.'

A moment or two later his customer walked out of the shop a little richer and once again, Bill Baxter, against his better judgement, had become a receiver of stolen goods.

*

The next day, their last in Bournemouth, Izzie's employer decided to take some of her artefacts from South America to the Russell-Cotes Museum on the East Cliff. After breakfast she'd asked Izzie to fetch a box from the hotel safe. Izzie brought it to her room.

Mrs Shilling opened the box with her key and took out a leather case. 'Put that on the table for me will you?'

When Mrs Shilling opened the leather case, it contained a couple of bracelets with gemstones, a long link chain necklace with seven oblong shaped pieces hanging from it, and a pair of earrings with what looked like a coin at the top. Beneath the coin there was a horse shoe shape which held several long tassels. It was obvious that they were all made of gold. There were also several small statues, which were shaped like birds and fish. Mrs Shilling ran her fingers over them lovingly.

'When I die,' she said, 'all these will belong to the museum. I should have handed everything in a long time ago. Still, it's already been hidden for five thousand years, and I wanted to look at it occasionally.' She placed one of the bracelets over her left wrist and sighed. 'I remember the day I found this one . . .' And she was off again, recalling the excitement of the dig and its discovery.

The walk up the East Cliff was a struggle – Mrs Shilling wasn't a heavy woman but the hill was steep – and Izzie kept thinking about their discussion the day before. Should she really try and contact her mother? Should she talk it over with Linda first? And what about her father? He would probably go bonkers but the more she thought about it, the more she wanted to do it. Her mother had been in hospital but which one? Maybe she should start with that. If she found out when her mother had been discharged, they might tell her where she was. But what if she was still unwell? She had to do it soon. Izzie couldn't bear the thought that if she left it too long it might be too late.

*

All too soon, the holiday came to an end and Mrs Shilling's chauffeur took them back to Worthing. Izzie had enjoyed every minute. Because of her employer's generosity, she'd had time to herself and she had been a guest in a luxurious hotel. She'd enjoyed the meeting in the Russell-Cotes Museum and while Mrs Shilling and the curator talked business in the office, Izzie had been given a personal tour of the exhibitions by one of the staff. She had learned that back at the turn of the century, fifty years ago, the museum had been the home of Sir Merton and Lady Annie Russell-Cotes. Situated on the cliff top, overlooking the beach and with a beautiful garden, it was such a romantic place. Like Mrs Shilling and her husband, Sir Merton and Lady Annie had collected artefacts over a lifetime of travelling. As Izzie walked around listening to the stories behind the exhibits, she knew she would remember this trip for the rest of her life.

Back in Worthing and with an exhausted Mrs Shilling resting in her room, Izzie emptied the suitcases and put the washing into the laundry room. She was just about to leave when Esther called her.

'She wants to see you,' she said.

'Who?'

'Old Mrs Shilling.'

Mrs Shilling was in her bed. The nurse had given the old lady her medication and even though it was only six-thirty, it was obvious that she was more than ready for sleep.

'Oh Izzie,' she said, pushing an envelope into her hands. 'I wanted to thank you for helping to make this trip so special. You've been so patient with me and so helpful. I want you to have this.'

Izzie tried to refuse the gift. 'You've already given me so much, Madam,' but her employer was insistent.

When Izzie opened the envelope in the privacy of the toilet she found a five pound note. She caught her breath. She'd never seen one before let alone owned one. She smiled. What an amazing person Mrs Shilling was. This would boost her leaving home fund quite a bit.

*

When Izzie got home to Chandos Road the house was in an absolute shambles. She left her things by the stairs and set about clearing up the mess in the kitchen. Linda hadn't even bothered to wash up her own breakfast things let alone the things in the sink and her father had obviously come in and done a fry up at lunch time. The greasy pan rested on the top of the pile of plates in the sink. On the table, the loaf of bread had been hacked to death on the board. As she walked past the cooker, Izzie's foot almost went from under her. Clearly someone had dropped and broken an egg, leaving it where it fell on the floor. She frowned crossly. It would take her ages to clear a space before she could even start to get the tea ready. Resentfully, she crashed the dishes from the washing up bowl to the draining board and put the kettle on to boil some water. There were two empty beer bottles on the table and the ash tray was over-flowing. As she picked it up to empty it, she caught a faint whiff of perfume in the air. That's when she heard the sound of voices upstairs. Izzie froze. Someone was in the house? But who? Izzie's heart began to thump. After a minute or two and hearing nothing else, she went to the bottom of the stairs. She cocked her ears and listened.

'Hello? Is anyone there?'

There was a shuffling sound and her father called down, 'Only me. I'm having a bit of a lie down. I'll be down in a minute.'

Suddenly concerned she called, 'Are you all right, Dad?'

She heard hushed whispering before he called out, 'I'm fine. Just a bit tired, that's all.'

The kettle had boiled so Izzie returned to the kitchen to make a start. As she tipped the ash tray into the bin, she noticed one cigarette was stained red at the tip. Then she heard the sound of a woman laughing and glancing up at the ceiling, her heart went cold.

A little while later, she heard voices in the hallway and then the front door slammed. A second later, her father appeared in the doorway. His face was flushed. 'So, you're back.'

'Yes, I got in about ten minutes ago,' she said. 'I didn't expect to find you here.'

For a second or two, when she'd heard the woman's laughter, she had toyed with the idea of charging upstairs and confronting them both, but then she'd decided she didn't really want to know who it was or what they were doing. Somehow, she knew it wasn't her mother.

'Let's give you a hand with that love,' he said in an uncharacteristically cheerful voice, as he'd picked up a tea towel. He dried a plate then said, 'I've just taken your sister over to your grandmother's.'

Izzie's heart went into her mouth. 'Is Granny all right?'

'Fine,' her father said with a grin. 'Seeing as how you've been swanning about in Bournemouth I thought your sister could do with a little break too.'

Izzie returned to the sink and they carried on working in silence. When they finished, Izzie put the clean crockery onto the dresser.

'Aren't you going to put the kettle on?' her father asked as he flopped into a chair and shook out his newspaper.

Izzie sighed. No, 'How was your week, Izzie? Did you have a good time? Nice to have you back.' She picked up the kettle and walked to the sink. Yes, the sooner she was out of here, the better.

⨉

Alone in her room later, Izzie got the five pound note out again to look at it. She would have to get a Post Office Savings book. It was far too much money to leave lying around the house.

With her other savings, she probably had as much as eight or maybe nine pounds by now although she hadn't counted it for a while. With a happy smile, she pulled her tin from the drawer but when she opened it Izzie gasped in horror. Instead of finding a tin half full of money, there were only a few coins left. Where had it all gone? She tipped the money onto the bed and counted out twelve shillings and tuppence. The disappointment reduced her to tears. When she'd set out for Bournemouth she definitely had a lot more money than this. She'd been the victim of theft and there was only one person who could have taken it.

Linda.

Eight

'I hope you jolly well had it out with her. What did she say?'

Izzie and Esther were returning to Worthing on the bus. Izzie had just told her friend about the missing money and Esther was so indignant she could hardly contain herself.

Izzie shook her head. 'Not yet. She's still over at Granny's. My father sent her away for a week's holiday.'

'Which is probably why she pinched the money!' cried Esther. 'You will confront her when she gets back.'

'You bet!' Izzie said emphatically.

A woman passenger in front of them turned around to stare. As she turned back Izzie stuck her tongue out and the two girls grinned at each other.

They had spent the afternoon together in Brighton and now they were returning to Esther's house to get ready to go out to the pictures for the evening.

Their time in Brighton had been brilliant. They'd wandered through the Lanes doing a bit of window-shopping and then walked up to Hannington's department store to look at the make-up counters and the dresses. Neither of them could afford anything but that didn't stop them trying on dresses and coats and even some shoes. By four-thirty they'd walked back to Poole Valley to catch the bus back to Worthing.

As the conductor rang the bell and called out 'Worthing

Central,' the two of them stood up to get off. They waited for the crossing gates to open then walked over the railway line to Esther's house in West Court Road. Mrs Jordan had already invited Izzie to stay for tea so it wasn't long before they were tucking into a plate of shepherd's pie and cabbage. After they'd eaten, Esther took Izzie upstairs to her bedroom to change. On the way back from Brighton, she'd suggested going to the dance but Izzie had declined. She'd made the excuse that she was really tired but the truth was, she couldn't afford it. Esther had tried so hard to persuade Izzie that she decided to confide in her friend about the theft.

'I cannot get over how heartless your sister was,' Esther cried. 'How cruel.'

Her passion suddenly made Izzie feel disloyal. Linda might be a rotten cow but she was still her sister. Perhaps she should have kept what had happened to herself. Maybe she shouldn't have confided in Esther. 'You won't tell anyone will you,' she said anxiously. 'She didn't take it all but I was saving up.'

'For something nice?'

Izzie took a deep breath. 'I want to leave home.'

She waited for the backlash but to her surprise Esther said, 'Good for you. I'm leaving home too.' Izzie's face must have registered her shock because she added, 'Oh don't get me wrong. I love my home and my parents are sweeties but in this day and age it's important for a girl to be independent, don't you think? Anyway, I can't bear the thought of working in that dreary job for ever.'

'What will you do?' asked Izzie.

Esther waved her hand in the direction of a pile of books on the shelf. 'I want to join the police force. That's why I'm studying.'

Izzie was taken aback. She'd been annoyed when her father had taken her out of school early but it had never occurred to her to pick up her studies in her spare time. She had simply rolled over and accepted that there was no chance of going to college or university for people like her so why bother.

'Gosh,' said Izzie. 'You're brave, but surely you have to wait until you're old enough before you can join?'

'I do but it's not long now,' said Esther. 'A couple of years ago they lowered the entry age to twenty.' She grinned. 'Only a few months to go.'

Izzie was surprised. She knew Esther was older than her but she had no idea she was nearly twenty. She certainly didn't look it. Only five foot four, she was a pretty girl with blonde hair and a porcelain complexion. Izzie fingered the book at the top of the pile, *The Modern Police Force*. Lifting the front cover to take a peek inside, it looked as dry as dust.

'What do you plan to do when you leave home?' Esther asked.

Izzie was immediately placed on the back foot. She hadn't got that far either. All she wanted to do was get away from her father and Linda. Quite what she was going to do once she'd actually packed her bag she hadn't a clue. She shrugged hopelessly. 'I haven't really thought about it,' she admitted rather sheepishly.

Esther got up and pushed Izzie down into the chair in front of the mirror. 'Shall I do your hair for you?'

It seemed a bit silly when they were only going to sit in the dark all evening but Izzie found it very relaxing as her friend brushed her hair. 'The trick is to think of something you really enjoy,' said Esther. 'Something you're good at.'

Izzie's mind went blank. What was she good at? Housework, recognising bird song, listening to people, a bit of typing . . . where on earth could that take her?

'You're very good with Mrs Shilling,' Esther remarked. 'What about training to be a nurse?'

'Oh no,' said Izzie with a small shudder. 'I can't bear the thought of all that blood and vomit. I'm far too squeamish.'

'Care of the elderly?'

Izzie wrinkled her nose. 'They're not all as nice as Mrs Shilling.'

Esther chuckled. 'You might be right there. What about writing?'

'I'm not clever enough for that,' said Izzie.

'Don't put yourself down, Izzie,' Esther scolded. 'You've done wonders with that book of Mrs Shilling's. Everybody says so.'

'I've only written what she told me,' said Izzie.

'There,' said Esther, stepping back and patting Izzie's hair.

It looked amazing. With a few deft strokes of the hair brush she had made Izzie look very grown up.

'Shove over Princess Margaret,' said Esther, putting on a posh accent. 'Here comes Lady Isobelle Baxter.'

And they both laughed.

The film at the Dome (Esther's choice) was quite good. Starring Norman Wooland and Sarah Churchill, it was a comedy drama about a failing newspaper and two down-on-their-luck reporters who expose a corrupt property tycoon. As the credits rolled the two girls stood to their feet. 'That Norman Wooland is really dishy,' Esther said out of the corner of her mouth as they waited for the National Anthem to finish.

Izzie wasn't thinking about him but the film had given her food for thought.

*

Back from Granny's, Linda was also at the pictures. Terry, a boy she'd met on the bus back home, had asked Linda to go out with him so she'd agreed to meet him outside the Rivoli in North Street on the other side of town. Linda was very excited as this was her first ever date. Because she had assured Terry that she was over sixteen, he was taking her to the early evening showing of *The Queen of Spades,* an H rated film. You were supposed to be sixteen to go to a horror film so he obviously thought she was a lot older. They met in the foyer. He was quite good looking although she could see now that she was up close to him that he did have rather a lot of spots. His hair was brushed into a quiff and when she'd complimented him on his roll cuff denim jeans he'd told her they had cost him three weeks wages. Linda hung back until Terry bought tickets. They were for the back row.

Almost as soon as the lights went down, Terry held her hand and Linda shivered with a delicious sense of naughtiness. She felt ever so grown-up but what would her father say if he knew she was here? What would Izzie say?

The film, which was quite scary, was about a woman who sold her soul to the devil so that she could win at cards and a soldier who became obsessed with discovering her secret. During one spooky bit, Linda jumped and cried out. Terry took the opportunity to pull her towards him and then he began to kiss her. Her heart was thumping as his mouth covered hers and his tongue went between her teeth. At first, it felt as if she was being sucked right inside and swallowed alive and her initial reaction was 'is this what they write songs about?' but after a few moments, she began to enjoy it. When he began kneading her left breast with his hand, her heart beat even faster and it quickly became overwhelming. Linda tried to push him off but that only seemed to enflame his passion. His hand drifted up her skirt and between her legs. She tried desperately to stop him touching her knickers but it wasn't until the usherette shone her torch their way that he moved away. Trembling and dishevelled, Linda sat up straight. The usherette moved on and a moment later Terry grabbed her again. This time he pulled her hand towards his crutch and she shrank away in shocked surprise at the huge bulge between his legs.

'Don't,' she whispered as loudly as she dared. But the more she tried to regain her composure, the more excited he became. The next time the usherette shone her torch at them, Linda jumped to her feet.

'Where are you going?' he hissed.

'To the ladies.'

She worked her way along the row and followed the usherette back into the foyer.

'You all right, love?' the woman asked.

Linda nodded dully but wasted no time in getting out of the cinema. As she pushed open the swing door onto the street, she heard Terry behind her calling her name. Panicking and scared, Linda just ran. Charging up North Street towards Richmond Road, her plan had been to turn into the darkened street and head straight for home but she had forgotten to bring her torch. Added to that, when she glanced behind, Terry was running after her, and worse still, gaining ground. Something told her to stay in an area where there were street lights and other people. It was better to avoid the dark twittens. With that in mind, she kept heading towards the centre of town.

A group of young people had gathered on the steps of St Paul's Church for a group photograph. Linda mounted the steps to the side of them and stood at the back.

The photographer was standing on the street complaining. 'I can't see everyone. Shorter people in the front please.'

A second later, Linda found herself being propelled towards the front of the group. She spotted Terry standing on the corner of Chapel Road and Union Place, doing his best to look nonchalant with his hands in his pockets.

The photographer shouted 'Say cheese,' and the huge bulb

on the side of his camera exploded in a flash of white light. As Linda slunk around the back of the group again she saw Terry give her two fingers before he continued down Chapel Road towards the bus station.

'Coming in for some refreshments?'

Linda swivelled around to face a girl about her own age. She shook her head.

'I've never seen you at the youth club before,' said the girl.

'My first time,' said Linda.

'Oh, please come in,' said the girl. 'You'd be very welcome.'

Linda glanced around. Everyone was roughly her own age but they all looked a bit old fashioned and boring. The girl was keen to get Linda inside. 'We're going to have a warm drink and something to eat and we've got a table tennis table or you can dance if you want.'

Linda caught sight of a couple of good looking boys and smiled. 'Have you got a group in there then?'

The girl laughed. 'No, not tonight, but we do have a fairly decent gramophone and some really good records. By the way, my name is Ruth. What's yours?'

Linda hesitated and while she dithered, one of the better looking boys came up to her. 'You coming in then, doll?' he said in a fake American accent.

Linda nodded. This couldn't have been more perfect. If her dad checked up on her she could tell him she'd been to a *church* youth club and if she could name a few names so much the better. And when the paper came out later in the week, she would be right at the front of the photograph to prove it.

'Yeah,' she said with a lazy smile. 'Why not?'

Nine

On Sunday morning, Izzie was so tired, it took ages to get out of bed. After a snatched piece of toast, she carried on with what was left of the mammoth task of clearing up the house. By eleven-thirty the place was looking better, but there was still no sign of her father or her sister. Her father would most likely stay in bed until the pubs opened and she guessed that Linda was avoiding her. And so she should. Izzie was dying to confront her about the stolen money. She'd been practising what to say for hours. In the end she couldn't wait a moment longer and knocked on her sister's bedroom door. Silence. She knocked again and pushed the door open. The room was a complete shambles with clean clothes and dirty things all over the place. The bed was crumpled but Izzie was fairly sure it hadn't been slept in. She took in her breath noisily.

A sound behind her made her spin round. Her father had just come out of his room. He was bleary eyed and yawned as he scratched his head. Something about her expression must have registered because he said, 'What's up?'

'Linda's gone,' said Izzie.

'Probably went out early,' he said.

'There was no sign of her when I got up,' Izzie said, 'and she's not here.'

'What do you mean?' Her father pushed past her and went into Linda's bedroom. 'Well where is she then?' he added accusingly.

'I don't know,' cried Izzie.

Her father turned to her with a face like thunder. 'You must bloody know. She must have said something.'

'Dad, I don't know where she is and I don't care,' Izzie snapped. 'She wouldn't tell me anything anyway. It's about time you realised she's a lazy good-for-nothing thief and a liar.'

Her father's move caught Izzie off guard but the stinging blow to her cheek sent her reeling. She only just managed to save herself from tumbling sideways down the stairs. 'Don't you dare say that about your sister,' he snarled. 'Do you hear me? Don't you ever.'

Tears sprang into Izzie's eyes as she put her hand to her throbbing cheek. 'But it's true,' she blurted out. 'Before she went to Granny's she stole my savings.'

'I don't believe you!'

'It's true, Dad. I had four pound something in my piggy bank and now there's only twelve and six. She just helped herself to *my* money.'

'Did you see her take it?' he barked.

'No, but—'

'Well then don't go accusing people when you've got no proof.'

'There's only the three of us in the house,' Izzie protested.

'Oh, so you're accusing me now?'

'No of course not.'

'You're always on at that girl.'

'Only because she never does anything around the house.'

'Linda is just a school girl,' he said. 'You can't expect her to do a woman's work.'

'I'm not much older than she is and yet you expect me to

do it all,' Izzie retorted. She turned away in disgust. It was hopeless.

'For God's sake,' he spat angrily. 'You're as bad as your bloody mother, always bleating on about something. You never know when to stop, do you Izzie. I'm sick of your whinging and complaining.'

Izzie stared at his receding back in shocked surprise as he went back into his bedroom. She couldn't believe what he'd just said. Always bleating on? Izzie put her hand back onto her stinging face. It really hurt. He'd never hit her before and she'd certainly never heard him say anything like that about her mother before.

'Your mother never bloody liked things the way they were,' he shouted behind the closing door. 'It didn't matter what I did, there was no pleasing her.' He reappeared, buttoning his shirt. He had his trousers on now. 'So where did Linda go last night?'

'I don't know, Dad.'

He hesitated then added, 'I'll get my things on and go and look for her. You stay here and tidy up this mess.'

Izzie opened her mouth to protest but thought better of it.

As her father thundered down the stairs they heard the kitchen door open. 'Linda,' she heard him say. 'Where the hell have you been?'

Izzie hurtled downstairs behind him.

'Sorry, Daddy,' her sister was saying. 'Ruth let me to stay the night at her house. I would have let you know but we don't have a telephone do we.'

A girl Izzie had never seen before stood in the hallway beside her. She was neatly dressed although her clothes were slightly prim, and she wore no make-up. 'We are sorry if we alarmed you, Mr Baxter,' she said, 'but this awful man was following Linda and she was so scared I took her back to the vicarage.'

'The vicarage,' the father said dully.

'My father is the vicar of St Paul's,' said Ruth. 'We would have come straight round first thing this morning but we got up late and Linda asked if she could come to church with us.'

'To church . . .' They could all hear the astonishment in his voice.

'I went to the church youth club last night, Daddy,' said Linda, threading her arm through their father's and smiling up at him. 'It was ever so nice.'

Izzie felt her lip curl. Couldn't he see Linda was just sucking up to him?

'Well I'd better be going,' said Ruth, putting out her hand to shake. 'Goodbye Mr Baxter. See you next Saturday, Linda.' And with that she was gone.

Linda batted her eyelids and smiled. 'I hope I didn't worry you, Daddy.'

'It doesn't matter, sweetheart,' he said, placated. They walked together towards the kitchen. 'You're home safe and sound now.'

Still standing at the bottom of the stairs, Izzie's eyes smarted with angry unshed tears.

*

If Izzie thought the fact that they had sent Mrs Shilling's manuscript to the publisher was an end to the matter, she was mistaken. They worked steadily on her next book but soon after their return from Bournemouth, she found that the South American script had been returned covered in squiggles and funny symbols.

'We have to go through it all again,' Mrs Shilling explained. 'The copy editor has found a great deal of mistakes and anomalies which have to be corrected.'

'But I typed it just as you said,' Izzie said.

'It's not your fault, dear,' said Mrs Shilling. 'It happens all the time. The good news is, they liked it so much, that they want to pay me an advance for the book about our travels in Africa.' She chuckled. 'It looks like you'll be working for me for a while.'

Izzie was pleased to have the opportunity to work with Mrs Shilling but it did make finding a new job and leaving Worthing more difficult.

Mrs Shilling frowned uncertainly. 'You're happy about that, aren't you, Izzie?'

'Yes, yes of course,' said Izzie. 'It took me by surprise, that's all.'

They set to work at once. At first the symbols on the page looked a bit like shorthand or a foreign language but the instructions were clear enough.

'So that "Y" shape means I have to insert a space between those two words,' said Izzie pointing down at the page.

'And that mark which looks a bit like a doorstep, means we should have started a new paragraph there,' Mrs Shilling added. 'Oh dear, I'm afraid you really will have to type the whole thing again.' She smoothed out the page of instructions and put it beside the typewriter.

'It'll be fine,' said Izzie, anxious to get started.

By lunch time she had worked her way through twenty or more pages and it was agreed that she would begin typing them up again while Mrs Shilling had her nap.

The trouble was, as soon as Izzie was on her own, it was hard to keep her mind on the job. Over the past few weeks, she had done a lot of serious thinking. After her latest altercation with her father, Izzie had made up her mind that come hell or high water she was definitely going to try and find her mother. He'd treated her like a child but from now on, she didn't care what her father said and she wasn't even going to ask his permission. Although, at seventeen, she was still very much a minor (you had to be twenty-one to be considered an adult), Izzie felt competent enough to begin the search for her mother by herself. But where should she start? Esther was a good friend but Izzie felt she needed an older, wiser head on the subject, so she made up her mind that after Mrs Shilling had had her rest she would ask the old lady's advice.

'Do you think your mother may be living locally?' Mrs Shilling asked when Izzie spoke to her about it.

Izzie shrugged. 'I have no reason to think otherwise, but the truth is, I don't know.'

Mrs Shilling looked thoughtful. 'Izzie this may take some time. You'll have to take it one step at a time. I think the first thing is to put an advertisement in the paper.'

Later that week, at her employer's suggestion, Izzie placed an advertisement in the *Worthing Herald*, the *Littlehampton* and the *Worthing Gazette* and the *Brighton Evening Argus*.

If you have any information about the whereabouts of Doris Baxter of Elm Grove, Worthing, last seen on February 25th 1947 in Worthing, Sussex, please contact . . .

*

When she got back home, Izzie didn't bother to mention what she had done to her father, or to Linda, for that matter. Her father seldom read the papers so unless a customer mentioned they'd seen it, there was a good chance he would never even know. Izzie decided to risk it. Mrs Shilling had also advised Izzie for safety's sake to use a box number.

'It's better not to let people know your address,' she'd said.

'There are a lot of cranks out there who might try and take advantage of you.'

'I can look after myself,' Izzie said stoutly but she took the advice anyway.

Now all she had to do now was wait.

*

Doris Baxter hurried along Upper Rock Gardens in Brighton, hugging two portions of fish and chips wrapped in newspaper. She'd slipped them inside her coat to keep them warm and the delicious smell of salt and vinegar so close to her chest was making her mouth water. Hurrying through the pub door, she went behind the bar and upstairs. She would have to be quick. It was almost a quarter to six and Arthur was a stickler for time.

She'd left two plates warming under the grill. They'd be red hot now. She hadn't counted on the queue in the fish and chip shop. Arthur came to the table and watched as she tipped an enormous piece of fish onto his plate. She had a smaller piece and she gave him half of her portion of chips as well. Their bread and butter was already waiting under a damp tea towel.

'This looks good enough to eat,' Arthur said and she chuckled even though she'd heard the same joke a hundred times before.

They began to tuck in. Doris glanced up at him. For all of his size, he had good table manners. They'd taught him that at the orphanage, but not with kindness.

She poured him some tea. 'How was Isaac?'

Arthur shook his head. 'Not good,' he said sadly. 'I fed the dog and took it for a walk, but I told him it would be better to take it to the PDSA or the vet.' He helped himself to some more bread. 'I told him, Isaac, I said, you're in no fit state to look after that dog. It's not fair on him and it's not fair on you.'

'It'll break his heart if the dog goes,' said Doris.

'Maybe,' said Arthur, 'but he can't go on like that.'

Doris nodded. Arthur was right. Isaac Farrant, one of Arthur's regulars, had a bad chest but this year it was much worse. Nobody said anything but his forty a day habit had caught up with him and the old boy was heading for the hospital. Kind-hearted as he was, Arthur went round to see Isaac most days. Doris also did a bit of shopping for him and kept his room clean and tidy.

'I'll pop in and have a word with the doc in the morning,' said Arthur.

They ate silently. Doris' eye drifted towards the screwed up newspaper she had yet to put in the bin and she blinked. 'That's my name,' she said. 'My name is in the paper.'

'Fame at last,' Arthur chuckled.

Doris spread the paper out. '*If you have any information about the whereabouts of Doris Baxter of Elm Grove* . . . Oh Arthur, it is me!'

She positioned the paper for him to see. '*Please contact Miss I Baxter P.O. Box 376, Worthing.*' He looked up with a frown.

'That's my daughter,' she said. 'My Isobelle.'

Arthur smiled. 'Then you must write to her.'

Doris was shaking. 'Oh Arthur . . . I never dreamed . . .' A tear trickled down her cheek. 'Bill told me they never wanted to see me again.'

He reached across the table and grasped her fingers. 'What did I always tell you? Blood is thicker than water my lovely.'

Doris looked at the paper again. 'But what about Bill?' she asked anxiously.

'He doesn't know,' said Arthur. 'That's why she's used a box number.'

Doris put her finger tips to her lips. 'Oh Arthur, what am I going to say?'

'Just tell her you love her and you want to see her again.'

They looked at each other and then they laughed together.

Arthur glanced up at the clock. 'I'd better be going. It's nearly six.'

She watched him go down the stairs to open up and, her dinner forgotten, Doris stood up to fetch her Basildon Bond.

Ten

Wearing a pretty yellow dress with tiny white flowers under her winter coat, Izzie was ready to leave the house. She hadn't told her father or Linda the real reason why she was going to Brighton in December, but when her father had pressed her as she called out her goodbyes she'd told him she was just going to look round the shops.

Since she'd received the reply to her advertisement, Izzie had written several letters to her mother, each time using the box number. She'd kept the letters at work. She had also been thinking a lot about her own future. Esther would be leaving her job soon because she had been accepted as a policewoman cadet. Excited, she was looking forward to a twenty-six-week training course beginning in January, after which she would become a woman police officer. The only drawback, as far as Izzie was concerned, was that she wouldn't be allowed to work in the area of her home in case she was tempted into corruption by people she knew. For that reason, Izzie knew her friend would soon be leaving not only the Shilling household but Worthing as well. She would miss her dreadfully.

Esther's determination to succeed in life had been a real inspiration to Izzie. She now knew it was time to stop dreaming about a better tomorrow and do something to bring it into being.

The day she'd come home from Bournemouth and her father had surprised her by helping her with the dishes, she couldn't bring herself to talk about the woman he'd had upstairs. She never mentioned the cigarette end she'd put in the bin either. When they'd finished the clearing up, her father had surprised her again when he suddenly said, 'Izzie I'm sorry I got a bit narked with you the other day.'

She'd felt her face heating up.

'I know I can be a bit sharp at times,' he went on, 'but it doesn't mean anything.'

Izzie said nothing. He was just trying to butter her up because he had some tart upstairs, that's all.

'You do know that, don't you?'

She'd sucked in her lips because she didn't want to give him the satisfaction of saying she believed him so she just gave him a curt nod. It wouldn't make any difference anyway.

'I'll try and mend my ways,' he'd said with a smile.

And strangely enough, he did. Her father had been more thoughtful towards her over the next few days.

It was when she was alone in her bed at night that Izzie mulled things over. Her father was bound to want to bring that woman home again and he might even want to make it a more permanent thing. She kept thinking what changes having another woman about the place would bring and frankly the idea appalled her. True, the housework would be shared, but Izzie couldn't bear to think of her father horsing around in his bedroom at his age. It was disgusting. And what should she say to her poor mum? What if Mum wanted to come back home? How could she if Izzie's father had some floosy in tow? The idea of moving on was scary but it was becoming more and more attractive. Maybe she could move in with Mum. Yes, why not? They could make a home together. Izzie liked that idea.

'Okay, I'm off now,' she'd called as she'd headed for the door.

'Be back by four-thirty,' her father had said.

Four-thirty! Izzie felt the old irritation flare. What soon to be eighteen-year-old gets told to be home by four-thirty? 'Actually, after I've been shopping with Esther,' she said airily, 'I'm going to visit one of my old school friends who is in Brighton hospital, and you know what hospital visiting hours are like.'

Her father had given her a disbelieving frown. 'Why couldn't she go to Worthing hospital?'

Izzie felt her face go pink as she plunged on with the lie. 'Woman trouble,' she'd said.

He glared at her suspiciously but he had let her go.

Izzie was so nervous as she waited on the platform at Worthing. Her mind was full of what-ifs. What if her mother didn't turn up? What if they both waited in the wrong place and missed each other? What if she didn't recognise her; after all it was four and a half years since her mother had disappeared. She was twelve the night her mother disappeared, thirteen the next day. What if the person she was meeting wasn't her mum but one of the hoaxers Mrs Shilling had warned her about? Her stomach churned. That would be almost too much to bear. When she heard Esther call her name Izzie had never been more delighted to see her friend.

The two girls chatted amiably until they approached Hove station. 'Nervous?' Esther asked.

'Terrified,' said Izzie.

'Aah, you'll be fine.'

'Oh,' cried Izzie. 'I nearly forgot. Tell me about your interview.'

'Bit embarrassing really,' Esther confided. 'I had to strip down to my underwear.'

'Gosh,' Izzie said, raising her eyebrows.

'Then they called me into this room,' Esther went on, 'and there was this panel of people sitting behind a long desk all staring at me. I had to stand on a sheet of brown paper and bend over and touch my toes.'

Izzie gasped. 'Whatever for?'

Esther shrugged. 'To see if I could do it I suppose.'

'And that was it?'

'More or less,' Esther said. 'The doctor listened to my heart and asked me to show him my hands and yes, that was about it.'

Izzie was speechless.

When they arrived in Brighton, Esther walked with her down North Street until they reached the clock tower in the middle of the town. Izzie had arranged to meet her mother outside the old air raid shelter opposite Timothy White's, the chemist. At first glance there was nobody waiting there. The two girls watched the cars and buses going by and a couple of times Esther nodded in the direction of some woman heading into the chemist but Izzie shook her head that it wasn't her mother. Apart from a few young lads dressed in flashy suits who hung around near the public toilets waiting for their friends to come out, everybody else was concentrating on getting across the road or heading towards the shops. The run up to Christmas was in full swing.

'What does she look like?' Esther asked eventually.

'Tall,' said Izzie, struggling to remember. 'And she has dark brown hair with a slide.' There were no photographs of her mother at home and as she spoke Izzie was alarmed to realise how quickly her memory had faded. 'She hasn't come.' Tears of disappointment were already stinging the backs of her eyes.

'Come on,' said Esther, taking her arm encouragingly. 'Let's walk down to Freeman, Hardy and Willis and try on some shoes.'

They were just about to move on when a small voice behind her said, 'Izzie? Is that you?'

Izzie spun around and came face-to-face with a middle-aged woman the same height as herself. 'Mum!'

'Oh my dear girl,' said the woman. 'Haven't you grown into a fine young woman.' Despite her beaming smile, her mother had tears in her eyes. She put her arms out hesitantly and Izzie went to her. 'Just look at you,' her mother said, pulling her back and touching her face with chilly featherlight fingers. 'I hardly knew you. And you're so pretty.'

It was weird looking at her; like looking at a much older version of herself. Now she understood why Gran had told her she was the spitting image of her mother.

Izzie laughed nervously. 'I nearly missed you, Mum. I was looking for a much taller person.' The two of them stood looking at each other until Esther cleared her throat. Izzie turned to her with a smile and said, 'Mum, I want you meet my friend Esther.'

'Pleased to meet you, Mrs Baxter.'

The two women shook hands. 'Call me Doris, please.'

'Well, I'd better be off,' said Esther.

'You don't have to go,' Izzie said awkwardly.

'Yes I do,' said Esther, stepping away from them. 'I planned to do some window shopping and you two have a lot of catching up to do, remember? Have a nice time. Byeee.'

They watched her sail off down the road towards the shoe shop then Izzie turned to her mother. They shared a shy smile. 'Let's find a café and have a sit down,' said Doris. 'Then we can talk.'

There was an attractive place nearby where the tables had pink table cloths and the waitresses wore pink dresses with a white apron.

'Everybody loves this place,' said Doris. 'They do some amazing cakes and things. It's run by Italians.'

They went inside and Doris picked out a table near the back in a small alcove. As they sat down, the waitress came to take their order. Without hesitation, Doris asked for a pot of tea and two slices of cake.

'My treat,' she said.

Izzie studied the woman sitting opposite her. Her mother was older than she had remembered and of course, because she herself had grown up, she seemed much shorter, somehow more vulnerable. Her straight hair was grey, a little old fashioned because it was caught up by a Kirby grip at the side but she wasn't dowdy. Under her brown and black flecked coat, she was wearing a smart grey pleated skirt with a pale blue hand knitted jumper. At her neck she wore a pearl necklace, only Woolworth's, Izzie supposed, but it looked very pretty. Her mother was smart all the way down to her polished black court shoes and a neat handbag.

'I can't believe I'm here with you at last,' said Doris as the waitress walked away. 'You have no idea how long I've dreamed about meeting you.'

Izzie gripped her mother's hand across the table. 'Me too, Mum.'

Doris' bottom lip quivered but she quickly regained her composure. 'So tell me about yourself. What are you doing? Have you got a job? And what about Linda? Is she still at school?'

Izzie began a résumé of her life so far, painting a very rosy picture. She left out the fact that she and her father didn't get on and that half the time Linda was a pain in the bottom.

The tea and cake came and her mother was right. Having put a beautiful china tea pot and two cups on the table, the waitress actually brought six slices of cake on a cake stand, two of each sort so that they could choose. 'Chocolate sponge, fruit cake, orange chiffon,' she said, pointing to each type in turn. 'Enjoy your tea, Madam.'

Izzie was used to having lovely teas with Mrs Shilling but this was special and the cakes looked delicious.

Having decided on a slice of the orange chiffon cake, Izzie told her mother about Granny and Grandad and her life at Dial Post. 'When we came back to Worthing to live with Father, I worked in a green grocer's shop and then I went to work for Mrs Shilling. I've been helping her to write her memoirs.'

Her mother shook her head slowly. 'I'm so proud of you, Izzie.'

Izzie blushed. 'It was only because Mrs Shilling encouraged me to put the notice in the paper that I'm here,' she said. 'I would never have thought of it otherwise.'

'I don't usually bother with the newspaper,' her mother confided, 'but,' she added with a small giggle, 'it was wrapped around our fish and chips.'

'Our?' said Izzie, picking up on what she'd just said.

Doris' face coloured. 'My gentleman friend,' she said, lowering her eyes. 'Arthur. We've been together for a couple of years now.'

Izzie frowned as her own dream bit the dust. She had been hoping to persuade her mother to come back home but if she had a gentleman friend . . .

'I couldn't go back to Worthing,' her mother said, as if reading Izzie's thoughts. 'And I can't go back to your father.' Her voice became a low murmur. 'How can I live with the memory of what that butcher did?' She looked away and the hand that held her cake fork suddenly trembled.

'Mum?'

'Don't ask me, Izzie,' Doris said, her voice thick with emotion. 'I can't talk about it. It will spoil the afternoon and I want it to be special.'

Izzie's mind whirled. What on earth had her father done? Why was her mother so upset about him? She reached across the table and touched her mother's hand. 'It's okay, Mum.'

Her mother gave her a watery smile. 'Tell me more,' she said deliberately changing the subject.

It took everything Izzie had in her to resist asking her mother more questions but Doris listened happily as she talked about her trip to Bournemouth with Mrs Shilling. Every now and then the waitress floated by to ask if they needed more tea or hot water, but they didn't. They finished their cake then shared one piece of fruit cake to have with the last of the tea in the pot.

After a while, Izzie noticed that the level of conversation in the café had become somewhat muted and the atmosphere was charged with excitement. She turned her head to see that everybody's attention was drawn to a rather attractive man who had entered the room. He began walking around the tables, chatting amiably to the customers and making a fuss over some of them. He was older than her, in his late twenties or maybe as much as thirty, dark haired and handsome, wearing a smart waistcoat over a crisp white shirt. On anyone else the waistcoat would seem rather old fashioned but on him, it was very attractive.

'That's him,' her mother whispered as he came nearer.

'Who?'

'Mr Semadini. He always comes round the tables to talk to the people who come here.'

'And 'ow are you today Mrs Ellis,' she heard him say to the woman at the next table.

Judging by her reply, Mrs Ellis, a middle-aged woman with a rather tired expression, was more than flattered by his attention. 'Much better now, thank you Mr Semadini.'

He kissed her hand. 'I missed you last week.'

'Thank you for your concern.'

'It is nothing,' said Mr Semadini, his accent coming out strongly now. 'I am glad to see you back in your usual place.'

As Mr Semadini came to their table, Izzie saw her mother's face light up.

'Mrs Frobisher,' said Mr Semadini. 'So she come? This must be your lovely daughter.' He shook her mother's hand and squeezed her finger tips, then reached for Izzie's hand. He had a surprisingly warm and firm handshake. His dark brown eyes sparkled as he smiled down at her. 'Bella, bella,' he murmured. Izzie felt an unaccustomed flutter in her chest and a heat in her cheeks.

'Your mama has been so excited that you come,' Mr Semadini continued. He waved his hand over the table. 'Now, please to enjoy, enjoy . . .'

With a broad smile, he moved on to the next table.

Izzie gave her mother a puzzled frown. 'Mrs Frobisher?'

Ignoring her query, her mother glanced at her watch. 'Oh dear, is that the time? I have to go.'

Izzie suddenly felt bereft. Oh no, what had she said wrong? She stared helplessly at her mother as she called for the waitress to bring the bill. Mr Semadini had called her Mrs Frobisher. Was her mother upset because she didn't want her to know she was married again? Dad hadn't mentioned a divorce.

Her mother leaned towards her and squeezed her hand. 'Shall I walk you to the station or shall you be meeting your friend again?'

Still slightly bewildered by the suddenness of it all, Izzie shook her head. 'She'll make her own way home.'

The unanswered questions looming large above her, Izzie and her mother walked back to the railway station arm-in-arm and parted by the big gates near the taxi rank. They arranged to meet, same time, same place after Christmas. Izzie kissed her mother's cheek and said her goodbye. As she sat in the train, the memory of their afternoon together and the way her mother rushed off gradually faded. Someone else filled her thoughts. Mr Semadini with his dark eyes and warm handshake. After a while, Izzie closed her eyes to relive every magical second.

*

By the time Izzie's train neared Worthing Central, somewhere in Kemp Town, Brighton, Arthur Frobisher heard the front door open and slam. He jumped to his feet and hurried into the passageway. Doris was taking off her coat. 'Well?' he said anxiously.

'Oh Arthur, she's lovely,' Doris said as she beamed from ear to ear. 'She's ever so pretty and we had a wonderful time. I took her for tea, just like you said.'

'Somewhere nice I hope,' he said, enfolding her in his big embrace.

'Semadini's.' She snuggled into his chest and felt his chuckle welling up inside him long before it erupted. 'Thank you, Arthur. I couldn't have done it without you.'

He kissed the top of her head. 'My pleasure, darlin'.'

She pulled back and gazed up at his dear face. 'I still can't quite believe it,' she said.

'That you've found your daughter?' he asked.

She shook her head firmly. 'That I found someone as wonderful as you.'

Eleven

Before she'd set off to Brighton that morning, Izzie had taken the time to prepare the tea so that all she had to do was put a taper under the saucepans and light the oven. At five forty-five, Linda came in.

'Hello.'

''lo,' Linda grunted as she went upstairs.

Their father came in a few minutes later and it came as a bit of a relief to Izzie that he didn't mention her sick friend or ask how she was. It was obvious that his mind was on other things.

'Where's me clean shirt?' he said gruffly.

Oh hello, dear. And how was your day? Did you have a nice time in Brighton? Izzie thought to herself as she said dully, 'Hanging in the wardrobe upstairs.'

He washed in the downstairs bathroom then went upstairs to change. They all sat at the table and Izzie dished up the potatoes, cabbage and a slice of pie. After her father and Linda had finished their meals and left the table, all the old resentments came flooding back.

As soon as their father had gone out, Izzie scanned the *Evening News* she'd bought at the station in Brighton for the jobs section. She still hadn't actually decided what she wanted to do but it wouldn't do any harm to see what was on offer.

Mrs Shilling's manuscript was almost finished and she'd made good headway with the book about Africa.

Her sister sat at the kitchen table, propping their father's shaving mirror next to the tea pot as she got out her make-up bag. Izzie couldn't help noticing that it was bulging. Where did Linda get the money to buy all that stuff? Her paper round money wouldn't stretch that far, surely? And as for that lipstick she was using, it must have cost a fortune. Was she pinching again? After the theft of her money they'd had one hell of a row and now Izzie kept her savings in the Post Office Savings Bank. Even though her small change was well-hidden, that didn't mean Linda wasn't up to her old tricks again.

Izzie looked up. 'Are you going out?'

'I'm going to church.'

'Church?' Izzie said incredulously. 'On a Saturday night?'

'The youth club,' Linda said with a tired sigh.

'Oh,' said Izzie. 'Yes of course.' She was surprised that her sister was still going to the church youth club. The few people she'd met from St Paul's seemed very nice but she had been quite convinced Linda would be bored with them by now.

Izzie turned the page of the newspaper. 'What are you doing?' Linda asked.

'Looking for a job.'

Linda brushed her hair vigorously. 'I'm not surprised. It's about time you chucked in that job with that awful family.'

Ignoring the barbed remark, Izzie carried on scanning the *Jobs Vacant* column.

'They say that Mrs Shilling is as stingy as hell,' Linda went on, 'and yet they must be flippin' rolling in it.'

The room remained silent.

'Why don't you get a job as an usherette or something,' suggested Linda as she glanced up. 'You could see all the best films for free.'

'I want something where I can meet people,' said Izzie, running her finger down the column one last time.

'You meet loads of people in the cinema,' said Linda, twisting up her new lipstick.

'But you can't talk to them,' Izzie said, putting the paper down. She watched her sister patting her face with some Max Factor Pan-Cake and chewed at her bottom lip. Now might be a good time to tell Linda that she'd found Mum. It didn't seem right keeping it from her. 'There's something I want to tell you—' she began, but she was interrupted by a tap on the door.

'That's John,' Linda said breathlessly.

'John?'

'My boyfriend.'

Izzie stared, wide-eyed, and Linda's eyes flashed. 'And before you say anything,' Linda snapped, 'no, Dad doesn't know about him and you're not to tell. Okay?'

Her sister rose to her feet and grabbed her cardigan from the back of the chair.

'Why don't you bring him in to say hello?' Izzie suggested.

'Oh Izzie, you are so square.' Linda snorted. Stuffing her arms into the sleeves of her cardigan, she grabbed her handbag and swept out of the room, leaving behind nothing more than a whiff of *Evening in Paris* perfume in her wake. Izzie listened to their hushed voices in the hallway as Linda opened the door to let him in and he helped her on with her coat. A few moments later the front door slammed. Rushing to the sitting room window, Izzie pressed herself against the wall and moved the lace curtain slightly to look outside. Her sister was walking down the street with a tall languid looking fellow dressed in a long jacket and very thick soled shoes. He looked a bit like one of those Spiv types but his heavily Brylcreemed hair was cut in the fashionable DA style at the back. She'd read in the paper that they called it that because it looked like a duck's bottom.

She caught in her breath noisily. He didn't look like the sort of boy who went to church, and did he realise that Linda was only fifteen? What on earth would Dad have to say if he knew she was going out with a boy who looked like that?

*

When Izzie returned to work the next morning, Mrs Shilling wasn't very well. She had been listless for a couple of days but when she complained of a headache and that the vision in her left eye was blurred after her lunch time nap, Izzie went to tell Muriel Shilling. It was unusual for her to be in during the day but all morning Cook had been baking for England as young Mrs Shilling was having what she called a 'soiree' this afternoon. The doorbell had been ringing nonstop for the past half an hour.

Hearing the buzz of happy voices, Izzie knocked lightly on the sitting room door.

'Yes, come in.'

Izzie pushed the door open. As she stepped into the room, every eye turned in her direction. For a brief moment she was dazzled by the spectacle before her, a sea of beautifully dressed women sitting elegantly on chairs or standing around in small groups. They were obviously enjoying afternoon tea. The table by the window was overladen with cakes although nobody seemed to be eating them. Mrs Shilling stood near the French windows, a cigarette in a long ivory coloured holder in one hand and a dainty triangle shaped sandwich in the other. The buzz of conversation faded.

'This is the girl helping my mother-in-law with her book,' Muriel announced to the assembled company. Addressing Izzie, she said, 'What is it, dear?'

Embarrassed, Izzie blushed. 'May I have a word with you please, Madam?'

'Can't it wait?'

Izzie shook her head. 'I'm afraid not.'

With an exaggerated sigh, Muriel Shilling put her sandwich down onto a plate on the top of the piano. 'Do excuse me for a moment everybody.' She walked towards Izzie and grabbed her arm, pulling her from the room. 'What is it?' she snapped in a hissy whisper as she pulled the door closed behind them. 'I told Esther I wasn't to be disturbed.'

Izzie blinked in surprise. 'I think Mrs Shilling is unwell.'

'You think?' Muriel said. 'Oh for heaven's sake girl, use your brain if you've got one. Call the doctor.'

Izzie turned to go.

Muriel paused, her hand still on the door knob. Her mind was in a whirl. Although most people used the new National Health Service, she had persuaded her husband to stay private. Muriel had no desire to sit in a waiting room with the more common of society – you never knew what they might have – and though Doctor Kearney charged a pretty penny for a home visit, Muriel deemed that it was worth it. The thing was, why incur the extra expense for her mother-in-law? 'No, wait,' she said, glancing up at the grandfather clock in the hall. 'The nurse will be here in less than an hour. Just put her to bed and tell the nurse when she comes. And don't come back unless she's . . .' Mrs Shilling hesitated. 'Well, I'll leave it to you but I really can't be interrupted again.'

She waved her hand irritably, indicating that Izzie should leave, and then pushed the sitting room door open. 'I'm so sorry about that,' she exclaimed in an exasperated tone as she closed the door again. 'Really, what would they do without me?'

Furious, Izzie walked back to the old lady's room. How could young Mrs Shilling be so uncaring and heartless? The old lady was already on her bed so Izzie covered her over with a blanket and tried to get her to sip some water. Mrs Shilling seemed

95

unresponsive and drowsy so Izzie sat beside her and spent a very worrying hour until the nurse came. After giving her an examination, the nurse went downstairs to telephone for the doctor but when she came back her face was flushed and angry.

'I picked up the telephone but her daughter says there's no need. She insists that Mrs Shilling has simply overdone things and all she needs is a day or two in bed.'

'But you think it's more than that?' Izzie pressed.

The nurse nodded. 'I'll have a word with the doctor when I get back.'

*

Across town, Brenda Sayers turned the open sign to closed in her haberdashery and wool shop and pulled the blinds down. It had been a good day in the Woolly Lamb. She'd sold a fair bit of stock and put several bags of wool in layby. It was a good system. When she took over the shop she realised that most of her customers who wanted to knit a jumper or something for their babies didn't have enough money to pay for all the wool at once. As she didn't want to lose their custom, she agreed to let them buy a couple of balls at a time while she put the rest of the wool they needed in a bag with their name on it and kept it for six weeks. That way all the balls would have the same dye number so there would be no risk of their garment coming out in stripes. The idea was popular with her customers because it was affordable.

There was a bit of stock-taking to do then Brenda settled down for a cup of tea before she began the long walk home. She loved it here and in some ways she knew she'd been luckier than most. The shop was doing well and she enjoyed chatting to her customers. 'When you're on your own, as I am,' she used to tell them, 'there's nothing like a friendly natter.'

She'd been here since 1943. She loved the area and the people. In fact the only fly in the ointment was the discovery that Doris Baxter lived only six hundred yards down the road. They avoided each other, of course, but it rankled every time she saw the woman walking past the shop. What an irony. You couldn't make it up. Two friends, one dead child, an investigation which went on for weeks, then moving away to make a new start only to find that they were practically neighbours!

When Doris had gone missing, Brenda was almost glad. If someone had asked her, she would have told them she'd hoped Doris had found a fancy man and run off with him. At least that would have meant she wouldn't be coming back. However, it did make her feel a bit uncomfortable when she heard them say Doris had been found but that she'd been declared insane and taken off to the lunatic asylum. Although she still blamed her one-time friend for what had happened to Gary, Brenda wouldn't wish that on her worst enemy. In her mind's eye she could see Doris now, standing in the witness box and trembling like a leaf. As she put the kettle on, Brenda shook the memory away.

When the postman had called this morning he'd brought three letters. Brenda hadn't had time to look at them so she'd propped them up on the shelf in the kitchen. Two were bills but the other had a London post mark and she could tell from the handwriting that it was from her sister. It began with the usual dull chit-chat but Thelma ended with,

I'm worried sick about Ray. He's a good boy but he's got in with the wrong crowd. You know what kids are like. They don't seem to worry about ending up in trouble. As if I haven't got enough to worry about with Lennie getting into trouble with the police, and now Ray's been hanging around with that Charlie Davenport.

Brenda frowned. He was always trouble, that boy. Not like her Gary. She sighed. She didn't wish her nephew harm, but could somebody please explain to her, why was it that only the good died young?

The long walk home gave her time to think. She and Thelma had always been close. Thelma had been an absolute marvel when Gary died. Brenda was convinced that she would have topped herself if it hadn't have been for her. Maybe now it was her turn to help Thelma. Ray was probably a bit of a handful but only because he'd got in with the wrong crowd. What if she offered to have him here for a little break? He'd behave himself then, wouldn't he? Of course he would. There was nobody around here to lead him into trouble. As she put her key in the door Brenda had decided. She would write to Thelma tonight inviting Ray to come to Worthing and post the letter in the morning. It would probably do them both good and it would be nice to have a little company again.

Twelve

Mrs Shilling had only made a slight recovery when Izzie turned up for work the next day, nevertheless, she wanted a blow-by blow account of Izzie's meeting with her mother. They both giggled when she told her employer about her mother spotting her notice wrapped around her fish and chips. Mrs Shilling seemed very tired and her speech was a little strained but she didn't complain of anything other than a headache. Esther told her that the doctor had come soon after Izzie had left the day before. According to Mrs Dore, he had said she may have suffered a slight stroke but he'd only prescribed bed rest. She shook her head. 'Poor old soul.'

Half expecting Muriel Shilling to seek her out and tell her what had happened to her mother-in-law, Izzie went straight to the garden room to carry on with the manuscript. She was left alone all morning. At lunch time, Izzie offered to take her employer some lunch. Mrs Dore had prepared a small plate of scrambled egg with bread and butter but Mrs Shilling only managed a few mouthfuls. She seemed very tired. Izzie didn't bother her about the manuscript but helped her to the toilet then covered her over in bed again.

'What time is the nurse coming?' Izzie asked Esther and Mrs Dore when she took Mrs Shilling's tray back to the kitchen.

'Usual time, I suppose,' said Mrs Dore.

'I'm quite worried about her,' Izzie confided. 'I know Mrs Muriel doesn't seem very bothered but I think she really doesn't look at all well.'

They heard the sound of a footfall by the kitchen door. The door burst open and an irritated voice said, 'And that is your medically qualified opinion, is it?' It was Muriel Shilling.

Amid the sound of scraping chairs, they all rose to their feet and Izzie blushed profusely. 'No Madam. Sorry Madam.'

'I should think so,' Muriel snapped. 'How much more of that typing have you got to do?'

'It's almost done,' said Izzie. 'I'm on chapter thirty-one and there are thirty-six altogether.'

'Then I suggest that you stop wasting your time gossiping about me and get on with it!' Muriel hissed. 'Esther, I've been ringing the bell for ages. There's no salt in the salt cellar.'

Izzie made her way back to her typewriter while Esther hurried to fetch fresh salt and followed Mrs Shilling back into the dining room.

By Thursday, Izzie had done everything she needed to do. She had checked and re-checked it and was satisfied that the manuscript was the best it could possibly be.

'Shall I put it in the post for you?' she asked her employer. Old Mrs Shilling waved her hand wanly and nodded but Izzie wasn't too sure that she had understood what she had said. However, she tidied the manuscript anyway and wrapped it securely in brown paper and string, before dropping sealing wax onto the knots. All that remained was to ask Mrs Shilling's daughter-in-law for the money for the postage. She did and it was given, if grudgingly.

'After you've brought back the receipt and the change,' Mrs Shilling said icily, 'you can take the rest of the day off.'

'Thank you, Madam,' Izzie said, but a glance up at the grandfather clock in the hallway told her it was already three-forty.

By the time she'd got to the Post Office and back, she would probably only have fifteen minutes working time left.

As it turned out, there was a queue a mile long at the Post Office and as she was walking back upstairs to say goodbye to her employer, the clock in the hall was already striking five. 'See you on Monday, Mrs Shilling,' she called cheerfully from the door. The old lady gave her a half smile and laid her head back on the pillow.

*

The weekend promised to be good fun. Izzie was going to the pictures with Patsy on Friday and the two of them had arranged to meet Esther outside the pier pavilion on Saturday. This would be the last time the three of them would get together for a while because Esther was off to Peto House, Oxford Street in London on the following Monday. She would be living there for thirteen weeks while she did her basic training at the Police Training School in Hendon.

Patsy had got tickets for a fashion show. The three friends met outside the pier pavilion and joined the snaking queue outside. It took a while to get in and then they struggled to find three seats together. A long wooden 'runway' went out from the stage into the audience. As soon as the first model came on, she walked along the runway, pausing every now and then for the audience to admire what she was wearing. Everything was very chic and colourful with bold geometric designs. Izzie, Esther and Patsy loved it.

After the interval, there was a slot for local talent and to Izzie's immense surprise one of the models for the St Paul's sewing group was a very familiar face. She gasped. 'That's my sister!'

Her two friends gaped in surprise as Linda walked purposefully down the ramp before posing with her hand on her hip. She was wearing a red and white polka dot dress with a halter neck and a very full skirt. As she twirled towards them, her layers of petticoat peeped from beneath the hem of her dress. To complete the ensemble, Linda wore red high heel shoes and red clip-on earrings. Her accessories were a small straw bucket bag and a matching wide-brimmed straw hat. The level of applause grew louder as the girl who had designed and made the dress, Ruth Squires, took a bow by the curtains. Izzie was left speechless.

'She was amazing,' Patsy said with a gasp.

'I had no idea your sister was a model,' said Esther.

Izzie shook her head in disbelief. 'Neither did I.'

*

'There's a newspaper reporter here and he wants to take your photo.'

Linda was standing in the wings watching the audience as they made their way out of the theatre. She felt a little nervous. She hadn't expected to see Izzie in the crowd and now she was worried that her sister would say something to their father. If that happened then all hell would be let loose because Linda hadn't got parental permission to be on the stage in the first place. Ruth had asked her to model her outfit because she said Linda looked slim and pretty. It had never occurred to her to ask Linda how old she was. Everyone assumed that she was sixteen because she was going out with John Middleton, but that wouldn't happen until later in the year.

'Linda?'

She turned towards Ruth who had come to join her. 'I said there's a reporter . . .'

'I know. I heard but I'm not sure.'

'Oh please,' said Ruth. 'You don't know what this means to

me. I want to get on the dress designing course at Worthing College and if there's a picture of my frock in the paper, who knows where it might lead.'

'Cor,' said John, coming up behind them both. 'You look fab in that dress.' He slipped his arm around Linda's waist. Linda didn't say so but he didn't look so bad himself. Like a lot of boys his age, he loved the Edwardian look that was becoming so fashionable. He already had some thick soled shoes they called creepers and he'd saved for ages to buy the drape jacket with four inch lapels. Last week he'd managed to get the boot-lace tie, which was worn in a long bow, so all he had to get now was the flashy silk weskit with a fob watch and chain to be a fully-fledged member. He leaned towards her. 'All the lads are dead jealous 'cos you're my girl.' He kissed her cheek and a camera bulb flashed.

'Hey!' Linda protested as she stepped away from John. 'If that gets in the paper my dad will go loopy.'

The photographer was unrepentant. 'Can I have a picture of you posing by the curtains, love?'

'No you can't,' said Linda, pushing her nose in the air.

'Linda, please . . .' Ruth cried but Linda was already on her way back to the dressing room.

With Ruth and photographer hurrying after her, Linda barricaded the door by putting a chair under the handle then took the hat off and flung it across the room. Someone began hammering on the door. Linda looked at herself in the mirror one last time, then undid the side zip and took the dress off. It was a pity she had to give it back. She loved it and it was made for her, quite literally. She dressed in her own things then folded the dress on the dressing table and put the shoes, bag and hat on top. Having tidied her hair and removed all traces of her make-up, Linda took the chair from under the door. By this time everybody had gone so she slipped out of the theatre without being noticed. As she put her hand into her pocket, she felt quite pleased with herself. She'd had a brilliant time and she'd acquired a pretty pair of red earrings.

*

'Did Dad know you were going to be in the Pavilion?'

Linda glared at her sister. 'No, and you're not to tell him.'

Izzie was making a cup of cocoa. She poured the boiling milk over the cocoa powder then stirred it vigorously. Linda was getting ready to fill her hot water bottle.

Izzie yawned. 'It was a very pretty dress.'

'I know,' said Linda with a sigh. 'Ruth is very clever. She wants to go to the same college as Alma Cogan.'

Izzie was impressed. Alma, a local girl made good, was getting to be famous after she'd won five pounds in the Sussex Queen of Song competition and had been recommended by none other than Vera Lynn for a variety show in Brighton's Grand Theatre. Alma designed her own clothes and everyone agreed that they were to die for.

'Do you ever think about Mum?' Izzie asked tentatively. Now might be a good moment to tell Linda she was seeing their mother.

'Not anymore. Why should I?'

'I was just thinking how much she would have liked to see you tonight.'

Linda put the kettle back on the stove. Having filled her hot water bottle she laid it down horizontally to get all the air out then put the stopper in firmly.

'Linda?'

'Look,' her sister said, 'Mum ran out on us ages ago. She didn't give a stuff about us back then and I don't give a stuff about her now.'

'Linda, she was ill,' Izzie protested.

'So?' Linda challenged. 'She got better, didn't she, but she still never bothered to come back home.'

Izzie frowned. 'How did you know she got better?'

'When I got upset that time, I talked to Dad. He told me she was a silly bitch who ran off with another bloke so she can go to hell for all I care.' With that, her sister flounced out of the room leaving Izzie shocked and bewildered.

Thirteen

The bus had barely stopped before Izzie jumped from the platform. She was late, late, late. Threading her way through the crowded streets she tore up the hill towards Brighton station, dodging a small queue outside Divall's Café, where they sold Tiddyoggies, a popular beef, onion, carrot and potato pasty. A taxi horn sounded as she dashed across the road towards the railings at the top of the hill and the big sign which promised passengers they could be in London in one hour. Thank goodness she already had her return ticket in her coat pocket. No time to buy one.

Once again she had spent a lovely afternoon with her mother. Thankfully, the weather was good although it was quite cold. They'd walked past Brighton Pavilion to stroll in Old Steine Gardens, a large open space where in times past the local fishermen used to store their boats and dry their nets. Over the past few weeks, Izzie and her mother had become close.

'I've got something to show you,' said Izzie. She'd reached into her handbag and drawn out a newspaper cutting. It had been on the front page of the *Worthing Herald* and was of Linda wearing the polka dot dress. In it she looked slightly surprised as a good looking young lad planted a kiss on her cheek.

'Is that my Linda?' Doris said breathlessly.

Izzie nodded. The headline said, *Local beauty in winning dress.* Doris looked up sharply.

Izzie chuckled. 'No, she didn't make the dress, Mum. She was just the model.'

Her mother had stopped walking and stared at the picture long and hard. 'She's very pretty.'

Izzie nodded as her mother handed the cutting back. 'No, you keep it.'

Doris put it in her bag. 'Have you told her about me yet?'

Izzie thought back to her brief foray into that territory on the night of the fashion show and shook her head. They walked on arm-in-arm, pausing beside the Victoria fountain where its three large cast-iron cups towered above them. In the summer, water cascaded over the rims, shrouding the huge dolphins which supported the fountain in a water mist, but because the winter was not yet over, the water was switched off.

'I'm thinking about getting another job,' said Izzie.

Her mother looked surprised. 'I thought you really loved your job.'

'I do,' said Izzie, 'but Mrs Shilling is getting weaker all the time and I honestly don't think her daughter-in-law wants me there. I want to find another job before I get pushed.'

'What will you do?' said her mother as they resumed their stroll.

'I don't know, Mum. Esther said I should find something to do with writing but I have no experience.'

'But you do have some experience,' said her mother. 'That's what you've been doing with Mrs Shilling, isn't it? Could you become a secretary, perhaps?'

'I'm nowhere near quick enough for that, Mum.'

'What about secretarial college?'

'I'm not sure Dad would allow it,' said Izzie. 'He needs my money to help run the house.'

Her mother shook her head. 'That man.' She sighed sadly.

They had almost done a circuit of the park. Izzie took a deep breath. 'Mum, what did happen that night? Why did you run away?'

She felt her mother's body tense. 'I want to tell you, Izzie, but I'm too ashamed.'

'But I have a right to know, Mum.'

Doris turned her head and looked at her. 'Oh Izzie. How can I explain? It was the war. Things were very difficult and your father was – still is – an ambitious man. He did something very, very stupid and got into a lot of trouble.'

Izzie frowned. 'What do you mean? Mum, please tell me.'

Doris sighed. 'Bill never was a prisoner-of-war. That was just a story I told you to spare you. Please don't ask me to tell you any more but because of what he did, your father went to prison for a long time.'

Izzie was deeply shocked. They had stopped walking. Her father in prison? A prisoner-of-war was one thing but being in prison for a crime was a different thing altogether. She could scarcely take it in. 'Mum . . .?'

'Izzie, no,' said her mother, beginning to walk on again. 'You can ask all you like but I won't tell you anything else.'

'Just one thing,' Izzie insisted as they linked arms again. 'Has it got something to do with Mrs Sayers?'

She felt her mother's body stiffen again but Doris remained silent. Izzie bit her tongue. However unfair it seemed, it was obvious that the subject was closed. She'd have to let it go. The one thing she didn't want to do was to fall out with her mother. Not after all this time. They reached the edge of the pavement and headed towards the Honey Bun café.

'Izzie,' Doris had said deliberately changing the subject. 'Have you ever thought of going to night school?'

*

Charging through the big gates at the entrance of Brighton station, Izzie almost fell onto the concourse. Which way should she go? The trains didn't always go from the same platform. She looked frantically this way and that. A quick glance up at the wooden board told her the Worthing train was leaving platform two in two minutes. Disregarding the stitch in her side that threatened to cripple her, she sped towards the barrier just as the ticket collector prepared to close the gate. Another passenger, ticket outstretched, overtook her. The collector waved him on with barely a glance while Izzie fumbled in her pocket for her ticket. Breathless, she handed it over and the collector clipped it.

'Better hurry, Miss,' he said unnecessarily. 'The train's about to leave.'

Safely on the platform, Izzie hurled herself towards the electric train, which was gathering momentum. The man who had run in front of her threw his coat carelessly over his arm and as he did so, something fell from his pocket. It was a wallet.

'Hey,' Izzie shouted after him. 'Excuse me. You dropped something.'

With one hand on the door handle and his foot on the step of the train, the man turned as she thrust it at him and for a split second, their eyes met. Izzie's heart lurched. It was Mr Semadini. His carriage was almost full, but a man inside stood up to offer her his seat when he saw Izzie on the platform. At exactly the same time, the guard blew his whistle long and hard. In an absolute panic, Izzie reached for the door of the next carriage, a Ladies Only. As she heaved herself into the compartment, slamming the door behind her, the train was already moving. Sinking into the seat, she did her best to calm herself and get her breath back. Thank goodness she'd caught the train. She had enough on her mind without having to face the wrath of her father for being late as well.

Her travelling companions looked up; one a middle-aged woman who was knitting what looked like some cotton gloves on four needles, and the other, a much older woman who was reading a book. Neither of them spoke but the younger of the two stood up and very purposely pulled down the window blinds.

A minute or two later, as her temperature cooled and her heart stopped thudding, Izzie closed her eyes. Her mother's anxious expression as they'd said their goodbyes filled her thoughts.

They'd had their tea in the Honey Bun café rather than the usual place and they'd talked about what Izzie could do now that she'd finally made up her mind to leave the Shillings. Izzie didn't know where she would find the time but the thought of training to type properly was attractive. She wouldn't plump for a typing pool or being a secretary. She'd told her mother she fancied being a journalist or working in publishing, something like that. If she brushed up on her skills as her mother had suggested, she could present herself at the offices of either the *Worthing Herald* or the *Worthing Gazette*.

Having settled on that, Izzie and her mother talked about Linda and what she would do now that she had left school. Then they talked about her father and the success or otherwise of the emporium. Izzie at last admitted what a disaster it had been when she'd helped him out on her days off.

'Bill always did cut corners,' said Doris, 'and he never did like to be told.'

Izzie nodded but she felt uncomfortable saying all this. She didn't want to bad mouth her father even though her mother was the only person who seemed to understand how she felt. In the end, the two of them talked about the weather and tourists and the up and coming Festival of Britain . . . anything except the one thing Izzie wanted to talk about, namely her father being sent to prison. What had he done? Why was he on the wrong side of the law in the first place? Oh, he made her so angry! Should she confront him about it? *By the way, Dad, I know you've been in prison.* Izzie pursed her lips. No, she couldn't. She could just imagine his reaction and it wouldn't be pretty.

Another thought crossed her mind. She still didn't know anything about her mother. Apart from discovering that she was going by the name of Mrs Frobisher (something she'd only discovered when Mr Scmadini spoke to her the day they'd first met), Izzie knew nothing of her mother's life. Who was Mr Frobisher? Where had he and her mother met? Where did they live? Izzie frowned. It was all so frustrating.

As she drew closer to home, Izzie relaxed and allowed other less traumatic thoughts to come into her mind. She smiled to herself. Fancy Mr Semadini being on the Worthing train. Just the thought of him being so near and yet so far away made her heart flutter. He seemed such a nice man. She wondered where he was going. It was just her rotten luck that there was a carriage wall between them. If only this was one of the newer trains with a corridor. She closed her eyes and tried to imagine what it would have been like if they had struck up a conversation. After a few minutes she opened her eyes again. How ridiculous. She was far too grown-up for school girl crushes and silly day dreams.

*

On the other side of the carriage wall, the Italian sighed. For a moment he struggled to recall where he'd seen the pretty girl who had picked up his wallet but then he remembered. She was Mrs Frobisher's long lost daughter. They had come into the shop a few times. He wondered vaguely where the girl was going. At every station along the way, Hove, Preston Park, Shoreham . . . he'd looked out of the window to see if she got off before him but he was disappointed.

After a few stops there was only one other man in his carriage. The stranger, solidly built, his long legs stretched out in front of him, was dozing. When he finally pushed his hat away from his eyes, he gave Mr Semadini a quizzical stare.

'Travelling on business?' he said as he nodded towards the small attaché case Giacomo was carrying.

'I'm on my way to see a shop in Worthing,' Giacomo explained.

'A shop?' said the man. 'What sort of shop?'

'At the moment it's empty,' he said, 'but I plan to sell beautiful pastries and Italian ice cream.'

'Sounds good.' The stranger smiled affably. 'I wish you luck although I have to say that Worthing isn't exactly a forward looking town.'

Giacomo shrugged. 'My shops are popular,' he said confidently. 'I have one in Brighton and another in Hastings. For me, Worthing is the next step.'

'Three shops?' said his companion, clearly impressed. 'You're an ambitious man. You must enjoy cooking.'

'Like most Italians, I enjoy seeing people eat my food.' Giacomo smiled.

'Have you been in this country long?' the man asked.

'All my life,' said Giacomo. 'I am British and my family regard themselves as so. We were very happy until the whole family was interned.'

'Ah,' said his companion, 'the war.'

'Yes, the war.'

It was an awkward moment until the man moved forward and held out his hand. 'My name is Roger Hughes, and I'm a cinema projectionist.'

'And I am Giacomo Semadini,' said Giacomo returning the handshake.

'How do you spell that?' Roger asked.

'G-i-a-c-o-m-o, but it's pronounced Jack-o-mo.'

'Pleased to meet you Giacomo.' Roger sat back and smiled. 'And now you plan to take Worthing by storm.'

Giacomo grinned. 'Why not? We Romans once conquered the whole of Britain. For me. . .? Just the south coast.'

They both laughed.

By the time the train reached Bridge Halt in East Worthing it was tipping it with rain and Giacomo was wishing he'd brought an umbrella. If that girl got off the train at Worthing Central, it would have been the perfect excuse to offer her shelter. Never mind. Perhaps he could offer to share a taxi with her instead. But as he alighted onto the platform, the door to the Ladies Only carriage remained resolutely shut and he couldn't see inside as someone had pulled down the blinds.

*

The minute Izzie lifted the edge of the carriage blind she was thrown into a panic. She must have nodded off because although she was vaguely aware of slamming doors, it wasn't until the guard blew his whistle that she fully woke up and saw the sign for Worthing disappearing into the darkness behind the train. She'd missed her stop. She got out at West Worthing with a plan to head for the bus stop until the ticket collector stopped her.

'If you get out here,' he said firmly, 'you'll have to pay another sixpence.'

'But I didn't mean to travel on,' she protested.

'Sixpence,' he insisted.

Izzie's eyes pricked with tears. How could she tell him she was stone broke?

'Look,' he said, his voice softening. 'Take my advice and cross over to the other side of the line and catch the next train to Victoria. That'll take you back to Worthing Central.'

Izzie nodded and walked to the end of the platform to cross over as the gates opened. She felt a bit of a fool getting upset over such a trivial thing but it had been a difficult day.

Fourteen

When the alarm went off at six-thirty on Monday morning, Izzie's first thought was for her sister. She'd seen Linda setting off at around six-thirty with John yesterday evening and though she had expected her to be back home around nine, when she went to bed at ten, Linda still wasn't in. Izzie had fought sleep until nearly midnight when she heard the back door closing. Thank goodness her sister was back. What on earth was Linda thinking? Didn't she realise what sort of a reputation she would get if she was out until all hours?

As Izzie walked downstairs to the loo, a quick glance through the partially open door of Linda's room reassured her that her sister was in her bed. Their father's deep snores behind his bedroom door told her that he would be in bed for at least another hour. Izzie hurried downstairs. There seemed to be so little time in the mornings and she had to be at work by nine-thirty.

Izzie boiled the water in the kettle and used half to make a pot of tea, while the rest went into a bowl which she took into the bathroom to use for a strip wash. The geyser in the bathroom was unsafe so until their father could afford to pay for a new one, everyone had to put up with boiling the kettle. In the depth of winter it was perishing cold in there but it was becoming a little more pleasant this time of year. It was still cold but with the early morning sunshine streaming in through the window somehow everything seemed better. Her clothes were folded over the clothes horse so after her wash, Izzie dressed quickly. When she came back into the kitchen she found a bleary eyed Linda sat at the table, scratching her head as she waited for the kettle to boil for her own wash.

'What time did you get in last night?'

'Half past midnight.'

Izzie gasped. 'Blimey. What on earth did Dad say?'

'He was already asleep,' said Linda, pouring herself some tea. Her hair was all over the place and she still had traces of make-up on her face.

Izzie cut herself a slice of bread and put it under the grill. How did Linda do it? If she'd stayed out until all hours, there would have been hell to pay yet her sister got away with it every time. Their grandmother always used to say Linda could fall down the toilet and come up smelling of roses and it seemed as if she was right. All the same, Izzie couldn't help voicing her concern.

'About that boy . . .' she began.

'Oh don't start,' said Linda irritably. 'John is fine.'

'Yes but you'll get yourself a bad name.'

'Just listen to yourself, Iz,' Linda snapped. 'You sound like an old woman. Stop trying to organise my life.'

'I'm not,' Izzie protested. 'It's just that—'

'John is all right I tell you,' Linda interrupted. 'He hangs around with a few mates but that's all, so give it a rest.'

But Izzie wasn't about to give up; not just yet. 'Where did you go?'

The kettle boiled so Linda stood up. 'To church and then we had a squash in someone's house.'

Izzie frowned. 'You played squash?'

'No,' said Linda exasperated. 'We had a squash. It's when

everybody is invited and we all squash in. If you get a seat you're lucky, if not you sit on the floor.'

'You couldn't have been there until half past midnight,' Izzie retorted.

'I wasn't,' said Linda. Standing with the kettle in her hand she looked at Izzie with a wicked grin and laughed. 'I'll tell you one thing, John is a great kisser.'

Izzie's mouth dropped open.

'Oh, the look on your face!' Linda laughed. 'Don't worry sis, I know what I'm doing. John won't make me do anything I don't want to do.'

'But if Dad ever found out . . .' Izzie insisted.

Her sister tossed her head. 'Well, Dad isn't going to find out, is he,' she said coldly. 'Honestly you're driving me mad. You better get used to it because I want to enjoy my life and you with your prissy ways are not going to stop me.'

'I was only looking out for you,' Izzie said dully as her sister flounced off to have her wash.

'I don't need looking out for,' Linda said through gritted teeth, 'so leave off.'

*

Although he would never admit it, Giacomo Semadini was a slightly superstitious man. For a start, he always took the small teddy bear with him whenever he was on the move. People called it his lucky mascot. He never bothered to correct them because it saved him having to tell the story again. After he'd dressed with care, he fondled the soft fabric and put the bear in his pocket. He was certainly going to need some luck today. His Italian grandmother, a great one for reading the tea leaves, had always said the bear would help him find a new love but there was only space in his heart for one girl and that was

Maria. She had been gone for some time now and it had crossed his mind that he was being foolish, but it was hard to break the habit.

Giacomo had become a restless spirit. He never really settled anywhere until he was absolutely sure that it was the right place. Seeing that lovely girl again was a good sign. How fortunate he'd been that she'd picked up his wallet, and how honest to give it back. He smiled to himself. She was so striking. Her brown hair brushed back and clipped at the nape of her neck shone and she had the most beautiful eyes; a deep blue, no, more beautiful than that . . . violet.

Meeting the kindly projectionist who had offered him a place in his taxi was another good sign. Funnily enough, as he looked out of the cab window, even the town itself seemed very pleasant despite Roger's disparaging remarks. The roads were leafy and the streets were clean. Further along, in Chapel Road, he could see clear signs of the lingering scars of war. Scaffolding shrouded some of the shop fronts and high up on the sky-line Giacomo spotted pock-marked walls, a sure sign of enemy machine gun fire in times past. Now that he thought about it, France was only just across the water so places like Worthing would have been right on the front line during the war. It came as no surprise then, that the ravages of the conflict had penetrated even this sleepy town.

The taxi dropped him very close to his friend's house and Roger wouldn't hear of accepting Giacomo's offer to pay half the fare.

'When I open my shop,' he told Roger as he grasped the young man's hand in a warm handshake, 'you will have free pastry.'

'You're on there, mate.' Roger chuckled as he wound up the window and the taxi moved off.

The shop Giacomo had come to see the next morning was

in Ann Street, just behind the Town Hall and, at a stretch, within sight of the pier. It was an ideal spot for visitors to the town to relax over a pot of tea and one of his pastries. His appointment with the letting agent was for nine but Giacomo was early. He spent several minutes walking around the area to get a feel of the place. When Mr Friend finally arrived he was full of apologies.

'Mr Sem-merd-denny,' he said as he extended his hand. 'I am mortified that I'm late. So pleased to make your acquaintance.'

'Semadini,' Giacomo corrected as they shook hands.

While Mr Friend unlocked the door, Giacomo stepped back and looked up at the shop front. Although in a small side street, it was close to the main thoroughfare, double fronted, with a central door and a private door at the side leading to accommodation above. He nodded. Yes . . . he could see prospects here. The tour of the premises and the flat above didn't take long and although he was convinced that this was exactly the sort of shop he wanted, Giacomo was a shrewd businessman. He didn't want to appear too keen.

'I think I'll take a walk before I decide.'

'Yes, yes of course.' Mr Friend's eager expression had dipped a little, which was no bad thing as far as Giacomo was concerned. If the man was unsure of the sale he might be willing to drop the price a little. They agreed to meet up again at twelve noon and Giacomo set off for the seafront.

He knew immediately that he'd love it here. Disappointingly, the beach was pebbles, but the sea air was bracing, the promenade wide and even at this time of year, visitors were plentiful. He was already forming a plan. He'd sell Italian cream water ices in the summer, hot chocolate in the winter and all year round he'd bake his delicious pastries for the ladies and make cream jellies for the children. Just as in Brighton and Hastings, all he needed was a few weeks to make Semadini's the most popular place to be in Worthing.

*

The house where she worked was still silent as Izzie let herself in through the back door. In the distance the hall clock was chiming nine-thirty and Mrs Dore was busy rolling out some pastry for a meat pie. 'Morning.'

'Good morning,' Izzie said cheerfully.

'The missus wants you to leave the old lady to have a rest until lunch time,' she said as Izzie hung her coat up. 'She wants you to tidy up her study instead.'

'Did she have another funny turn then?' asked Izzie.

Mrs Dore shrugged. 'Not as far as I know. The new maid took her up some breakfast this morning. The lazy mare left the dishes in the sink after.'

'Did she eat much?'

'A bit,' said Mrs Dore. 'A little porridge, that's all.' She glanced around with an uncomfortable expression then moved a little closer to whisper, 'The pair of them had a big bust up last night.'

'What, the new maid and Mrs Shilling?'

'No,' said Mrs Dore, exasperated. 'Young Mrs Shilling and her mother-in-law. She doesn't like her spending her money.'

Izzie frowned. 'It's so unfair. It's her money. Why shouldn't she enjoy her life?'

Mrs Dore nodded sagely and went back to her pastry. 'She's never forgiven her for that trip to Bournemouth.'

'She's jealous, that's all,' said Izzie. Grabbing a duster, she headed towards Mrs Shilling's study.

*

At a quarter to twelve Giacomo strolled back to the estate agent's. As he came through the door, Mr Friend looked up from his desk. He seemed agitated and Giacomo noticed beads of perspiration along the man's top lip.

'I'm sorry Mr Semerdenny, but you've had a wasted journey,' he said. 'The property is no longer available.'

Giacomo stared at him in disbelief. 'But only an hour ago—'

'The owner has found another buyer,' Mr Friend interrupted.

Giacomo frowned.

'There's nothing I can do,' Mr Friend said with an apologetic shrug. 'I'm sorry.'

Outside the shop, Giacomo was unsure whether to be angry or despondent. Everything had looked so promising. Why had the man so suddenly changed his mind? It was certainly perplexing but Giacomo wasn't a man who was easily put off. As he'd walked back to the estate agent's he'd noticed a vacant property at the bottom of South Street. He paused outside and saw that it was up for sale, not for rent, and with a different agent. If anything, this property was in an even better situation than the first. It was certainly worth making enquiries. He crossed the street and headed for the offices of Mr Friend's rival.

Half an hour later, he was looking round a shop which was in need of a refurbishment, but because it had been a café before, Mabel's, it wouldn't require a complete renovation. It was a sound building and suited his purpose very well. The family had already agreed that his two cousins, Umberto and Benito, could come from Hastings to join him and the tour of the living quarters convinced him that the flat was large enough to accommodate the three of them. He and the agent walked back to the office where Giacomo agreed to buy the property there and then.

By the time he was dozing on the train back to Brighton,

he was already making plans for his new Italian ice cream empire on the doorstep of Worthing pier.

A voice interrupted his reverie. 'Tickets please. Your tickets, please.'

As Giacomo reached into his wallet for his ticket, he remembered the pretty girl with the violet eyes. With a smile, he wondered what she was doing now.

*

Izzie was carrying a tray up to the old lady's room. It was lunch time and Mrs Dore had prepared a small fish pie. As she walked through the door, the smell of urine was overwhelming. Izzie immediately regretted that she hadn't come up sooner. She should have ignored Muriel Shilling's edict. For the smell to be this bad, Mrs Shilling probably wet the bed ages ago so the poor old soul would be feeling very uncomfortable.

'Good afternoon Mrs Shilling,' Izzie said cheerfully. She put the tray on the table and drew back the heavy curtains. The light flooded in. When she turned, the figure in the bed stared back at her but made no sound. 'I hope you've had a nice lie-in?'

She walked to the bed but it wasn't until she got up close and put her hand onto the old lady's shoulder that the penny dropped. Old Mrs Shilling was dead.

Fifteen

The first thing Izzie did was to look for a quiet place to have a cry and the best place was Mrs Shilling's private bathroom. She sat on the lid of the toilet, her hands still trembling. It was such a shock. It was a wonder that she hadn't cried out. She had never seen a dead person before and the expression on the old lady's face didn't look very peaceful. What would happen now? She wasn't expected to do anything, was she? Muriel Shilling was always looking for ways of saving money. Surely she wouldn't want her to lay out the body or something? Izzie shuddered. No, she told herself crossly, the undertaker would be required to do that. Oh poor Mrs Shilling. Izzie blew her nose and wiped her tear stained face. Somehow she had to pull herself together before she went downstairs.

When she came onto the landing, young Mrs Shilling was downstairs in front of the hall mirror getting ready to go out. Izzie remembered that today was the day she went to her bridge club. Hurrying down the stairs Izzie called out to her.

'Not now, Izzie,' said Muriel irritably.

'I'm afraid it can't wait, Madam,' Izzie said. 'It's your mother-in-law . . .'

Muriel opened the door. 'You deal with it.'

'I can't,' said Izzie, her voice rising. 'She's . . . she's dead.'

Muriel froze on the doorstep.

'I'm sorry, Madam,' Izzie blundered on. 'I shouldn't have told you like that but I went up to give her some lunch and she . . . It must have happened some time ago.' Izzie burst into tears. 'I'm so sorry.'

Muriel Shilling came back into the house and slammed the door. 'For heaven's sake, stop blubbering,' she said, taking off her hat. Dumping her coat on the hall chair she pushed Izzie aside and went upstairs. 'Why did this have to happen now? I was really looking forward to this afternoon.' She paused by the bedroom door for a second or two before grasping the door handle and walking in. 'Good God, it stinks in here.'

Izzie watched her as she went to the bed and peered down at her mother-in-law. After a second or two, Muriel reached out and touched the dead woman's face. The minute she did, she snatched her hand back as quickly as if she had been scalded. She showed no emotion apart from irritation that her plans for the afternoon had been thwarted.

*

As soon as the body was gone, Izzie helped the new maid take the soiled linen to the laundry room. They wouldn't wash it. Muriel Shilling had ordered that the gardener burn it at the bottom of the garden, along with the ruined mattress. Izzie felt numb. It played in her mind that the old lady may have felt neglected and miserable as she died all alone.

Muriel Shilling spent most of the rest of the day on the telephone. Everybody else in the house seemed genuinely upset. Mrs Dore got on with her work but every now and then she disappeared into the pantry before coming out red-eyed and blowing her nose in her hankie. Even the new maid wept.

Alone in the garden room cum office, Izzie typed letters for Mrs Shilling's publisher, her editor and her printer. She didn't sign them, of course, that was for Muriel Shilling to do, but she felt it might help if she did the donkey work. At the end of the afternoon, before she left, Izzie left them on the hall table.

The next day, Izzie and the new maid thoroughly cleaned the bedroom and put all Mrs Shilling's clothes in a suitcase for the Red Cross. Anything of value, such as the brooches on the lapels of her jackets and her silk stockings left over from the war, had already been removed.

Mr Shilling, now home for a period of time, was obviously distressed about his mother but Muriel Shilling behaved as if her spoiled afternoon was all Izzie's fault and a terrible inconvenience. A steady stream of visitors came to the house bringing flowers and sympathy but far from a melancholy gathering in the sitting room, the place was filled with the buzz of conversation and laughter.

Izzie had been told to pack up Mrs Shilling's books. Apparently they were to be put upstairs in the loft and she'd been given two medium sized trunks to put them in. As she pulled them from the shelves, so many of them brought back happy memories. She'd leafed through this one when they were typing up that chapter about Quipu and Mrs Shilling needed to refresh her mind about something. Izzie had been fascinated to learn that the Incas didn't have a written language but they kept records by tying knots on a piece of string.

'Different coloured string had different meanings,' Mrs Shilling had explained. 'They still do it now. Our guide knotted one cord whenever my husband paid him and another cord if he had to spend money. The word Quipu means knot.'

Izzie smiled sadly. Her employer had opened her mind to so many wonderful things. She would miss her dreadfully.

She was working hard when Mrs Dore came to tell her Muriel wanted to see her. Izzie went at once. The funeral was to be next week so Izzie was expecting to be asked to act as a maid for the wake. She would do it of course; not for Muriel, but for the sake of her old employer.

As she walked into the room, young Mrs Shilling was relaxing on the sofa smoking a cigarette. She was alone. Muriel didn't look like a person in mourning. She was dressed not in the customary sombre clothing but a white pleated skirt and a sailor style blouse with blue piping.

'Ah, Izzie,' she said standing and going to the writing bureau. 'Thank you for all you did for my mother-in-law. Of course now that she's gone we have no need for your services. Your wage is in this envelope and I have written you a character reference.' She thrust two envelopes into Izzie's hands, leaving her in a state of shocked surprise.

'That will be all,' said young Mrs Shilling, resuming her seat and her cigarette.

Izzie was shaking when she got back into the hall. Tears smarted her eyes when she opened her wage packet to find she hadn't even been paid for a full week. Today was Tuesday and she'd only been paid for two days. How mean can you get? How could she possibly get another job by tomorrow? The money in the envelope was less than a third of her normal wage. She looked around. All this wealth and that stingy woman could not even be bothered to show a little gratitude.

Now Izzie was in a quandary. It was half past one. Should she carry on packing Mrs Shilling's books into the trunks or walk out now? She was so angry it was hard to think.

'What's up, duck?' Mrs Dore said as she walked into the kitchen.

Izzie explained what had happened.

'The tight fisted old bag,' Mrs Dore murmured. 'If I was you, I'd walk out right now. You've got your reference haven't you?'

Izzie hesitated. She hadn't had a chance to read it and right now she hadn't the stomach for it. It was probably rubbish anyway. Part of her wanted to stalk out of the house and slam the door behind her but another part of her thought of Mrs Shilling's stoicism in the face of her daughter-in-law's animosity towards her. Izzie took a deep breath and made the decision to go back and finish the job. She would pack the books carefully and view it as the last thing she could do for dear old Mrs Shilling. If she left the packing for Muriel, she would probably throw the books into the trunk any-old-how or get the gardener to burn them.

Miserably, she made her way back to the garden room. As she reached the hallway, Mr Shilling came down the stairs.

'Ah, Izzie,' he said affably. 'Last day I hear. Everything all right?'

Izzie's cheeks flamed with anger. 'Actually, Mr Shilling,' she began haughtily, 'now that I'm leaving, there's something I wanted to say—'

'You know you were a bloody marvel with my mother,' he interrupted. 'I know she could be a difficult old biddy at times but she was like putty in your hands. She was awfully fond of you, you know.'

'That's all very well but . . .' Izzie began again.

'Don't think it wasn't appreciated,' he went on, completely taking the wind out of her sails. 'You're very young but I've never in all my born days known such a capable gel.' With that, he thrust something in her hand. Izzie didn't look but it felt like folded money. Mr Shilling put his finger to his lips and came closer. 'Don't tell the Memsab, eh?' Izzie blinked in surprise. 'Now what was it you wanted to say?'

'Um . . .' Izzie flustered as she blinked in surprise. 'I . . . I'm sorry about your mother, Sir. I shall miss her.'

Mr Shilling chuckled. 'Apart from me, you're about the only one who will,' he muttered as he walked away.

Izzie pushed the money into her apron pocket and went back to the job in hand. By three forty-five the shelves were bare and the trunks were full of dusted books. Izzie turned her attention to the writing desk. Most of the paperwork still there was to do with Mrs Shilling's publisher but there were a few scraps of paper which Mrs Shilling had used to jot down her notes or something she wanted to look up. Izzie classed them as rubbish, which she screwed up and put in the bin, but then she came across a notebook she didn't remember. As she was fanning the pages to see what was in it she came across a small envelope with her name on it. Izzie eased herself into the chair and opened it.

On the back of the envelope old Mrs Shilling had written, 'Found in newspaper archive. Show Izzie.' It contained a newspaper cutting. Izzie spread it out. The stark headline was *Local boy dies.* Underneath there was a picture of a small boy holding a jam jar containing a minnow. Izzie read the article itself.

Five-year-old Gary Sayers died in hospital last night of suspected food poisoning. Gary was one of fifteen children who were taken ill after eating meat pies and sausage rolls prepared for a Christmas party put on by the council for evacuee children who had returned home. The event, which was held in the Town Hall, was attended by some forty youngsters. Suspicion has fallen on a batch of sausage rolls which came from a local butcher and have been sent to a laboratory for analysis.

Izzie frowned. Which newspaper had Mrs Shilling got that from? She never went out except when Izzie went with her. Did someone send it to her? There was no date or newspaper reference, so when did it happen and what on earth had it got to do with her? Izzie knew Mrs Shilling had been anxious to help her find her mother. Was this something to do with it? She read it again and her blood ran cold. Gary Sayers. Mrs Sayers was the mysterious woman who came into the green grocer's and she remembered her father's reaction when Izzie had asked about her. Had she told Mrs Shilling about her? Izzie couldn't remember. She remembered Mrs Sayers crashing into the wheel-chair outside the bus stop but had she told Mrs Shilling her name? And what had her mother to do with this? Izzie fanned the pages of the notebook again but there was nothing else inside. How odd. Mrs Shilling obviously planned to give it to her, otherwise why would her name be on the envelope?

Izzie slipped the envelope and cutting in her pocket and looked around the room. Everything looked neat and tidy. It was time to go. What a good job she hadn't walked out when Mrs Shilling had given her the sack. She didn't know where the cutting would lead her but she was so glad to have found it.

A few moments later, and in the privacy of the toilet, she unfolded the money Mr Shilling had given her. She was holding five one pound notes.

*

Bill was in a quandary. As he examined the three pictures the old man had brought in, it was obvious that one of them was worth a bob or two. The beach scene and the waterfall were fairly good but only worth five quid each at the most. The picture of a Victorian gentleman was in a different league altogether. Should he tell the old boy or offer him just a few quid for the lot? He had two things to weigh up: his reputation and his chronic lack of funds. On the one hand, if he offered his customer a fair price, he might have other gems he could bring in. On the other hand, he could offer him fifteen quid for the three, not exactly an unreasonable amount, then sell the cheap ones in the shop and take the better quality painting to the auction rooms.

He opened his secret drawer in the desk. The William IV sterling silver table box was gone, as was the slightly smaller dark blue enamel box – he'd shifted them a couple of weeks ago to another dealer from Bognor, no questions asked – but the Edwardian silver box was still there. It was always a risk when passing on stolen goods and he didn't really have the stomach for it anymore. Hadn't he told himself he was going to be totally legit this time? It was all right ducking and diving when you're young but not now. Not at his age. One taste of prison was enough to last a man a lifetime; which brought him back to the pictures. He sighed. Picking them all up, he went out onto the shop floor to chat with his elderly customer.

Sixteen

Izzie arrived back home with mixed emotions and went straight upstairs to her room. She was still upset about Mrs Shilling's death and now she was reeling from the shock of being given the sack. She'd always known Muriel Shilling was a bit of a cow but to get rid of her in such a callous way was a bit rich, even for her.

It should be reasonably easy to get another job but it meant her dreams of going to night school would have to take another back seat. Not only that, but also she would have to work a week in hand, meaning she wouldn't have any money for two weeks. What a good job Mr Shilling had given her that five pounds. She wouldn't use it unless it was absolutely necessary but it was a comfort to know it was there should she need it. She re-opened the envelope and spread the notes on the counterpane. As soon as she could she would put it into her Post Office Savings Bank. Once that was done she would have seventeen pounds twelve shilling. It should have been a good feeling but she suddenly felt bereft of an old friend and found herself succumbing to tears. A little later she heard the front door bang and Linda pounded up the stairs. Her sister turned her head as she went past Izzie's room.

'Oh hello. What are you doing home so early?'

Izzie blew her nose. 'I got the sack.'

Linda gasped. 'Blimey. What did you do?'

'Nothing,' Izzie said miserably, 'but now that old Mrs Shilling has gone, they don't want me anymore.' She lifted her head and added bitterly, 'They no longer require my services.'

'Poor old you,' said Linda, eyeing the money on Izzie's bed. 'I thought you were going to say you'd been caught nicking something.'

'I don't steal,' Izzie retorted as she snatched the notes up. 'Mr Shilling gave this to me, if you must know.'

Linda raised an eyebrow. 'Did he indeed? Dirty beggar.'

'For heaven's sake Linda,' Izzie snapped. 'You've got a mind like a sewer. He gave it to me for being kind to his mother.'

'Okay, okay,' said Linda, putting her hands up in mock surrender. 'I was only teasing. Lucky you.' She turned away and headed for her bedroom.

'And you can keep out of my room,' Izzie shouted after her. 'I don't want any more of my money going walk-about.'

'As if I would,' Linda shouted as she slammed her door.

Izzie looked around for a place to hide the money. She didn't trust her sister as far as she could throw her. She kept her Post Office Savings book taped above the dressing table drawer. She reasoned that a thief (like Linda) might pull the drawer out and look on the bottom but they wouldn't reach inside and feel the underside of the dressing table top. The Post Office book was quite flat but if she added five more notes there was a chance that it would be seen when opening the drawer. She looked around the room for another hiding place but almost all of them were immediately obvious. In the end, she put the money behind the photograph of her and Linda walking along the seafront, which stood in a frame over the fireplace.

*

Her father wasn't very happy when she told him. They were all sitting together at the dinner table for a change. Usually one or the other of them was out, but tonight all three of them were in together. Izzie had waited until the meal was almost finished before she told her father the news.

'Well you'd better get out there and find another job PDQ,' he said crossly. 'You're not a kid anymore. You can't expect me to support you.'

'I wasn't going to,' Izzie said indignantly.

'And you can hand over your wage packet now.'

'There's not much in it,' Izzie said mildly. 'She only paid me for Monday and today.'

'But Mr Shilling gave her a fiver,' Linda piped up.

Izzie glared at her. Her father beckoned with his hand. 'Hand it over.'

'I need that money,' Izzie protested. 'Even if I get another job tomorrow, I won't get a wage packet until Friday week.'

Her father continued to beckon.

'Dad, please . . .'

But Bill Baxter was unrelenting. Izzie rose from the table, her cheeks flaming and her eyes stinging with unshed tears. She mounted the stairs with a mixture of anger, disappointment and pain. Why was he always so horrible to her? She recalled what Gran once told her. *He never was much good with women and you look so like your mother.* So why take it out on her? It was so unfair. I bet if Linda lost her job he'd be really nice to her, she thought bitterly.

Back downstairs she threw the five pound notes on the table in front of him. 'I hate you.'

Her father winced. 'Please yourself.'

Izzie turned away but not before she saw the sly smile on her sister's face.

*

133

By the end of the week, Izzie had got a new job. What with the references Mrs Shilling had given her (which turned out to be not as bad as she thought they might be) and the glowing reference Mr Allen the green grocer had given her the previous year, she found a job in a sweets and tobacconist shop close to Worthing station. She was to start first thing on Monday. The wage wasn't brilliant, three pounds ten shillings, which after stoppages left her with three pounds one and five pence a week. Any hopes of saving much money looked rather slim. Izzie felt more stuck than ever and it was a bitter pill to swallow.

As Izzie walked into the house after her interview, Linda was in a state of undress. She had her back to the door and she didn't hear Izzie coming. Her sister was just stepping out of her skirt and under it she wore another one with the price label still attached.

'That's nice . . .' Izzie began but the shifty look her sister gave her aroused her suspicion. Linda hadn't bought the skirt, had she; she'd tried it on in the shop and then walked out with it under her own clothes. Izzie stood with her mouth open.

'Oh shut-up,' said Linda before Izzie had said a word. 'Everybody does it.'

'Oh no they don't,' said Izzie, snatching at the label to see which shop it came from. 'If you keep this up you're going to get caught.'

'I'm too clever for that,' said Linda as she gathered her things and flounced upstairs.

*

Having a whole weekend with nothing to do except the washing and the ironing was a God-send. Izzie decided to go and see her grandmother instead. Granny had sent her two pounds in her birthday card, so she caught the early bus to Horsham and got off at Dial Post. She hadn't had the opportunity to write and tell Granny she was coming so she kept her fingers crossed that the old lady would be in.

Granny had moved since Grandad died as the cottage where Izzie and Linda had spent two years after their mother disappeared was too big for her to manage. Fortunately, there was a small dwelling on the edge of the village but it was in a bad state of repair. Out of respect for her grandfather, the owner of the estate, the landlord of the local pub and some villagers got together to make it habitable. Her advancing years made change hard for Granny but so long as she had her chickens and the vegetable garden, she was content. As Izzie walked up the lane and saw her hanging out some washing her heart surged with love. Her grandmother looked a little more stooped than usual but the sight of her in her colourful wrap-over apron brought a smile to Izzie's lips for the first time since old Mrs Shilling had died.

'Hello, Gran.'

Ada Baxter turned sharply. 'Izzie!' she cried. 'Oh what a lovely surprise.' When she enfolded her granddaughter into her arms, Izzie almost collapsed. Ada smelled of lavender talc and Izzie's mind was filled with a rush of childhood memories. She bit back the tears. 'Whatever's wrong, child?' she said, then added, 'Come you on in and I'll put the kettle on.'

Izzie sat at her grandmother's kitchen table while the old lady filled the tea pot. She told her all about Mrs Shilling, about Muriel giving her the sack and how her father had taken all of her money. The only silver lining, she told her, was that she'd managed to find a new job starting on Monday.

'My, my, you've had quite a busy week, haven't you my dear,' Gran teased in an affectionate way.

Izzie managed a wan smile. 'Everything seems to be going wrong for me Gran. Everything.'

'Oh Izzie my dear,' said her grandmother, 'it really will do no good thinking like this. Life is what you make it. I know you've had a bit of a setback but the trick is not to let it get you down. Things will get better, I promise you.'

'I wish I could believe you,' Izzie said miserably. 'You don't know what it's like. Dad and Linda take advantage of me all the time. He spoils her rotten and I get lumbered with all the work.'

'I hope you're not feeling jealous of Linda.'

'Of course not!' Izzie cried. 'But I get so fed up with it all.'

'Has your father said you have to do all the work?'

Izzie hesitated. 'Well, no, but if I don't do it, who will?'

Her grandmother rose to her feet and kissed Izzie's forehead as she put their empty cups in the sink. 'Try not to be a martyr, my dear.'

Izzie frowned crossly. She knew her grandmother meant well but she could have been a bit more understanding. Anyone could see that right now her life was so horribly unfair.

Ada Baxter turned on the tap to do the washing up. 'Just remember that when the winter has gone, spring and summer are just around the corner.'

Izzie set her face. She didn't want pious platitudes. She wanted sympathy.

Wiping her hands, Ada cupped Izzie's face and smiled lovingly at her. 'Now, dry your tears and come with me to the village hall. There's a sale in there this afternoon in aid of the RSPCA and I'm after some of Freda Bishop's lardy cake.'

By the time Izzie caught the five o'clock bus back home she had spent a very happy day, despite her grandmother's apparent lack of sympathy. It was fun being back in the village hall where she caught up with old friends, drank gallons of tea and sampled some wonderful cakes. She had brought a little money with her so she managed to buy a couple of books and a rather pretty trinket box from the bric-a-brac table. When they got back to her grandmother's cottage, they had one last cup of tea before she went to the bus stop. Izzie took the opportunity to show her grandmother the newspaper cutting.

Ada's face paled. 'I always hoped you would never have to know about this,' she said with a sigh. 'Who gave it to you?'

Izzie explained that she had found it in an envelope while clearing old Mrs Shilling's desk. 'I'm guessing she didn't show me because she wasn't one hundred per cent sure of the connection or maybe she found it just before she got ill. I don't understand it, Gran. What has this got to do with me?'

'Your mother and Mrs Sayers were best friends,' Ada said cautiously.

Izzie frowned. 'You say they *were* best friends; why did they fall out?'

'Because Brenda always blamed your father for Gary's death.'

'Dad?' Izzie said, puzzled. 'But why?'

'Because . . .' said Ada. As Izzie raised her eyebrows, she added quickly, 'No, your mother never wanted you girls to know. I made a promise and I'm going to keep it. You'd be wise to let sleeping dogs lie.'

'Gran . . .' Izzie began again.

'No,' her grandmother said firmly. 'I've already said far too much. I want you to forget all about this. It's all in the past. What's done is done and the price has been paid.'

It was frustrating but Izzie knew her grandmother well enough to know that she wouldn't say any more. On the bus back home she read the cutting again. *Suspicion has fallen on a batch of sausage rolls which came from a local butcher . . .* Had her father once owned a butcher's shop? Izzie frowned to herself. She couldn't imagine him working as a butcher but come to think of it, the night she ran away, her mother had said something about a butcher; now what was it? '*How can I live with what that butcher did?*' Clearly something awful had happened and as a

137

result a little boy had died. And what did her grandmother mean when she said '*the price has been paid*?' Was that why her father had to go to jail? It was all very puzzling and Izzie knew she couldn't complete the story until she had all the pieces.

*

Izzie's new employer, Sid Pierson, had run the sweet shop and tobacconist near Worthing station for more than thirty years. It looked as if the shop itself hadn't changed since Edwardian times, when Sid's father opened it way back in 1907. As far as Izzie could see, the décor badly needed updating and everything needed a good clean, but her new employer lacked interest. Certainly his smoker's cough meant that she was left in the shop on her own for a good part of the day but Izzie didn't mind. She enjoyed making the place look more presentable. When it was quiet, Izzie first cleaned then filled the shelves, remembering to put the old stock right at the front and the new at the back. Sweets were back on ration. The government tried lifting rationing of confectionery in 1949 but the demand was so overwhelming that the whole country looked as if it were sliding towards anarchy so they'd had to reinstate it. Tobacco had never been rationed and because most people smoked, the shop did a brisk trade in cigarettes and pipe tobacco. By the middle of the week, Izzie felt settled and happy and she'd already made quite a few friends among Mr Pierson's customers.

*

By the time Izzie had been at the sweet shop for two weeks, the shop looked cleaner and brighter than it had done in quite a while and Sid Pierson let her have a relatively free hand.

It was during a very busy period that the police came into

the shop. Izzie was serving a man who wanted twenty Craven A and a quarter of toffee crunch. Mr Pierson was serving another customer who wanted a measure of tobacco for his pipe. Sid was weighing it on the scales. The policemen, one a sergeant and the other a constable, walked up to Izzie.

'Miss Isobelle Baxter?' the sergeant asked.

Surprised that he knew her full name, Izzie said, 'I'll be with you in a minute.'

'I'm afraid that will have to wait, Miss,' the sergeant said in booming tones.

Izzie looked surprised.

'Isobelle Baxter,' he continued, 'I'm arresting you on suspicion of theft. You are not obliged to say anything unless you wish to do so, but what you say may be put into writing and given in evidence.'

Izzie stared at him in disbelief.

'Come along with me now please, Miss.'

She turned towards Sid who stood with his mouth open. 'There must be some mistake,' he said.

'There's no mistake, Sir,' said the sergeant. 'The young lady is to come along with us.'

As they came out of the shop, the constable bumped right into a young man and a much older woman. The woman cried out in shocked surprise and the lad, who was carrying a suitcase, said gruffly, ''ere, watch out!'

Izzie was horrified to see that the woman was Mrs Sayers. What sort of sod's law was it that the woman should be outside in the street the moment Izzie had been arrested? Her face burned with shame.

'Excuse me, Madam,' said the constable, saluting her with his forefinger on his helmet.

'You wanna watch where you're going,' the young man called after them. 'My aunt ain't so young as she used to be.'

Izzie turned to glance back at the pair. Mrs Sayers was clearly annoyed by the reference to her age because Izzie saw her hit the young man's arm crossly. 'You mind your manners, Raymond.'

Izzie tried to say something but the two officers, one either side of her, simply marched her towards Union Place and the police station.

Seventeen

''ere Bill, your Izzie has been arrested!'

Bill Baxter, who was sitting in the office of his shop, leapt to his feet in shocked surprise. 'What? How do you know?'

The bearer of the bad news was his lorry driver, Mick Osborne.

The two of them were having a fairly quiet day. They'd collected a large consignment of furniture as part of a house clearance the day before and were spending today sorting out the rubbish from the good. As was always the case with a house clearance when somebody had died, they were asked to take everything down to the butter in the butter dish. The occupier of this particular house had been elderly so most of the bedding, curtains and clothing was so old they would only be good for rags, but Bill was lucky enough to find the odd promising item. The garden tools were in good nick, as was the silver cutlery set that he'd found in the attic. The cutlery box itself looked pretty dilapidated and was hidden behind an old trunk full of books, which led him to suppose that that was the reason why the relatives had missed it.

Sorting through everything for hours on end was a bit tedious, which was why Mick had popped out to buy a pie from the station café and get some fags from the corner shop where Izzie worked.

'I just seen her being marched off to the local nick.'

'What's she done?' Bill gasped.

Mick shrugged. 'Nicked summat, I suppose.' He laughed, revealing brown and uneven teeth. He had a twinkle in his eye as he added, 'The apple don't fall far from the tree, do it?'

'Nothing to do with me,' Bill said defensively.

'Yeah, right,' said Mick. 'Tell them that when they're giving your place the once over.'

Bill's face paled. 'I just have to nip out for a minute,' he said, grabbing his coat. The sound of Mick's raucous laughter followed him into the street.

*

It was some time later when Izzie was taken into an interview room. It was cold and bare, with four tubular steel chairs with canvas seats, two on either side of a scrubbed wooden table. The same sergeant came into the room but this time he was with another man, a policeman in plain clothes. They introduced themselves as Sergeant Parker and Detective Inspector Norris.

'You understand why you are here?' asked the inspector.

Izzie shook her head. 'I don't. You said it was theft but I've never taken anything that didn't belong to me. What is it I'm supposed to have done?'

The two men said nothing but the inspector shuffled some papers in a buff coloured folder.

Until she'd come into this room, Izzie had waited in a cell. That was cold as well and it smelled of urine. The walls were tiled in white with a line of dark green raised tiles about waist high all around. There was a window but it was high up and very small so she couldn't see out. All she'd had to sit on was

142

a bed with a very hard mattress covered with an army surplus blanket. The door had a slide over peep-hole in the centre through which someone used to look in on her every now and then, which was a bit disconcerting. Izzie had stared at the blank wall opposite. Too bewildered to cry, she spent her time going over everything she could think of to see if she could work out why she'd been brought here. Had someone spilled the beans about Linda? Had Linda, in turn, accused her of stealing that skirt? It was a possibility but Izzie had the feeling it was much more serious than that.

'Until two and a half weeks ago, you worked for a Mrs Shilling?' the inspector said.

'Yes, but she died.'

'And you were asked by her daughter-in-law to tidy her office room.'

'Yes,' said Izzie. 'I used to act as her secretary. I'm not trained, of course, but old Mrs Shilling didn't mind that. I typed up her manuscripts and saw to her post. When she passed away, I was asked to pack up all of her books and bring the correspondence up to date.'

'Mrs Shilling senior had some valuable pieces of jewellery, didn't she?'

Izzie began to tremble. Was this what all this was about? They were accusing her of stealing the old lady's jewellery? 'Yes.'

'Where did she keep that jewellery?'

'In her bedroom. She had a white leather case on her dressing table.' Izzie leaned forward and said earnestly, 'but I never touched it.'

The policemen glanced at each other. 'Last autumn, you went away with Mrs Shilling, didn't you?'

'Oh yes, I may have touched it then,' Izzie conceded. 'She asked me to put it in her suitcase.'

The inspector leaned back in his chair and flared his nostrils. His expression gave Izzie an awful sinking feeling in the pit of her stomach.

'We went to Bournemouth,' she ploughed on. 'She had just finished writing her book and was in need of a rest. We stayed at the Royal Bath Hotel.'

Her mind was working overtime. If someone had pinched some of Mrs Shilling's jewellery, could it have happened at the hotel?

The questioning went on for some time. Izzie had to tell them when she was alone in the garden room, how often and how many times she'd been left alone in the bedroom while Mrs Shilling was ill. They particularly wanted to know about her movements since she'd been sacked, how she felt about Muriel Shilling, her relationship with other members of the household. Izzie answered truthfully and did her best to stay calm.

Eventually she was taken back to the cells and for the first time since this terrible thing started, she gave way to tears.

*

Bill Baxter and his youngest daughter sat at the kitchen table, each wearing an expression on their faces as if butter wouldn't melt. For the past hour, two policemen had been snooping around the house, looking into drawers and cupboards. Bill was uneasy. All this reminded him of another time and another place when the outcome was far from good.

For her part, Linda hoped she could trust an unsuspecting Ruth not to look in the bag she had asked her to put in the church hall.

'I've brought a few things my sister wants to give to the

church jumble sale next Saturday,' she'd said when Ruth opened the door to the vicarage.

Ruth had thanked her and invited her in for a cup of tea but Linda explained that she couldn't stop. She might be tempted to stay for tea when she went back after the police had gone. She would apologise profusely and tell Ruth she'd made a dreadful mistake. She'd brought the wrong bag earlier that day, and could she have it back please?

'Have you ever seen your sister with anything out of the ordinary?' one bobby asked her. He was quite young for a copper and good looking too.

Linda opened her eyes wide. 'I don't know what you mean,' she simpered.

'Any jewellery, or any money?'

'Well she did come home with five pounds a couple of weeks back,' Linda said innocently. She glanced at her father. 'Isn't that right, Dad?'

Bill nodded. 'She said the old boy gave it to her.'

'Old boy? Which old boy?'

'Mr Shilling,' Linda said batting her eyelids. 'But I'm sure she didn't do anything she shouldn't have, Officer.'

The young bobby looked away quickly.

Bill took in a breath and rolled his eyes. Why couldn't Linda just keep her big trap shut? If she didn't belt up they'd be thinking Izzie had hidden money in the house and the last thing he wanted was the coppers turning the whole place upside down. He had too much to lose. Upstairs under the floorboards by his bed, he still had that ruddy Edwardian snuff box he'd got off that posh bloke down on his luck. It was too distinct to get rid of just yet and if the coppers found it, he could be facing a hefty prison sentence for receiving stolen goods. That wasn't the only hot stuff he'd got. He didn't know why he'd done it but he'd squirrelled away a couple of brooches, a gold bracelet and a pair of pearl earrings. Right now they were in a bag he'd chucked into next-door's coal hole. He knew his elderly neighbour, Mrs Knowle, was in hospital having her varicose veins seen to so it had been easy enough to open the door and shove the bag inside for the time being.

'We've found a Post Office Savings book hidden in her room,' said the other policeman. 'She deposited five pounds in there.' He opened it to show his colleague and pointed to an entry.

The good looking copper nodded and looked up at Bill. 'We'll be taking this back to the station for a while.'

They left soon after. 'Did you know she had money in the Post Office?' Bill asked Linda.

Linda shook her head and arched her eyebrow. 'I bet it was the money she accused me of pinching.'

Bill sighed. 'I suppose I'd better go down to the station and see what's going on,' he said, reaching for his coat.

'And I have to see a friend about a bag,' said Linda, following him to the door.

*

'So where did you get this money?'

The inspector had called Izzie back into the interview room. She felt drained and terribly afraid. What if they didn't believe her? What if they sent her to prison for something she didn't do? She'd heard of such stories and always dismissed them, but what if it were true? What if it happened to her? Her Post Office Savings book was open on the table between them.

'I saved it.'

'How?'

'Out of my wages, of course.'

'Your sister said you came home recently with five pounds.'

'Mr Shilling thanked me for looking after his mother and he gave it to me when I left.'

The inspector pointed to an entry in the book. 'Is that it?'

'No,' said Izzie. 'Old Mrs Shilling gave me that five pounds after we got back from Bournemouth. It was a gift.'

'They were very generous.' The inspector gave her a sceptical look. 'You see, I'm wondering if you didn't steal that jewellery and sell it on for five pounds.'

'Look at the date when I deposited it,' Izzie said tetchily as she drummed the entry in the book with her finger. 'I had that five pounds ages ago.'

The inspector shifted uncomfortably in his seat. 'So what about the five pounds Mr Shilling gave you? What did you do with that?'

'My father took it off me,' said Izzie. She was conscious that her voice was becoming more shrill but it was hard not to show her anger. This was an absolute nightmare. 'Look,' she continued, 'would you just tell me what jewellery I'm supposed to have stolen?'

The inspector opened the buff cover and looked at a piece of paper. 'A gemstone bracelet, a pair of gold earrings, a small statue . . .'

Izzie let out a cry. 'Mrs Shilling took them with us to Bournemouth. I didn't steal them. She gave them to the Russell-Cotes Museum!'

The inspector frowned.

'You don't believe me but it's true I tell you,' Izzie wailed. 'They were part of her treasure trove and she gave them to the museum. I took her there in the wheelchair myself. Ring them up and ask them.'

The inspector glanced up at the clock on the wall. 'It's too late to ring them now.'

Izzie leaned back and closed her eyes with relief. 'So can I go now?'

'The constable will take you back to your cell,' said the inspector, 'and you can be sure that first thing in the morning I shall be on the phone to them.'

*

In Brenda Sayers' sitting room on the other side of town, her nephew Raymond Perryman looked around and sighed. He was already bored out of his skull and he'd only just arrived in Worthing. Ever since he'd come here, Auntie Bren had been harping on and on about his cousin Gary and what a lovely boy he'd been.

It was seeing that chick being arrested by the rossers that triggered it all. He wondered vaguely what she'd done. As for his cousin being so lovely, Ray had heard it all before and he didn't believe a word of it. Back then, when Gary was alive, he'd been the one who'd got them into trouble. Of course Ray was upset when Gary died. Young as he was, he knew he could so easily have gone the same way. Auntie Bren seemed to forget that he'd been pretty ill himself.

At nine, he made his excuses and went upstairs to bed. By nine-thirty he'd switched off the light and ten minutes later he was shinning down the drainpipe and legging it away from the house. He caught a bus to town and after wandering around a bit, he found a basement club called The Cave. It was a bit tame compared to what he was used to in London but the skiffle band was quite good and he'd made a couple of friends already; a lad called John Middleton, who worked on the railway, and Paul Dawkins, who was an apprentice motor mechanic. With a few illicit drinks inside him, Ray got into a punch up with some other lads and somebody called the cops. He ended up having to hide down some dark alley-way between the shops, which the locals called a twitten, until the coppers had gone. After that he felt much more at home.

*

Izzie woke with a back ache. She'd had a terrible night. It seemed as if the hours of darkness would never end. The lights were only dimmed at ten o'clock and the police cells were far from quiet. She heard drunks singing at the tops of their voices and someone banged on a door for what seemed like hours, begging to be let out. Policemen stopped by to tell someone to 'shut-up', and there was a constant sound of jangling keys and banging doors. Someone came in at stupid o'clock to take her to the toilet and she was allowed to have a quick wash, but she had nothing with which to brush her hair or her teeth. Breakfast was a slice of toast with margarine and a mug of very strong tea.

With no watch and no means of knowing the time, it seemed an age before the door finally flew open, and the inspector said, 'You are free to go.'

Izzie stared in disbelief. So, that was it? She'd been paraded through the streets like a common criminal, accused of stealing and stuck in a police cell overnight and now all he said was, 'you are free to go'? She swallowed down the desire to rant and rave about the unfairness of it all, afraid if she made a fuss he'd lock her up for disorderly behaviour or something.

'You rang them?' she said coldly.

'Yes and they verified your story.'

'Does Mrs Shilling know?'

'My officer has gone round there to explain.'

Izzie waited. No apology. Nothing. He stepped back and

she flounced past him with her nose in the air. In the custody room she was handed back her handbag and the bits and pieces she'd had in her pockets and then they opened the door. And oh the joy when she stepped out into the street.

Eighteen

Giacomo Semadini stepped back and looked around his new premises. The past few weeks had been a lot of hard work getting the paperwork done but everything was finally coming into shape. Before it opened, the Café Bellissimo had to be perfect. First he planned to change the brown and tan walls of Mabel's café; Giacomo would paint them a very delicate shade of pink and the window frames would be white, giving the whole room a much lighter, brighter ambiance. The high backed chairs with crushed velvet cushions had arrived and soon they would be placed under the small round tables which would be covered with snow white table cloths. All that was left now was to sort out the kitchen and once his two cousins got busy in the kitchen, the counters would groan with their delectable cakes and pastries.

Giacomo smiled to himself as he fingered the precious little toy mascot in his jacket pocket. Who knows? Perhaps his grandmother was right. Maybe one day this little bear would bring him luck and the girl he loved. He looked around once more and let out a satisfied sigh. There was no doubt about it, his creation for Worthing would be a masterpiece, a tea room unlike any other and a place where women (for most of his customers were women) would be seen and pampered according to his own unique style. All he needed now was to find some really good waitresses but, as always, he would be picky about his choice. The girls working in his shop had to be just right.

*

On a bright sunny afternoon in March, Izzie stood outside the Café Bellissimo smoothing down her coat and making sure her beret was on straight. She paused and looked up at the shop front. Newly refurbished, it looked much more attractive than it ever had done when it was called Mabel's. She experienced a pang of loss which constricted her throat for a fleeting moment as she recalled the times when she used to wheel old Mrs Shilling past Mabel's.

When the feeling had passed, Izzie drew in a deep breath and wondered if she could face another disappointment. The past few weeks had been utterly awful. Since her arrest, the stigma had followed her everywhere like a bad smell. It didn't seem to matter that she had been proven completely innocent. The fact that half the town had seen her being marched along the street between two burly policemen was all it took to label her as 'unemployable'.

'There's no smoke without fire,' people whispered behind her back.

She'd become so desperate, she'd even asked her father if she could come back to the emporium.

'It didn't work before,' he'd said bluntly. 'You need to bring in some cash. I can't afford to pay you.'

Izzie had been for interview after interview but as soon as she said her name the job vacancy she'd seen advertised had either been filled or they would 'let her know', which of course they never did. She couldn't go back to Mr Pierson's tobacconist shop either. He had been 'taken bad' the day she'd been removed from the shop and was still in hospital. The shop was permanently closed and rumour had it that if Mr Pierson died, it would be sold, the first to be bought under a compulsory purchase order from the council who were keen to redevelop the area around Teville Gate.

If Izzie had expected a little sympathy from her family, she was sadly mistaken. Nothing was said about her arrest but every day her father demanded to know if she'd got another job. He didn't say anything when she told him no but she knew what he was thinking. She was useless and a liability. Linda behaved as if nothing had happened. On top of that, having no spare money meant that Izzie couldn't go over to Brighton to see her mother. She wrote a letter to explain and her mother had kindly sent her a couple of pounds in the post to tide her over.

To keep herself busy, Izzie began to decorate the house. Her father gave her wallpaper and paint, mostly from house clearances he'd done, and Izzie made a good job of it even if some of the rooms were papered with two different designs. She was slowly transforming the house from dowdy to bright.

The only other support Izzie had came from Esther and Patsy. She wrote long letters to Esther and she'd met Patsy to go to the pictures just after she'd got back home from her night in the cells. Patsy was very supportive but she had a new boyfriend, Dick, and it seemed things were getting serious. Patsy was all apologies but she explained that she and Dick were talking about getting engaged. She wouldn't have much time for girlie nights out she said, and they hadn't met since.

Esther wrote back immediately. She stated her belief in her friend and went on to tell her in a chatty and fun way about her training. She was coming home on leave for a weekend in May and she promised that they would meet and catch up. Izzie was looking forward to seeing her but at the moment her meagre savings were so sadly depleted and if she didn't get a job soon, she wouldn't even be able to afford a cup of tea with Esther.

The Café Bellissimo, as Mabel's was now called, was Izzie's last chance to find a place of work in Worthing. She would have preferred something more challenging but since her very public arrest, she had little choice. The café would be busy in the summer months although she wasn't sure if it would have the same number of customers in the winter. There was every possibility that this could end up as a seasonal job, which was a bit disconcerting because she would then have to face another round of job hunting as soon as the summer season ended. Added to that, there was plenty of competition with Lyons tea rooms near the Old Town Hall and the two other cafés within shouting distance in South Street. Still, so long as the owner paid her wages every week, Izzie decided it didn't matter. A job was a job and having been out of work for so long, she needed this one desperately.

The tea room was crowded. The notice on the window said 'Waitress wanted. Apply within,' but Izzie was reluctant to go into the shop by the front door and run the risk of a public humiliation. She decided to go in the back of the shop and went in search of the tradesman's entrance.

The alleyway behind the shops was crowded with doorways but it was easy enough to find the one belonging to the Café Bellissimo. Several cats hovering around the dustbins fled as she approached. Izzie walked to the kitchen door and knocked. Immediately, the door burst open, making her jump, and a large man, aged about forty or forty-five, stood in front of her. She noticed his hair first. It framed his face like a million charcoal grey and black bubbles. His eyes, dark as oak, sparkled with mischief and he sported a small old-fashioned waxed moustache over his generous lips.

'Look atta this!' he exclaimed loudly as he threw his hands in the air and showered her with flour. 'The Blessed Virgin has sent us an angel from Heaven.' Then he threw the door wide open so that those inside could see her.

Izzie blushed with embarrassment as he roared with laughter, his dark eyes twinkling and his giant belly wobbling under a big white apron smeared with pastry finger marks. Someone else appeared at his shoulder. He was a much younger and slimmer man but the similarity between the two was apparent. Izzie felt sure the two men must be related. Gently pushing the older man aside, he said with a smile and in a much less pronounced accent, 'Have you come about the vacancy?'

Izzie nodded.

'Please come in,' said the younger man, stepping back. He was holding an icing syringe. 'We already have two other ladies waiting.'

The heat in the kitchen hit her like a wall. Izzie looked around. Sparkling pots and pans of every size and shape hung from hooks on the walls. On the kitchen table, a large chocolate sponge and a great many delectable pastries stood in rows and on wire cake racks. The younger man had been decorating a large cake covered with Royal icing. Tiny, perfectly formed pink roses waited for their place on the top of the cake. He threw the syringe down beside it as the big man who had opened the door went back to kneading a piece of dough on the huge table in the middle of the room. As she walked past him, Izzie caught a glimpse of someone else in the scullery doing the washing up. For someone who had grown up with the privations of war and now peacetime rationing, the whole kitchen seemed like Pharaoh's store house.

The younger man didn't speak as he led her through the kitchen into a dark passage between the kitchen and the shop but a white aproned waitress carrying a tray of tea who bustled past them smiled. The man motioned for Izzie to sit down next to two other women who sat on wooden chairs outside a door marked 'office'. One, a blonde girl, heavily made up, was very fashionably dressed. Her pointed bra divided her breasts in a seductive way under a tight white sweater and she wore a brown pencil skirt. She didn't wear stockings but she had a pair of bobby socks and her flat lace-up shoes had a brown flash down the sides. The other woman was a lot older and a complete contrast. Her grey coat was shabby and her shoes down at heel. She sat bolt upright clutching her handbag, which she fingered nervously. Izzie couldn't help noticing that her fingernails were bitten down to the quick and that she exuded a slightly unwashed aroma. Izzie sat on the chair in between them and waited.

Izzie was the last to be called. When the other two came out of the office, they gave no indication as to how their interviews had gone, just made their way into the restaurant and sat at one of the tables where they were offered a free cup of tea.

'Miss Baxter.'

Izzie stood up nervously.

The office itself was spacious. There was a desk with two chairs either side of it, a filing cabinet, a fairly solid looking wall safe and a small leather sofa. Izzie gaped in surprise when she saw the man who was about to interview her. It was none other than Mr Semadini, the owner of the café in Brighton where she and her mother had first met.

He sat on one side of the desk with his head down, studying Izzie's references. He was much as she'd remembered. She stared at the top of his dark hair, waiting for him to look up. He wore a smart suit with a colourful waistcoat. As he looked up he blinked in surprise. 'Oh, it's you,' he said as he handed her references back.

Izzie's heart sank. Oh no, not again. It seemed as if her reputation had been sullied around here for ever.

'Well, Miss Baxter,' he went on in flawless English, 'there is no contest. I have no hesitation in offering you the job. Your references are exemplary and because you had no hesitation in

156

handing me back my wallet when I dropped it on the station in Brighton that time, I already know how honest you are.' He rose to his feet and extended his hand for her to shake. 'If you would like to come and work in the Café Bellissimo, we should be very pleased to have you on board.'

Izzie beamed as they shook hands and they agreed that she should start work on Monday.

Nineteen

The rules in the Café Bellissimo were strict and the customer always came first. All waitresses were expected to be well turned out; their pink gingham dresses neatly ironed and the detachable Peter Pan collar absolutely spotless. They had a cherry coloured bow at the throat and their small white aprons were slightly starched. As soon as she got the job, Izzie was relieved to discover that Mr Semadini used a reliable laundry service so she wasn't expected to wash her own uniform herself.

There were even rules about their hair. Izzie's was short (as soon as she knew she'd got the job, she'd treated herself to a Bob) so she was all right but the other girls had to have their hair in a neat roll at the nape of the neck or swept up at the sides with combs. The shop opened at nine but everybody had to be at work by eight-thirty for inspection. Mr Semadini lined them up before looking at their hands and finger nails. As soon as he deemed them fit, the menus were placed on the tables.

He had modelled the Café Bellissimo on Lyons Tea Rooms with its famous Nippies, but the menu wasn't nearly as comprehensive. As well as wonderful cakes and pastries, they offered simple affordable fare which would appeal to the locals as well as the day tripper. Crumpets, currant buns and fairy cakes stood alongside crab salad, egg sandwiches, bacon and onion pudding and locally caught fish with chips. For dessert, Café Bellissimo offered something completely unique in Worthing: freshly made Italian ice cream.

It didn't take long to work out that certain customers liked to sit in the same seat. Mr Pressley from the family jeweller's sat near the back of the restaurant, he wanted privacy to look at some paperwork, whereas Mrs Templeton made sure of a table in the middle of the restaurant so that she could enjoy eavesdropping on other people's conversations. Miss Cheeseman, head of ladies fashion in Bentall's department store, preferred the window seat.

There were several occasions when Izzie noticed Mr Semadini watching her. At first it unnerved her. She worried that she had done something wrong. Had she forgotten something? He never reprimanded her or questioned what she was doing but if she looked up and caught his eye, he would smile pleasantly and move on. In the end, she decided that it didn't mean anything. It was just his way.

When it came to his customers, Mr Semadini had a wonderful gift of knowing exactly what to say. With some he was almost familiar. 'How are we today, my darling?' he would ask some elderly woman as he kissed both of her wrinkly cheeks. With others he was more formal. Holding out his hand to shake, he would say in his reappearing Italian accent, 'I'm delighted to see you again. We have missed you. I hope you have been keeping well?' He'd have just the right sort of banter for the men as well. 'Looks like the perfect weather for a bit of sea angling, George. Are you going to join the boys on the pier?' Or if he saw someone struggling with the sleeve of his coat he'd say, 'Here, let me help you with that, Sir.' And when he found out that one old lady had a sick grandson in Worthing Hospital, he put an empty sweet jar next to his lucky mascot by the till and told his customers he was saving odd change for the children's ward. It wasn't long before the coins in the jar began to creep up the sides. Kind gestures like that meant Izzie was thinking about him all the time. At home, she wrote letters to her mother and Esther telling them all about it.

*

When Christmas came around, Izzie and her fellow waitresses were pleasantly surprised to receive several gifts from customers and Mr Semadini gave everyone an extra two pounds in their wage packet. Between them, the girls exchanged Secret Santa presents. Izzie's gift was a lovely woollen scarf guaranteed to keep out even an arctic winter.

At home, she wrapped presents for her father and Linda and prepared a Christmas meal. This year, she was determined that they celebrate with roast chicken, carrots and Brussels sprouts, and roast potato, followed by tinned peaches and custard. There had been no time to make a Christmas pudding but she had managed to win a small Christmas cake in a raffle. The meal was a success and the three of them got on quite well. Her father had already told them he would be out in the evening so Linda had invited John to the house. He, Linda and Izzie played Monopoly until it was time for him to go. Climbing wearily into bed, Izzie wished every day could be as happy as this one had been.

*

On New Year's Eve, a large car drew up outside in the street and young Mrs Shilling came into Café Bellissimo with a couple of friends.

'Good heavens, Izzie!' she cried as she was handed the menu. 'Well, I never expected to see you here.' There was a condescending sneer in her voice.

I bet you didn't, Izzie thought to herself as she smiled sweetly.

Her old employer was looking every inch the lady in a very expensive day dress and a matching jacket. Obviously Muriel had come into quite a bit of money when the old lady died.

As Izzie had expected, Mrs Shilling was an awkward customer who demanded instant service even though she could see that Izzie and the other girls were rushed off their feet. She fingered a cake, then said she didn't like it, telling Izzie to, 'take it away, girl,' in ringing tones. After that, she complained that the tea was cold. Izzie was tempted to tip the tea pot over her head but she had a shrewd idea that to arouse her temper was exactly what Mrs Shilling wanted. Izzie smiled and apologised in a professional way. Mrs Shilling left the café announcing in a loud voice that she wouldn't be returning and that she much preferred the tea room in Hubbard's department store. She left no tip.

'Do you know that lady?' Mr Semadini asked as he helped her prepare the table for the next customer.

'She was the mother-in-law of my old employer,' said Izzie.

Mr Semadini shook his head. 'You must be a saint to put up with the likes of her.'

Their eyes met and Izzie grinned.

Izzie loved her work and the people she worked with were a happy-go-lucky bunch. Mr Umberto, the large man in the kitchen, was always jolly and the younger man, Mr Benito, was serious minded but very kind. She discovered that they were all cousins and lived in the flat above the shop although it was rumoured that they were all looking for houses in town. It was also a source of gossip that Mr Semadini had a habit of starting a business and then leaving it in the capable hands of a relative before he moved on to the next project. His first restaurant in Hastings was run by two of his brothers and the one in Brighton had been left in the capable hands of his uncle and another cousin. He clearly had a flair for business planning but Izzie hoped he didn't move on to pastures new just yet.

The man she had spotted doing the washing up in the back kitchen the day she had come for interview was Ken. Injured during the war, he was delighted to have the work, so much so that he never stopped whistling. Izzie's fellow waitresses, Lucy, Helen and Carol, were easy to work with although their days were split into shifts. Mr Semadini made it clear that he didn't want his staff stressed or over stretched, which meant that Izzie wasn't always working with the same girl. She enjoyed being with them all and they often went to the pictures together.

'You coming to the dance, Izzie?' Helen asked.

'I can't,' said Izzie. 'I already have a date.'

She didn't mention it was with the Bex Bissell and a duster. She'd have to finish off the housework on New Year's Eve because she was seeing Mum again on New Year's Day.

*

Linda would never have known the coffee bar they called The Cave was there if she had passed the door in the day time. It was New Year's Eve and she had heard on the grapevine that this was the place where all the young people came to hang out. Just around the corner from the National Provincial Bank and within sight of the Old Town Hall, it was behind a battered brown door and down some steep steps. There was no handrail and the stair wasn't well lit so as soon as she went through the door it felt creepy and exciting. She could feel the heat from sweaty bodies coming up to meet them as she and John walked down.

At the bottom of the stairs she was met by a wall of sound. Loads of people were crammed into the relatively small space and because of the dim lighting it took her a moment to focus her eyes. John led her across the room through the mass of gyrating dancers to a table right at the back. As soon as she sat down, he went to the bar to buy her a coffee. She could tell he didn't really want to be here but she was bored with the church youth club. There were only so many games of table tennis a body could stand. This was more like it. She wanted to rest her arms on the top of the table but it was sticky. Clearly something had been spilled on it and it hadn't been washed.

Linda looked around with mounting elation. In one corner a skiffle band played some indeterminate music on a guitar, a drum made out of an old tea chest with a piece of string attached to a broom handle, and a washboard strummed by a lad wearing thimbles on each finger. Another chap who stood in front of the instrumentalists was the singer. Their efforts were mostly drowned out by the level of chatter in the room and a blue haze of cigarette smoke hung in the air. Most of the boys in the room, and Linda was only interested in the boys, wore long jackets, white shirts and bootlace ties. Some, like John, only had part of the new Edwardian look, probably saving up for the rest of the gear. It wasn't cheap. A complete suit could set a boy back a whole month's wages.

There were a few girls in the coffee bar as well. They had their own unique style of dress; drape jackets, tight sweaters, pencil skirts and flat shoes. Linda felt a little out of place in her flowery skirt and white blouse.

'First time here?' asked the girl sitting at the other side of the table.

Linda nodded.

'Thought so,' said the girl. 'My name is Maureen but everybody calls me Mo.'

'Linda,' said Linda.

'I'm Ray's Judy,' said Mo, opening her compact and studying the wild curls at the front of her hair. She tugged at one or two so that they sprang back. The rest of her hair was scraped back into an elastic band like a pony tail. Linda wondered what a Judy was, but she didn't dare ask. Mo snapped her compact shut and stared directly at Linda. 'So keep off him, okay?'

Linda blinked.

'Hey, Doll.'

They both looked in the direction of the male voice. A boy on the other side of the room was beckoning. Mo rose to her feet and threaded her way through the crowd immediately. Linda stared after her, admiring her wiggle. When Mo stopped by a boy with the biggest quiff she had ever seen, Linda's heart skipped a beat . . . or maybe three. He was easily the dishiest looking boy in the room; medium height, dark-haired and with a gorgeous smile. As Mo approached, the boy took her handbag and turning his back on her, began rummaging through it until her found her purse. Mo was tugging at his arm trying to get it back from him but he elbowed her aside roughly and only gave her purse back to her after he'd helped himself to some money.

'There you are,' said John, suddenly appearing and placing two glass Pyrex cups of coffee onto the table. Linda jumped. They were the smallest cups she had ever seen and half the content was in the saucer.

'Two bloody bob they cost me,' said John, crashing into the seat beside her. He picked up his cup and sipped the coffee. 'Ugh, it's cold.'

Linda looked away, irritated. Why did he always have to put the dampener on everything?

The skiffle band began to play a tune she recognised from the radio. Linda smiled. This was great. She loved it here. She looked around and spotted Mo and the good looking boy again. They had linked their fingers together and were dancing The Creep. Her other hand was on his shoulder but his other hand was kneading her bottom. Linda felt both a frisson of excitement and a pang of jealousy.

'Great in here, isn't it?' said John, bringing her back to earth.

Yes, she thought acidly, as she gave him a cursory nod, and it would be even better without you.

'See that bloke over there,' said John, jerking his head towards Ray. 'He's from London. They say he was in the Mile End fight.'

Linda gave an involuntary shiver. The papers had been full of it. Two rival gangs had met on a bomb site, which was being developed into a park, and a vicious fight broke out.

'Was Ray in the gang then?' Linda asked breathlessly.

'Na,' said John. 'He's all right. He's come to Worthing to stay with his auntie.'

Linda was doing her best to look casual. 'What does he do?'

'Do?' said John. 'People like Ray don't *do* anything.'

Twenty

Izzie and her mother strolled along the seafront. There was nothing much to do because it was cold and blustery. Izzie wondered why her mother didn't invite her to her home. Was it because she lived in a poor area of town? Or maybe it was because she lived in a shared tenement. All the same, it was a bit odd that they were wandering around in the open rather than being indoors. Eventually she suggested they should find somewhere warmer and Doris suggested a pub near the seafront. They went into the Ladies Snug. Doris had a sherry and she bought Izzie a lemonade. They sat huddled by the fire.

'Tell me about your life, Mum,' said Izzie, 'before you met Dad.'

Doris chuckled. 'Not very exciting I'm afraid. I was born in Bethnal Green, near Weaver's Fields. They're pulling down all the old cottages to make way for a new park.'

'Weaver's Fields?' Izzie queried. She'd never heard of it before.

'It was where the Huguenot silk weavers lived,' said Doris. 'They were French refugees.'

Izzie nodded. 'There's a chapel belonging to them in the Lanes.'

'My family were originally costermongers,' Doris went on. 'My father and his father before him.'

'That's what Dad did, wasn't it?'

'Your dad sold everything and anything,' said Doris. 'My family were famous for Polly's meat pies.'

Izzie grinned. 'Sounds delicious.'

'They were.' Her mother smiled. 'Made to a secret recipe handed down from the eighteen hundreds.'

Izzie's interest was kindled. 'Have you ever made them?'

'Of course.'

'Will you share the recipe with me?'

Doris' face clouded. 'I haven't done any since . . .' She faltered and Izzie's heart constricted. It always came back to what happened to Gary Sayers didn't it. It hung over everything like a thick dark cloud.

When she got back to Worthing, Izzie spent the evening with Esther and her parents. They'd played silly games and eaten for England. All in all, Izzie had really enjoyed herself. Mr Jordan brought her home in his car and as she and Esther embraced to say goodbye, she somehow knew that 1952 was going to be a momentous year for both of them.

*

As he sat at Auntie Bren's kitchen table flicking through the newspaper, Raymond Perryman was beginning to wish he'd never agreed to come to Worthing. He faced a long afternoon by himself and there wasn't even anything decent on at the pictures. *The Long Memory* starring John Mills was showing at the Plaza. Apparently it was a smuggling story beginning with a charred body being found in a boat. Ray curled his lip. He could guess the plot already. His eye moved down the paper. *House of Wax* starring Vincent Price was on at the Odeon. Vincent Price was quite good but did he want to see the film? Ray turned the page with a sigh. He was sick of looking at wedding pictures and reports about children's Christmas parties. Nothing ever happened here. The whole place was full of newly-weds and nearly dead's and now that it was winter it was worse than ever. With the cold weather all the girls were bundled up in coats and scarves so he couldn't eye-up any classy chassis on the prom. Even the dances in the Assembly Hall were a dead loss, full of middle-aged spinsters and old duffers in dress suits, which was hardly surprising when the music was so deadsville. The Cave was just about the only place that was hip but even that was losing its appeal.

Auntie Bren was okay. She might be a widow but she was no soft touch. She was quite capable of giving her nephew a clip around the ear if necessary. There were times when his blood ran cold at the thought of his mates seeing him bringing in the coal or putting the dustbins out but he knew better than to go against her. He was supposed to be looking around for another job but so far he'd managed to keep one step ahead of that one; any lifting involved and he had a bad back, he was no good at sums so he couldn't work in a shop, and if deliveries were involved, he hadn't got a driving licence yet. He was determined to keep off the radar because the one thing he really wanted to avoid was getting his call-up papers for National Service. He turned the page of the newspaper. *The Cruel Sea* was showing at the Odeon cinema and *Cosh Boy* at the Rivoli. Now, that was more like it, but a quick feel in his trouser pocket told him he didn't even have enough for even the cheapest seat in the house. It looked like he'd have to help himself to a bob or two from his auntie's purse again.

He didn't like taking money from Auntie. He'd found himself a nice little gold mine in Mo and she was only too willing to do anything he wanted. Now that she was his Judy he'd taught her a thing or two and she was so keen she'd given him a golden opportunity to have her in comfort tonight. She'd invited him over to her place because her mum and dad were going out.

'Come at eight,' she'd told him. 'They're going to the Connaught Theatre so they won't be back until after ten.'

He was looking forward to it. Anything was better than doing it in some draughty doorway with the ever present risk of being caught by some passing copper, or having her on the beach where the shingle rubbed the skin off his knees. The only trouble was, from the moment he'd got her knickers off, she'd started talking about wedding bells and marriage.

'Cut the gas,' he'd told her impatiently, but her constant chatter drove him crazy. He wasn't ready to get circled yet. He wanted to make a name for himself first.

Ray made his way to the sitting room, to where Auntie Brenda had left her handbag beside her chair, but just as he was about to slip his hand inside, she came along the corridor. 'Oh Raymond, would you do me a favour? Could you get the big red case down from the loft? I've got some curtains in it. They'd be much nicer for the summer months than the ones already hanging up but I have to do some repairs first.'

Ray sprang to attention. When he'd known he was coming to Worthing, Ray's brother Lennie had asked him to hide some stash. 'It'll be safe as houses at Auntie Bren's,' he'd said, handing him something wrapped in an old vest.

Ray must have looked puzzled but when Lennie said the cops were watching him he understood. 'One false move,' said Lennie, 'and I'll be back in Borstal quicker than you could say flick knife.' So Ray had agreed.

It was handy that Auntie Bren had asked him to go into the loft. It gave him the ideal opportunity to hide Lennie's stuff somewhere he knew she wouldn't be snooping around. At the moment, he had it at the back of his wardrobe so there was always the risk that Auntie might find it. She couldn't climb the ladder to the loft anymore so it would be safe from her prying eyes up there.

As soon as he'd arrived in Worthing he had unwrapped Lennie's parcel. It was a little disappointing at first, just some bits of old jewellery and a watch, but there was also a flick knife. The blade had been wiped clean but where it met the hilt he could see a small stain. Ray guessed it was blood. As he turned it over in his hands, Ray wondered why his brother hadn't chucked it into the Thames. But even as he posed the question, he knew the answer. It was obviously some sort of a trophy.

Auntie's loft was packed to the rafters with all sorts of junk but in between the battered old chairs, rolled bits of old carpet, and even half a bike, he spotted the red suitcase. It weighed a ton and as he manhandled it towards the loft opening, he knocked an old tennis racquet down, which in turn sent a small package wrapped in sacking and perched on a rafter, flying.

'Whatever was that?' His aunt was standing at the bottom of the ladder looking up.

'I knocked some things over,' he said. 'Don't worry, I'll go back and tidy up.'

Once the case was downstairs and his aunt was fiddling about with the curtains, Ray slipped back into the loft with Lennie's stuff. Picking up the package he'd knocked over, he pulled the sacking away to reveal a gun. A gun! He searched the loft for bullets and found a box on one of the overhead beams. The gun looked very old and he guessed it was a relic from the First World War, but all the same, it was still a gun!

There was an old mirror in the corner propped against a trunk. The glass was foxed but Ray spent the next twenty minutes waving the gun around and pretending to be James Cagney. The last time he'd gone to the pictures in London was to see his gangster film *Kiss Tomorrow Goodbye*. With a gun like this, Ray could be a real gangster. He couldn't wait to show Mo.

Eventually his aunt called to the ladder. 'You all right up there, Ray?'

'Yes, Auntie,' he called back. 'Just coming.'

*

Despite the fact that spring was just around the corner, it looked like snow. Thick iron coloured clouds hung in the sky like a lead ceiling. A chill wind from the sea made Izzie hunch her shoulders and sink her chin deep into her woolly scarf as she dashed to the offices of the *Worthing Herald*.

'Oh, it's freezing out there!' She turned and the receptionist, a plump woman dressed in a grey skirt and a grey knitted jumper gave her a warm cherubic smile. She wore round rimmed glasses and her grey hair was piled untidily on the top of her head in a chaotic yet oddly attractive way. The only relief from a sea of grey was a cream coloured cameo brooch at her neck. Izzie guessed she was a woman in her fifties.

The reception itself was neat and tidy but a tad old fashioned. A paraffin stove made a noble but failing effort to warm the premises and its dark walls were covered with framed and faded back-dated front pages from the paper.

'Can I help you?'

Izzie stepped towards the desk hesitantly. 'I'm not sure. I hope so.' She opened her handbag and drew out the cutting. 'I want to find out a little more about this.'

The older woman peered at the cutting. 'It's definitely from one of our papers.'

Izzie was surprised. 'It is? How do you know?'

The woman chuckled. 'Believe me, I've worked here for nearly thirty years and I'd recognise our style anywhere.' She paused, frowning. 'I remember this. Terrible business. The whole country was up in arms. I believe the man in question went to prison.'

Izzie sucked in her lips lest she showed any emotion. If everyone in the country was up in arms, this woman might have strong feelings herself.

'I think it was 1941 or maybe 1942,' said the woman. 'Would you like to look at some back copies?'

'Yes please,' said Izzie, not realising she could do that.

The woman went through a door, leaving her alone in reception. Izzie looked around, studying the pictures on the walls, anything to help her keep control of her feelings. There was one from a 1921 issue when the war memorial outside the new Town Hall was unveiled in April. The front page photograph showed a large crowd of sombre townspeople standing with heads bowed as the drapes were being pulled away from a statue of an English Tommy with his rifle pointing down and his helmet held high in a victory salute. Nearby there was a more recent one, taken in 1945 when the crowds gathered on the steps of the Old Town Hall to cheer and celebrate VE day. Izzie squinted to see if she recognised anybody, maybe her mother, but she didn't.

The woman came back with two very large leather bound books. One was for 1941 and the other 1942, and to Izzie's surprise she found that they contained every copy of the *Worthing Herald* for those years.

'I think it happened around Christmas time,' said the woman, 'so perhaps if you look at January and February first, it might save a little time.'

She put the books on a shelf near the window and Izzie began to thumb the pages. She found the article in the February 20th edition 1941. It made headline news, of course, and in the issues which followed she found other references to the incident. It made grim reading.

'I can probably find some old copies,' the receptionist said. 'You'll have to pay for them, of course.'

'Of course,' said Izzie dully. 'Can I have the April 17th and April 24th editions?'

'The trial,' said the receptionist.

Izzie nodded.

'I remember it was delayed because Easter was at the beginning of April that year,' said the receptionist, getting ready to leave the desk again. 'Give me a minute or two.'

Half an hour later Izzie walked out into the rain with two old newspapers that had broken her heart stuffed into her handbag.

Twenty-One

As Izzie walked to work one week in February, the streets of Worthing were strangely quiet. She became aware that the few people about had sombre faces and a woman was crying in the doorway of Woolworth's as the manager opened the door to let her in. By the time she reached the café, Izzie was feeling very unsettled. Carol opened the door, her face streaked with tears.

'Whatever's happened?' Izzie asked but Carol only put her handkerchief to her mouth to suppress a sob.

'Haven't you heard?' said Helen. 'It's the King. He's dead.'

'What? When?' Izzie put her hand to her mouth in shocked surprise. 'I didn't listen to the wireless this morning.'

'They'll announce it again at nine o'clock I shouldn't wonder,' said Mr Semadini. 'We shall not be opening today, so come into the office.'

Everyone, including Mr Umberto and Mr Benito and Ken, squeezed into the office and Mr Semadini switched on the wireless. After listening to sombre music, John Snagg came on at nine.

'This is London. It is with the greatest sorrow . . .'

Izzie's mind froze. So he'd gone. George VI had been king virtually the whole of her lifetime. She was only two when he came to the throne, and now he was gone. Like everyone else in the room, she felt a great and yawning loss.

'. . . that the King, who retired to rest last night in his usual health, passed peacefully away in his sleep early this morning . . .'

Carol was sobbing now. Izzie slipped her arm around her shoulders and at the same time they heard someone trying the café door.

Mr Semadini frowned. 'Go and tell them we're closed.'

Izzie took a deep breath. 'Excuse me, Sir, but if you don't mind me saying so, I think you should open.'

He glanced up at her in shocked surprise and she heard Helen take in a breath.

'But out of respect . . .' Mr Umberto began.

'I think a lot of your customers regard you as friends,' Izzie went on, 'and when something terrible happens, don't you seek out those closest to you for comfort?'

Mr Semadini shook his head. 'I don't want to be seen to be making a profit out of this.'

Everybody looked thoughtful.

'I for one would be willing to donate my day's wages to charity,' said Izzie.

They all looked from one to the other and began to nod. 'I don't mind doing that,' said Carol.

'Nor I.'

'Include me in that.'

While everybody left the office, Mr Semadini began to write a notice and Izzie went to the door to let in the first of their bereaved customers. Her suggestion proved to be the right thing to do. It turned out to be an emotional day but their regulars, especially those who lived on their own, were grateful to have somewhere to go. When they read Mr Semadini's notice by the till, the gifts left in the sweet jar exceeded the usual total by several pounds. Mr Semadini decided to donate the money to the Queen Alexandra Hospital Home, where veterans of the

First and Second World Wars were cared for. King George VI's newly widowed Queen Elizabeth often visited there.

'I think we really helped those people,' Mr Semadini said as he stood by the shop door to lock up after them at the end of the day. 'I can't thank you enough, Isobelle.'

She smiled up at him and as their eyes met she was afraid he could hear her heart thudding. He leaned forward and kissed her lightly on both cheeks. Her face flamed.

'*Buonanotte, mia cara.*'

She slipped past him and he locked the door. Izzie had no idea what he'd just said to her but it sounded lovely.

*

They buried the King at St George's Chapel in Windsor nine days after the announcement came. The café had closed for the funeral, of course, and like millions of others, Izzie and her family gathered around the wireless. Linda sat painting her nails and though for a brief second Izzie felt sure she saw her father wipe away a tear with the back of his hand, for the most part he sat grim-faced behind a bottle of stout. As soon as the broadcast was over, he left the house without a word – for the pub, she presumed.

'Are you all right, Linda?'

Her sister shrugged. She wasn't very talkative these days. Izzie wasn't sure why but she reasoned that if Linda had a problem, she would tell her. Thankfully, she was a little more helpful in the house these days, which had eased their relationship quite a bit.

'Is it just because you're sad?' Izzie probed.

'Oh stop going on,' Linda snapped as she left the room in a huff.

Izzie sighed and rolled her eyes heavenward. She was always treading on egg shells as far as Linda was concerned.

On the Saturday following the funeral, Izzie got to see her mother again. The weather had been mixed; the snow had gone and spring was making a valiant attempt to get going. The fact that there were far fewer crowds along the parade meant that they'd walked quite a long way.

They sat on a bench in a tiny public space near the station. Not big enough to be called a park, it sat back from the main thoroughfare like a small green oasis. A few sparrows hopped among the pigeons, looking for scraps, and a lone daffodil waved at the edge of some railings. It was cold but the thin sunshine gave the illusion of a nice day and so long as they pulled their coats around themselves tightly, it was quite pleasant.

Izzie and her mother had enjoyed their usual cup of tea in a café near the station and this was the walk back for Izzie to catch the train. When Izzie showed her the newspaper cuttings from the *Worthing Herald*, she was shocked by her mother's reaction. Doris turned her head away and was clearly upset.

'Oh Mum,' she said helplessly. 'I'm sorry. I didn't mean to make you cry.'

Doris struggled to compose herself.

Izzie had been trying to pluck up the courage to tell her mother about the cuttings the whole time and now that she had, she wasn't quite sure how to cope with the fallout.

'Mum, I know you'd rather not talk about what happened, but I hate the not knowing.'

Doris put her hand over Izzie's. 'I know,' she choked, 'and I promise . . . I promise I will tell you. I will.'

Izzie chewed her lip. 'I have to get the train soon,' she ventured. 'Next time, eh?'

Doris looked relieved. She nodded. 'Next time. I promise.'

They embraced and parted and Izzie walked the rest of the way up the hill towards the station. She was hardly aware of entering the station concourse and still deep in thought when a man's voice, though gentle, startled her. With only half an ear open for the tannoy, she'd been thinking about the time she'd just enjoyed with her mother and how much she regretted producing the newspaper cuttings right at the end of her visit. It was a bad mistake; too much of a bombshell. She could see that clearly now. She should have shown them to her sooner, maybe in the café, not then, not when she was so close to catching her train.

Tired from the walk back up the hill, she had found a seat to rest on.

'Forgive the intrusion . . .'

When she looked up, the light was behind him so his face was in shadow. She didn't know him so she lowered her eyes without speaking. Obviously some chap trying to pick her up. She'd heard of people like him, preying on young girls at stations. They usually hung around places like Victoria Station in London, or King's Cross or St Pancras, on the look-out for run-aways or girls on their own. The men would befriend them, and after buying them a cup of tea in the refreshment room, they'd offer to find the girl accommodation at a reasonable price. If the offer was accepted, the girl would find herself on a slippery slope to prostitution. *The News of the World* was full of such stories every Sunday. Izzie turned her head to look at the revolving notice board.

'You probably don't remember me . . .'

Good heavens, he was persistent.

'. . . but I saw what you did for Giacomo and I just wanted you to know I thought it was admirable.'

Izzie frowned. For what she'd done? What was he talking about?

She turned to look at him as he began to move away. It was only then that she recognised him as the man who had stood up to offer her his seat on the train the day Mr Semadini had dropped his wallet on the platform.

'Oh,' she exclaimed. 'I'm so sorry. You must think me very rude. I didn't realise who you were.'

He paused and smiled. 'That's quite all right. I just wanted you to know how much I admired your honesty.'

'I only did what anyone else would do.' He hovered awkwardly so she added, 'Are you catching the Bournemouth train today?'

'Yes, but I'm only going as far as Worthing. That's where I live.'

'Worthing! But that's where I live too.'

'Really?' he said with a smile. 'May I?' He lowered himself carefully onto the edge of the other end of the seat.

They chatted amiably and before long she discovered that his name was Roger Hughes and that he was a cinema projectionist who worked in the Plaza. When the announcement came over the tannoy that their train was on platform one, they walked to the ticket barrier together. Roger opened a train door and stood back for her to enter so it was perfectly natural to sit in the same carriage. By the time they reached Worthing, they seemed like old friends. She'd found out that he was living in digs in Rowlands Road. She told him about her job in the Café Bellissimo and he was delighted to hear that Giacomo had made such a success of it.

'The day I met him, I warned him that he might find it hard to make a go of things in Worthing,' he said with a chuckle. 'Looks like I was wrong about that.'

They walked together from the station, and said their goodbyes at the end of Chandos Road. Izzie walked indoors with a smile on her lips. She'd really enjoyed being with him and she was sure he'd liked being with her too, which was why she had been delighted when he asked her out.

Twenty-Two

A couple of weeks later, after Izzie ran down the hill from the station to Brighton seafront, she found her mother waiting by the railings. Having crossed the road, they hugged each other, all smiles and 'how are you's?'

Since the war ended, Brighton was a town of contrasts. The rich dined in the Grand Hotel and drank expensive Champagne while the people living in the east of the town on Albion Hill didn't even have electricity in their homes. Day trippers thronged the front during the summer months but as soon as the autumn temperatures arrived, the queues of coaches waiting to take them back home would be much shorter.

A small crowd had gathered along the promenade so, curious, Izzie and her mother strolled towards it. Down on the beach a baby elephant and its mother, both the property of Billy Smart's circus had taken to the waters. They had come by train, part of a herd of fifteen elephants which had paraded down Queen's Road to the Old Steine the day before. Performances in the big top, which could seat four thousand people, were held daily on The Level. The two women found a small space by the railings and watched the elephants enjoying a few minutes of carefully managed semi-freedom.

'Mum,' Izzie ventured, 'you promised to tell me about the

cuttings and I want to know what happened between you and Dad.'

Her mother patted her arm and sighed. 'I wish you would let it go, love. You shouldn't be fretting about our past mistakes. It's all water under the bridge now.'

'I'm not a child anymore,' Izzie insisted. 'You don't need to protect me. Tell me, Mum, please.'

Doris Baxter turned her head to look out to sea. 'You've read the cuttings so you already know that your father went to prison at the end of 1941,' she said quietly. 'And you know what he did. When he came back, he promised me things would be different.'

'But they weren't.'

'No,' Doris said bitterly. 'It only took him five minutes to get up to his old tricks again. That's why I was upset. I couldn't bear to go through all that shame and embarrassment again.'

Izzie frowned. 'But you were quite happy to go off and leave me and Linda to deal with it,' she said coldly.

Doris turned to face her daughter. 'Is that what your father says?'

'He says you went off with another man,' said Izzie, 'that you deserted us and he calls you rude names.'

Her mother grimaced. 'Well, it doesn't surprise me, but it's just not true.'

'So what did happen, Mum? I want to know your side of the story.'

'Izzie, I've always tried to protect you and Linda,' said Doris. 'Sometimes I went about it all wrong but I promise you I didn't just desert you.'

Her mother took her arm and they began to walk towards West Pier. 'I was an idiot and I was too young. Your father and I had to get married because he sweet-talked me into going all

181

the way and I ended up having his baby. You. But I can't simply blame him. It takes two to tango and I certainly never regretted having you.'

A street photographer took their photograph and stepped in front of them to give them his card. 'It'll be ready at the booth,' he said, pointing in the direction they had just come, 'by two o'clock this afternoon and at the shop on the corner for a week.'

Doris took the card and nodded absent-mindedly. The two of them walked on.

'Your father was a market trader. Like I said, we got married and then you came along.' She looked up and smiled at Izzie. 'You were such a lovely baby, with a great mop of dark hair and such a cheeky smile.' Her mother touched Izzie's cheek lovingly. 'You haven't changed a bit.'

Izzie felt her throat tighten. It had been a long time since someone had said something so nice to her, and it coming from her mother made it doubly sweet.

'We tried to make a go of it but your father was ambitious. I'm not exactly sure how or when he got in with the wrong crowd and I was too much of a coward to ask, but something told me what he was doing wasn't kosher.'

'Kosher?'

'Not quite right,' Doris explained. 'Not honest.'

'Why do you say that?'

'There were terrible shortages because of the war and a lot of black market stuff going on. You could make good money so it was easy to get sucked into it but I wasn't comfortable about it.'

'Didn't you tell him?'

'Of course I did, Izzie,' her mother cried in exasperation, 'but you know your father as well as I do. When he's got his mind set on something, does he listen?' She pulled away from her daughter and frowned. 'Look, if you're going to keep inter-rupting me . . .'

'Sorry, sorry,' Izzie said. Doris reached for her handkerchief and angrily wiped a tear away. 'Please don't be cross with me. I didn't mean to upset you.'

Her mother nodded and Izzie took her arm again.

'Let's find somewhere to sit down,' said Doris.

They found a seat facing the beach within sight of the Victorian bandstand, an octagonal building consisting of eight beautifully decorated cast iron arches, close to the more opulent West Pier. They could hear the band playing but the music wasn't intrusive. Izzie waited for her mother to begin again.

'Bill's family came from a long line of villains and thieves,' said Doris. 'Stupidly, I thought I could change him.' She laughed sardonically. 'I really thought that with a little love, he'd put his old ways behind him.' She turned her gaze towards the sea. 'They were trying to shift unregulated meat.'

Izzie was dying to ask what unregulated meat meant but thought it better to hold her tongue. Now that her mother was willing to talk she daren't risk her clamming up again.

'They got hold of some manufacturing meat, the sort of stuff you use for sausages and pies,' Doris went on, 'but they had to keep it longer than usual because the inspectors from the Ministry of Food were clamping down on people flouting the rationing rules.'

'And the meat went off,' said Izzie.

Doris nodded. 'It must have done. Your father sold it to a butcher who made sausage rolls for a Christmas party.' She began to cry. 'Oh Izzie, it was awful. So many little children and they were so sick.'

'And that's why he went to prison.'

Doris nodded again. 'And what's even worse, I made a batch

183

using Polly's secret recipe and gave it to my best friend as a present.'

'Mrs Sayers?' Izzie said quietly and her mother choked back a sob. Izzie put her arm around her as she wept. Things were starting to fall into place. So Gran was right. Mum and Mrs Sayers had been best friends and her father was partly responsible for the death of Mrs Sayers' son. No wonder her grandmother didn't want to talk about it and no wonder Mrs Sayers was so cold towards her.

Doris dried her eyes and sat up straight. 'I'm sorry, dear. It still upsets me to think about it, even after all these years.'

'I know, Mum,' said Izzie. 'I know.'

Doris turned to watch the elephants as they walked further up the beach and sighed. 'When he came out of prison, I just didn't love him anymore. I tried but I couldn't bear him touching me,' she said quietly. 'He got so frustrated and angry.'

'I heard him the night you left,' said Izzie. 'I wish now I'd helped you.'

Doris caught Izzie's hand and pressed it to her chest. 'Darling, you mustn't blame yourself. You were only a child.'

'I was nearly thirteen,' Izzie protested.

'A child,' her mother insisted as she kissed Izzie's gloved fingers.

They lapsed into silence and Izzie frowned. 'So, what did happen the night you ran away?'

Her mother nodded. 'I told him I didn't want to be his wife anymore and then I said something I wished I'd kept to myself. After that I just had to get away.'

'And that was the winter of '47, the coldest on record,' Izzie said sagely.

Doris nodded. 'They said I would have died if Walter Patterson hadn't found me.'

'Oh Mum,' Izzie said again.

'I don't remember a lot about it but they tell me I was in hospital for three weeks and then because of what your father told them, they sent me to Graylingwell,' said Doris.

Izzie frowned. 'The mental hospital?'

Her mother nodded again. 'That's why you and Linda went to stay with your Gran. It broke my heart.'

Izzie slipped her arm around her mother's shoulders. 'Oh Mum, I'm so sorry.' She kissed her cheek. 'Why didn't you talk to the police?'

Her mother snorted bitterly. 'What would be the point?' she said. 'It was a domestic. Nobody gets involved where a husband and wife are concerned.'

'If only I had known,' said Izzie brokenly.

'You couldn't have done anything my dear,' said Doris. 'Like I said, you were a little girl. I only wished you'd stayed with your Gran until you were all grown up.'

'I wanted to but Dad came to take us back home,' said Izzie. 'Grandad was ill. Dad said he missed us but I wasn't convinced. I reckon he only wanted us because I could go out to work and he needed someone to look after him.'

'He finds it hard to show affection,' said Doris. Her mother grasped Izzie's arm. 'Promise me you won't stay at home and let him waste the whole of your life,' she said earnestly. 'You're still very young and there's a whole world out there waiting for you.'

'But what about you Mum?' said Izzie.

Her mother smiled coyly. 'I think you already know I've already met somebody very special.'

'Mr Frobisher,' said Izzie.

Her mother nodded.

'So did you and Dad get a divorce?'

Doris chuckled. 'No. Your dad refuses to divorce me. I think he wanted to punish me for rejecting him. Well, I may be what they call "living in sin", but I'm happy.'

The elephants and their trainer were leaving the beach now. Someone handed Doris a flyer for the circus and she glanced down. 'Now that I've told you everything,' she said quietly, 'will you still consider bringing Linda one day?'

'It would be easier if you came to Worthing.'

Doris shook her head sadly. 'I'm not allowed to, Izzie. After they put me away, I was only allowed out if I promised not to go back to Worthing. They said I was too unstable. Your dad made me sign a paper and if I do go back there, the authorities will make me go back to Graylingwell.'

Izzie gasped. 'Can they really do that?'

'Your father sent me a solicitor's letter telling me so.'

Izzie sucked in her lips. 'Then I will try and persuade Linda to come, Mum,' she said gently. 'Give it time, eh?'

Doris nodded sadly. 'Give it time,' she repeated with a wan smile.

Izzie looked thoughtful. 'Mum, next time I come, can I meet your Mr Frobisher?'

'Oh, that would make me so happy, dear.' Doris grasped her hand and squeezed it. 'He's a wonderful man,' she said, her eyes lighting up. 'He's no oil painting but I love him to bits.'

'That doesn't matter, does it?' Izzie declared. 'And if he makes you happy, I'd like to meet him.'

Doris smiled wistfully. 'All right, I'll ask him.'

Twenty-Three

As the train pulled into Worthing station, Izzie leaned out of the window and waved frantically. 'Esther, yoo-hoo.'

She had arranged to meet her friend on her return from Brighton. Esther ran towards Izzie's carriage and as she alighted onto the platform the two girls embraced warmly. 'It's *so* good to see you,' Izzie cried.

'You too,' said Esther, slipping her arm through Izzie's. 'How was your mum?'

'Fine,' said Izzie. 'Oh Esther, I have so much to tell you.'

The two girls walked from the platform and showed their tickets to the collector; Izzie, her return ticket from Brighton, and Esther, her platform ticket. Then, stepping through the doors and into the Worthing sunshine, they turned right to walk towards the railway gates and eventually Esther's home.

'Well,' said Izzie. 'How do you like being a policewoman?'

'It's not quite what I expected,' Esther said in a flat tone of voice. Her face was set.

Izzie blinked in surprise. 'Oh. I am disappointed for you. You were so excited about it. Is it truly awful?'

'It's not that,' Esther admitted. 'It's the men. Sometimes they're so annoying.' They paused at the crossing gates while the London bound train pulled into the station. 'Do you know,' Esther continued, 'the first day I got my posting, some

187

big-headed sergeant at the desk asked me if I was a dyke or a bike and when I said neither everybody fell about laughing.'

Izzie wasn't sure why that was so funny but she didn't like to say. Instead, she frowned and shook her head. 'Can't you do something about it?'

'Absolutely nothing, so it would seem,' Esther continued. 'One girl on my course packed up and went home.'

Izzie gasped. 'Why?'

'When she was standing in the queue in the canteen, one of the older men shoved his truncheon up her skirt,' said Esther. 'She went to the station sergeant to complain but he said if she was upset about a silly thing like that, she shouldn't be a police-woman. He said she would get far worse from members of the public, so she left.'

'But that's awful,' Izzie cried indignantly. 'Why should they be allowed to behave like that? It's disgusting.'

They had reached Esther's front gate. 'Not a word to my mum,' she whispered, 'or she'll be wanting me to come back home.'

'You're not going to let it stop you then?'

'Absolutely not!' cried Esther. 'No jumped up little twerp is going to stop me doing what I want.'

Izzie giggled.

Esther's mother was pleased to see Izzie again but apologised that she and her husband had to go out. 'I've left half a crown on the kitchen table,' she told her daughter. 'Get yourselves some fish and chips from round the corner and make yourselves at home.'

Twenty minutes later, they were tucking into two plates of cod and one portion of chips, which meant they'd managed to get a bottle of Coca-Cola to share as well. It was so good, Izzie was sure she was in food heaven.

'So tell me about your new job,' said Esther.

Izzie told her about the Café Bellissimo and a little more about the girls she worked with. 'Lucy is about the same age as me. She's got two brothers, both called up and doing National Service. They've been sent over to Germany and they're a bit homesick so she asked us all to be pen friends. Helen and Carol are writing to her brothers but they found me another chap.'

'Ooh,' said Esther, 'what's he like?'

Izzie reached over and got his photo from her handbag. When she saw it, Esther nodded approvingly. 'Not bad looking.'

'I know it sounds awful to say it but I don't think he's very bright,' Izzie went on. 'He told me he comes from "Litter Hamton", and he said he lived with his mum on a "bawt".'

'Oh dear, not good at spelling then,' said Esther with a chuckle. 'What about the other waitresses?' she said. She was screwing up the newspaper their meal had been wrapped in and putting it in the bin. 'What are they like?'

'Helen and Carol? They're nice girls. We go to the pictures together sometimes although I've told them I can't do it very often.'

'Because of your dad?' said Esther, filling the kettle to make them some tea.

'No,' said Izzie with a grin, 'because I'm doing a correspondence course.'

'Izzie that's great!' cried Esther. 'What are you studying?'

'Journalism,' said Izzie. 'It costs an awful lot of money but they are letting me pay for it in monthly instalments.'

Esther filled the tea pot. 'How long will it take you?'

'There are ten parts,' said Izzie. 'I wanted to do it quickly but I have to wait for my tutor to return my last assignment before I can send the next.'

'I'm sure you'll be fantastic,' said Esther. 'Are you enjoying it?'

'Loving it.' Izzie cupped her hands around the cup of tea

her friend had given her. 'My only problem now is getting a typewriter. They're letting me do the lessons in long hand for the moment but I really have to find one soon.'

Esther pulled a face. 'Second hand shop? Rag and bone man?'

'I've already tried,' said Izzie. 'I think I went to just about every second hand shop on the planet but no joy.'

'How odd,' said Esther. 'You'd think they'd be ten a penny.'

'There's something else,' Izzie began again. 'Remember that newspaper cutting I wrote to you about?'

'You asked your mother?'

Izzie nodded. 'But first I went to the offices of the *Worthing Herald*. Did you know, they have an archive of all of their newspapers?'

'No I didn't, but go on.'

'It took me no time at all to look through the books and I found it. Then I had to go forward to see what happened next.'

'Isobelle Baxter,' Esther said with a giggle. 'I may be a police-woman but you are definitely the detective.' Izzie blushed and smiled shyly. 'So go on, don't keep me in suspense, what was it all about?'

Once again Izzie opened her handbag. This time she drew out several different cuttings. 'I'd be as excited as you,' she said, 'if it weren't about my own father.' Izzie spread the scraps of paper out. 'The *Herald* have plenty of old copies,' she continued, 'and the woman at the desk managed to find this one for me.'

Under the headline *Tragic Death* there was a picture of two boys, one holding a jam jar containing a small minnow. '*Just hours after this picture was taken,*' Esther read, '*Gary Sayers, aged five, was dead and his cousin, Raymond Perryman, was seriously ill. Last night, market trader William Baxter was arrested for an offence against the Ministry of Food regulations. It is believed that he knowingly sold Manufacturing meat as Ration meat. The meat had been condemned as contaminated. Baxter was remanded in prison until his trial.'*

The second cutting under the first read, *Market trader sentenced to five years in prison with hard labour.* Esther glanced up with a look of surprise.

'So your father was in prison?'

Izzie nodded. 'My mother always said he was in prison,' she said bitterly, 'but she led me and Linda to believe that he was a prisoner-of-war.'

'And Mrs Sayers is Gary's mother?'

Izzie nodded.

'What are you going to do?'

'There's nothing I can do, is there,' Izzie said with another shrug. 'As shocking as it is, it's ancient history now.'

'And your mother?'

'I told her what I'd found out,' said Izzie, 'and she cried. Esther, my dad had her locked up in a mental home. There's a court order forbidding her from coming to Worthing.'

'Crumbs,' said Esther.

'At least now I understand why she doesn't want to come back to him.'

'It was wrong, yes,' Esther began again, 'but surely it was just a ghastly mistake.'

'Apparently not,' said Izzie, shaking her head. 'My mother told me that my father knew the risk and that he took a chance. That's why she's still angry with him.'

Esther laid her hand on Izzie's. 'I'm so sorry,' she said. 'It must be awful for you.'

Izzie nodded. 'But far worse for poor Mrs Sayers.' The atmosphere had become sombre. 'Sorry,' Izzie said suddenly, 'let's talk about something else; something a bit happier.'

Esther nodded.

'I didn't tell you, did I?' Izzie began again, this time a little brighter, 'Mrs Shilling came into Café Bellissimo.'

'Never,' Esther said with a gasp. 'So did she apologise for what she put you through?'

Izzie laughed sardonically. 'You must be joking.' She told her friend what happened and Esther laughed.

'What's your boss like?'

'Mr Semadini?' said Izzie looking away. 'He's a lovely man.'

'Half a mo,' Esther teased. 'I can see something in your eyes. You're a bit in love with him, aren't you?'

'Don't be daft,' said Izzie scornfully. 'He's years older than me. He's at least twenty-eight. I don't suppose he's even noticed me.'

Her friend smiled knowingly as Izzie felt her cheeks heating up.

*

Back home in Chandos Road, Izzie was alone in the house. She had no idea where her father was and even less idea where her sister was. Linda came through the front door just as Izzie was finishing her wash in the bathroom.

'Hello.' Her sister's call seemed animated and happy.

Izzie put her towel onto the rail. Now seemed as good a time as any to tell her about Mum. 'Nice time?' Izzie called out in reply as Linda came into the kitchen.

'The best,' said Linda. 'I went to that new coffee bar at the back of the Old Town Hall again.'

'The Cave?' said Izzie. She was about to add, be careful, as she'd heard the girls in the café saying it didn't have a good reputation, but she bit the words back just in time. 'Did you go with John?'

Linda nodded dreamily. 'They've got a skiffle group and they

192

serve really cool coffee in special glass cups. It's very expensive.'

'Sounds fun,' said Izzie, putting the toothbrush into her mouth. 'And how are you liking your new job?'

Linda shrugged. 'I left.'

This was Linda's fourth job since leaving school. She had worked in a small dress shop but all at once her employer didn't require her services anymore. Izzie guessed she'd been up to her old tricks again but luckily her employer didn't press charges. From there, she'd gone to work in a shoe shop where her manager was a bit of a dragon. Then she was an usherette in the cinema for a while and now she'd left her job behind the counter of a shoe repair shop.

Izzie must have looked a little surprised because Linda said, 'I'll soon get something else. And anyway, I won't need a job for long. I shall probably get married before I'm twenty.'

Izzie turned her head away to spit out the toothpaste. What an absolute waste! Didn't Linda want to do anything with her life? Their father had let her stay on at school so that she could go to college but she'd bunked off too many times and the headmistress had asked her to leave just before Christmas 1951. Izzie would have jumped at just such a chance but Linda didn't seem to care that here it was, the middle of May, and she'd just quit yet another job. How did she get away with it? And as for getting married, once the wedding was over, Izzie was willing to bet real money that her sister wouldn't even like being married. She hated housework and when the babies came along . . . Izzie rinsed out her mouth and patted it dry with the towel.

'Linda, there's something I've got to tell you. When you've had your wash, come to my bedroom.'

'What is it? Something horrible?'

Izzie shook her head. 'I'll tell you when you're ready for bed.'

Linda knocked softly on Izzie's bedroom door about fifteen

minutes later. She was in her nightdress and Izzie was sitting up in bed. 'Okay,' said Linda, 'what is it?'

'I hope you won't be too upset,' Izzie began, 'but for several months now, I've been seeing Mum.'

Linda lowered herself onto the edge of her sister's bed. 'I know.'

Izzie's eyes widened. 'You know! But how?' Then the realisation dawned. 'Oh, don't tell me. You were snooping about in my room again and you found something.'

'One of her letters,' said Linda, completely unabashed.

Izzie sighed. 'I do wish you would stop doing that. What gives you the right to go through my things?'

Linda shrugged. 'I was looking for a handkerchief.'

Izzie didn't believe her for one minute but she wasn't about to get into some sort of distracting argument. 'Mum wants to meet you.'

Linda said nothing.

'I know you're angry with her for going off like that,' Izzie went on, 'but you should hear her side of the story. Mum didn't have a choice.'

Linda looked up sharply and Izzie could tell she wasn't convinced. 'I was just as sceptical as you are right now,' said Izzie, 'but now that I've met her I believe what she says. She really does love you Linda and she wants us to be friends again.'

'What about Dad?'

'She's not interested in Dad, but she wants to see us.' Linda remained silent so Izzie ploughed on. 'If it's any consolation, I don't think Dad wants to be with her again anyway. He's got someone else.'

'I know,' said Linda. 'He's had several girlfriends already.'

Izzie blinked in surprise. 'What?'

'I've seen them,' said Linda. 'He spends a lot of time with them in that back room in his shop. I caught him at it once,' she added with a smirk. 'I popped in on my way home from school and he had his trousers around his ankles. He tried to make out she was the district nurse and she'd come to look at a boil on the top of his leg. Didn't fool me though and I got a quid out of him to keep quiet.'

The two girls stared at each other for a second before bursting out laughing. They heard the front door open and slam shut.

'I'd better go,' whispered Linda.

'So can I tell Mum you'll meet her?' Izzie said softly.

Linda hesitated by the door but only for a second. 'I'll think about it.'

Twenty-Four

True to his word, Giacomo had made the Café Bellissimo the most popular eating house in Worthing. Every day was busy. People were willing to queue for a table and he often had customers waiting in the street to come in. It had taken a while but he'd finally got permission to have a few tables and chairs outside, so long as he didn't block the thoroughfare, and of course that led to even more customers. By June he had taken on another two waitresses and Umberto and Benito were working flat out in the kitchen.

Even though life was hectic, Izzie was loving every minute. People were generous with their tips and she'd made quite a few friends. She was still working hard with her correspondence course and so far she'd had top marks for every assignment although her tutor was beginning to press her to get a typewriter. Izzie had tried everywhere but she just couldn't find one. It was so frustrating.

The rest of the course was still challenging and fun. She'd learned how to do a market study of a magazine to see if she could write for it, she'd brushed up on her grammar, how to precis a piece of writing and she was exploring her own writing style. She felt as if she was being drawn towards real people and their lives and for her next assignment, she was to conduct an interview. Her problem now was, whom should she ask?

If Mrs Shilling was still alive, Izzie would have had no problem, and the old lady would have been a fascinating subject.

Izzie had toyed with the idea of asking her new neighbours but it seemed a bit intrusive. Her father wouldn't want his private life on public display, so he was a no go. The only other possibility was her grandmother, but when would she find the time to go out to Dial Post?

It was only as she held out her hands for his morning inspection that Izzie had the idea of asking Mr Semadini. Of course, he would be ideal. A relative newcomer to Worthing, he was a successful businessman and a foreigner; what could be more interesting? But did she have the courage to ask him for an interview? Her heart was already beating wildly at the thought. She finally plucked up her courage when she took his morning coffee to the office and she was pleasantly surprised that he agreed to do it straight away.

'I think Monday at the end of the day would be good,' he said, glancing down at his diary. 'Monday is always quiet compared to the rest of the week. Will that suit you?'

'Absolutely,' cried Izzie. It would give her plenty of time to prepare her questions.

*

As he had predicted, Monday was a quiet afternoon although they had enough customers to keep them busy. Carol had already changed several table cloths in preparation for the next day when Mr Semadini called Izzie into the office. He closed the door and sat at his desk.

'So, you are doing a correspondence course?' he said amiably.

'Yes, Sir. I should like to be a journalist.'

Mr Semadini nodded approvingly. 'Good for you Isobelle.

I can see that you are a very modern woman.' He leaned back in his chair to make himself comfortable. 'Okay, fire away.'

Izzie loved the fact that he always used her full name. He was the only person in the world who did, and the gentle lilt he used when saying it was so attractive to the ear. She opened her notebook and began. 'Were you born in this country?'

He smiled and Izzie realised her first mistake. Of course he wasn't. He was Italian, for goodness sake! She felt herself colour with embarrassment.

'My father came to this country in 1924 and I was born later the same year,' he said. 'Well spotted that I'm only Italian by my parentage.'

Izzie shifted in her seat. 'Can you tell me something about your childhood?'

Mr Semadini launched himself down memory lane and she heard all about his school in Dover, which didn't have the facility for school dinners. 'Some of my mates brought a large potato to school with their initial carved on it,' he went on. 'Our teacher baked it for them on the coke stove for their dinner. I was lucky. My father sent me with a meal in my lunch tin.'

Izzie tried to imagine this good looking man as an untidy school boy. 'Did you enjoy school?'

'I was good at the three R's,' he said with a shrug, 'and I had the chance to do woodwork but they wouldn't let me do the one thing I wanted.'

'Which was?' Izzie began, then realised.

'Cookery!'

They had said it together and now they laughed. Her eyes met his and she felt her whole body tingle. Izzie hurried on with the interview. 'So you left school at fourteen? What did you do then?'

'I went into my father's restaurant,' he said. 'I worked there until we were interned at the start of the war.'

Izzie raised an eyebrow. 'Your family was interned?'

'My father and brothers,' he said, 'along with a couple of thousand other Italian men.' He laughed sardonically. 'They thought we were a threat to the country; my father who hated everything to do with Mussolini, the very reason why he left Italy.'

Izzie felt the need to apologise. 'I'm sorry.'

Mr Semadini shrugged. 'These things happen in war time. I was sixteen. We were sent to the Isle of Man.'

She left him to describe the Victorian boarding house where he and his father and uncles spent their time playing cards, putting on concerts and plays, and competing in snooker competitions while they worried about his mother and the business back in Dover.

'Eventually they sent me to work on one of the farms,' he said. 'I was surprised to find I enjoyed it. In fact, I stayed there until I joined up in 1943.'

'After the way you were treated, you joined up?' Izzie squeaked.

'This is my country,' he said fiercely and Izzie felt her face colour again.

There was a sharp knock on the office door and Mr Umberto came in.

'I lock up,' he said putting the shop keys onto the table.

Mr Semadini scooped them into a desk drawer. His cousin stood watching them for a minute and Mr Semadini said something in Italian. Izzie hadn't a clue what it was but in reply, Mr Umberto nodded and gave his cousin a knowing smile before leaving the room and closing the door. Izzie's employer put his hand out to indicate that she should begin again.

'So, how did you become the owner of three restaurants?' she asked, deliberately changing the subject.

'After the war, I went to work with my father,' he continued. 'I married my wife in 1946 and her father wanted to retire so I took over the running of his restaurant in Hastings.'

'You're married?' said Izzie. Her heart sank. No-one had ever mentioned his wife. So where was she?

'I had a wife and a son,' he said quietly. 'They were killed. A hit and run. The driver was drunk.'

'Oh I am so sorry,' Izzie blurted out. 'I had no idea. I wouldn't have asked . . .'

'But you should,' he said good-naturedly. 'A good journalist ferrets out everything.'

Izzie was flustered. 'Um . . . what made you decide to come to Worthing?'

'I'm not sure,' he said. 'I suppose I didn't want to stay in Hastings. After my wife . . . It was too painful. My brother had a small café, the place near the station in Brighton, but it wasn't doing too well so we decided to go in together.' He smiled encouragingly. 'It's the place where I met your mother and saw you for the first time.'

Izzie looked away. He wasn't flirting with her, was he?

'How is your mother?'

'Very well, thank you, Sir.' Izzie regained her composure. 'So, can you tell me your first impressions of Worthing, and why you wanted to stay here?'

They spent the next ten minutes or so talking about his dreams and ambitions now that he'd landed in the town. After that, Izzie dried up. She wasn't sure she'd got enough for an article but she couldn't think how to go on. Gathering her things, she rose to her feet murmuring, 'Thank you.' He followed her to the door and they both grasped the door knob at the same time. As their hands touched, a rush of feeling went through Izzie's whole being like a bolt of electricity and she took in her breath.

'Sorry,' he said quickly as they both took a second or two to compose themselves. As soon as he took his hand away from the door, Izzie flung it open and fled.

*

The following Saturday, Roger took Izzie to see *The Silver Whip*, a western staring Dale Robertson at the Odcon.

'Bit like coals to Newcastle for you isn't it?' she quipped as they walked in and he laughed.

Although Dale was quite dishy, it was hard to concentrate on the story. She and Roger sat close together, not actually touching but Izzie hardly noticed. She couldn't stop thinking about Mr Semadini, which made her feel a little guilty. Roger was really nice and Mr Semadini was her employer. He was much older than her and he probably never thought of her in that way. It was all so silly and yet every time she'd looked at him since the day of the interview, he'd left her feeling breathless. When she'd got home that night she'd thought of a million things she should have asked him. Had he encountered any prejudice since he'd come to town, what were his long-term plans for the future, how did he source his ingredients? What was his wife's name? How old was his son? Do you look at me that way because you like me? Ah well, she told herself, you learn by your mistakes. The next time she did an interview she would plan her questions more carefully beforehand.

The film over, Roger offered to walk her home and asked her about her family.

'I live with my father and my sister,' Izzie said pleasantly.

'Oh, I thought you said your mother lives in Brighton.'

201

'She does,' said Izzie. 'My parents are separated.' He stayed silent, as if waiting for more. 'The war, you know,' she said, and he nodded.

Twenty or thirty years ago, it might have been shocking to hear that her parents were living apart but these days it came as no great surprise. In the weeks, months and years after VE Day and VJ Day, the divorce rate had peaked. The men who had returned from the front in 1945 were not the boys who had left home in 1939. Years of staring death in the face, the horrors of POW camps and the deprivations, not to mention the temptations at home for their wives, had taken their toll. Some were sick in body, others sick in the mind. The compliant young wives they'd left behind had changed as well. Because women had been expected to go out to work or join one of the uniformed organisations, many had gained their independence and were no longer financially dependent on their husbands. Those who were not married came back home to find that their sweethearts had cut their hair, wore their skirts short and smoked in public. Their women were stronger than they had thought, capable of doing a man's work and liberated.

'What about you?' Izzie asked. 'Tell me about your family.'

'I have a mother and two brothers,' he said reaching for her hand. 'My mother lives in Rye and one of my brothers lives in Rottingdean. That's where I go on my days off.'

They had reached the end of Chandos Road.

'I'd rather you didn't come right to my door, if you don't mind,' she said. 'My father is rather strict.' It seemed better to put it that way rather than say he'd probably make a scene and more than likely send Roger off with a flea in his ear if he saw him.

'Fair enough,' said Roger.

'But thank you for a lovely evening,' she added quickly.

'Care to do it again?'

'Yes,' she said. 'I'd like that.'

Roger bent his head and brushed her cheek with his lips as she turned to go. Although it felt pleasant enough, there was more than a tiny part of her that wished that kiss had come from Mr Semadini.

Twenty-Five

Worthing was proving to be popular with day trippers and holiday makers alike. The promenade was heaving with visitors and the shops, especially those near the beach, were doing a roaring trade. The Café Bellissimo was no exception. The girls took it in turns to work on the tables outside because it could get very hot and crowded. It also meant a lot more running around.

The morning Izzie was assigned to the outside tables there was a bit of a commotion when some young lads, who were running amok through the town, went past the café and tipped over several chairs.

'Hooligans!' one customer yelled after them. There was a collective gasp as one boy turned around and gave her two fingers.

People began whispering, 'Young people of today . . .'

'Disgraceful. What they need is a taste of the birch.'

'How rude. That wouldn't have happened when I was young.'

Izzie was surprised too. That rude boy was John Middleton.

After picking up the tipped over chairs, Izzie served two women with Mr Umberto's Baked Alaska, a layer of sponge with jam and ice cream on the top, cleverly topped with a baked meringue shell. It was the talk of the town because no-one could work out how he managed to serve ice cream inside a hot meringue. The mood outside changed as her customers squealed with delight as she placed the dish in front of them.

As Izzie turned to go back inside with a tray of dirty crockery, she came face-to-face with Mrs Sayers. 'Oh!'

Mrs Sayers eyed her coldly. 'I didn't know you worked here.'

She wasn't sitting at one of Izzie's designated tables but Izzie felt bound to speak to her. 'Can I get you something?' she said, putting the tray down and getting out her notepad.

But Mrs Sayers was already gathering her things. As she stood, Izzie put her hand up in mock surrender. 'Look Mrs Sayers, I'm really sorry about your son, but I honestly had no idea.'

'Who told you about Gary?' she said accusingly. The buzz of conversation had died again as every customer eavesdropped on their conversation.

'My mother,' Izzie said awkwardly.

Mrs Sayers raised an eyebrow and leaned back a little. 'Your mother!'

'You remember the first time I saw you, in the green grocer's, and I told you my mother was missing?' Izzie lowered her voice almost to a whisper and ploughed on. 'Well, I found her and she told me about you. I can't tell you how desperately sorry she is for what happened.'

Mrs Sayers had picked up her handbag and began threading her way through the tables. 'Mum would do anything to turn the clock back,' Izzie went on. 'She has suffered so much.'

Mrs Sayers froze, then turned and rounded on her. '*She* has suffered,' she hissed. 'She's suffered. How do you think I've felt?'

Izzie shook her head desperately. 'No, no, I didn't mean it like that.' She gulped. 'Of course it's been much worse for you, but believe me, my mother is so, so sorry.'

'She was my *friend*,' Mrs Sayers said angrily.

'I know,' Izzie said helplessly.

'My *best* friend.'

What could Izzie say? Whatever came out of her mouth, it wouldn't help. Mrs Sayers glared angrily at her for a second or two and then turned on her heel. As she watched her sailing down the street, Izzie could have wept.

*

Linda was absolutely boiling. She was beginning to hate this job. Standing all day long in a small kiosk dishing out ice cream was hardly her idea of fun. For two pins she felt like jacking it all in and going home but she'd had so many sackings and walked out of the job so many times that it was proving harder and harder to get past the interview for a new one. She touched her hot cheeks. She had no sun cream. Her face was going to look like a flipping lobster before the day was through. She'd been working non-stop all morning serving customers with ice cream, candy floss and sticks of Worthing rock. The kiosk was positioned in such a way that she had her back to the sea but every now and then the breeze would lift the flaps up and she could see the water glistening. It was so tempting. If only she'd brought her swim suit she could have had a dip in her lunch hour. Lunch hour, she thought bitterly. If her boss didn't come to relieve her soon, she wouldn't even get a lunch hour.

'Hello.'

Linda was bending down to push an empty box to the back. She looked up to see John Middleton leaning over the counter in front of her. 'Oh hello,' she said uninterestedly. 'What are you doing here? Shouldn't you be at work?'

He laughed. 'Maybe I should,' he said, 'but maybe I thought I'd have a day off and come and see you. Isn't that right, Ray?'

He stepped to one side and Raymond Perryman came into view. Linda's heart skipped a beat. God, he was gorgeous; even more so in daylight. He fitted every girl's idea of a dream boat in his white shirt, bootlace tie, and some highly fashionable drainpipe trousers – not exactly beach wear but gorgeous all the same. Linda patted the back of her hair self-consciously.

Ray gave her a lazy smile. 'You look hot, darling.'

Linda felt herself blushing. What did he mean? Hot as in sweaty or hot as in hot? A small boy waved a stick of rock at her. Linda snatched it from him and threw it into a paper bag. 'Two bob please,' she said holding out her hand. The boy handed her a half crown and Linda ran up the till. By the time she'd turned back with the sixpence change, the boy had gone.

'I'll have a sixpenny wafer with that tanner,' said Ray.

Linda hesitated, but then reached into the refrigerator box and cut off a slice from the Lyons Maid block. Putting it between two wafers, she handed it to him.

'And me mates'll have one too,' he drawled.

Linda looked around nervously. There was nobody about so she cut two more slices and put wafers either side of them. The three lads sauntered off licking their ice creams. Linda was furious. How dare they? They obviously had no intention of paying. Didn't they know she could get the sack for doing something like that? And no 'thank you' either. Cheeky pigs. But when the boys had gone about a hundred yards, Ray turned around and winked, making her go weak at the knees all over again.

'Excuse me,' said an irate voice.

Linda turned to face an angry looking man, aged about forty, with an open neck shirt and a knotted handkerchief on his head. The small boy stood beside him.

'Yes?'

'My son bought a two bob stick of rock,' the man began. 'I gave him half a crown but he didn't get the change.'

'I'm sorry, Sir,' said Linda, unflinching and looking him

straight in the eye. 'I remember the little boy but I definitely gave him the change. Sixpence wasn't it, dear? He must have dropped it on the way back to you.'

*

A couple of hours later, Raymond Perryman, John Middleton and Paul Dawkins were back at Ray's auntie's place. The three of them had decided it was such a nice day they'd bunk off work. As soon as his Auntie Bren had gone to her shop, Ray met the other two boys by the phone box on the corner. First John had pretended to be Paul's dad as he rang the garage where Paul worked as an apprentice mechanic.

'My lad is proper poorly,' he'd told the person in the office. 'In fact, I may have to get the doctor to him.' Ray and Paul, who were holding the phone box door open, nudged each other and stifled a laugh. There was a pause then John said, 'I dunno, mate. He's got pains in his legs. They don't work proper. I fink it's his appendix.' By now, Ray and Paul were helpless with laughter.

The person at the other end obviously asked another question because after another short pause John said, 'I dunno. Look mate, I'm late. I've got to go to work meself. Just tell the boss my boy's sick, really sick. He won't be in today.' And with that, he hung up.

Next, Paul rang the railway yard where John worked to say the same thing. Ray didn't have a job so they didn't need to ring anybody to make an excuse for him.

They caught a bus to Worthing, pushing their way in with a crowd and running upstairs. Ray got his penknife out and began changing the sign at the front. By the time he'd finished, *Please lower your head* said, *fleas love your head* and John and Paul had a good laugh.

When the conductor came upstairs they dashed downstairs

again before he could ask them for the bus fare and as soon as he followed them back downstairs, they hopped off the bus and walked the rest of the way. They had no money and it promised to be a boring day, but taking a lead from Ray, they mucked about around the town, making a nuisance of themselves. They shouted and whooped all the way down Chapel Road and South Street, bumping people on the pavement and pulling over the chairs outside the Café Bellissimo near the pier. The butcher's boy also had his delivery bike knocked over, spilling the joints and sausages onto the pavement, and though the boy managed to grab most of it and put it back into the basket on the front of the bicycle, a mangy looking dog grabbed a bag of lamb chops. Somebody tried to get it off him, but the dog wasn't about to let that happen. Growling fiercely, it disappeared down a nearby twitten with its booty.

The boys tried a bit of shop lifting in Woolworth's but some woman, probably the store detective, followed them round so they gave up. When they came out of Woolworth's they saw somebody's dog chained to a railing outside and released it. Ray yelled at it and, terrified, the poor animal ran as fast as its legs would carry him, dodging cars, buses and people in its panic to get away. That was good for a laugh until the owner came out of the shop and saw that his mutt was missing. A lot of fist shaking and a threat to call the police meant the three of them had to make themselves scarce.

Safe again, they wandered along the seafront and spotted John's bird working in an ice cream kiosk. It was easy enough for Ray to persuade Linda to give them all an ice cream.

After a while of wandering aimlessly, they saw a woman put her bag down to place her toddler in the pram. While she was strapping her little boy in, Ray bent down and lifted her purse from her open bag. They all ran and ended up in a quiet street at the back of the shops. The purse contained nearly seven pounds which meant they could have a slap up meal at the fish and chip shop before they all went back to Ray's auntie's place.

Ray leaned back on his chair with his feet on the table. They had the back door wide open because they'd been smoking some Senior Service cigarettes they'd bought with some of the money they'd nicked from the purse.

'There's something I want to show you,' Ray said suddenly. He disappeared upstairs and they heard him pulling down the loft ladder.

'What's he up to?' said John. Their curiosity got the better of them so they waited at the bottom of the ladder, looking up expectantly.

Ray came back down with something wrapped in a piece of old cloth which he stuffed into his back pocket. They watched him put the loft ladder back then his friends followed him into the kitchen where he laid whatever it was onto the table. Tossing the cover back, he said, 'Nobody touches it except me.'

It was the gun.

John and Paul gasped in surprise. 'Blimey,' said Paul. 'Is it real?'

''Course it is,' said Ray with a cocky grin. His friends were glancing nervously at each other. It was rather satisfying to see their reaction.

'Where did you get it?'

'Never you mind.'

'Got any ammo?' John reached out to pick it up.

''Course I have.' Quick as a flash, Ray knocked his hand away. 'I said, nobody touches it 'cept me,' he snarled and John sprang back.

'What you going to do with it?' said Paul.

'Rob a bank.'

His friends laughed.

'I'm serious,' he said. 'I want to be something in life. I'm gonna be famous.'

John raised his eyebrows and gave him a sceptical look. 'And how are you going to do that?'

'Easy,' said Ray, picking up the gun. 'Nobody's going to argue with this, are they?'

'You wouldn't really shoot someone, would you?' Paul asked nervously.

'Don't be daft,' said Ray. 'It's just to scare them.'

Paul pointed two fingers at John. 'Give us the money you dirty rat,' he said, gangster style, and they laughed. After that, they all stared at the gun for a full minute.

'If we rob a bank, we'll need to make a quick getaway,' said Paul. 'How are we going to do that?'

'Which bank?' said John eventually.

'Doesn't matter, does it,' Ray snapped. 'Anywhere where there's plenty of dosh.'

'We ought to have a practice run first,' said John. 'A bank is a big job.'

'A practice run,' Paul scoffed.

'No, hang on,' said Ray. 'He's right. We should look for something local. Somewhere where there's bound to be a safe. Somewhere away from street lights and prying eyes.'

'The emporium,' said John. 'Easy as pie to break in there.'

'Where's that?'

'Back of the station,' said John. 'Black as pitch down there.'

Ray's face lit up. 'They got a safe?'

John nodded. 'My chick's dad runs the place. I've seen it.'

'If they know you,' said Paul, 'you'll never get away with it.'

'We will if we plan it,' said Ray. They heard the front gate squeak. 'Auntie's coming back,' Ray hissed.

Snatching the gun and its wrapping he dashed from the room and belted upstairs. Seconds later they heard the key turning in the front door. When it opened his auntie came in. She was surprised to see the two boys sitting in her kitchen.

'Good afternoon, Mrs Perryman,' said Paul.

'Mrs Sayers,' Brenda corrected. 'And who are you?'

They heard the lavatory chain flush and Ray came down the stairs. 'I hope you don't mind, Auntie, but my friends had a day off work so we thought we'd meet up.'

'Of course not, dear,' said Brenda. 'Your friends are always welcome.'

'We have to go out now, Auntie,' Ray announced. 'Paul's mum wants some shopping.'

The three of them trooped out of the house and headed towards the sea. Once they were safely out of sight, John said, 'I hope you don't mind, Auntie . . .' in a perfect imitation of Ray's virtuous expression and the three of them fell about, helpless with laughter.

Twenty-Six

In the middle of the night, Izzie woke up with a brilliant idea. Why not go back to the *Worthing Herald* offices and see if they had a spare typewriter in their typing pool? She could hardly wait until her lunch time and when it came she hurried back to Warwick Street.

The same middle-aged woman was on the desk and to Izzie's surprise, she actually recognised her. 'Come back to look through some more back issues?' she asked pleasantly.

Izzie explained her problem and was disappointed to see the woman shake her head. 'I'm afraid the management don't keep old typewriters as a rule,' she said, 'but I'll tell you what. There's an old shop at the end of Clifton Road. It's a general repair shop but I'm pretty sure I've seen a typewriter in the window.'

Izzie got the address and glanced up at the clock. She had twenty-five minutes before she had to be back at the café. Did she have time to go to Clifton Road? She was desperate to go now because if she waited until she left work, the shop would be shut – everything closed at five thirty. But even if she ran all the way she couldn't get there and back in such a short space of time. Frustrated and disappointed, Izzie thanked the receptionist and opened the door. Deep in thought, she bumped into a man who was coming in.

'Beg pardon,' he said raising his hat. 'Oh it's you, Izzie. How are you my dear?'

It was Mr Shilling. Izzie couldn't hide her delight to see him as they exchanged niceties. Yes, his wife was well and yes, Mrs Dore still worked for him. He was pleased to hear that Esther was a policewoman at last and eventually he asked Izzie what she was doing.

'At the moment I'm working in the Café Bellissimo,' she explained, 'but I want to improve myself so I'm doing a correspondence course in journalism.'

'Good for you,' he cried. 'So it looks like my mother's love of writing has rubbed off on you.'

'I suppose it has,' Izzie agreed. 'I enjoyed working for her.'

Mr Shilling raised his hat. 'Well, I must get on. I've come to place an advertisement for a new gardener and I want it to go in the next edition. Goodbye, my dear, and good luck.'

Izzie turned to go.

'She's looking for a typewriter,' said the receptionist.

Mr Shilling turned back. 'A typewriter? Well why don't you have Mother's old one?'

Izzie gasped. 'Really? Oh could I?'

'I don't see why not,' he said. 'It's just sitting there doing nothing. The Memsab doesn't care for it, so you have it my dear.'

Izzie was so excited she could have kissed him.

'Call round for it,' he said, raising his hat a third time. 'Any time you like.'

*

The last of the summer was proving to be wet. Dark clouds and heavy rain sent the holiday makers packing and the coaches normally so full of day trippers were almost empty. Those who

214

were brave enough to come to the beach begged to go home early because it was cold and wet, and more often than not, the chairs outside the Café Bellissimo were redundant.

If the people of Worthing thought they had it bad, it was even worse in North Devon. On Saturday August 16th the whole country woke up to hear on the wireless that there had been a terrible disaster. Ninety million tons of water, enough to satisfy the people in the area for one hundred years, had cascaded down the hills towards the sea. The small villages of Lynton and Lynmouth, known as a honcymooner's paradise, were overwhelmed and the people there had lost absolutely everything.

The newspapers were full of horrific stories; a postman swept away, the bodies of two unidentified boys being recovered, houses demolished under the weight of the water, and stories of amazing bravery, like that of the motorcyclist who raced through the villages ahead of the wall of water trying to warn people of the danger to come.

Like many others in the country, the customers of the Café Bellissimo were united in a feeling of helplessness so Mr Semadini turned over the money in his sweet jar to the Mayor's relief fund which pleased everybody. It also gave them the freedom to share their personal stories of tragedy and heroism from the war.

'Water,' said one man, 'is like fire; a good friend but a bad master. I should know. I was on board the HMT *Lancastria*.'

'Oh my goodness,' Miss Cheeseman exclaimed, 'were you really. 1940 wasn't it?'

Izzie couldn't help overhearing their conversation but she didn't want them to know she was listening so she took her time putting the dirty cups onto her tray.

The man nodded. 'They say nearly two thousand men died when that ship went down, but I reckon it was much more than that. There were hundreds of them trapped below deck. They had no chance.'

'How come you were there?' said a lady customer.

'I was part of the British Expeditionary force,' said the man, rising to his feet and picking up his trilby. 'Private Cecil Davison.' He snapped to attention and saluted.

'Bit different in Devon,' another man observed. 'Those people were asleep in their own homes when the water came.'

'I understand that,' Mr Davison said tetchily, 'but water is water and I'm telling you when it comes in at that kind of speed, it's a bugger.'

The bell on the shop door jangled as he left and as Izzie took the laden tray into the kitchen for Ken to wash up, her mind was buzzing. Most people were discouraged from talking about their war-time experiences. The common consensus of opinion was, 'let sleeping dogs lie and get on with the rest of your life,' but it occurred to Izzie that if no-one wrote these things down, they would be lost for ever. Perhaps someone, somewhere, should be writing down these war-time experiences for future generations. Her latest lesson from the correspondence course said she should think of a long-term project she could begin now and work on throughout her career. *What did you do in the war?* Now that really was an interesting idea.

'You look miles away, Isobelle,' said Mr Semadini. He was standing in the doorway of his office. Izzie jumped as he spoke and he chuckled.

'Oh,' she said joining in with him, 'yes I was, wasn't I.'

'Everything all right?'

'Yes.'

'Thinking about your next project?'

Izzie hesitated for a second. Should she ask him if he'd answer some more questions? Dare she ask? 'Actually, I was wondering . . .' she began.

'If I would talk to you again,' he said, finishing the sentence for her.

She nodded shyly. It was strange how sometimes they both knew what the other was thinking.

He patted her arm. 'I should be delighted, Isobelle. Shall we say next Monday?'

She nodded quickly and with a smile on her lips, hurried back into the café to wipe down the tables. She could feel her cheeks flame and her hands were shaking. Why, oh why did her heart pound like this every time he spoke to her?

*

John, Paul and Ray waited until the streets were deserted. The cinemas were closed and the pubs were empty as they crept along Teville Gate towards Baxter's Emporium. The bobby on the beat had just gone by so they were reasonably sure that they could do the job and be on their way before he came back.

Ray hid behind some bins and motioned John to try the door. It was locked. The three lads made their way round the side of the building where Paul noticed the toilet window was slightly open. He was the smallest so they gave him a leg up and he squeezed inside. A couple of minutes later, all three of them were inside.

'Stupid bugger left the key in the back door,' Paul whispered.

They found themselves in a place stuffed with all kinds of flotsam and jetsam. With only one torch between them, they decided it was best to stick together. In the office, they found the safe.

'How are we going to get into it?' John whispered.

'Find me a cushion,' Ray said to Paul.

'What d'you want a cushion for?'

'Just get it!'

Paul found one and Ray made the other two hold it over the lock on the safe. John took in his breath noisily as Ray produced the gun from his back pocket and fired. The noise was quite loud but not as loud as it might have been. Feathers filled the air as the ruined cushion fell away and the door of the safe swung open. Ray got down on his knees and began pulling everything out. They were elated to find a silver cigarette case, a gold charm bracelet, a silver box, some pearl earrings and a couple of watches. There was also a quantity of cash and some papers. The papers were not much good to them but the rest made a pretty good haul. The lads made their way back to the door and Paul bolted it after them before making his own exit through the toilet door. Then they all legged it.

*

Izzie asked Roger to come with her to The White Lodge. She was no coward but she didn't want to face Muriel Shilling alone and she knew from experience that the typewriter was quite heavy. Mr Shilling was a sweetie but there was every likelihood that he would forget to tell his wife that he'd given it to Izzie. If that happened it would be too embarrassing for words. As second projectionist, Roger had a gap after Saturday morning pictures and the first of the afternoon showings so he was happy to oblige. Izzie also took the opportunity to ask him if he would be willing to talk about his job.

'Sure, I'll do it for you,' he said, 'but who is going to want to read it?'

'The rest of the world and his wife when I've finished with it,' said Izzie and he laughed.

They took the precaution of going around the back and knocked on the kitchen door. Mrs Dore opened it and gave Izzie a very warm welcome. Five minutes later they were sat at the kitchen table eating one of Mrs Dore's delicious cakes and drinking tea while Izzie caught up with all of her news.

'The Missus was that mad when the police told her old Mrs Shilling had given all of her artefacts away,' said Mrs Dore. 'I'm afraid she blames you for that.'

'I don't know why,' Izzie said stoutly. 'I was just a kid. What influence did I have over the old lady?'

'Quite,' said Mrs Dore. 'Anyway, between you and me and the gate post, she did all right. The old dear left a lot of money. So what are you doing with yourself these days?'

Izzie explained about her correspondence course and the problem she had sending her articles to magazines. 'Mr Shilling said I could have the old typewriter,' said Izzie. 'That's why we're here.'

'I know,' said Mrs Dore. 'He told her last night. She's left it in the hall.'

'I was half wondering if she would stop me from having it.'

Mrs Dore walked towards the door leading from the kitchen to the house.

'I'll get it if you tell me where to go,' said Roger. 'Those typewriters can be heavy.'

When they came back, Izzie beamed but her smile soon died. The typewriter ribbon was missing and two of the letters had been deliberately locked together.

'Mean old cow,' said Izzie.

'I can fix it for you,' said Roger. 'It might not be perfect but I reckon it'll do.'

Mrs Dore reached for her purse and pulled out a ten bob note. 'Here,' she said, 'this'll help pay for the repairs.'

'Oh no, I couldn't,' cried Izzie.

'And I shall be offended if you don't,' Mrs Dore insisted.

Izzie put her hand on Mrs Dore's shoulder and kissed her cheek. 'Thank you.'

'Ah, away with you,' the cook scolded.

They stayed for a few minutes more before Roger said they had to go or he'd be late for the afternoon showing. Mrs Dore waved them goodbye from the doorway calling, 'And don't forget to show me a copy of the magazine after it's published.'

Twenty-Seven

'We've been robbed,' said Mick Osborne as he stepped over the papers strewn on the floor in the office.

The two men had just arrived at Bill Baxter's emporium. They'd found the office door wide open and the room a wreck. Bill frowned crossly. 'I can bloody see that!'

'I reckon they got in through the small winder,' said Mick. 'Looks like they've emptied the safe, dunnit. I'll get on to the police.'

'No!' said Bill.

Mick gave him a quizzical look.

'I'll do it later,' said Bill, 'when I've worked out what's been nicked. You get over to Jeffries Lane and pick up that piano.'

Mick gave him a toothless grin. 'You been up to naughties again?'

Bill bristled. 'Just get on with it will you?'

Cackling with laughter, his driver cum handyman left the emporium while Bill set about clearing up the mess. The money tin was empty, of course. There must have been at least sixty quid in it – maybe more, damn it – but of course he wouldn't be phoning the police. If he did, he'd have to tell them what else was in the safe. He kicked the side of the desk in rage. He never should have done business with that bloke. He'd tried to turn over a new leaf. He'd given that old boy good money for those paintings and taken the better one to auction for him. His commission on the sale had been a tidy penny but it hadn't gone nearly far enough to cover his debts. He'd had a gut feeling when he'd agreed to take some more knocked-off stuff it was a bad idea. And now look what had happened. He kicked the desk again and winced in pain. Throwing himself into the chair he took his shoe off and rubbed his sore toes. If only he could get his hands on the toe-rag who'd done this.

*

It didn't take long for Roger to bring back the typewriter, all fixed. Izzie was incredibly grateful but even so, it was hard work getting the rest of her assignments typed up and sent off to the writing school. Normally, there was no official time scale but for her interview of a local worthy, Izzie had a deadline. Her tutor explained that it was all part of the discipline a journalist needed. She had gathered quite a lot of information from Mr Semadini, meeting with him on two more consecutive Monday evenings, and she had augmented it with background statistics from the library. A lot of war-time events were still covered by the Official Secrets Act, but she had found plenty of information about previous immigrants in Worthing, including their historical family involvement in the beginnings of the St Mary of the Angels church. Built on land bought by the owner of Offington Hall, Thomas Gaisford, it was Worthing's first Catholic church, and had encouraged a small influx of Italians to the town. Izzie went back to the *Herald* offices to look at the newspapers. The archive wasn't terribly helpful but she did find a small reference to some Worthing-based Italians being removed to internment camps at the beginning of the war in 1939. Where there was a name she recognised, she wrote a polite letter asking if the person would agree to talk to her.

Two people did and Izzie spent one of her days off meeting these people, one in the morning and the other in the afternoon. She'd collected a lovely lot of material she could use for other personal interest articles as well. The more she researched, the more she loved it.

Izzie's only problem was her father. As time went on, he became more demanding. Izzie did what she could but even she could see their home was getting more untidy and in need of a good spring clean.

'Look at the state of this room!' Bill complained. 'It's worse than a pig sty.'

'I'll tidy up in a minute, Dad,' she'd said, in the vain hope that he would go away. She needed to shut everything else out and concentrate on the article she was writing.

'You spend all day on that bloody typewriter, clack, clacking away,' he grumbled. 'I don't know what you think you're playing at.'

'I have to get my assignment done, Dad.'

'Assignment,' he scoffed. 'Just listen to yourself. Who do you think you are, Marj bloody Proops?'

Izzie stopped typing and gave him an impatient stare. 'No, Dad, I don't. Marjorie Proops is an agony aunt. I want to be a journalist.'

In the end, Izzie found her best means of defence was to ignore him so she let him carry on and just said, 'yes Dad,' or 'no Dad,' every now and then. If she argued with him, it only made things ten times worse. Becoming a writer and learning how other people overcame huge obstacles to fulfil their dreams or to survive in war time had given her a new strength.

Linda was still a bit of a madam, but Izzie didn't get stressed about that either. If Linda complained that the dress she wanted was still waiting to be ironed, Izzie would say, 'There's the iron,' and her sister would be forced to do it herself. Gone were the days when she'd worried about alienating them if she refused to do the chores and funnily enough they treated her with a new found respect.

Izzie's deadline was Monday September 15th, and she got her manuscript in the post on Thursday 11th. As the assistant took the foolscap envelope across the counter, Izzie had mixed feelings. She felt elated that she'd finished on time, nervous in case she hadn't done enough, and bereft that the course which she had so enjoyed was at an end.

*

In the rooms above the fish and chip shop, Bill Baxter hauled himself up the bed and reached for his packet of Player's Navy Cut on the bedside table. Pulling out a cigarette, he lit it and took a deep breath. He looked down at the woman beside him and smiled. He didn't remember feeling like this before. He was tired of being on his own and he really liked being with Mavis. She was fun and she was a good laugh. She may have been around the block a few times but she was all woman and she knew how to give a man a good time. He watched as she stretched luxuriantly and opened her sleepy eyes for a second and smiled. His loins still tingled with the thrill of her and now that she was awake, he wanted her again.

He leaned over her on his elbow. 'Come and live with me Mavis,' he said, giving her boob a tweak. 'I'll take care of you.'

He'd been with her on and off for a few months now and whenever she invited him into her bed, the sex was good. Of course there had been a few times when he was too pissed to remember but she was always willing. He ran his finger between her breasts then touched her nipple with his tongue.

She opened one bleary eye and grinned. 'Naughty boy,' she

said sleepily, but he could feel her fingers moving across his thigh and getting close but not quite touching his member. They kissed each other hungrily.

'I want you with me Mav,' he said hoarsely. 'A man needs a good woman.'

'I know what you need,' she said, sending him into ecstasies of delight as she stroked him.

'Oh Mav,' he groaned. 'I'll divorce the bitch and we'll get married if you like.'

She laughed softly. 'I tried marriage once. It didn't work.'

'We'll make it work,' he said desperately. 'I've got a nice house.'

'I know you have, sugar,' she said, putting her tongue in his ear. 'But I couldn't share my kitchen with another woman. I don't get on with me own daughter so how do I know I'll get on with yours.'

'I'll kick 'em out,' he said, turning back to stub out his cigarette. 'It's about time they stood on their own two feet.'

She held him and a fiery heat flooded his body. 'Would you really do that for me Bill?' she said coquettishly.

He was fully aroused again and eager. 'I'd do anything for you Mav.'

'You don't think much of them, do you?' she said.

'It's not that,' he said. 'I was only seventeen when the bitch got herself pregnant. I had to marry her, didn't I. Linda's all right, I suppose, but Izzie always reminds me of her.'

'It's not their fault, sugar.'

'I know,' he said, feeling chastened and there was a note of sadness in his voice. 'I've tried but they won't have me. I can't remember the last time Linda talked to me, I mean really talked to me, and Izzie's always so bloody angry all the time.'

He rolled onto her and grasped her wrists above her head. 'Oh Mav, I want you with me. I want you in my own bed without worrying that one of them will come back and disturb us. I'll make sure we have the place to ourselves.'

She struggled to free her hands but Bill pinned her down and kissed her roughly. 'Whadda you say?'

'I'm not the sort of woman that breaks up families.' She positioned herself to accommodate him. 'I'll think about it.'

'Oh Mav . . .'

He let go of her wrists and she clawed at his back. 'Come on then, sugar. Let's make it a good one.'

*

It wasn't until a few days after she'd sent her last assignment to the writing school that Izzie realised how tired she was. She had spent the last few months juggling so many balls in the air, her shifts at the café, the housework, seeing Roger at least once a week, as well as doing her course far into the night, and now the most demanding thing had come to an end. Most of the other girls had already had a break but now Mr Semadini gave her a week's holiday and there would be a staff outing at the end of the season. It would have been lovely to go away somewhere but most of her savings had been used up on course fees. Izzie did, however, take the bus over to Dial Post to see Granny for a couple of days.

'Your Mr Semadini sounds very nice,' her grandmother said.

'He's not *my* Mr Semadini,' Izzie protested mildly.

'But you like him more than Roger.'

Izzie pretended to be shocked.

Granny smiled. 'And your face lights up when you talk about him.'

Izzie looked away.

'Does he know how you feel?'

'No and he won't,' said Izzie. 'Granny, he's years and years

226

older than me and far more experienced in life. He's been married and he lost his wife and child. He doesn't want to settle down again and even if he did, he'd never be interested in someone like me.'

'Don't sell yourself short, dear.'

'I'm not,' Izzie said stiffly. 'Anyway I need to find something else to write about.'

Her grandmother shrugged. 'Remind me sometime to tell you about the typhoid epidemic in Worthing.'

Izzie's eyes grew wide. 'Typhoid!'

'Oh yes,' said Granny. 'I was only seven at the time and my friend Josie died. The Girl Guides carried her coffin into church.'

'I never knew that!' cried Izzie and she reached into her handbag for her notebook.

*

Linda agreed to come to Brighton with Izzie to meet their mother. They caught the bus down by the pier. It took twice as long as the train but the fare was much cheaper. They managed to get the front window seat on the top deck, giving them a panoramic view all the way. This was the first time in ages that the two girls had been alone together.

'What will you do now that the summer season has virtually ended?'

'My boss has offered me the same job in the spring, but I've had enough of looking like a lobster and selling ice cream,' said Linda. 'I might try working in a dress shop, but then again, Ray says he's got some contacts in the filming business in London. They're always looking out for models. He's says they'd bite his hand off to meet a looker like me.'

Izzie frowned. 'Ray?'

'John's mate,' said Linda. 'Of course, Dad's girlfriend says I

227

should be careful and they're not all they're cracked up to be, but if Ray is with me it should be fine.'

'Dad's girlfriend?'

'Oh wake up, Izzie. He's been seeing Mavis for ages.'

Izzie recalled the time she'd come home and been sure he was upstairs with some woman, but that was months ago. 'What's she like?'

'Big and brassy,' said Linda with a chuckle. 'I think she looks like a right tart but Dad seems to like her. She lives over the fish and chip shop at the end of Prospect Road.'

'She's got a fish and chip shop?' Izzie gasped.

'No,' Linda said impatiently. 'That's where she lodges. She works as a barmaid in The Buckingham.'

Izzie was stunned into silence. She had no idea her father had a regular girlfriend, let alone that he was serious. She stared at Linda who had a smirk on her face. 'All right, all right, I suppose I have been too preoccupied to notice. What about you? Are you still seeing John?'

'I suppose so, but I like Ray better,' said Linda as she studied her finger nails. 'He's got a girl at the moment but I can tell he's bored with her. I'll soon have him eating out of my hand.'

'Oh, well, good luck with that one,' said Izzie.

Linda put her feet on the sill at the front of the bus and relaxed until they reached Hove, when Izzie saw a visible change in her sister. With Brighton on the horizon, she seemed nervous and edgy.

'It'll be all right,' Izzie said by way of comfort. 'Mum is very nice and I know she's busting a gut to see you.'

'She should have been there,' Linda said dully.

'Where?'

'At home with us.' There was irritation in Linda's voice.

Izzie squeezed her sister's forearm. 'I know.'

'I wanted to tell her so much,' Linda went on. 'She should

have been there when I left school, when I got in the paper . . .' Her voice trailed.

'She knows that,' said Izzie. Linda turned her head and Izzie saw tears in her eyes.

'I showed her the cutting from the *Herald* and she keeps it in her bag. She's so proud of you.'

'Well, I'm telling you now,' Linda announced, 'if she gets up my nose, I'm off.'

When they got off the bus at Pool Valley, Doris was waiting for them on the other side of the road. She waved nervously and greeted them both with a smile. She and Izzie hugged each other but Linda walked just out of reach.

'It's so lovely to see you,' Doris said, but her youngest daughter remained tight lipped.

'Linda,' said Izzie. This was embarrassing. Was she going to behave badly all afternoon?

'Let's go and find somewhere to sit down,' said Doris, putting her hand gently onto Izzie's forearm.

They walked towards the pier and would have stayed on a bench nearby but Linda wanted to walk on the pier itself. Despite the fact that the summer season was almost over, it was still crowded. They wandered through the crowds, watching the people playing games, having a go at darts, eating shell fish out of small hand dishes you could buy for sixpence, dozing in deck chairs and queuing to see Madam Sylvia, the famous palmist. Linda wanted a go on the penny telescope and then she insisted they pose for a photo. The photographer placed them behind a huge wooden frame. They each had to push their heads though a hole which turned out to be part of a picture of Tarzan, Jane and a monkey. Izzie could tell her mother wasn't very keen but she did it to please Linda. Mum was Tarzan, Linda was Jane and of course Izzie got lumbered with being the monkey.

At last her sister was persuaded to come off the pier and into a small café. It smelled of chip fat and bacon but all three were hungry after being in the fresh air for such a long time. Izzie and Linda had sausage, egg and chips while Doris opted for a pork pie and chips. They each washed it down with a mug of tea.

Doris tried to get things going by asking Linda about herself but she was sparing in her replies. 'I wrote to you. Didn't you get my letter?'

'I tore it up,' Linda said sulkily.

Izzie was shocked and the atmosphere between them grew tense. Anxious to lighten the mood Izzie said, 'Linda's starting a new job next week, aren't you.'

'Oh, and where's that?' said Doris.

'In a hair dressers,' said Linda. Her tone was flat. 'It's not much money but I get a free shampoo and set every week.'

Doris smiled proudly.

'What about you, Mum?' Linda said. Izzie could hear the sarcasm in her voice. 'What are you doing with your life now?'

'I am a driver,' Doris said with a smile.

'You never told me that, Mum,' said Izzie.

'That's because I've only just started,' said Doris. 'I've spent the past few months learning to drive and now I help out with a mobile shop.'

'That's marvellous, Mum,' said Izzie. 'Do you enjoy it?'

'Love it,' said Doris. 'I get out in the countryside and I've met some lovely people. It's great fun.'

'What sort of stuff do you sell?' Izzie asked. Everything was beginning to feel forced and uncomfortable.

'Everything from paraffin to soap,' said Doris. 'And Arthur persuaded me to bake pies again.'

'Is that the man you ran away with?' Linda said cuttingly.

Doris looked slightly taken aback. 'I don't know what your father has told you, but I didn't run away with anyone.'

'But you left Worthing,' Linda challenged.

'Yes,' Doris said cautiously, 'because I was ill. I met Arthur after that.'

Linda scoffed.

Doris looked at Izzie helplessly.

'D'you know what?' said Linda, 'I don't believe it. Dad told me about your fancy man. He said he did his best to persuade you to stay but you still ran off with him. Ran off and left your own children without a backward thought.'

Doris reached her hand across the table. 'That's not true, darling. Your father had me sent to a mental home.'

'Oh a *mental* home, now is it?' Linda challenged. 'Well that sounds about right.'

Izzie gasped. 'Linda!'

Her sister stood. 'I've had enough of this. I'm going.'

Their mother looked stricken. 'Linda, please darling . . . Let me explain.'

But Linda was already on her way to the door. Everyone was staring at them. Izzie didn't know which way to turn. Should she go after her angry sister or stay to comfort her mother who looked very close to tears?

'You go, Izzie,' said Doris, taking her handkerchief from her sleeve and shaking it out. 'Your sister needs you. I'll be fine.'

But the shattered expression on her mother's face made Izzie's heart constrict so she sat back down.

Twenty-Eight

The postman came just as Izzie was about to leave for work. There was a large envelope from the writing school, probably containing her last assignment with comments and corrections. She'd worked hard with this one, taking all the information she had about Mr Semadini's life story and breaking it down into several sections. She'd figured out how to make it into at least five different articles for five completely different magazines. When aiming for the woman's magazine market, she had emphasised the attractiveness of the café and the wonderful cakes which were on sale. For a more upmarket serious magazine, she had majored on the war-time internee made good. Any company in-house magazine such as that of a chocolate factory or a major food retailer, would welcome an article about new recipes such as Mr Umberto's Baked Alaska, while a Worthing-based magazine might be more interested in the amount of custom the popular Café Bellissimo had brought to the town. Finally, she had written an article about the companionship and camaraderie among the customers which had resulted in a significantly generous gift going to the people of Lynmouth caught up in the terrible and disastrous flood. The common element of each article was, of course, Mr Semadini, but she had been careful not to repeat the same phrases. There was no time to look at the comments now though, and Izzie knew she would be in agony until she could open the envelope and see if she'd got it right.

There was also another letter in a long envelope bearing the same crest as the writing school. She knew her course had come to an end, so she supposed this might be a letter concerning her overall marks; pass or fail. She stared at the envelope for a second then glanced up at the clock. It was no good. She couldn't wait.

Linda sauntered into the kitchen, yawning, as Izzie ripped open the envelope. Pulling out a piece of paper edged in gold she smiled. 'I've done it,' she said breathlessly. 'I've got my certificate from the writing school. There's going to be a presentation although they don't say when.'

Linda picked up the kettle and shook it. 'Bully for you,' she said in a totally uninterested voice. 'You could have left some water in the kettle for me.'

Izzie was a bit hurt. 'Sorry,' she murmured.

'When is Dad going to get the geyser in the bathroom fixed?' Linda complained.

'Next week,' said Izzie, her mind still on her course marks.

Linda didn't reply but carried on getting her breakfast ready.

The two of them had barely spoken to each other since their disastrous trip to Brighton to see their mother. Izzie had stayed in the café after Linda had left, doing her best to offer her mother a little comfort over a second mug of tea. Doris managed not to break down but Izzie could see that she was in bits. It was frustrating that Linda was so determined not to believe her. After about half an hour, Doris had squeezed Izzie's hand.

'Don't worry about me anymore darling,' she'd said, putting on a brave smile. 'I'm all right now.'

'Well, if you're sure?'

Doris had nodded. 'Do you think Linda is waiting at the bus stop for you?'

'I shouldn't think so,' Izzie had said with a chuckle. 'Knowing her, she's either gone shopping or to the pictures.'

Just then, they'd heard someone knocking on the window pane. When they looked up, a man was waving at them. He was solidly built but not fat, with a weather beaten face and twinkly eyes which almost disappeared as he smiled.

'Oh that's my Arthur,' said Doris. 'Would you still like to meet him?'

'I'd love to,' Izzie had said with a nod and Doris waved him in.

'All right, my lovely?' he'd said as, introductions over, he sat at the table with them. 'Where's the other girl?'

Doris had sniffed into her handkerchief so Izzie had told him what had happened. Arthur was very sympathetic and Izzie could see he was concerned for her mother.

'She'll come round,' said Izzie, trying to sound confident but she'd had a pretty shrewd idea neither of them really believed her. It was now time for proper introductions. They sat together for another half an hour just talking. Izzie's impression of Arthur was that he was a good and caring man. Her mother had been right. Mr 'call me Arthur' Frobisher was no oil painting but he obviously thought an awful lot of Doris.

'We used to go to the same school when we were nippers,' he'd said adding with a smile, 'I fancied her something rotten, even back then.'

'Arthur!' her mother had scolded but the pair of them gave each other a loving smile.

As they stood to leave some time later, Arthur had handed Izzie a small business card.

'If ever you need anything,' he'd said. 'Just phone, okay?'

Back at home, Izzie had desperately tried to get Linda to talk about it but she had gone into non-speaking mode.

'You still here?' Her father's appearance made Izzie jump and brought her back to the here and now. 'You'll get a flea in your ear if you're late for work.'

'I was just looking at my letter,' she said. 'I've got my certificate from the writing school.'

He sat at the table yawning and scratching his head. 'Hurry up in that bathroom,' he shouted at Linda. Izzie pulled on her coat. Now she was feeling a bit teary. They could have shown a bit more of an interest. They knew how hard she had worked for this. I bet Mum and Arthur would have been more forthcoming, she thought bitterly. Leaning the large envelope next to the best tea pot on the kitchen dresser she hurried through the door and ran all the way to the Café Bellissimo.

It was mid-morning when the telegram boy came through the door. Every customer regarded him with an anxious stare and then with relief as he went straight through to the office. A couple of minutes later Mr Semadini came into the café and beckoned Izzie to come with him. Izzie frowned. Conscious that everybody was watching her, she hurried to follow him. Once inside the office, he closed the door behind her. It was only then that Izzie was aware that one of the other waitresses, Helen, was already in the room, along with the telegram boy.

'This is Miss Baxter,' Mr Semadini said and the telegram boy handed her the yellow envelope. 'Isobelle, you might like to sit down.'

Izzie's throat closed and her heart began to thump. She couldn't imagine why on earth someone would send her a telegram unless something awful had happened. Who could it be? Granny? Mum?

She lowered herself into a chair and peeled back the seal.

Helen moved closer and put a comforting hand on her shoulder. Izzie struggled to make her panicking brain take in what she was reading and then she began to laugh.

'Quick,' said Mr Semadini, jumping up and waving his hand towards Helen. 'Get a doctor. She's hysterical.'

'Any reply?' the telegram boy asked.

'No,' said Izzie, still smiling broadly. 'And I'm not hysterical. It's not bad news.' She held it up and read aloud, 'Congratulations. Stop. You are our star pupil. Stop. Highest marks ever recorded. Publicity on its way. Stop. D. Lloyd-Scott, Principal of London Writing School.'

'You've done it!' cried Helen, her eyes sparkling. 'You've finished the course.'

Izzie nodded, her face lit up with excitement as Helen gave her a hug.

Mr Semadini beamed. 'Congratulations, Isobelle!' Reaching across the desk, he shook her hand vigorously. 'I never doubted you for one minute. You are a very clever girl.'

Izzie felt a tear trickle down her cheek but she couldn't stop smiling.

Back in the shop, Mr Semadini broke the news to the anxious customers who burst into spontaneous applause as Izzie re-entered the room. Everywhere she looked there were smiles and handshakes and cries of 'Well done, dear,' and 'Congratulations.' Izzie couldn't have been happier and Mr Semadini looked fit to burst with pride.

'Such an amazing girl!' she heard him say to one customer. And to another, 'Such a talent.'

The day that followed was utterly astonishing. The news was passed from outgoing customers to those coming into the shop so Izzie seemed to spend the whole time thanking people for their good wishes and collecting huge tips.

Late in the afternoon, the bell jangled as two men entered

the shop. One had a large press camera. When they asked for Izzie, she discovered they were from the *Worthing Herald* and wanted her story. Izzie was at a loss to understand how they could have known when a familiar figure came through the shop door. It was the man whose face adorned the front of the folder from the Writing School, none other than Mr Lloyd-Scott himself. She could hardly believe her eyes. The principal himself had come all the way down from London just to see her!

With apologies to Mr Semadini, he posed with Izzie as he briefed the newspaper reporter about her achievement. Then he posed with Mr Semadini and Izzie.

'I believe you have a wonderful new dessert,' he said. 'Baked Aladdin, wasn't it, Miss Baxter?'

'Alaska,' Izzie corrected.

'Then I should like to try some if you don't mind.'

Mr Semadini sat him down and Izzie could only imagine the rush in the kitchen to get it ready. Fifteen minutes later, Mr Umberto swept into the café with a plate of Baked Alaska on his finger-tips. He bowed as he delivered it to his customer and watched as Mr Lloyd-Scott took a mouthful. The photographer's camera flashed, catching Mr Lloyd-Scott's delight at what was on his spoon. Mr Umberto beamed, looking from one person to another as Mr Lloyd-Scott declared it was quite the most amazing thing he had ever tasted and the camera bulb flashed again. Izzie and the girls shared a mischievous grin.

When everyone had gone, the girls cleared up and Helen counted out the tips. Even though most of them were meant for Izzie, she had put them into the shared pot. Each waitress ended up with at least five bob more than she would have normally got. Izzie was quite happy to leave things as they were, but her generosity was reciprocated. The girls took some of their extra cash and pooled it for Izzie so that she had the lion's share.

Their last customer of the day came in about half an hour before closing time. It was Roger.

'Hello,' said Izzie, 'what are you doing here?'

They were interrupted as Mr Semadini came over. 'Ah, you come for your pastry at last,' he cried extravagantly, his Italian accent at its most pronounced. 'Isobelle, give this man whatever he wants. It's on the 'ouse.'

Roger protested but Mr Semadini wouldn't hear another word. 'When I came to this town, you welcomed me to Worthing,' he said. 'Now I welcome you to the Café Bellissimo.'

Izzie grinned, and following her employer's instruction, she served Roger high tea. She knew he'd be starving anyway. He was always saying his landlady didn't feed him enough.

'You two know each other?' Mr Semadini said eventually. He had obviously noticed the familiarity between them.

'Izzie and I are going out,' said Roger and Izzie saw something flicker in Mr Semadini's eyes. Embarrassed, she turned away quickly. Why should he look so surprised? Roger was a nice person. He'd behaved as if he'd liked Roger, especially as he'd given him tea on the house. She paused. Could it be possible that Mr Semadini . . .? No of course not. He'd never given her any impression that he liked her in that way. That she liked him went without saying but the thought of her feelings being reciprocated . . . well, that was impossible . . . wasn't it?

As Izzie placed the cake stand in front of him, Roger leaned forward and whispered. 'I only came to ask if you would like to come to the local amdram with me. I've managed to get two tickets.'

'Amdram?' Izzie gave him a vague smile. 'What's that?'

'The amateur dramatic society,' he said. 'They meet in the Sussex Road school hall.'

'When?'

'Tonight.'

Aware that Mr Semadini was still watching her, she said quietly, 'I'd love to.'

Roger left a few minutes before they were due to lock up. Mr Semadini had asked the staff to come back into the office before they all went home. It was a bit cramped and some had spilled into the corridor but a moment later Mr Umberto made another grand entrance, this time with a huge chocolate cake. It was a lot bigger than it might have been a year ago because at long last sugar was off ration.

'Congratulations, Isobelle,' cried Mr Semadini, and everybody clapped.

Izzie could hardly believe her eyes. What an amazing surprise.

As the cake was shared around, Izzie knew that for once she'd be late getting home. Her father would be annoyed that his tea wasn't on the table, but she didn't care. She was having a wonderful day and she wanted to savour every moment of it. The only problem was that as they all ate cake and drank a glass of sherry she could no longer look Mr Semadini in the eye.

Izzie insisted that she stay behind to help with the clearing up, so as it turned out, she was the last person to leave.

'You are a fantastic girl, Isobelle,' Mr Semadini said as he stood by the shop door to lock up after her. 'One in a million. We are all very proud of you.'

'And I can't thank you enough for what you've done for me, Sir,' she said shyly. 'I've had a wonderful time.'

'You are very welcome,' he said, helping her into her coat. He handed her the rest of the celebration cake to take home.

She turned and for one moment she thought he was going to kiss her on both cheeks, Italian style. Their faces were so close together she could feel his breath on her skin. She felt herself growing pink with embarrassment and her heart pounded so loudly she was positive that he could hear it. Then, to her immense disappointment, he stepped back and, looking slightly awkward, said, 'Erm, well, good night, Isobelle.'

Lowering her gaze, Izzie murmured, 'Good night, Sir,' as she fled through the door.

Twenty-Nine

Izzie was dog-tired when she came into work the next morning. The day before had been the most stunning day of her life, the zenith being the impromptu party in Mr Semadini's office. She had never been happier. Just imagine, she'd got top marks and her picture would be in the newspaper.

Roger had taken her to the amateur dramatic society play in the evening and although it was enjoyable, she couldn't stop thinking about Mr Semadini. Standing next to him as he raised a glass of sherry and called for a toast for 'a very special young woman' was perhaps the most wonderful moment of her life. She recalled the warmth of his hand on her shoulder as the photographer snapped yet another picture, his smile, that chuckle of delight and his beautiful dark eyes . . . Of course it was impossible that there could ever be anything else between them. There was so much against it. He was much older than her; he had been married before and she was ignorant about love and men; she was his employee and he was her boss. And even if it ever came to anything, they could never marry because he was Catholic and she was Church of England. Izzie didn't care tuppence about such things but she knew plenty of people would; her father, for a start.

The play had been great fun. A thriller, the actors had them all on the edge of their seats for the final scene and they richly deserved their three curtain calls.

As she and Roger strolled home through the quiet streets of the town, he'd taken her hand in his. Izzie left it there but the thought crossed her mind that though she should feel a little excited, she didn't. She could just as easily have been holding the hand of a small child. Roger was a nice boy but nothing more. She would have to tell him. It wasn't fair to string him along.

As they'd reached the end of her street, she was just beginning to pluck up her courage to say something when Roger had said, 'I'd like to take you home to meet my parents.'

For a second or two Izzie hadn't known what to say. Meeting his parents would move everything up a gear and she couldn't let that happen. Not with Roger. On the other hand, she didn't want to hurt him. 'I'm sorry, Roger, but what with my writing and all, I'm going to be a bit busy for a while.'

'That's all right,' he'd said. 'We can do it when you're ready.'

Izzie chewed at her bottom lip. 'The thing is, Roger, I don't feel ready for a serious relationship right now.'

He'd nodded – she could see – bravely. 'You can't blame a chap for trying.'

'I'm sorry,' she'd said awkwardly.

He'd nodded again. 'Bye then, Izzie.' And with that he'd walked off.

For a split second, Izzie had felt so guilty she almost called him back but in her heart of hearts she knew, abrupt as it was, it was probably for the best.

*

Saturday saw an endless stream of customers coming in to congratulate her. There was a moment when she worried that the other girls might not like all the attention she was getting, but the truth was, nobody minded. The tips were good and the ambiance was warm and friendly. Mr Umberto made Baked Alaska all day long and Mr Semadini toured the tables as usual but with a proud look on his face.

'Did you enjoy your trip to the theatre?' he asked Izzie one moment when they met in the corridor. She was on her way into the kitchen with a tray of dirty crockery and he was just about to go into the café to greet his customers again.

'It wasn't actually a theatre,' she explained, her heart thumping wildly at the closeness of him, 'but they were very good.'

'I suppose you will be giving in your notice,' he ventured. She must have looked shocked because he added, 'now that you are a celebrity journalist.'

'I wasn't planning to,' she admitted. 'Would you prefer it? I don't want to cause any disruption.'

'No, no, no!' he cried. 'You can stay as long as you like, Isobelle. We like to have you in the Café Bellissimo.'

Mr Benito squeezed by them on his way to take a large order for a box of cakes into the shop. They were for the Mayor's tea party for some German exchange students visiting the town.

Izzie smiled shyly. 'Well, I'd better get these into the kitchen.'

'Yes, yes,' Mr Semadini said, flustered. 'Don't let me hold you up.'

*

'You should have told her,' said Benito.

'Told who what?' Giacomo feigned surprise as his cousin came up behind him in the office. It was Sunday morning and they were all preparing to go to Mass.

'You know exactly what I'm talking about,' said his cousin.

'When you and Izzie were talking in the corridor yesterday, I saw the way you looked at her. You should have told the girl how you feel about her. It was a golden opportunity.'

'I've no idea what you're talking about,' said Giacomo, looking away quickly.

'You love her,' said his cousin. 'I've seen the way you look at her.'

'Rubbish.' Giacomo took his rosary beads from his desk and put them into his jacket pocket as he glanced up at the clock. 'Hurry up or we'll be late.'

'If you can't be honest with me,' said his cousin, 'be honest with yourself.'

Giacomo couldn't deny his feelings for Izzie but he wasn't comfortable with them for several very valid reasons. For a start, being attracted to another woman still felt like he was being disloyal to Maria. It might be coming up for six years since that drunken fool had mounted the pavement and smashed into her and their baby son, but he couldn't forget them. There were times when it seemed like only yesterday. Another reason why he struggled to tell Izzie how he felt was that she was on the brink of forging a new career out of her writing. And then there was Roger. He'd had no idea she was seeing someone. Perhaps they were serious. Roger certainly looked as if he liked and admired her. Giacomo had seen it in his eyes.

Benito positioned himself in front of him and grasped his upper arms. 'Listen to me, *caro cugino*,' he said gravely. 'Maria and Gianni are gone. Maria wouldn't have wanted you to spend the rest of your life on your own. She would have wanted you to be happy. Izzie is a lovely girl. Tell her.'

'How can I?' Giacomo said helplessly. 'She is young. I am twenty-nine years old next birthday. She is only eighteen. In her eyes, I am an old man.'

Benito waved his hand in frustration. '*Non esagerare*,' he said.

'The English have a saying, "Faint heart never won fair lady."
She likes you. Tell her.'

Giacomo shook his head sadly. 'If I tell her she may leave.'

'If you don't,' said Benito, giving him a cuff on his arm, 'she
will probably leave anyway. Take the opportunity to tell her on
the outing.'

Giacomo turned away. 'I couldn't bear it if she wasn't here,'
he said brokenly. 'This way I keep her close.'

Benito frowned. 'But not close enough. Tell her.'

*

Raymond Perryman sat with Paul and John in his aunt's kitchen.
He handed round some cigarettes, this time the more expensive
Player's Navy Cut they'd bought from the proceeds of the
robbery, and struck a match. Brenda Sayers had gone to church.
Not the one just around the corner between Elm Grove and
Ripley Road but to the Ebenezer Baptist church in Portland
Road so he knew she would be gone for a while.

Having helped themselves to tea and some of her cake from
the tin, the three of them were reviewing their haul from the
robbery. They still had the pearl earrings, the snuff box and
the gold bracelet but they had sold the watches, no questions
asked, one in Lancing and the other in Littlehampton. And
they'd already spent the money.

'Here,' Ray said, fishing into his pocket, 'you have the earrings
and Paul can have the bracelet. If you can sell them, keep the
money or give them to your mum if you want to. It's up to
you.'

John and Paul were delighted.

'We need to do somewhere else,' said Ray. 'Somewhere with
plenty of cash.'

'What I don't understand,' said John, prodding the *Worthing*

Herald and the *Worthing Gazette* on the table, 'is why the robbery was never in the papers.'

'Maybe it'll be in next week,' said Paul. 'The whole thing is full of that girl from the café this week.'

Ray pulled the article towards him. 'Not bad looking,' he said, making a fist and thrusting it into the air. 'I wouldn't mind giving her one.' He laughed coarsely.

'She's my girlfriend's sister,' said John. 'From what Linda says, I reckon they're raking it in down there.'

'What that Italian place?' said Paul.

John nodded. 'It's always packed out.'

'I hate Italians,' said Ray. 'My old man had a mate who was killed in Italy during the war.'

'Time they was taught a lesson, then,' said Paul, his excitement mounting.

'What, do the café instead of a bank?' said John.

'Why not?' said Paul.

'It'd be difficult with people around,' John said nervously.

'We don't do it when the shop is open you numpty,' said Ray, giving John a smack on the side of his head. 'We wait until after dark.'

John rubbed his sore ear. 'There's people living upstairs,' he cautioned.

'And we've got a gun,' said Ray, leaning towards him.

'Your money or your life!' cried Paul.

They fell silent, all of them trying to take in the gravity of what they had just said.

'We shall need a good car,' said Ray, looking at Paul, 'to make a clean getaway.'

'Hang on a mo,' cried Paul, putting his hands up. 'If I nick a car from work, they'll know it was me.'

'You won't have to,' said Ray. 'Just leave a door open and leave the rest to me.'

The boys went silent again, each lost in his own thoughts.

'Are we going to do it then?' John said, stubbing out his cigarette.

'Yeah,' said Ray. 'Like you say, there'll be plenty of dosh floating round. It'll be a cinch.'

They heard the sound of the key in the front door. Ray sat up sharply and waved his hands frantically in the air to get rid of the cigarette smoke. Paul flung open the back door and John sat bolt upright, pushing the overflowing ash tray into the sink. All three sat back down and waited, doing their best to look innocent as Brenda Sayers came into the kitchen.

'Hello Auntie,' Ray called cheerfully. 'You're back a bit earlier than I expected. I hope you don't mind my friends popping in.'

'No, no, of course not,' said Brenda, slightly flustered. She frowned and sniffed the air. 'Have you been smoking in here?'

'Sorry Mrs Sayers,' said Paul. 'It was me. Filthy habit. I ought to give it up.'

'I did open the back door, Auntie,' Ray said innocently.

Brenda frowned but said no more. John turned his head, struggling not to laugh out loud.

'How was your service?' Ray asked. His voice had become high pitched and squeaky.

'Very good,' said Brenda. She looked around her kitchen. 'Well, I think I'll go and have a little sit down.'

Ray rose to his feet. 'Good idea, Auntie. Do you want to read the paper? I'll make you a cup of tea if you like.'

'Oh would you, Raymond?' she said, turning to go. 'You are a good boy. But I won't read the paper today. It's the Sabbath. Leave it there for tomorrow.'

But as she started to leave the room, her attention was caught by the picture on the front page. 'Oh!' Her face paled and she swayed slightly.

Ray looked surprised. 'What is it, Auntie?'

Brenda picked up the paper and opened it out with a trembling hand. 'That's Doris Baxter's girl, isn't it?'

Ray frowned. 'Who's Doris Baxter?'

'Her husband, that girl's father, was responsible for my poor Gary,' said Brenda. Her voice sounded hard and bitter. The three boys looked at the press photograph with renewed interest as she contemptuously threw the paper back onto the table and walked from the room.

'What was all that about?' John whispered.

Ray jerked his head towards the photograph of him and Gary on the dresser. 'My cousin,' he said, lowering his voice and looking down at his hands. 'When we were kids, we went to a party. She goes on and on about it but I can hardly remember. I do know we stuffed ourselves silly and it made us ill. And I remember waking up in the middle of the night with a terrible stomach ache and being taken to hospital. My mum came to see me but when I got better, they told me Gary had died.'

'Blimey,' said Paul. 'But what's it got to do with her dad?' He was staring at Izzie's picture in the paper.

'I'm not sure,' said Ray. 'They don't talk about it much. Not even Auntie. I think he was some kind of wide boy. He must have sold them some black market stuff I suppose.'

'What happened to him?'

Ray shrugged. 'He got put in the clink.' He stood up and poured water into the kettle. 'I'd better get the old lady her tea.'

'Oh he is a good boy,' said John. grinning at Paul. He didn't even notice the tea caddy coming until it hit him on the back of his head.

Thirty

On the day of the staff outing there was a change in the weather. The week before had been overcast and getting cooler but the sun came out and the wind dropped. Izzie was excited as she packed her sandwiches and a flask. Everybody was talking about it. According to the notice on the door, the Café Bellissimo would be closed and everybody from the Brighton café would be included. Izzie was wearing a summer dress and she had a bathing costume and a towel in her bag as well as her cardigan. It was well known that the wind off the sea at Littlehampton could be very cold so she wasn't going to take any chances.

The coach was already waiting outside the Café Bellissimo when Izzie turned the corner, and was already half full with the staff from the Brighton café. They'd taken the best seats but Izzie and her fellow waitresses didn't care. Everyone was determined to have a good time no matter what.

Mr Semadini, Mr Benito and Ken were allocated the seats nearest the driver and a block of four seats had been labelled 'reserved'. A moment later Mr Umberto pulled up in a taxi with his family. Izzie had never seen them before. His wife, who spoke little English, was plump with dark hair and had a rather loud voice. Three children aged between seven and two piled on the coach behind her, leaving Mr Umberto to put a mountain of baggage into the boot. The moment the older children sat down, Mrs Umberto pulled the little one onto her lap. Izzie couldn't help noticing that the middle child had a calliper on her leg. Her heart went out to the little girl. She didn't know why she was in the leg iron but chances were that she'd suffered from polio, a dreadful disease which usually started as a sore throat or maybe a headache. Of the victims who made a recovery, many were left with useless limbs or damaged internal organs. It had blighted so many children's lives. As soon as Helen arrived, pink-faced and out of breath from running, they were off. The coach buzzed with excited chatter and already Izzie and her friends were having a laugh on the back seat.

'There's a funfair just off the beach,' said Carol. 'Anyone fancy going?'

'I'm up for it,' said Helen.

'I want a boat ride,' said Molly, one of the newer waitresses.

'I'd enjoy that,' said Izzie.

As they made their plans for the day, Mr Semadini came down the aisle of the coach.

'Just to let you know,' he was telling everybody, 'you can do whatever you want but at five-thirty I want you back by the brick shelters because I have arranged for a fish and chip supper. That will give you time to eat before we go to Dick Chipperfield's circus on the big green.'

There was a rumble of excited chatter and everyone was so busy talking they didn't notice Mr Semadini giving Izzie a wink before he went back to his seat near the front.

'Can you believe it?' Carol asked nobody in particular. 'How many other employers give their waitresses an outing like this?'

Traffic was light at this time of the morning and it didn't take long to get there. The coach pulled up near the rows of beach huts on Littlehampton seafront and everybody got off. They found a spot on the sands fairly near the public toilets and began to make it their own. Before long, Mrs Umberto and the men had deck chairs, and the children were already running across the sands to the sea. The little girl with the calliper seemed reluctant to venture very far until Izzie offered her a hand. Her name was Liliana and she and Izzie became instant friends as they walked to the water's edge and paddled.

When she wasn't helping Liliana with her sand castle, Izzie and her friends spent the morning paddling, swimming and sunbathing. For Izzie, it was wonderful not to have to think about meals and housework for a change.

'Oh this is so relaxing.' Helen sighed and closed her eyes as she lay on her towel next to Izzie. 'Don't you find it relaxing, Izzie?'

'Umm,' said Izzie. If she was being truthful, she couldn't relax that well with Mr Semadini sitting so close. He hadn't spoken to her beyond being polite, but she had to force herself not to stare at him. It was funny how you can be so aware of someone and yet not communicate.

At noon, they re-arranged themselves on deck chairs and blankets for lunch. Before long the air around the circle was pungent with the smell of egg sandwiches and flasks of tea. They'd never tasted so good as they did out in the open air, even if they were a little sandy.

Mr and Mrs Umberto were staying with the children on the beach so Izzie and her friends packed their things behind their deck chairs and set off for the entertainments.

Izzie and Carol queued for a boat ride on the Gee Whiz. It was only a small wooden boat with a motor on the back but the passengers in the back seat got very wet from the spray. Some much younger lads were keen to be at the back so the girls opted to sit next to the driver. By the time they stepped ashore, Carol had found out that his name was Des and she had arranged to meet him to go to the pictures the following Saturday.

They crossed the road to join the others in Smart's Amusements Park. 'Come on,' cried Helen when she saw them. 'We're going on the carousel.'

The funfair was loud and the rides were expensive. The crowds wandered around in a haphazard way and spilled out onto the green. Izzie almost turned back when she saw it was a shilling a go, but Carol urged her on.

'You're only young once,' she cried.

Izzie gazed up at the fantastic ride. It was so beautiful and it had a kind of magic all of its own. Its solid wooden horses, three in a staggered row, resplendent in their bright gaudy colours, rose and fell gracefully with every turn of the machine. In the centre, the organ was belching out a marching tune, and over the great pipes, a hundred little mirrors reflected the lights on the canopy in a swirl of silver stars.

The ride slowed to a stop and almost before the riders could get down, the next swathe of customers jostled and pushed to get the best seats. Izzie, overwhelmed by the mass of people, hesitated until she felt a strong arm pull her up the steps and steer her towards a golden horse in the centre. She had just enough time to stand on the foot rest and swing her leg over before it began to slowly rise. As she settled into her seat, she turned to thank her helper and found herself looking down on Mr Semadini, who was sitting on a green dragon beside her. When the barker came round for his money, Mr Semadini paid for them both.

Izzie tried to protest but he was firm. 'My treat,' he said, waving his hand.

Izzie smiled. Her mother had used the same expression the first time they'd met in Brighton. That was the first time she'd seen Mr Semadini as well.

Izzie glanced around and caught Carol grinning at her. Her face went scarlet but as the ride speeded up, Izzie loved every minute. It was pure madness; idiotic, ridiculous and wonderful . . . As she held onto the golden pole, she leaned back as the laughter bubbled from inside her.

When he helped her down after the ride was over, she thought he was going to say something, but then the other girls were pulling her towards the Mouse House big dipper. Mr Semadini raised his finger to his forelock in a mock salute and then, as the crowds swirled around her, he was gone.

They came back to the beach just in time for the fish and chip supper, though quite how Mr Semadini had managed to get it to them all piping hot nobody knew. While everyone else on the beach was making their way home, they sat under the brick shelters on the edge of the promenade and enjoyed every mouthful. After that, they strolled towards the big circus tent on the green.

Izzie had never been to the circus before. They all filed in and sat together on long wooden seats. Liliana came to sit with Izzie and Mr Semadini was immediately in front of her. She only had to reach out her hand to touch his hair, but of course she didn't. The show was amazing. They saw horses parading around the circus ring, girls bare-back riding, elephants on podiums, lions jumping in a cage beside their keeper and clowns spilling buckets of what looked like water, which turned out to be nothing but coloured pieces of paper. The sound of the band and the animal smells only added to the fun of the occasion. Izzie wasn't sure if she was comfortable with magnificent wild animals performing silly tricks but she wasn't about to spoil the occasion for anyone else.

At eight o'clock, tired out, they trudged back to the coach to journey home. Mr Semadini had Liliana on his shoulders and Mr Umberto carried the little one in his arms. She was fast asleep. Back in the coach someone struck up 'We'll Meet

Again' and they spent the journey back to Worthing singing silly songs.

As they drew up outside the Café Bellissimo, the rest of the coach happened to be singing, 'If You Were The Only Girl In The World'. Mr Semadini was there to help all of his staff down the coach steps. Izzie smiled shyly. She was at a loss to know what to say.

'Thank you for a wonderful day,' she managed.

Thirty-One

One of the useful tips they'd given Izzie at the writing school was to forget what you'd just sent out in the post and get on with the next assignment. That being the case, after all the excitement of her graduation, Izzie grabbed every moment she could to write more articles and life settled back to normal. She returned to the same old juggling of her time between her shifts in the Café Bellissimo, housework, writing and keeping in touch with her mother and grandmother.

Doris had been desperately disappointed that Linda had walked away from her but as soon as she saw the article about Izzie in the *Brighton Evening Argus*, she sent her a lovely card. If her father saw the article, or the card sitting on the mantelpiece for that matter, he made no comment, but then he'd never said anything about Linda's picture in the paper all that time ago which convinced Izzie that she was right to think he hardly ever looked at newspapers.

Linda was more envious than anything.

'The front page!' she'd squeaked. 'How cool is that.'

With autumn well under way, the menu in the Café Bellissimo was changing. From now on there was to be less emphasis on ice cream and cool desserts because Mr Umberto had turned his hand to putting steak and kidney pudding and other heart-warming dishes on the menu.

Izzie sensed that Mr Semadini was getting restless for change as well. There were a few awkward moments when he and Izzie were alone in the restaurant but apart from giving each other a shy or embarrassed smile, nothing of a romantic nature passed between them. She wished it would but he didn't seem to want it. He did, however, talk to her about his plans for the future.

'The whole country is changing, Isobelle,' he said as they tidied up the counter during a slack time. 'Italian coffee bars are becoming more popular.'

Izzie couldn't help chuckling at his enthusiasm. 'So what makes them so different from English coffee bars, Sir?'

'Italians specialise in serving "frothy coffee" from imported Gaggia coffee machines.'

Izzie raised an eyebrow. 'I've never seen one of those before.'

'It's a system which extracts coffee oils from the bean,' Mr Semadini explained, his face lit up with excitement, 'and it's served with a layer of crema naturale on the top.'

He went on to say that these new coffee bars attracted young people who liked to listen to jazz and skiffle music on the premises. 'But I don't honestly think they will work here.'

Izzie must have looked puzzled because he added, shaking his head sadly, 'Worthing has too many old people. Opening a coffee bar wouldn't be good business sense.'

Izzie decided he was probably right.

A couple of days later, she overheard him saying that his relatives in London had told him that Italian bistros were also becoming popular in the capital. Apparently, they were characterised by their red and white checked table cloths and a candle in a Chianti bottle on the table. It soon became an open secret that Mr Semadini wanted to launch his own bistro but finding the capital to start was a problem.

The Italian community in Worthing, however, saw a fairly young, attractive man with ambition and drive to be successful;

a man who had a good track record having given a start to several members of his own family in the restaurant business. He was all these things and unmarried. They, of course, had unmarried daughters, good Catholics and Italian by blood, so it wasn't long before Mr Semadini became the most popular bachelor in town. By the end of September, the Café Bellissimo bulged at the seams with pretty young Latin women who dined with their mothers, and waited with excited anticipation for Mr Semadini to make his rounds. The more embarrassed and awkward he became the more overbearing the mamas seemed to be. Izzie couldn't fail to be amused by it all but she dreaded the outcome.

'I need a guinea-pig,' he said to her one day. 'Would you do me the honour of sampling a menu for my new bistro one evening?'

Surprised, Izzie laughed. 'You mean serve in the evening?'

'No,' he said more carefully, 'I mean, will you be my guest, while I serve you?' She must have looked confused because he quickly added, 'Purely to see what it's like from the customer's point of view.'

He looked so earnest that Izzie couldn't help saying, 'Yes.'

*

Esther wrote to say that she was coming home. She had been thrilled to hear of Izzie's success and begged her to let her know when her articles would be published. In truth, Izzie didn't know. So far she had sent out eight unsolicited manuscripts but hadn't heard from any of the editors. She had been warned that it took several weeks before she could expect a response so she moved on to other topics. She had written a piece about the forthcoming bonfire celebrations, but that winged its way back to her fairly quickly. Apparently, she had sent it to the magazine far too late for publication, breaking one of the writing school's golden rules. Izzie filed the article to send out next year, probably to a different magazine. There was every possibility that next year being coronation year, Worthing would have another bonfire celebration. She would send it out around August, leaving plenty of time for acceptance in a November issue. The article was timeless, but she would add something up-to-date, and she was sure that in 1953, coronation year, there would be plenty of things to draw from. That left seven articles still out there. Izzie was already planning another idea but first she was to meet up with her mother's gentleman friend, Mr Frobisher.

Izzie could hardly contain her excitement as she got closer to Brighton. The weather was terrible; squally rain and cold. It was hard to see out of the windows of the bus. They remained grimy even with the rain lashing down outside. She had an umbrella but she doubted if she could keep it up.

Her mother was waiting at Pool Valley, as arranged. They kissed and then Doris said, 'Arthur's brought his car.'

She led Izzie to a bend in the road where a black four door Ford Prefect was parked. She opened the back door and Izzie climbed in. Her mother sat in the front passenger seat. Arthur turned to greet Izzie with a smile. 'Nice to see you again, lass.'

'Ooh Arthur,' said her mother, shivering, 'it's freezing out there.'

'Let's get you home in the warm, my lovely,' he said, starting the engine.

They drove along St James's Street and into Upper Rock Gardens.

'Nearly there,' Mr Frobisher called out cheerfully over his shoulder. 'Are you very wet?'

'Not too bad,' said Izzie, though the hem of her coat did feel rather soggy.

They pulled up outside a small corner pub called the Earl of Egremont. Mr Frobisher had got as close to the door as he could so Izzie and her mother were able to dash inside without getting much wetter. At first glance, it was a homely place, very small and rather dark inside, probably because the walls were panelled. Taking her head scarf off, Izzie's mother glanced up at the clock and bent to light the fire in the grate.

'The first of the regulars will be in soon,' she said. 'Arthur likes to get the place warm for them.'

She took Izzie through a door and upstairs into a cosy sitting room and a few minutes later Mr Frobisher himself came in. As he took his coat off, Izzie could see the bulging muscles beneath his shirt. His fingers were as thick as sausages and he had a misshapen nose which looked as if it could have been broken at one time. Her mother made some tea.

He asked Izzie about herself and listened enraptured as she told him about her love of writing and her work in the Café Bellissimo.

'You should ask him about his time in children's homes,' her mother said, coming back with a tray. 'That would make a story and a half. Honestly, the way they treated those poor kids . . .'

Arthur leapt to his feet to take the tray from her and he put it on the table. 'I doubt anybody would be interested in that, my lovely,' he said, shaking his head.

Izzie felt a little awkward. She didn't know what to say.

They sat drinking tea and enjoying each other's company until it was twelve o'clock.

'I'd better get going,' said Arthur. 'They'll be hammering down the door before long.'

As he hurried down the stairs, her mother said, 'Well, what do you think of our little home?'

'It's very cosy, Mum.' As she looked round, Izzie saw the

photo the street photographer had taken of her and her mum had pride of place on the mantelpiece. Izzie felt quite moved.

'And my Arthur?'

'He's a lovely man,' said Izzie.

Her mother relaxed into her chair with a warm smile. 'Yes, he is.'

When the pub shut again at two, they had some dinner. Doris had baked a pie. It was delicious and Izzie said so.

'It's an old family recipe,' she said.

'It's got a secret ingredient,' said Arthur, 'but she won't say what it is.'

Doris chuckled. 'But I'll share it with you, my darling girl,' she told Izzie confidentially. 'If you keep it in the family.'

It was a wonderfully intimate moment and Izzie felt so happy.

Arthur insisted that he run Izzie all the way back to Worthing. He had to be back to open up again at six so they set off just after four o'clock. Izzie hugged her mother tight. 'Thanks for a lovely afternoon,' she whispered in her ear. 'I love you, Mum.'

She heard a small sob in Doris' throat. 'And I love you too, darlin'.'

Arthur was quite chatty on the way back home and he dropped her in Chandos Road. 'Try and persuade that sister of yours to come next time,' Arthur called out as Izzie got out of the car. 'Your mother is broken-hearted without you both.'

'I know,' said Izzie. 'I'll do my best, I promise.'

*

The following Monday, Izzie finished work as usual but at seven o'clock she was back at the Café Bellissimo. Izzie had taken a lot of trouble with her appearance and as she knocked on the shop door, Mr Semadini opened it.

'Come in, come in,' he said. 'Isobelle, you look lovely.'

She stepped inside and gasped. Most of the restaurant looked much the same as when she had left that evening, but in the far corner he had set a table with a red check table cloth and dimmed the lights. In the middle of the table stood an attractive Mateus Rosé bottle with a lighted candle pushed into the neck. Behind the table was a large picture poster of an Italian gondolier on the water. She could hear Italian music playing in the background and realised it came from a gramophone tucked away in the small alcove where they usually kept extra cups and saucers in case they had a rush and no time to do the washing up. Izzie turned to him with a smile. 'It's beautiful,' she breathed. 'Where is that place?'

'*Venezia*,' he said, using the Italian way of pronouncing the word. 'The English call it Venice. It's in the north east of Italy and part of a group of one hundred and eighteen islands all linked together by bridges and canals.'

They turned their heads at the same time and their eyes met. Izzie trembled.

'They say it's very romantic to ride on a gondola with the person you love.'

Izzie smiled shyly. 'Have you ever been there?'

He shook his head. 'Never been beyond these shores.'

He took her coat, then motioned her to sit down. Mr Semadini looked amazing in a smart suit, a crisp white shirt and a black bow tie. Izzie was wearing her new pale blue poodle skirt with a white blouse. At her neck she had a black and red neckerchief tied in a jaunty knot and her black belt matched her black shoes with an ankle strap. Her hair was brushed back.

'You look very beautiful Isobelle,' he said softly, sending her heart into a wild beat and her face scarlet.

He lowered himself into the chair opposite and clicked his fingers. A second later, Mr Umberto, all smiles, came in with a basket of bread. 'Tonight,' he announced, 'we have spaghetti Bolognese or hand cut tagliatelle with meat sauce.'

Izzie smiled, and taking a bread roll from the basket, she ordered spaghetti Bolognese even though she hadn't a clue what it was.

Mr Semadini went for the tagliatelle.

The meal was wonderful although she struggled a little with the length of the pasta until Mr Semadini showed her how to roll it in a spoon. It was a lot easier then. He offered her a taste of his dish and that was delicious too.

'It's a special family recipe,' Mr Semadini said confidentially, 'handed down from my grandmother.'

'Oh we've got one of those,' cried Izzie.

'For tagliatelle?' Mr Semadini gasped.

Izzie chuckled. 'No, for Polly's pies. Apparently my great-great-grandmother started baking them in Victorian times.'

Mr Semadini looked impressed. 'I must try one.'

Izzie swallowed hard. She'd have to persuade her mother to teach her how to make one first!

They talked and talked. It began as small talk, the price of their cups of tea now that tea itself was off ration and the petition circulating the town to get meat off ration.

'What made you start writing?' he asked, so she told him about Mrs Shilling and her memoirs.

'Sounds like a lot of hard work,' he said.

'It was,' Izzie agreed, 'but when we'd finished, she took me to Bournemouth with her to have a little holiday.'

'Bournemouth,' he said. 'What's it like?'

Izzie couldn't help enthusing about it; the hotel, the gardens, the pavilion, the shops and of course the aqua show. When she finally drew breath Mr Semadini laughed.

'I take it that you liked Bournemouth,' he teased.

Over coffee, they talked of the forthcoming bonfire

celebrations and where Mr Semadini would be spending Christmas.

'You must miss your wife and child,' Izzie said sadly.

'It is always hard at times like Christmas and birthdays,' he said. Izzie could hear just a hint of sorrow in his voice. 'But my cousin is right. I must move on with my life.'

Izzie nodded sagely. 'Tell me about your wife.'

He spoke of Maria and Gianni with tenderness and as she listened she could tell that his loss was still painful. 'You must have loved her very much.'

'I did . . . I still do, but I cannot change the past,' he said. 'She will always have a special place in my heart but now my heart is big enough to love again.'

Izzie cast her eyes down to the table cloth.

They sipped their wine. 'Your turn,' he said with a smile. 'Tell me about your family.'

When she started, Izzie had planned to be frugal in what she said. The continuing feud between her parents and how it had affected her and Linda wasn't a pretty story, she knew that, but somehow he had made her feel so comfortable that she told him far more than she meant to. 'I'm sorry,' she blurted out when she was done. 'I didn't mean to tell you all that.'

'No, no,' he said kindly. 'I'm glad you did.'

Izzie ran her finger around the rim of her wine glass, making it sing. 'You must think me pretty awful to say such things about my dad.'

Mr Semadini smiled. 'You say these things because you are hurt and angry.'

Izzie frowned, puzzled. 'Am I?'

There was a moment of silence then Mr Semadini said, 'Sometimes it is simply better to leave all that pain behind; to turn the page and start again.'

Izzie felt the tears spring to her eyes.

'He is your father,' Mr Semadini went on. He had his head down and was fiddling with his napkin on the table. 'You cannot change what has happened between him and your mother, Isobelle. And it's not your quarrel.' He looked up and caught her dabbing her eyes. 'Oh I am so sorry. I didn't mean to make you cry.' He put his hand over hers. It felt warm and comforting but the moment was lost when Mr Umberto bustled back into the room to take away the empty plates and Mr Semadini snatched his hand away.

After coffee, they parted and he kissed her on both cheeks, Italian style, sending her into ecstasies of delight. As she walked home, it crossed Izzie's mind that she hadn't actually said much about the meal, which was the whole purpose of her being there. But one thing was for sure. She would remember this magical evening for a very long time.

Thirty-Two

'How about Bonfire Night?' said Paul.

It was Friday evening and the three lads were sitting in Paul's kitchen this time. His mum and dad had gone to the pub for the evening, leaving Paul to babysit his kid brother. Brian was six and in bed asleep, or if he wasn't, he was too scared to come downstairs after all the threats his big brother had made. John had managed to buy beer even though, strictly speaking, he was still under age. Paul took the caps off with a bottle opener and filled three glasses.

Ray frowned. 'What about Bonfire Night?'

'Why don't we do the job that night,' said Paul. 'It'd be perfect.'

'You mean break into that Italian place?' said John.

'Good idea,' said Ray. 'Kill two birds with one stone.'

John frowned. 'How do you work that one out?'

'I told you I hate Italians,' said Ray. 'And that tart who upset my auntie works there.'

'Time they was taught a lesson, then,' said Paul, his excitement mounting.

Ray leaned back and put his feet on the table. 'You really reckon it's true that they're raking it in there?'

John nodded. 'And the thing about Bonfire Night is that all the shops are staying open until late. It'll be too late for them to go to the bank with the takings. The safe will be stuffed full of money.'

Ray sat up, spat on his handkerchief and leaned down to wipe a scuff mark from his brand new brothel creepers.

'So, while the Bonfire Boys are coming down the road we could be in there chucking money in the air like it was raining,' Paul said excitedly.

'The streets will be crowded,' said John.

Ray nodded. 'But we'll have a car, won't we.'

'Getting away should be a piece of cake,' Paul chortled, enjoying his own pun.

'I reckon we should park it up just around the corner, in Bath Place,' said Ray. 'Then, as soon as it's done, we can head up Montague Street and make a clean getaway.'

'Bonfire Night it is then,' said John.

'We'll have to lie low for a bit,' Ray cautioned. 'We can't go spending the money or everyone will know it was us.'

'So how long do we have to wait?' Paul wailed.

Ray shrugged. 'Maybe as much as a year.'

'A year!' Paul choked. 'That's too long. I want to buy a motorbike.'

Ray slapped Paul's head. 'Don't be so daft. You do that and the cops will come down on you like a ton of bricks.' He put on an authoritative accent and added, 'Now then, my lad, where did you get the money for that there bike?'

John thought that was very funny. Paul scowled.

'Anyway, we need to get that car first,' said Ray.

'And we need to do a recce to find out where the safe is,' said Paul.

'How are we going to do that without raising suspicion?' said John.

They sat in silence for a few minutes then Ray looked at John and said, 'I can't come to The Cave this week. My old lady and the old man are coming to Worthing to see me but next Saturday tell your chick you're taking her out to tea the following week.'

Paul lifted his little finger as if drinking tea from a posh cup. 'More tea, Vicar?'

John gave him a playful thump.

'In fact,' said Ray, 'we'll all take her to the café. That'll give us all the chance to have a good look around.'

*

Izzie had had a letter from Esther. She would be back on the day of the bonfire celebrations but sadly too late to take part.

I've learnt to drive, she wrote, *and Dad says when I come home on leave, he'll let me borrow his car.*

Izzie wrote back by return of post. *How exciting! You drive somewhere and we'll find a nice restaurant. My treat.* She'd thought long and hard before penning the next few sentences. *You remember I told you that my father had a stall in the market and he got sent to prison? Well, I've managed to piece together most of the story but I get the feeling there's more. Is it possible for you, being a WPC, to find out exactly what happened? I know you can't go looking at police records without a good reason, and I don't want to get you into trouble, but could you ask around? Some old copper who's been in the job for years might remember something. I would be so grateful, Love Izzie.*

*

With a brand new Queen, who was to be crowned the following year, the country had entered what was called the New Elizabethan Age. For that reason, the council had agreed that the tumbling of the barrels, popular in Victorian Worthing, could be brought back to life as part of the town's November 5th celebrations.

There had been a lot of discussion about it in the local newspapers. Some were concerned that having lighted tar barrels trundling through the town would be too dangerous. However, in the end, the council had agreed to revive the old tradition. Provided the crowds were kept well back they would be perfectly safe. The barrels would come down Chapel Road and South Street on their way to the beach where a large bonfire would be lit at Splash Point before a public firework display on the pier. It promised to be an amazing spectacle.

Bill had been away for a few days but Izzie had heard him coming in at around eleven o'clock the night before. To avoid yet another confrontation with her father, Izzie made a calculated decision to get up very early the next day. She planned to sneak out of the house as quietly as possible but, to her horror, as she opened the stair door he was already sitting at the table. She hurried to the bathroom without a word but he was still there when she came out.

'Sit down,' he growled.

'Dad I have to get ready for work. I'll be late.'

'Sit down!'

There was no getting away from it. Izzie lowered herself onto a kitchen chair and waited for the onslaught.

'I want to know how long you have been seeing your mother,' he said coldly.

Izzie looked away.

'She's seen her loads of times,' said Linda, coming through the stair door. She'd obviously only just woken up. Her hair was wild and her eyes pink. She yawned and added, 'The pair of them are as thick as thieves.'

Bill fixed Izzie with a malevolent glare.

'You went against me to look for that woman?' His eyes were

bulging. She'd never seen him this angry before. Izzie suddenly felt afraid.

'I'm sorry,' she said, 'but she is my mother.'

Her father's eyes narrowed. 'So where is she?'

'Brighton,' said Izzie.

Her father thumped his fist on the table making the crockery rattle. His face was distorted with rage. 'I told you to have nothing to do with her,' he shouted, his spittle spraying the table cloth. 'I won't have it, I tell you. The pair of you can get out of my house.'

The girls looked at each other in shocked surprise. 'Get out?' Izzie murmured faintly. 'You can't mean that.'

'That's what I said,' their father bellowed. 'I don't want you in this house a moment longer.'

'I don't see why you should take it out on me,' Linda protested angrily. 'It was all Izzie's doing. I didn't even want to see Mum.'

Their father rose to his feet. 'End of next weekend,' he said, snatching his hat from the peg. 'I want you out by Sunday.'

'You're joking!' cried Linda. 'You can't just chuck us out. Where will we go?'

'I don't know and I don't care,' said Bill, struggling into his coat. 'I'm going to ask Mavis to move in with me and I want the both of you gone.'

Linda burst into tears. Izzie had been struck dumb. What he was saying refused to sink in. It wasn't so long ago that he'd begged and pleaded with them to come home and be a family, and now he was kicking them out for no reason at all. She didn't know whether to be angry or upset.

'You haven't given us much notice, Dad,' she said, trying to sound calm and reasonable. She needed to take the heat out of this argument if she was going to buy them some more time. 'We may not be able to find anything suitable by the end of this week.'

'That's your problem,' said Bill, heading towards the door. 'You're out by Sunday.'

'But that's not fair,' Linda wailed after him.

As soon as he'd gone, Linda rounded on Izzie. 'This is all your fault. If you hadn't found Mother, this wouldn't have happened. You knew he'd be angry. Why on earth did you tell him?'

'I didn't,' said Izzie. 'I can't help it if he saw Arthur dropping me off at the door.'

Linda threw her hands in the air in exasperation. 'You idiot!'

'I'm sorry,' Izzie said, her voice thick with emotion. 'It'll be okay, I promise. Once he's calmed down he'll change his mind.'

'Fat chance of that!' Linda retorted and pushed past Izzie as she headed for the bathroom. As she slammed the door she shouted, 'I hate you, Izzie Baxter. I hate you!'

Izzie put her head in her hands. What a family. Why were they always at logger-heads with each other? Mr Semadini had said it wasn't her quarrel. He'd told her to leave the pain behind and start afresh but how could she when they were all so bloody unreasonable. Now she had no time at all to find lodgings in a town with a desperate housing shortage. That would mean she would have to spend every spare minute she could traipsing around, knocking on doors, answering advertisements and looking up cards in shop windows. Oh, how could he do this to his own family!

*

The Saturday before the bonfire celebrations, The Cave was buzzing with the news that Ray and Mo had split up. Nobody knew the exact details but apparently he'd been having his leg over in her mum's sitting room when Mo's parents had come home early and caught Ray in nothing but his dangly bits, helping himself to some of her dad's whiskey. Quite which of the two couples was the most shocked was open to suggestion but there had been a humungous row which ended with Ray being kicked out . . . literally. The next day, so the story went, Mo had been packed off indefinitely to her granny's place in Cornwall.

Linda's heartbeat quickened when she saw Ray lounging on a chair near the coffee bar. Every time John asked her to dance she made sure she looked good but she was keen not to look too happy. She didn't want Ray thinking she was stuck on John.

'You feeling all right?' John asked when she refused to do The Creep with him.

'Just because I want a bit of a rest doesn't mean I'm ill,' she snapped.

'Okay, okay,' said John. 'Keep your hair on.'

When he set off to chat to a mate, she was glad to see him go. Now she could spend her time watching Ray. She was beginning to think that the old adage that if you stare at someone's back long enough they turn around, was an old wives tale, but then he turned and their eyes met. Without breaking his gaze, Ray got out his comb and put it through his hair. Linda blinked dreamily as she struggled to look cool. It was just like the pictures. The rest of the room full of sweaty bodies and noisy people faded away and it was just Ray and her. Linda's racing heart almost stopped as he put his comb back into his coat pocket and gave her a lazy smile. He blew a kiss. He was amazing. His hair looked especially good when it looked like it did right now with a few strands flopping over his forehead. Jet black, it glistened with Brylcreem. Tonight he was wearing a lurex waistcoat she'd never seen before and she couldn't help admiring his luminous socks. When he slowly wet his lips with his tongue, Linda almost passed out with delight.

Then John told her Ray wanted to take her to the Café Bellissimo and she could hardly believe her luck.

'I was thinking of taking my auntie there for Christmas,' Ray explained, his voice as smooth as silk. 'People say it's really nice, but I have to check it out for myself, see?'

Linda gazed at him starry eyed.

'They'll let us in if I was with a nice girl like you,' he went on. 'You could pretend you're my sister.'

With Izzie working there, it would be impossible to pretend to be his sister, but Linda wasn't going to tell him that. 'I'd love to help out,' she cooed.

'Okay,' said John, 'so I'll book a table for four.'

'Four!' Linda squeaked.

'Yeah,' said John. 'Ray, you and me, and Paul's coming too.'

Linda nodded and smiled although she could have wept. She would much have preferred it to be just her and Ray. John looked around the room. 'Oh there's Paul,' he said. 'I'll go and tell him it's on.' And he hurried off.

Linda looked up at Ray. 'When?'

'When what?' said Ray, brushing his finger against her breast.

Linda could hardly breathe. 'When are we going to the café?'

'Next Saturday, if that's okay?' he said. 'You off on Saturday?'

Linda nodded. She wasn't, but she'd make out she wasn't feeling well on Friday and get Izzie to phone in that she was sick on Saturday.

Ray leaned over her. She could feel his breath on her face. 'Would have been even better if it was just you and me, wouldn't it doll?' She closed her eyes as he brushed his lips across her cheek and slid his hand over her bottom, squeezing.

'I really like your durex waistcoat,' she murmured.

Ray threw back his head and laughed.

'What?' she exclaimed.

'It's lurex darlin', not durex.'

Thirty-Three

All day long in the Café Bellissimo, Izzie did her work efficiently and with a smile, but she was all churned up inside. She was in shock. Fortunately, no-one seemed to notice, or if they did, they didn't say anything and Mr Semadini wasn't around. Apparently he'd gone away for a few days.

Izzie had less than a week to find somewhere to live but it was proving to be extremely difficult. Esther once told her she could approach her mother if she ever wanted digs, but she could hardly expect Mrs Jordan to take in both her and Linda, could she?

Worthing itself was undergoing radical changes. Some of the buildings in the High Street were ear-marked for demolition to make way for a new construction which was to be built once the Old Town Hall was demolished. There was a possibility that a condemned house might have rooms to rent for a short period but the only way she could find out was by doing some leg work. It wasn't a very palatable proposition.

Although Linda had pleaded with their father, it was no use. They had to go and that was that.

*

It was Carol who first noticed something was wrong. 'You're looking very pale,' she said. 'Are you worried about something, Izzie?'

Izzie told her and swore her to secrecy but before the afternoon was out, Mr Umberto called her into the office. The café was running like a well-oiled machine and he had been left in charge while Mr Semadini was gone.

Izzie's first reaction was to be annoyed. 'I asked Carol not to say anything!'

'About what?'

Izzie was suddenly embarrassed. 'Nothing.' So her friend hadn't told him after all.

'I asked you in here,' Mr Umberto began, 'because you are not your usual cheery self, Izzie. Something is wrong and whatever it is, I should like to help.'

He listened very sympathetically as a tearful Izzie told him everything. Then he came round from his desk and stood over her as he handed her his handkerchief. For a second his hand hovered above her shoulder but he didn't touch her. It felt too much like taking advantage.

'I may not be able to help,' he said, going back to his seat, 'but I promise to try.'

As soon as she'd left the office, Mr Umberto picked up the telephone. He had to be careful about this. He didn't want anyone to misconstrue his request. Both his own and Izzie's reputations had to be preserved at all costs. With that in mind, he tried various trusted friends and acquaintances but to no avail. In the end, he telephoned his parish priest.

'She may not be a Catholic,' he explained, 'but this is a perfectly respectable girl who works for my cousin. Giacomo wouldn't want to lose her. Do you know anyone who would rent her a room?'

When he finally put the phone down, he told Izzie to go to a house in Queen's Street to see a Mrs Noyles.

*

As arranged, Linda met John outside the fish and chip shop to talk about their forthcoming evening out. Paul and Ray were waiting too. As soon as she saw them, Linda burst into tears. The boys stared in embarrassment and at first they just wanted to shut her up.

'If she's going to make that racket,' Paul said in a savage whisper, 'I'm clearing off.'

John put his arm around Linda's shoulders.

'Is she up the duff?' said Ray, looking down his nose at John. 'Have you been dipping your wick you mucky bastard?'

'No I haven't,' John said indignantly.

'Then sort it out,' said Ray. 'We'll be in the chip shop when you've finished.'

As soon as she and John were alone, Linda poured out her heart. John listened but there wasn't much he could do. His mum would never allow Linda to doss down at his place, he told her. Never in a million years. Eventually, he persuaded her to join the others and said he would buy her some tea.

They sat together in a corner near the back of the chip shop, a place where they couldn't be easily overheard. John bought Linda a piece of cod and six-pennyworth but she only picked at her meal.

'Her old man is kicking her out,' he told his friends. 'Come Sunday she's got nowhere to live.' Linda was pleased to see a measure of sympathy for her now.

'I've got an uncle near Portsmouth,' said Ray. 'He runs a caravan park. I reckon I could get you a place there.'

'A caravan?' Linda squeaked.

'Sure,' said Ray. 'He's got plenty. No takers – winter time, see?'

Linda gazed at him starry eyed.

'We could use Paul's car,' Ray went on.

'But I haven't . . . ow!' Ray had kicked Paul's shin.

Ray leaned over the table and patted Linda's hand. 'We'll take you to my uncle on Saturday after we've had that meal.'

Linda dried her eyes. 'That would be wonderful!' she whispered. She was feeling quite pleased with herself. She'd had no intention of finding a place of her own, and she knew her dad wouldn't really kick her out, but the more she thought about it, the more she liked the idea of being with Ray. Far away from Worthing she could be his Judy and nobody could stop her.

They arranged to meet her at four outside the Café Bellissimo.

'Shall I bring my suitcase?'

Ray seemed confused.

'So that I can stay in your uncle's caravan.'

'Yeah, yeah,' said Ray.

'But my sister might ask me why I've got it,' she cried.

'I'm sure you'll think up an excuse,' said Ray. 'A clever girl like you.'

After they'd eaten, Ray lit up a fag while Paul went to the toilet and John reached for his coat.

'Thank you ever so much, Ray,' Linda simpered.

Ray leaned towards her. 'My pleasure, darlin'.' And Linda went tingly all over.

They parted outside and John walked her home.

'Ray's very grateful that you agreed to do this for us,' he said. 'He thinks the world of his auntie.' He pulled her close to him and kissed her. Linda didn't much like it. It was wet and slobbery. 'Wear something nice, won't you.'

Normally Linda would have bitten his head off, telling him she always looked nice, but instead, she smiled dreamily. Yes she would look nice. More than that, she'd look sensational. She'd use her lunch hour to go out and nick a really posh frock and she'd spend Saturday morning doing her hair.

John reached into his pocket and pulled something out. 'I want you to have these. They were my granny's and I know she would have wanted you to have them.'

It was difficult to see what he'd given her in the half light in the twitten, but she could tell it was earrings. 'Thanks,' she said, slipping them into her pocket and the next time he kissed her she let him knead her breast as well.

Alone in her bedroom, Linda took John's present out of her pocket and gasped. What he'd given her was a pair of pearl earrings and they looked a lot better than the ones in Woolworth's. Crikey, they might even be real.

*

'Mr Semadini tells me you are a respectable girl,' Mrs Noyles said stiffly.

'I am,' said Izzie. She had taken her references from Mrs Shilling with her and she was sure that Mr Umberto would have said good things about her too. She discovered that Mrs Noyles cleaned the Catholic church. She had a good reputation for being a stickler for cleanliness and she kept a spotless boarding house. Visiting priests sometimes stayed with her apparently.

'I don't allow young men in here,' said Mrs Noyles, handing the references back. 'Breakfast is at seven-thirty sharp and tea at five.'

Izzie chewed her lip. 'I don't finish at the shop until five-thirty.'

'I'm sorry,' said Mrs Noyles. 'I make no exceptions. If it doesn't suit you'll have to make other arrangements.'

Ah well, thought Izzie, I should be nice and slim by the time I leave here.

The room was small and she and Linda would have to share the bed, but it was neat and tidy. Izzie took a deep breath and agreed to take it. She had to pay two weeks' rent up front and Mrs Noyles said she would be expecting them on Saturday. It was far from ideal but at least Izzie had managed to get a roof over their heads until they could find something else more accommodating. She made up her mind not to tell Mr Umberto this was only temporary. She didn't want to cause trouble between him and Mrs Noyles but the small bed wasn't really suitable for a long-term arrangement.

*

It was weird going to the Café Bellissimo with John, Paul and Ray. Linda could hardly believe her luck that they'd asked her to tea. It was posh and respectable, not the sort of place she'd expected them to go. The four of them certainly raised a few eyebrows as they all walked in, even though the boys had smartened themselves up considerably. Only their quiffs and DA haircuts made them stand out as different from the usual customers. Linda was wearing her new outfit (she'd nicked it from Cloughda's in Warwick Street) and high heels. It was freezing cold outside but she hadn't bothered with a coat. It was old and frayed on the sleeves and she looked smarter without it.

Ray had already ordered tea and cake from Helen before Izzie saw them. She glanced around nervously. What on earth was Linda up to? Her sister had been a bit off with her since she'd told her she'd found them another place to live. Quite honestly, when she'd heard the news about their new digs in Queen's Street, she'd acted as if she couldn't have cared less. Izzie stared at the three boys sitting with Linda. Were they going to make trouble? She couldn't afford to lose this job, especially as she would be the one who would have to pay the lion's share of the rent. Her stomach was in knots as she hurried to their table.

'What are you doing in here?' she whispered desperately.

'Don't worry, sis,' said Linda as if reading her mind. 'We're not going to make trouble. Me and my friends just want to enjoy ourselves.'

Helen served them tea and although Izzie couldn't resist glancing over every now and then, all four of them were true to their word. Her sister was wearing a dress Izzie had never seen before and she had a lovely pair of pearl earrings. She sighed. Don't say Linda was shop lifting again . . .

The young people enjoyed the tea and the older lad, an attractive looking boy aged about eighteen, paid the bill. Just as they were about to leave, one of the other lads excused himself to go to the toilet but apart from that, the visit passed without incident.

Izzie went to the door with Linda to hold it open. 'I like your earrings.'

Linda touched one of them and smiled shyly. 'John gave them to me.'

'They were my auntie's,' he said.

'I thought you said they were your grandmother's,' Linda remarked with a puzzled frown.

'Oh yeah, yes that's right,' said John, slightly flustered.

Izzie raised an eyebrow and Linda laughed.

'If you're going to the bonfire on the beach tonight, don't forget we have to be at Mrs Noyles' place by seven,' Izzie reminded Linda.

'Of course,' said Linda, 'but first I have to go back home to change.'

'See you there then,' said Izzie, closing the door behind them.

'Friends of yours?' asked Mr Umberto, coming up behind her.

'My sister,' said Izzie.

Mr Umberto looked disappointed. 'Oh dear, dear. I wish you had told me, Izzie,' he said. 'She could have had her tea on the house.'

Thirty-Four

By the time Izzie got back home to change that night, her father was having his shave in the bathroom. 'Don't bother to get me anything for tea,' he said, coming into the kitchen and wiping the last of the shaving soap from the side of his face. 'Mavis is looking after me.'

Linda, who was sitting at the kitchen table doing her nails, sniggered. Izzie began to fill the kettle for a cup of tea.

'In fact,' their father went on, 'I'm bringing Mavis back here tonight. She'll be with me from now on so you'd better get used to it.'

'Well, we won't be here anyway,' Izzie said stonily.

Her father glared. 'What do you mean, we won't be here?'

'You told us to clear out, remember?' said Izzie. 'I've found us some digs.'

Bill looked crestfallen. 'You shouldn't have done that. I didn't mean it.'

'That's what you said,' Linda challenged.

'I was angry,' said Bill. 'This is your home. Our home; you two, Mav and me.'

'You don't mean you're going to marry her?' Linda squeaked.

'Don't be bloody daft,' said their father. 'How can I? I'm still married to your loopy mother.'

281

'I wish you wouldn't say that about Mum,' Izzie protested mildly.

'I'll never forgive her for what she did.'

'Then more fool you, Dad,' Izzie retorted. 'She tells me she's very sorry,' and continuing with Mr Semadini's words she added, 'You should let it go.'

But Bill wasn't listening. He was staring at Linda. 'Where did you get those earrings?' he demanded.

Linda put her hand to the pearl earrings as if she'd forgotten all about them. 'Oh, somebody gave them to me as a present. They're lovely aren't they. Do you like them?'

'Take them off,' Bill growled.

'Why?' Linda frowned.

Bill's face had gone puce with rage. 'Take them off!'

Linda rose to her feet. 'No, I won't,' she cried. 'Why should I?'

All at once her father struck her across the face with the back of his hand. 'I said bloody well take them off!'

Izzie drew her breath. 'Dad, what are you doing?'

Shocked and in pain, Linda removed the earrings and, trembling like a leaf, she dropped them into her father's outstretched hand. Izzie just stared at him in disbelief. Linda turned to run upstairs but her father blocked the way. 'Who gave them to you?'

There was still a vestige of defiance in Linda's attitude. 'I'm not telling you.'

Bill grabbed her wrist. 'I shan't ask you again. Where did you get them?'

'You're hurting me.' Linda was crying now. 'John . . . John gave them to me.'

'John?'

'John Middleton. He said they belonged to his grandmother and that I was special and so he wanted me to have them.'

'Grandmother, my eye,' Bill snarled. 'He nicked them from my shop.'

'I don't believe you,' Linda cried. 'John would never steal anything.'

He turned her wrist and Linda's mouth gaped open with the pain.

'Dad!' Izzie interjected.

'So where's the rest of it?'

'I don't know what you're talking about,' she protested indignantly as she finally managed to snatch her arm away.

'Dad, what are you doing?' Izzie began again. 'What's got into you?'

'You keep out of this, Izzie,' her father blazed. 'I had a whole lot more stuff pinched when these earrings went walk-about so who is this John Middleton? Where does he live?'

'I can't believe you just hurt me,' Linda said, rubbing her wrist.

'Then tell me.'

'He's my boyfriend,' Linda cried desperately. 'Izzie's met him. He's nice, isn't he? We all went to Izzie's café for tea—'

'We? Who's we?'

'Dad,' Izzie said a third time. She was trying to get between them but Bill kept elbowing her roughly out of the way.

'John Middleton,' Linda shouted defiantly, 'Paul somebody-or-other, I don't know his surname and Ray Perryman.'

Bill's eyes bulged. 'Perryman? You've been hanging around with a Perryman?'

He let out a loud roar and with one hand swept everything from the table. Plates, cups, saucers, the milk jug and even the tea pot went flying. When he'd finished, tea dripped down the dresser and a plate spun noisily on the floor before coming to rest. Izzie and Linda gaped in shocked surprise. Then their father turned back and struck Linda several times.

It was all too much for Izzie. 'Stop it, stop it!' She waded in and tried to separate them. In the scrimmage that followed, Izzie ended up with a punch on her shoulder and all three of them were yelling at the tops of their voices. At last, Linda managed to break free and she ran upstairs, sobbing loudly. Their father was about to follow but Izzie stood in the doorway, barring the way.

'No! Dad, listen to me,' she said. 'She didn't know. You could tell that by the way she reacted. If that boy pinched those earrings, Linda didn't know.'

He glared at her. 'Always got to put your five eggs in haven't you?' he said. He turned away, the steam suddenly going out of him. Bill sat down at the table and put his head in his hands. Izzie made a dash for the stairs.

The two girls sat together in Linda's bedroom in a closeness they hadn't experienced for ages. Izzie comforted her sister and they both wept. Neither of them had ever seen their father so angry before.

'You need to put a cold flannel on your face,' Izzie said. 'You'll have a big bruise if you don't.' She sucked in her lip for a minute. *Always got to put your five eggs in.* Why did he say that? She was just trying to help.

'What about you?' Linda said, sniffing into her handkerchief. 'He punched you didn't he?'

'My shoulder is a bit sore but it's not likely to show is it.'

'I can't believe he did that.' Linda whimpered.

Izzie waited until they couldn't hear him moving about and then she went to the top of the stairs. 'Dad?'

She heard a shuffling sound, then he said, 'You'd better get down here and clear up this bloody mess.'

Izzie glanced back at Linda. 'Wait here until I know it's safe.'

The room looked like a bomb had hit it. Her father, his anger spent, was still sitting at the table in his vest.

'If you're seeing Mavis why not finish your wash, Dad,' she said, picking up a fallen chair. She reasoned that if she kept calm, he would say sorry and make it up with them.

He stood up and went back into the bathroom. Izzie spent her time picking up broken pieces of china and the remains of the food which had been on the table.

Linda appeared and hovered by the stair door.

'He's trampled all over my make-up,' she said miserably. 'Pig.'

'Shh,' Izzie cautioned. 'He'll hear you.'

Their father came back into the room holding the towel to his face. 'And I'm telling you now, you two are not going anywhere tonight,' he ranted angrily. 'You can stay here and finish sorting this room out.'

'But it's Bonfire Night,' Linda protested. 'I've been looking forward to it all week and my friends are expecting me to be there.'

The look on his face was frightening. 'Tough,' he said, returning to the bathroom.

The girls looked at each other helplessly. 'Give me a hand and maybe he'll change his mind,' Izzie whispered.

They'd made a good start by the time he went back upstairs to change and no more was said when he reappeared all spruced up and ready to go out himself. He let them pass but as they both made their way back upstairs to get ready, they heard the bolt slide across the stair door.

Linda turned back and stared at Izzie. 'He's locked us in.' Running back downstairs, she hammered on the door. 'Dad? Let us out. You can't lock us in like this. We're not children anymore. Dad. Dad. Open this door!'

Izzie followed her down. 'It's no use,' she said. 'He's gone.'

Their father's bedroom overlooked the street so Izzie and Linda went in to look out. A crowd of about thirty or forty people had already gathered below. A buzz of excited chatter filled the cold November night air and the acrid smell of burning pitch swirled in the grey clouds of smoke above their heads.

'It's not damn well fair,' Linda complained. 'Why would he stop us going?'

'Because he's just like Mum always said,' Izzie said. 'He wants his own way all the time and he's angry.'

Linda rounded on her. 'Bit like you then.'

Izzie was shocked. 'What do you mean?' she said indignantly.

'Oh come on Izzie. You're always angry or complaining about something.'

'Because if I don't, nobody ever does anything!' Izzie cried.

'Yeah, right,' said Linda.

'But it's true,' Izzie said helplessly.

'Well maybe we'd be more inclined to help if you didn't criticise so much. Whatever we do, it's never good enough!'

Izzie's shoulders sagged. Was that really how Linda saw her? All right, maybe she did make the odd suggestion, but it was only to help Linda to improve. Saying all that was most unfair. But then she recalled what Mr Semadini had said that first evening they'd spent together in his experimental bistro. '*You only say this because you are hurt and angry.*' But she wasn't angry, was she? She was just trying to make the world a better place. She still firmly believed that everything would be different if she could just get her mother and father together in the same room . . . She pulled herself up short and glanced at her sister. Linda stood dejectedly with her forehead against the window pane. It wasn't going to happen, was it. She couldn't put the world to rights. She had to stop trying. It only made people unhappy.

'I'm sorry,' Izzie murmured.

'What?' her sister challenged. 'Oh my goodness, you're actually saying sorry are you?'

Annoyed again, Izzie frowned. They both stood at the window in silence, each lost in her own thoughts. Izzie felt her sister's hand very close to hers. Linda's fingers moved slowly towards hers. Nothing was said but the next minute they were both holding hands very tightly.

'Why did Dad get so annoyed when you said John's friend was called Perryman?' Izzie said eventually.

Linda shrugged. 'I don't know.'

Izzie scanned the eager faces down below. Despite being muffled up in scarves and woolly hats, she recognised several of their neighbours and friends. To enter into the spirit of the thing, some had smeared their faces with soot while others had gone to the other extreme. The neighbour from two doors down looked almost frightening. His face was chalk-white and in the eerie half-light, the lipstick (Izzie guessed that's what it was) around his eyes made them look red and bloodshot.

Before long they would all process through the town for the bonfire celebration on the beach. The men were carrying torches, primed and ready to be lit at the given signal, whilst the women stood in line, ready to begin banging their dustbin lids with metal spoons. Behind the adults, the children, some dressed as pirates, waited. Izzie searched the faces to spot any of her friends from the café but Linda was more interested in looking out for one person; John Middleton. She'd told Izzie he had walked back with her when they'd left the café and promised to wait while she'd got changed but now he was nowhere to be seen.

Izzie and Linda stepped smartly back from the window and hid behind each side of the curtains as they spotted their father chatting to someone at the corner of Chandos Road and Grafton Road. It was Mick Osborne.

'What's he doing with Mr Osborne?' Izzie said.

'Search me,' Linda murmured. 'Miserable old sod.'

They heard a voice near the back of the procession call out, 'Light up . . .' and all at once the little street was ablaze as every man lit his torch. There was a collective cheer and the procession moved off.

Izzie and Linda watched in silent misery as the crowd turned towards Montague Street. Linda suddenly turned and ran downstairs. It was obvious she was determined to get out. She began by rattling the door in the hopes of making the bolt slide back of its own accord. It was a badly fitting door but nothing happened. Then she dashed back upstairs to get some coat hangers. Back at the door, she tried desperately to get a hanger between the wood and the bolt on the other side but even that was proving to be quite tricky. The hanger was a tad too wide and not strong enough to slide the heavy bolt.

Izzie watched Linda's frantic efforts for a while then tried a different tack. She opened the back bedroom window and worked out that with one big stride she could get herself onto the roof of the bathroom. There was a large water butt on the corner of the house by the down pipe from the guttering. If she stood on the lid, the jump to the ground was a lot less scary. Tucking her skirt into her knickers as she used to do in PE lessons at school, she eased herself out of the window. The whole exercise went to plan and a few minutes later, she came back into the house through the open back door. Linda was shocked to feel the bolt slide back and even more so when she saw Izzie standing in front of her.

Anxious not to miss anything, the two girls dashed back up to change but it was only as they were almost ready that Izzie noticed that her sister had a suitcase in her hand.

'We'll come back for our cases later on,' said Izzie. 'Mrs Noyles isn't expecting us until seven.'

'I'm not going to Mrs Noyles,' said Linda.

Izzie was taken aback. 'But it's all arranged,' she said.

'I'm leaving now!' Linda cried. 'I'm not staying in this house a moment longer with that mad man.'

'You don't have to,' said Izzie, standing in front of her. 'She's offering us a nice room. It's a bit small but we don't have to stay there for ever. Just until I can find us a bigger place.'

'Izzie I don't want to be with you either,' Linda cried.

'But you can't go on your own.'

'I won't be on my own,' said Linda, her eyes sparkling. 'I'm going to be with Ray.'

Izzie was horrified. 'What?' she cried. 'But you can't.'

'Yes I can,' Linda insisted. 'His uncle has a caravan I can live in and besides, I'm sure Ray is going to ask me to be his girl.'

Izzie was appalled. 'Don't be ridiculous, Linda,' she cried. 'You can't do that. Think of your reputation.'

'For goodness sake, I don't give a hoot about all that,' Linda said as she headed for the door.

For a second Izzie was too stunned to move, then, grabbing her coat and scarf, she called out, 'Hang on. I'm coming too.'

Thirty-Five

Bill Baxter had stormed into The Buckingham, making such an entrance that every head turned in his direction when the door banged against the wall. Mavis, who was wiping glasses at the bar, looked up in surprise.

'I need to talk to you,' Bill said in a hoarse whisper.

She looked about her, then jerked her head towards the door marked 'private'.

He went through and found himself in a small stockroom.

'Whatever's wrong?' she said, coming up behind him.

'I've found out who nicked the stuff from my shop.' He paused for effect. 'Our Linda was wearing the bloody earrings,' he went on. 'She tells me it was her boyfriend and Perryman.'

'Perryman?' said Mavis. She frowned. 'But isn't that the name of the lad you told me was with the boy died of food poisoning?'

Bill struggled to control himself. 'Yes,' he said, 'so tell me what he's doing with my Linda?'

'Look, sugar,' said Mavis. 'This is between you and your girls. Anyway, why would he rob your warehouse?'

Bill flared his nostrils. 'To get back at me I suppose.'

Mavis turned to go.

'She was supposed to be going out with him tonight, but I've put a stop to that. I've locked her in.'

'Maybe you should have let her go and followed her,' said Mavis. 'She'd have led you straight to him.'

He calmed almost straight away and gave her a sheepish grin. 'See what I mean, Mav?' He came towards her and put his hands around her waist. 'You think things out, don't you, darlin'. You're clever.'

'Oh, get away with you,' she scolded. 'Look, get back home and say you're sorry. Let her go, then follow her. When he sees you, that'll put the fear of God in him and you'll get the stuff back.'

'Right,' said Bill. 'I'll do it now.' He hesitated by the door. 'I've told the both of them they've got to be out by Sunday,' he went on.

'You've kicked your own daughters out?' she said. 'Oh Bill, you shouldn't have done that.'

He shrugged. 'It's done now.'

'No,' she said. 'I can't have you doing that.'

He looked stricken. 'But you said . . .'

'Whatever I said, I never meant you to turf them out,' she said. 'They're family, Bill, and I told you before, I don't break up families.'

'But you will come, won't you Mav?'

She regarded him for a minute then said, 'Go and find Perryman and then we'll talk about it.'

They returned to the pub. 'Pint of Guinness, Mav,' said a customer standing by the bar. Bill headed for the door. As he left the pub he glanced back and Mavis blew him a kiss.

*

That afternoon when they took Linda to tea, Paul had never left the Café Bellissimo. Just before the bill came, he'd excused himself to go to the toilet. The plan had been for him to hide in the loo until everyone had gone, but they hadn't reckoned it would be outside in a small courtyard. As soon as he got there, Paul realised that if he hid in the bog there was every likelihood that he'd be stuck *outside* the shop unable to get back in, especially if the owner bolted the kitchen door.

He'd hung around for a bit until he was sure the kitchen was empty then dashed into the storage area to hide. There were some sacks of vegetables on the floor and being quite a small person, he was able to squeeze behind them and out of sight. His feet stuck out a bit and there was a breath-stopping moment when someone dropped a knife or something on the floor nearby, but he managed to stay hidden. It wasn't very comfortable. The floor was cold and the wall felt damp. The potatoes and carrots in the hessian sacks dug in all over him but fortunately he didn't have long to wait.

As soon as it was quiet, he made himself a little more comfortable and waited to make sure everyone was gone. Ray had said it would be a couple of hours before the barrels came down the road on their way to the sea so as soon as it was dark enough, Paul crept towards the door of the shop to disable the bell.

Ray and John hung around town after he'd said goodbye to Linda and then they split up. John went to fetch the car and park it in Bath Place. It had been easy enough to nick it. Ray had spotted it parked outside a house not far from the town centre a few days ago. The keys were still in the ignition and the engine was still running so it seemed easier to nick that one rather than risk Paul getting caught for stealing at the garage. The car was an Austin A40 Somerset Saloon which Paul said was capable of doing 70mph. He also knew there was an empty garage near where he lived so it seemed the obvious place to hide it until they needed it.

As the crowds gathered, Ray came back to the Café Bellissimo and waited in the shop doorway until it was time. Nobody took any notice of a lad having a fag. Every now and then he couldn't resist feeling the gun in his pocket. Its hardness had an amazing effect on him. Just wait until he told them back home what he'd done. His brother Lennie may have had a flick knife but he was only into small time stuff. This was a much bigger league. This was armed robbery.

A few minutes later, John sauntered up to the shop. Ray offered him a cigarette while they waited for Paul to open the door from the inside. Ray glanced up at the windows above them but the flat was in darkness. The two boys entered the shop silently. The feeling of elation and excitement was almost overwhelming.

Ray motioned them towards the back. The office door was closed but they were confident that no-one was there. Ray turned the door handle and they went in, closing the door behind them.

'So where's the safe?' he whispered as he turned on the light.

It was in plain sight in the corner.

'Blimey,' said Paul, 'it's pretty big.'

'Yeah but think of all the dosh inside,' said John, grinning from ear to ear.

'Find the key,' Ray ordered.

They searched the drawers and cupboards but to no avail. One drawer in the desk was locked so Ray forced it open. There was a loud crack as the wood splintered. They waited, holding their breath in case there was a vague possibility that someone was in the flat upstairs but everything was fine. Inside they found a set of keys but nothing fitted the door of the safe.

*

Upstairs in the flat, Giacomo was watching the gathering crowds from his sitting room window but he hadn't put the light on.

He had spent the past week visiting seaside towns along the south coast looking for the ideal spot for his new bistro. Now, at last, he was back home. All he could think about was Isobelle. In fact, she'd been on his mind all week.

He had just stepped out of the bath where he had spent the past half an hour soaking away the aches and pains of another exhausting day. He'd read three chapters of a thriller, struggling not to get the pages too wet as he raced through the exciting bits. Now all he wanted was a quiet evening to relax. Fat chance of that now. The crowds beneath his window were already several hundred strong and it was clear from the buzz and chatter that everyone was in a party mood. Parents stood with their little ones, the girls looking as pretty as a picture as the boys swung football rattles or banged two saucepan lids together to make a cacophony of sound. His heart constricted as he saw a man swing his son up onto his shoulders. The little boy held on tight, his small arms hardly reaching round his father's head. That should have been him with Gianni. He cleared his throat noisily to fight the tears which threatened. Umberto was right. He had to let go. He had to make a new life now and since he'd been away from her, he was very sure of what he wanted.

Swallowing hard, he turned his attention to a man with a drum making his way down the centre of the street as stewards made their last attempt to make sure people were standing well back before the lighted barrels came down. There was just enough time to pour himself a brandy before everything kicked off.

For the first time in years, Giacomo felt happy. Perhaps he had put the bitterness of internment behind him at last. He'd been stupid to hold a grudge for so long anyway. That first evening he'd talked to Isobelle had made that clear enough. He'd pointed out that she was angry and in pain because of her past but he might as well have been talking to himself. By the time he'd finished saying his piece, he'd felt ashamed of his own attitude. He would never forget his Maria, nor his baby boy, but perhaps he really was ready to start a new life. Every now and then the memories would creep up on him like just now but the pain was less raw these days. How he wished Isobelle was up here with him. He had been a fool. He had been too slow, too timid, too afraid to admit to the passion that beat in his breast. He loved her. He should have told her by now. Even forming the words inside his head triggered a deep, aching longing to be with her. Oh Isobelle, Isobelle my love . . .

*

Unbeknown to Giacomo, downstairs in the shop, the three lads tip-toed silently around but they couldn't find the keys to the safe. They helped themselves to some cake under the domes, cutting huge slices and agreeing that the chocolate was the best. Paul spotted Giacomo's lucky toy and stuffed it into his top pocket.

'What d'you want that for?' said Ray.

'My kid brother.'

Ray picked up the cushion on the office chair. If they were going to open the safe, there was nothing for it but to use the gun. Outside, the noise from the crowd was getting louder as the other two hid behind the big leather chair.

'I'll wait until there's plenty of noise outside,' said Ray. He braced himself and holding the gun with the muzzle in front of the lock, he held his breath.

*

The streets were packed with people, mostly locals. As Linda dodged the men with flaming torches, she looked around wildly to find John. She bumped her suitcase into people's legs causing a great many irritated curses and words of abuse. She shouldn't have put so much in it. It weighed a flippin' ton.

'Linda.' She could hear Izzie's shout from somewhere behind her. Linda didn't look back. 'Wait for me.'

But she didn't want to wait. This was her one chance for a bit of adventure, and she didn't want her big sister tagging along. She was tired of people telling her what she could and could not do. She was almost seventeen for goodness sake! She'd show them. She'd show them all. She was perfectly capable of looking after herself. She didn't need Dad and she certainly didn't need Izzie. Linda began to weave in and out of the swirling crowd in an attempt to lose her.

'Linda . . . Linda . . .' Izzie's voice was getting further and further away.

All at once, she realised she'd not only lost Izzie but that the first part of the procession was well under way. She stopped running and stood on tip toe, craning her neck for a sight of John. Oh, where was he?

Someone grabbed her arm. 'Steady on little Missy.' A dishevelled looking man pushed his bristly chin towards her and breathed his beery breath over her face. She could see bits of pie or meat or something in between his row of yellow teeth. Linda turned her head away in revulsion. 'Leave me alone,' she said sharply.

'Where are you off to in such a hurry?' he said. 'Your dad told me to stop you if I saw you.'

Now that she looked more closely she could see it was Mick Osborne. So that's why her father had been talking to him at the end of the street.

'I don't wish to be rude, Mr Osborne,' said Linda, desperately trying to shake off his grip on her arm, 'but I'm looking for my friend.'

'I think you'd better come with me,' said Mick, swaying slightly. 'Your dad's this way.'

Linda tried to resist him but he was holding her arm far too tightly to get away and besides, her suitcase impeded her escape. She began to panic as she realised he was pulling her back towards home. 'No! Let go of me!'

In an instant, Izzie was by her side. 'Let go of her!'

Giving Mick a kick on his shin, Linda aimed the suitcase at his private parts. As Mick cried out in pain and sank to his knees, Linda wrenched her arm free.

'Blimey!' Izzie cried. 'It's Mick.'

'He attacked me,' said Linda. 'You saw him.'

Izzie wasn't convinced but when she'd caught up with Linda, it certainly looked as if Mick was trying to take her somewhere against her will. Dad wouldn't be too happy that they'd laid into his employee but she hadn't realised who it was.

'Stick close by me,' said Izzie. 'I'll protect you.'

'Go away Izzie!' Linda snapped defiantly. 'You're not my mother and I'm perfectly capable of looking after myself.'

A great shout went up and Linda turned to see that the Bonfire Boys, fresh out of the Castle public house by the Broadwater Bridge had arrived. Dressed all in black with black woollen hats and a white skull and crossbones on the front of their jerseys, their flaming tar barrels rolled down the middle of the street in front of them. It was a fantastic spectacle. Linda was mesmerised.

It took a great deal of skill to keep the barrel on course. Each man pushed his dangerous cargo on its side using a gloved hand and a thick stick to keep it steady. The flames leapt from inside of the barrel in great red hungry tongues of fire and the thick black smoke which belched out almost engulfed the others following behind. As the first one went by, even from several feet away, Linda could feel the intense heat.

Above the Café Bellissimo, Giacomo had enjoyed watching the barrels come past the shops. The crowds had cheered and he'd marvelled at the skill of the Bonfire Boys. Then, to his delight, he saw Isobelle in the crowd. She was right outside Kinch and Lack, not more than two hundred yards away. He'd go down and ask her to join him, or if she preferred, he'd accompany her to the great bonfire on the beach. His heart lifted at the thought. Umberto and Benito were already down there. They had headed towards Splash Point where some of their friends from church had a beach chalet. There would be food and wine. He'd enjoy being there if Isobelle was with him.

Giacomo was just about to grab his coat when he thought he heard a muffled thud. What was that? It didn't sound as if it had come from outside. It sounded more like it had come from underneath where he was standing. Was someone in the shop? Giacomo looked around for something with which to arm himself but all he could find was an umbrella. His heart thumping, he opened the door to his flat and crept outside onto the landing.

Thirty-Six

They'd made a mess of the safe but it was open. Laughing and horsing about, the three lads stuffed anything of value into their holdalls, all caution gone. Disappointingly, most of it was paperwork but there were a couple of watches and a small box which contained a ladies engagement ring. Making their way back into the shop, Ray picked up the jar of coins at the other end of the counter. It contained mostly threepenny bits and pennies but the odd note was visible from the side and it weighed a ton. Tipping the jar into his holdall, they froze as they heard a creaking sound on the stairs.

'Shh,' Paul cautioned. 'Somebody's coming.'

From the doorway, they saw a shadowy shape on the wall. Ray stepped back into the hallway and the two of them saw each other.

'What the hell are you doing in my shop?' Giacomo boomed.

At the sound of his voice, Paul and John made a dash for the shop door.

Giacomo brandished his umbrella. 'You won't get away with this,' he shouted 'Help. Somebody help. I am being robbed.'

Ray gave Giacomo a slow smile, levelled the gun and fired.

Outside on South Street, a man turned to his neighbour. 'Did you hear that noise? It sounded like a gun going off.'

'Don't be daft,' said his companion. 'It was only the drum.'

Linda and Izzie clapped and cheered along with the crowd as another four barrels rumbled past. Once they'd gone, the people were on the move again as everyone headed for the beach.

Izzie slipped her arm through her sister's. 'Listen, Linda, don't do this. I know you think I'm being bossy but—'

'Just go away, will you!' Linda cried and as the crowd started to fold around itself, she suddenly crossed the street. It all happened so quickly. Linda thought she heard Izzie cry out, but she didn't look back. There was no way she was going to be dragged back to a boring life. This was her moment. She was going to have a bit of excitement before she had to settle down in some stupid lodgings. With her mind on other things, Linda didn't realise the last of the barrels was right behind her until it was almost too late.

It was only when a man's voice right behind her bellowed 'Get out of the way, girl,' that she turned to see a blaze of orange coming straight towards her. Linda froze. Her feet didn't seem to know which way to turn. It was still a small distance away but already the heat was terrific. A woman in the crowd screamed as the man rolling the barrel struggled to make it change course. Linda gaped in horror, rooted to the spot until she felt herself being propelled out of the way by a heavy blow to the back. As she struggled to stay upright, her suitcase hit somebody coming out of a shop doorway with such force that the two of them staggered together.

'Sorry, sorry . . .' As she stumbled, Linda caught sight of a pair of three tier wedge brothel creepers.

'Watch where you're going you silly moo,' a man's voice growled.

Linda fought to steady herself and the man grabbed her roughly by the arm.

'Are you all right love?' said a woman in the crowd.

'She's fine,' said the man in a softer tone of voice. 'Just pleased to see me, ain't you babe.'

Linda's mouth went dry and her heart pounded as she found herself looking up into Ray's face before he gave her a crushing kiss.

*

Outside the pier pavilion, Bill Baxter scanned the crowds. Mavis was right. He had been a chump not to let Linda go to the celebrations. If he had, he could have followed her and she probably would have led him straight to John Middleton. There was a good chance that the little toe-rag probably still had the rest of the gear.

Bill had come straight back to the house from the pub, only to find the two girls gone. He had raced back towards the town to find them but it was hopeless in this crowd. Needle in a haystack stuff. His only consolation was that when he'd bumped into Mick Osborne at the end of Chandos Road earlier, he'd told him to be on the lookout as well. Cursing and swearing to himself he was just about to give up when he saw Linda kissing some chap outside the Café Bellissimo. Bill's temper flared again.

Pushing his way through the melee he made slow headway. He and the crowd were going in opposite directions. She couldn't hear him or she didn't seem to, even though he bellowed her name loud enough.

Izzie was having great difficulty in crossing the street. As Linda crossed the road to avoid her, Izzie had seen the final barrel coming and yelled out but Linda ignored her. She had never been more terrified. If she hadn't been so anxious, she might have enjoyed the spectacle. It was a bit like watching the

301

sunrise in the morning. First there was a pink glow, then came the bright yellow light. The first lot of barrels had left a thick pall of black smoke and the acrid smell of burning pitch in their wake. A genuine expertise was needed to keep them on course because the road leading to the beach was fairly flat. Clearly the final Bonfire Boy wasn't as skilled as his companions.

When Izzie caught sight of Linda kissing a man in the Café Bellissimo doorway, she'd frowned, puzzled. That wasn't John Middleton. That was the cocky man who had come with Linda to the café. Ray, wasn't it? Ray Perryman, the name which had angered her father so much. Somewhere in her head a penny dropped. Of course! That was the same name as the boy who was taken ill at the same time as Gary Sayers had died. Her blood ran cold. What was he doing with Linda?

Izzie called out again, but to her horror, Raymond Perryman grabbed her sister's arm and they turned to run. Further up the road, she saw John Middleton and the other lad running ahead of them. What on earth was going on?

'Linda, Linda, wait for me!' Izzie was filled with blind panic but her desperate cries were swallowed up by the excited roar of the crowd as the final barrel reached Marine Parade and the beach.

Surprisingly, her sister and the man turned right at the junction where South Street met Marine Parade. She had expected them to turn left towards Splash Point where the huge bonfire had been created. By the time Izzie reached the corner, her sister was turning into Bath Place. Another shout went up and she saw her father only a few yards behind them.

As Izzie hurled herself around the corner, she saw Raymond Perryman standing by the back of a car, putting Linda's suitcase into the boot. Linda was climbing into the back seat and John made as if to get in beside her. Izzie saw Raymond slam the boot but she didn't see what happened next. Her father had caught up with them. He was shouting and there was some sort of an altercation. The rear door swung shut and the car began to reverse at speed towards Montague Street. Somehow or other, John had staggered backwards, hitting his head on a lamp post and her father was on top of him. When the driver reached the junction, he reversed around the corner then headed away from the centre of town. As the car disappeared into the darkness with the horn blaring, she saw someone stick his arm out of the window and give her father two fingers.

Her father struggled to his feet. 'Come back here you bastards.'

Izzie stopped running and stood in the middle of the road with her hands on either side of her head. Her chest hurt and she struggled to get her breath. Her eyes were filled with tears of despair and anger. Izzie bent over with her hands on her knees as her brain tried to make sense of what had just happened. Linda must have planned this whole thing but what on earth was she doing with these three men? She became aware of more shouting. Her father and John Middleton were arguing.

'Where's my daughter going, you little toe-rag?'

'I don't know.'

Her father took a swing at John but he ducked.

As Izzie hurried up the street towards them, she heard a whoop of encouragement and became aware of several other people running past her. It looked as if they had spilled out of one of the nearby pubs and were spoiling for a fight. Some of them had beer bottles in their hands and one man had picked up one of the sticks the Bonfire Boys had used to roll one of the barrels. Everything was beginning to look really ugly.

'And where's my stuff?' her father was yelling. 'You tell me now or I'll knock your bloody block off.'

John put his hands out in mock surrender.

'Dad,' she cried. 'What are you doing?'

'You keep out of this, Izzie,' he shouted.

As the other men joined them, John stumbled and slid down the wall. Her father's head snapped backwards as the man with the stick hit him on the back but the attack on John now took on a ferocity the likes of which Izzie had never seen before. Somewhere behind her she heard a policeman's whistle. John rolled himself into a helpless ball, but he was punched and kicked on the ground before the attackers broke up and ran off. Izzie tried to grab her father's arm but he'd obviously heard the policemen coming and was keen to get away.

As the drunks and her father took flight, the policemen, three of them, chased after them. Izzie knelt on the floor and cradled John's head in her lap. She couldn't believe the state he was in. There was blood all over his face and she saw him wince as she moved him. By now a crowd had gathered and someone had called a St John Ambulance man from the beach.

'What happened, love?' somebody asked.

'I don't know,' said Izzie. 'Some men just came out of the pub and attacked him.'

The St John Ambulance man took over, laying John down and trying to make him more comfortable. Izzie saw an ambulance driving slowly towards them and while everyone's attention was on John she started to walk away. When the police came back, they would start asking questions and she didn't want to tell them her father had been involved.

Filled with a mixture of confusion and concern, Izzie spotted something lying on the road. She frowned and bent to pick it up. It was the toy mascot Mr Semadini kept on the counter – the one he said brought him good luck. Izzie's blood ran cold. How had it got there? That was when she remembered that Raymond Perryman and her sister had been standing in the doorway of the Café Bellissimo. Had they been inside? She was too confused to work out what was going on but something told her it was bad. She had to get back to the Café Bellissimo and fast.

Thirty-Seven

The shop was in darkness but when she touched the door, it swung open.

'Hello.' Izzie called out and listened. The light switch was close to the door so she pressed it down and flooded the shop with light. The first thing she noticed was the mess. There were cake crumbs all over the floor, some trodden into the carpet. She called out again. 'Hello, is anybody there?' but there was no answer.

Her heart was thudding and she felt her throat tighten. She didn't want to go further but she felt compelled. If Mr Semadini was at home, he would have called back. Clearly something had happened here – something bad. Cautiously Izzie pushed open the kitchen door and put the light on. Everything appeared undisturbed.

She turned towards the hallway which led to the flat upstairs. As she put her hand on the newel post she became aware of heavy, distressed breathing. The shock of seeing someone or something on the stairs made her cry out and when she put the light on she almost stopped breathing altogether. Mr Semadini was laying half way down the stairs. His face was the colour of paper and there was a bright red stain on his shirt. For a nano-second Izzie was frozen to the spot but as soon as she saw his eyes moving under his closed eyelids, she dashed to his side. 'Mr Semadini,' she said desperately. 'It's Isobelle.' She had inadvertently touched his shirt and now her hand was red and sticky with his blood. 'Oh, oh Mr Semadini.'

Izzie had little medical knowledge; nothing more than how to bandage a cut finger or bring relief to an upset tummy but she could tell at once that he had been horribly injured. She jumped to her feet. 'Wait here,' she said rather stupidly. 'I'll get help.'

There was a telephone in the office and as she switched on the light, she saw the shattered safe and papers all over the floor. With a trembling hand, and her tears playing havoc with her vision, Izzie dialled 999.

*

Bill Baxter sat in the corner of The Buckingham public house next to the roaring fire. He had a glass of whiskey in his hand. He couldn't stop shaking and his stomach was churning. After a few minutes, Mavis came to join him. The pub had its regulars but tonight it was relatively quiet. Most people were waiting on the seafront for the fireworks to begin.

'What happened?'

'I found the little toe-rag who took my stuff,' said Bill, 'but he got beaten up.'

'Was it you? You look as if you've been in a fight.'

Bill shook his head. 'Half a dozen drunks decided to act all macho. I legged it when the coppers turned up.'

'But you found the girls?'

'I left Izzie there,' he said, taking a gulp from his glass and feeling the fiery liquid slip down his throat, 'but our Linda went off with them.'

'Went off with them?' Mavis echoed.

'In a car; one driving, the other blighter in the back seat with her.'

He stared into the fire. His mind was in a whirl. What was he going to do?

'Who did she go off with then?' said Mavis. 'I thought you said John was her boyfriend.'

Bill looked up. 'I don't know the one driving,' he said, 'but I'm guessing the other one must be that bloody Raymond Perryman.'

'Oh my lord!' Mavis cried, putting her hand to her mouth. 'Do you think it was deliberate? Is this about revenge?'

Bill went white. He hadn't thought of that.

Mavis put her hand on his knee. 'So what happens now?'

'I don't know,' said Bill looking at her helplessly. 'My God Mav, he's got Linda. He's got my little girl.' He put his face into his hands and wept. 'I've cocked up everything, haven't I?'

'Now, now, sugar, don't go blaming yourself,' she said. 'No time for all that now. Waste of time. You've got to work out how you're going to get her back.'

*

The police and the ambulance service turned up at the café shortly afterwards. As they came through the door, Izzie was still pressing clean linen napkins over the wound in Mr Semadini's chest to try and stem the flow of blood. She was also fighting her tears.

Mr Semadini was aware that she was there. He managed a faint smile and whispered something. She put her ear close to his mouth but whatever he was saying it was in Italian and she didn't understand. His breathing had become more laboured.

Izzie choked back a sob. 'Stay with me darling,' she whispered. 'Hang in there.'

'All right, Miss,' a voice behind her said. 'We'll take over now.'

Mr Semadini opened his eyes and mouthed a silent thank you.

As she stood to get out of the ambulance man's way, Izzie squeezed his hand. 'God bless you, my darling,' she whispered so softly that only he would hear. 'You're in safe hands now.'

But Mr Semadini had closed his eyes again. Izzie turned away, her heart breaking. It was only as the professionals took over that Izzie realised how cold she was. Trembling, she lowered herself onto a chair in the café and sat hunched forward until someone put a blanket over her shoulders. She looked up at the policewoman who had done it and smiled. Izzie's chin wobbled and she shook her head. The policewoman squeezed her shoulder. 'You did the best you could. That's what one of the ambulance men told me.'

Izzie wiped her eyes using the edge of the blanket. What a confusing mess this was. How would the policewoman react if she knew Izzie's sister had run off with two men who had quite possibly robbed Mr Semadini?

Her hands were covered in his dried blood and she had a sudden desire to wash them. 'Can I go now?' she whispered.

The WPC shook her head. 'Sorry, love,' she said stiffly. 'They may need to ask you some questions.'

'But I need to wash my hands.'

The policewoman came with her into the kitchen.

'Is Mr Semadini going to be all right?'

The WPC seemed slightly embarrassed by the question.

'It's just that he's my employer,' Izzie said, drying her hands on a towel. 'He's a very nice man.'

The WPC gave Izzie a sympathetic smile. 'I don't know, love.'

They were interrupted by a thick-set man in a raincoat. 'You can go now, constable,' he said, pulling up a chair and sitting at the table. He motioned Izzie to sit too and turned his head to address her. 'My name is Detective Sergeant Thorpe and you are?'

'Izzie,' said Izzie. 'Isobelle Baxter.' She swallowed the lump in her throat as she remembered the way Mr Semadini said her name.

'Now I want you to tell me everything you know,' said DS Thorpe, getting out his notebook, 'starting with what you were doing in the café at this time of night. Now that this is most likely a murder enquiry we need to move fast.'

Izzie blinked. 'Murder?'

'If you ask me, I'd be surprised if the gent made it into the ambulance, let alone to the hospital,' said DS Thorpe.

Izzie swallowed hard. Mr Semadini dead? Oh no, he couldn't be. She clamped her hand over her mouth to suppress a sob. Was it something she'd done? Maybe she shouldn't have pressed the wound so hard. Maybe if she'd got here sooner she could have prevented such a catastrophic blood loss . . .

DS Thorpe shifted impatiently. 'Look, love, I can see you're upset,' he said, 'but if we're going to catch the bloke what done it, we have to get a move on. Do you mind telling me what your relationship was with the victim?' He leaned back and glanced towards the stairs. 'Do you live here?' he said, adding suggestively, 'or maybe you just stay with him once in a while, is that it?'

Izzie was horrified. 'No I do not!' she cried indignantly. 'And how dare you besmirch his name. As I already told the WPC, Mr Semadini is my employer.'

'Okay, okay,' said the DS, putting his hands up in mock surrender. 'No need to get all aerated. I'm just getting the facts.'

And even as she began to explain, Izzie knew this was going to be an awfully long night.

*

The two lads in the getaway car were elated. Paul was driving very fast, the speedometer indicating fifty-five miles an hour.

'You should have stopped for John,' Linda said.

'I think you'll like it more without him,' said Ray, putting his arm around her shoulder.

'How could I?' Paul said over his shoulder. 'Those blokes would have stopped us all, given the chance. Who was that old geezer who was shouting at him anyway?'

'My dad,' said Linda. 'He was mad with John for giving me those earrings.'

Ray sniggered and she wasn't sure if he was just laughing or laughing at her. 'He gave *you* the earrings?'

'Yes,' Linda challenged. 'Why shouldn't he?'

'No wonder your dad was mad,' Ray sniggered. 'It was his place we done over.'

Linda's face flamed.

'You know, for one awful moment,' said Paul, changing gear, 'when that Iti came downstairs, I thought we were done for. How much do you think we got?'

Ray opened the bag at his feet. 'Not as much as if we'd robbed a bank,' he said, holding up a fistful of notes, 'but we're pretty rich.'

Beside him, Linda let out an audible gasp. 'Where did you get that?'

Ray pulled down the front of her dress and pushed in a handful of notes. He laughed. 'Feels good don't it, darlin'?'

'Where did it come from?' said Linda pulling out a couple of pound notes.

Paul turned his head slightly. 'We robbed the café,' he said over his shoulder.

Ray snorted. 'You're right about the Italian. I nearly wet meself when I saw him on the stairs. I had no idea he even lived there.'

Linda drew in her breath. 'What happened?'

'Nothing,' said Paul.

'I shot him,' said Ray matter-of-factly.

'You what?' Paul suddenly swerved and a horrified silence descended in the car. 'What did you say?'

'You heard,' said Ray, his eyes bright with excitement. 'The bloody old fool was yelling his head off. I had to shut him up so I shot him.'

'Oh God,' said Paul. 'You didn't kill him?'

'Dunno,' Ray said casually. 'Probably.'

Linda's heart was racing.

'But that's murder,' said Paul. 'You can swing for that. Listen, I ain't getting involved in no murder.'

Ray leaned forward. 'But you are involved, chum,' he sneered. And sitting back he looked at Linda. 'We're all involved.'

Linda put her hand to her mouth. Part of her thought, oh lord what have I done? While another part of her thought, this is like Bonnie and Clyde. Just like Bonnie, she'd run away with a bank robber – well, a café robber and a murderer. She shivered.

'Cold?' said Ray. He suddenly grabbed her hand and thrust it into the gap in his trousers. 'Have a warm on this.'

Linda made a feeble attempt to free her hand.

'Hey,' said Paul, watching them in the rear view mirror. 'Lay off her. She's John's chick.'

Linda took her hand away and she and Ray sat back. Ray took something out of his pocket and began poking the back of the driver's seat. It wasn't until they passed under some street lights and he pressed the muzzle up against Paul's cheek that she realised it was a gun.

'I'll do what I like,' he told Paul, 'and if I say she's my bird now, that's the way it is, right?'

'Right,' said Paul faintly.

Ray turned towards a white faced Linda and grinned. 'See? Nobody can stop the fella with the gun, 'cos he's the top man.'

Thirty-Eight

When Izzie finally got home the house was in darkness. A white piece of paper was pinned on the inside of the front door glass but with the nearest working street lamp several hundred yards away, it was impossible to read. Izzie squinted at it but to no avail.

She had little idea of the time. As she'd left the police station the clock on the Old Town Hall was chiming but she hadn't paid much attention to it. She'd spent what seemed like hours waiting to talk to the detective in the interview room. They'd been polite and a welcome cup of tea had appeared on the table but everybody seemed to have lost all sense of time.

There was no news from the hospital but as she left the police station, everybody was still talking about a pending murder case. Izzie was so exhausted she was only half listening. It was almost unbearable that Mr Semadini was gone. What a sad end to a lovely man. There wasn't a bad bone in his body. The people of Worthing would miss him too. She sighed as she thought how upset the matronly women who treated him like a son would be. The lonely who felt special when he was around would miss him as well. And as for the children who enjoyed his awful jokes . . . who would explain it to them? She was glad she'd called him darling. She hadn't meant to. It had just sort of slipped out. He'd never known what she'd felt about him

314

before, but she was glad she'd told him in the end. She wished she'd told him sooner, but he'd never given her even the slightest hint that he might feel the same way and she was too afraid that by telling him how she felt, she might be burning her bridges.

Izzie was also worried about her sister. Surely Linda hadn't gone willingly with those men? But then she remembered that kiss. One part of her told her that Linda might have been preparing to run away with John. But if Linda still liked John, what was she doing kissing that other boy? At first, Izzie had toyed with the idea that because of the way that Ray had hold of Linda's arm and was pulling her along, her sister was being taken hostage, but that couldn't be right, could it?

When Izzie finally got to speak to someone, every word she uttered was written down. Izzie told them how Linda was being dragged along, and how she'd seen her in the car but she didn't mention the kiss. Unfortunately, she did let slip that her sister was carrying a suitcase and immediately she sensed their sympathy evaporating. From that moment, they became more sceptical and suspicious.

Exhausted and longing for her bed, Izzie banged on her front door. 'Dad. Dad let me in, it's Izzie.'

When there was no answer, she rattled the letterbox and finally resorted to throwing small stones up to the window pane.

'Dad, it's me,' she called, but nobody came.

Izzie stared helplessly at the darkened window. She couldn't get in. He'd bolted the side gate from the inside and in the rush to catch up with Linda, she'd stupidly left her keys inside on the dresser.

What was she to do now? It was then that she remembered leaving her own suitcase inside. Of course, she was supposed to be going to Mrs Noyles tonight. She had totally forgotten.

Her father must have seen it and decided to lock her out anyway. A wave of misery and despair engulfed her. It was far too late to go over to Queen's Street now. 'Dad,' she called through the letterbox, 'let me in please. I'm sorry. I've nowhere else to go.'

Her next-door neighbour couldn't help either. She was in Norfolk with her son and daughter-in-law for a few days. There was nothing for it but to try to get to Mrs Noyles and appeal to her better nature. It was a long walk, especially when she was so tired, but Izzie couldn't bear the thought of sleeping outside in the street. She was lucky enough to get the last bus from the town centre and got off at the other end of Queen's Street. When Izzie knocked on her door, Mrs Noyles gave her short shrift. 'I was expecting you at seven, Miss Baxter,' she called down from her bedroom window.

'I know, Mrs Noyles, and I am dreadfully sorry but . . .'

'If you cannot stick to a perfectly reasonable time table, then I'm afraid I cannot offer you a room.'

'But I've already paid you two weeks' rent in advance,' Izzie protested.

'I can't help that, Miss Baxter,' Mrs Noyles said. 'And now I bid you good night.' And with that, she shut her bedroom window.

Izzie stared at the house for some seconds before she moved. Fighting to keep control of her emotions she tried to make her tired brain function. It was getting very cold and she could feel spots of rain. She had to find somewhere to shelter. She knew one of the waitresses in the Café Bellissimo, Carol, lived some-where around South Farm Road but she couldn't remember the number. Then she remembered that Esther had said her mother would help if ever she needed it. Esther was coming home on leave soon. She and Izzie had arranged to meet up tomorrow evening, but was she arriving in Worthing tonight or tomorrow morning? Whenever it was, Esther's mum was her only hope. Pushing her hands into her pockets, Izzie trudged towards Esther's home.

It was gone eleven when she got there and Izzie would have talked herself out of knocking the door had it not been for the rain. She was already very wet, cold and miserable. The house was in darkness. Izzie raised her hand over the door two or three times before she actually had the courage to knock.

The moment she did, a light went on upstairs and a few seconds later another light went on in the hall. She heard someone coming down the stairs. The front door opened and Mr Jordan stared at her, bleary eyed. 'Yes? What do you want?'

A voice behind him called, 'Who is it, George?'

'I don't know; some woman.' He turned to Izzie again. 'Who are you and what do you want?'

'I'm sorry to bother you Mr Jordan,' Izzie began. She was biting back the tears, 'but Esther said you and Mrs Jordan might be able to help me if I was in trouble. I'm Izzie . . . Isobelle Baxter.'

He hesitated but then she heard another voice behind him say, 'Izzie?' The next moment the door was flung wide open and Esther stood in front of her. 'Izzie,' she cried again. 'What on earth has happened? Come in, come in. You're absolutely soaked to the skin.'

Esther pulled her inside and helped her off with her wet coat. Her father leaned out of the door and looked up and down the street while Mrs Jordan appeared with a towel to dry her hair.

'Your teeth are chattering,' said Esther. 'I'll warm up some soup.'

'I'll light the fire in the sitting room,' said Mr Jordan.

'I think you'd better have a nice warm bath, my dear,' said Esther's mother, 'before you catch your death of cold.'

They all looked at Izzie who promptly burst into tears.

Everyone decided explanations could wait until morning so after her bath and some tomato soup, they made up a bed for her on the sitting room sofa. Safe and warm, Izzie was so exhausted she fell asleep almost at once.

Thirty-Nine

Linda was busting for the toilet. She had never been so frightened in her life. When Ray put the gun on Paul's neck, the tension in the car was palpable. Things had calmed down since then but she knew Ray was unpredictable. She stared out of the window into the inky darkness then glanced across at him. She'd have to tell him she needed to go or she'd wet herself in a minute. He sat motionless with the gun in his lap. A couple of times when he caught her looking at him, he gave her a sinister smile and pointed the gun right at her. The first time he did it, she honestly thought she was going to die. She'd screwed her eyes up and waited for the bang. When she'd finally plucked up the courage to open her eyes again, he'd laughed at her and pointed the muzzle at the back of Paul's head. She'd gasped. If he'd pulled the trigger while Paul was driving, they'd all die and from that moment she realised just how dangerous Ray really was.

'Where does your uncle live then, mate?' said Paul. He sounded nervous. 'Am I on the right road?'

Ray shifted in his seat. 'Portsmouth.'

'Where?' said Paul.

'Portsmouth!' Ray snapped.

'I know that,' said Paul, 'but where in Portsmouth?'

There was an awkward moment when all three of them realised Ray had no idea.

'We can't go banging on doors to ask the way at this time of night,' said Paul. 'If we do, we're bound to attract attention.'

'Shut-up,' Ray snarled. 'I'm thinking.'

'We've just passed a place selling caravans,' said Linda. 'Can't we get in one of them?'

'I said shut your gob, you dozy cow,' said Ray, waving the gun at her again. Linda began to cry. 'And stop that bloody whining!'

'Hang on a minute, Ray,' said Paul, slowing the car, 'she's got a point. We could kip there for the night and look for your uncle's place in the morning. It'll be easier to see the road signs in the daylight.'

'All right,' Ray said grudgingly.

Paul turned the car around and they went back.

The caravans were inside a wire fence and the gate was padlocked. Paul found a small torch in the glove compartment and they all got out of the car.

'I'll take the keys,' said Ray, beckoning with his hand. Paul handed them over.

The only building on the site was a small cabin which they presumed was the office. The whole place was in darkness and the nearest house was about half a mile away. Ray aimed the gun to shoot the lock but Paul put his hand on his forearm to stop him.

'The gunfire will be heard for miles,' he cautioned.

They skirted the perimeter of the compound, Ray holding onto Linda's arm in case she decided to run away. Paul went ahead of them and kept shaking the fence to look for a weak spot. In the end, several well aimed kicks loosened a dodgy looking fence post and both boys were inside the caravan park.

Still on the outside, Linda hesitated. Now was her chance to get away, but where could she go? It was pitch black and if she ran down the road, they could easily come after her in the car.

The best way to make an escape would be to run over the rough ground and hide in the undergrowth, but she had no light. Paul had the only torch. Besides, if she made a getaway, Ray would more than likely become trigger happy in case she went to the police. She must have been mad to come with them and she was still dying for the toilet. She watched them pick out a large luxury caravan at the back of the lot and shivered. She'd have to stick with them for now, wouldn't she. What choice did she have?

The boys walked around the caravan. When Paul shone the torch through the window, they saw a big bowl on the table laden with fruit.

'I'm starving,' Paul murmured and Ray pointed out that there was a loaf of bread and some cheese on the side.

Lucky for them, the dealer had left one window inadequately fastened so Ray prised it open and gave Paul a leg up. Once inside, he opened the door to let Ray in. The two lads pounced on the food, taking big hungry bites. Paul spat it out and cursed. 'Ugh, it's wax.' Ray lost his temper and began kicking everything in sight.

When Linda came in, the first thing she did was to squeeze herself into the tiny toilet. What a relief. When she came out, she was so tired she pulled the cushions off the sofa and lay down.

The lighting in the caravan wasn't great but the boys wanted to count the money. They'd got seventy pounds from the safe and several wage packets. As they ripped them open, Linda felt a bit guilty when she saw Izzie's name on one of them. The coins in the jar took a little longer to count but they discovered they had another eighteen pounds fourteen shillings and seven pence. That's when the argument started.

Ray wanted the lion's share. 'My idea,' he said doggedly. 'I planned it. My gang.'

'You should have worked out how to make a clean getaway then,' said Paul. 'And what about John?'

'What about John?' said Ray.

'You've got to give him his share.'

'It's not my fault he couldn't run fast enough.'

'You've got to.'

'I haven't got to do anything.'

They'd started bickering like quarrelsome and greedy pigeons at the bird table, pushing and shoving each other, one picking up some money and the other taking it from him.

'Oh for goodness sake,' Linda said crossly. 'Shut-up will you? Can't you let a girl get some sleep?'

Ray turned his head, his eyes narrowing. 'No bird ever talks to me like that,' he said, rising to his feet. He began to undo the belt on his trousers.

Terrified, Linda sat up. 'I'm sorry, Ray. I didn't mean anything by it.'

He made a grab for her but she gave him a shove and somehow managed to get past him. As she reached the door, he pulled her back by her hair. Linda was screaming and crying until one blow from his hand knocked her off balance and they both fell. All at once he was tearing at her clothes. Linda became desperate. 'No, no, Ray,' she shouted. 'No, stop it.' But the more she protested the more it seemed to enflame his passion.

'Come on, come on,' he growled. 'You were bloody gagging for it in The Cave.'

As she cried out in bewilderment Paul froze. 'No, no.' But Linda could do nothing to stop him as Ray pulled her skirt up and ripped at her underclothes. She fought like a tiger but it was obvious that there was only one thought in Ray's head and it made him too powerful. 'Paul help me. Help me!'

Paul had put his hands over his ears. He'd looked for a way to get out of the caravan but the two of them were sprawled across the floor in such a way that they'd completely blocked the exit. Paul was too scared of Ray to intervene. All he could do was sit it out. Although Paul had never been with a girl himself, he'd heard his parents at it sometimes in the early hours of the morning. He was used to moans and rhythmic creaks on the bed but this was something else altogether and she wasn't enjoying it. He felt both sickened and ashamed. All at once Ray gave a triumphant shout and it was over.

Linda was weeping. 'Oh shuddup,' he said savagely as he rolled from her. He lay on his back with a satisfied grin then his breathing became heavier as he fell asleep.

Paul picked up his money and stepping over a whimpering Linda, he slunk silently out of the door.

But as the door clicked shut behind him, Ray opened one eye and reached for his gun.

Forty

Early the next morning, the sitting room door opened and Esther popped her head around. 'Oh you're awake.' Izzie was sitting on the edge of the sofa with the blanket wrapped around her shoulders and staring into space. 'Can I come in?'

She nodded and moved over so that Esther could sit beside her. 'I can't thank you enough . . .' she began, but Esther waved her away.

'That's what friends are for,' she said. She gave Izzie a side hug. 'Are you ready to tell me what happened?'

It took a while and Izzie shed quite a few tears as she went through everything. Esther was a first-rate listener.

'Linda gets cross with me for telling her what to do all the time but I couldn't help it,' Izzie complained. 'Perhaps I've been too bossy, but we were so young when Mum went off and she looked up to me then.'

'I'm sure she knows that,' said Esther.

'And then there's my father,' Izzie went on. 'I think I made up my mind not to like Mavis. I just wanted Mum and Dad back together again.'

'But your mother has someone else,' said Esther.

Izzie nodded.

'And she's happy now,' Esther went on.

'I know,' Izzie said miserably. 'I've been really stupid. Mum told me her parents and Granny Baxter made them get married. I don't think they've ever been happy together and Dad ending up in prison like that just about finished it off.' She blew her nose noisily. 'I shouldn't have interfered.'

'But you meant well, Izzie,' Esther said gently.

Izzie sighed and went on to tell Esther how she had found Mr Semadini in the café. She sobbed as she told her friend about their last moments together.

'I'm so sorry,' said Esther. 'You really loved him, didn't you?'

Izzie nodded miserably. 'I don't think I realised just how much I did until the copper told me this would be a murder enquiry.' She wiped her eyes and blew her nose again. 'And it's all too late now.'

They sat together in silence for a short while. Esther had her arm around Izzie as she rested her head on Esther's shoulder. They heard someone going into the bathroom upstairs and Izzie sat up. 'But I can't dwell on my past mistakes,' she went on stiffly. 'I've got to find Linda.'

'So you're not convinced that she went of her own free will?'

Izzie shrugged. 'I honestly don't know. But I can't risk it, can I? And even if she did, she's still my sister.'

'Izzie, there's something I have to tell you,' Esther began cautiously. 'You remember you wrote and asked me to find out about your father? Well, I talked to an old police sergeant and he remembered the case quite well.'

Izzie sat up straight. 'Go on.'

'You were right,' said Esther. 'Your father was involved with the black market.'

'I had already pieced that together,' said Izzie.

'When those children were taken ill – when they ate those bad sausage rolls and Gary Sayers died – there was another lad, Raymond Perryman, who wasn't expected to survive.'

Izzie gasped. 'That's the boy Linda likes.'

'Looks like it.'

'Do you think Raymond Perryman knows about my dad?'

'Well, it's possible, isn't it,' said Esther.

'Then Linda could be in real danger.' Izzie gasped.

'There was something else which might throw light on why your parents' marriage broke up,' Esther continued. 'When your dad was arrested, it was because of a police tip-off.'

'I get the feeling you're going to tell me it was one of the Perrymans,' said Izzie.

'No,' said Esther. 'The sergeant remembered the police informant.' She paused and reached for her friend's hand. 'Izzie, it was your mother.'

'What?' Izzie frowned and something she'd overheard the night her mother ran away came back to her. '*I didn't realise it was so bad. I thought you'd just get a ticking off.*' A penny dropped. Her mother hadn't dreamt for one minute that her father would have to go to prison but because he did, she couldn't forget what he'd done and when he'd found out, he'd vowed never to forgive her.

'Are you okay, Izzie?'

Izzie rubbed her forehead. 'What am I going to do now?'

Esther rose to her feet. 'I suggest you have a wash and change your clothes. After that, we'll have some breakfast and then we'll go and get some answers from John Middleton.'

'Do you know where he lives then?'

'No,' said Esther, 'but if his beating is as bad as you said, my guess is they'll have kept him in hospital overnight. The doctor's rounds aren't until mid-morning so even if he's well enough to be discharged, he won't be sent home until this afternoon at the earliest.'

'Don't forget I have to find somewhere to live,' Izzie said dully.

'Nonsense!' Esther cried. 'You can sleep on the sofa until I go back to work and then you can have my room until you can find something more suitable.'

'Oh I can't . . .' Izzie began.

Once again her friend waved away her protestation. 'It's all fixed with Mum,' she said, 'so let's hear no more about it.'

*

Bill Baxter stared anxiously at the door. He had been in the emporium clearing out his stuff. There wasn't much of it left but if the coppers came to question him about last night, the last thing he wanted was a load of stolen gear on the premises. He pushed a holdall into Mick's hands.

'As soon as it's dark,' he said, 'chuck it off the pier.'

'Don't you want any of it?'

'No,' said Bill, 'and if I ever take another piece of gear give me a kick up the backside.'

He watched Mick hurrying off and for the umpteenth time he wished he'd never let himself get talked into all this. It seemed that no matter what he did, on the fiddle or going straight, he always ended up falling down the pan. What was the world coming to? Now that he'd been robbed himself, he knew how it felt. Was there no honour even among thieves these days? That's why he'd got so mad last night and it could have been a lot, lot worse. He'd been relieved when he'd heard someone in the pub say that John Middleton wasn't dead. He was in hospital and rumour had it that he'd robbed the Café Bellissimo.

But what of his girl? What of Linda? Perhaps Linda was in on it too? No, she wouldn't, would she? He was well aware that she was shop lifting. All those pretty dresses she had couldn't have come out of her wage packet. He should have said something long ago but how could he? What sort of an example had he set her?

Izzie was the only one who had stayed squeaky clean. That was probably why they fought so bad. She looked just like her mother. He shouldn't have let that get to him, but it did. Izzie had not only inherited her mother's good looks but she had the same pluck. In fact, she was turning out to be a girl to be reckoned with. Lord knows he tried not to let her prissy ways rile him but she always did.

His thoughts drifted back to Linda. What if Mav was right and that Perryman boy meant to do her harm? He shuddered. He'd never forgive himself if that happened. And where was his little girl now? The only person who was likely to know was John Middleton. He glanced up at the clock. What time were visiting hours? Perhaps a bunch of flowers for appearances sake – and, when no-one was looking, the threat of a fist – might encourage him to tell. It was the only way he might find out where his thieving mates had gone with Linda and with a bit of luck he'd get the rest of his stuff back as well.

*

John Middleton was on the men's ward. The sister told them it wasn't possible for him to go home just yet as he had sustained a rather nasty injury. She also told Izzie and Esther they were far too early for visiting but when Esther told the sister that she was a WPC and that Izzie had been the one who had saved John's life, she let them go in. John was at the very end of the ward behind some screens. They found him propped up in bed with four pillows on the back rest. His arm was in a sling and his face a mass of cuts and bruises. There was also a bandage over his right ear. He looked a sorry sight.

'Hello John,' said Izzie, and when Esther introduced herself she was at great pains to make sure he knew she was a WPC.

Izzie drew up a chair. Esther was already seated in the one next to the bed.

'They tell me I owe you my life,' said John, looking at Izzie as she sat down. 'I hear you tried to stop that maniac from beating me to death.'

Izzie felt her face colour. He obviously had no idea his first attacker was her own father.

'I can't thank you enough,' John whispered.

'Well I'm sure you'll understand that we're very anxious to find out where Izzie's sister Linda is,' said Esther, sounding very official. 'Any information you can give us will be most helpful.'

John turned his head away and said nothing.

Esther pursed her lips irritably. 'You could save yourself a lot of trouble if you help us now.'

'I'm no grass,' said John.

'Please John,' said Izzie. 'You like Linda, I know you do. Help me find her before she gets herself into even more trouble.'

'She wasn't part of it,' said John. 'I didn't even know she was coming.'

'She told me she was meeting you in town for the celebrations,' said Izzie.

'I only said that,' John admitted. 'I had no intention of meeting her.'

'Because you and those boys planned to rob the Café Bellissimo,' said Esther.

John nodded and Izzie gasped. Somehow she hadn't put the two together but of course, it was perfectly obvious now.

'You do know the police are treating this as a murder enquiry, don't you?' said Esther.

John winced as he sat upright. 'We heard someone coming downstairs but we legged it. There was no murder.'

'I found him,' said Izzie. 'He'd been shot.'

John's face paled. 'Shot?' He looked from one to the other

of them. 'Well, it wasn't me!' he cried desperately. 'I didn't fire the gun. Ray was the only one with a gun.'

'Ray?' said Izzie.

'Ray Perryman.'

'I don't know that name,' Izzie said innocently. 'Does he live in Worthing?'

John shook his head. 'He comes from London but he's staying with his auntie. That's where he got the gun from. It was in her attic. Look, if that guy got shot, it was nothing to do with me!'

'That won't make a lot of difference,' said Esther. 'You were there. You were part of it.'

John's eyes had filled with tears.

Izzie went to say something more but Esther tugged at her arm. 'Tell us where you were going so that we can rescue Linda.'

It was clear from the look on his face that John was torn between two loyalties. He sank back down on the pillows as the tears rolled down his cheeks. 'They'll hang me, won't they,' he said quietly. 'I swear to you, I didn't know. I didn't do it,' he added in a more desperate tone.

They were interrupted by a commotion by the door. It started with a shout of 'There he is,' and was followed by a scuffle just before a man and two policemen came crashing through the wooden swing doors. A bunch of yellow chrysanthemums flew across the polished floor. The two policemen and another man fell. On the other side of the swing doors, before they closed again, they caught a glimpse of the ward sister charging up the corridor to complain about the noise as several nurses scurried past to answer the bells rung by anxious patients.

The man on the floor was shouting, 'Get off me. Let me go!'

As Izzie rose to her feet she heard one policeman saying, 'You're nicked, sunshine.' The policemen got to their feet and dragged the man away.

'Izzie, tell them,' he was shouting. 'Tell them it wasn't me.'

But Izzie couldn't bear to look at him. She stared straight ahead, her face flaming. She'd recognised her father the minute he'd fallen to the floor. As Bill Baxter was being dragged away Esther leaned over John and Izzie heard her say, 'Listen John, we have reason to believe Linda could be in imminent danger. Anything you can tell us would be most helpful.'

John looked down the ward anxiously. 'Ray's got an uncle in Portsmouth.'

'Do you know the address?'

John shook his head. 'But I know the car they've got. It's a Ford Prefect, black, and the number plate is NNN 535.' He paused. 'No, hang on a minute. ONN 553.' He put his hand to the bandage on his head. 'Something like that.' He winced again. 'I've got a terrible headache.'

Izzie smiled grimly. 'Thank you, John. I hope you get better soon.'

With a tired nod, John put his head back onto the pillows and closed his eyes.

Outside in the corridor Esther shook her head. 'I'm sorry,' she said. 'I'm afraid that wasn't much help. We still have no idea where Raymond Perryman could have taken Linda.'

'We may not know,' said Izzie, 'but I think I know someone who might be able to tell us.'

Forty-One

First thing on Monday morning the bell on the shop door jangled as Esther walked into the Woolly Lamb on the Goring Road. Izzie, following close behind, closed the door, turned the sign to 'closed', and slid the bolt. Brenda Sayers looked up. She was busy restocking Paton and Baldwin wools in the purpose built square shelves behind the counter. 'Can I help you?'

'We hope you can,' said Esther, introducing herself. 'And of course you know Izzie.'

The two girls had driven to the shops in Esther's dad's car.

'I do,' Brenda said with a frown. 'Why have you turned the sign on the door?'

Esther ignored her question. 'Can you tell me where your nephew is?'

'At home in his bed I should imagine.'

'Are you sure?' Esther asked. 'I mean, did you actually see him this morning?'

Brenda hesitated and frowned. 'As a matter of fact I didn't,' she said. 'What's this all about?'

Esther told her about the robbery and how Raymond had been seen driving away in a car.

Brenda put her hands to her throat. 'That can't be right,' she said. 'He went to the bonfire celebrations and then he planned to stay the night with his friends.'

'And you haven't actually seen him,' Esther reminded her.

'The thing is, Mrs Sayers,' Izzie ventured. 'We think my sister is with him and that she may have been taken forcibly.'

'Forcibly?' Brenda gasped. 'Raymond may be many things but he's certainly not a robber or a kidnapper.'

'I don't want to offend you, Mrs Sayers,' Izzie blurted out, 'but we are very worried.'

Mrs Sayers glared at Esther. 'I can't think why you've brought her here.' Turning to Izzie she said malevolently, 'You and your family have caused me nothing but trouble.'

'We believe Raymond has an uncle in Portsmouth,' Esther went on.

'Silas?' said Mrs Sayers. 'What's my brother got to do with it?'

'Probably nothing at all,' said Esther, 'but Raymond's friend John seemed to think he and the other lad might go there. Can you give us his address?'

'I don't see why I should,' said Mrs Sayers, tossing her head.

'A man was shot,' said Esther.

'Shot?'

Esther nodded. 'Did you know Raymond had a gun?'

'He hasn't,' Brenda snapped. 'For goodness sake, I won't listen to this! Raymond is only a boy. He's not even old enough for National Service yet!' She waved her arm, accidentally knocking over a half filled cardboard box of Dewhurst cottons, which spilled on the counter and onto the floor. 'Now look what you've made me do,' she said irritably.

The three of them retrieved the cottons then Brenda said, 'Look, I know Raymond is a bit of a handful but he's a good boy really. You've got this all wrong. I'm telling you, my nephew wouldn't hurt a fly.'

Somebody tried the door handle and they looked up to see

a woman outside. At the same time, Izzie and Esther saw a police car drawing up beside the pavement.

'Go and open that door,' Mrs Sayers said crossly. 'You're losing me my customers.'

'So if we could have that address?' Esther said quickly.

'Oh for goodness sake,' Brenda snapped again. '42 Barrack Road.' Izzie began to walk towards the door. 'Thank you.'

'And stay away from my shop,' Brenda called after them.

Izzie paused and turned back. 'Mrs Sayers, I know you're upset but I did try to tell you that my mother still feels terrible about what happened all those years ago.'

'So you say,' Brenda said, her voice full of sarcasm. 'I don't suppose you know that your father never was a prisoner-of-war, like she told you. He was sent to prison for what he did.'

'Actually I did know,' said Izzie. 'But what I never realised was that my mother was the one who put him there. She was the person who informed the police of what he'd done.'

Brenda's jaw dropped.

As she opened the door to the shop, Izzie could see that she had completely taken the wind from Brenda's sails, but she didn't feel smug about it. It was all rather tragic and sad.

'Hurry up,' said Esther as they met on the pavement. 'I could end up making the tea for the rest of my life for doing this.' The two girls hurried towards Esther's dad's car and got in.

'I don't want you losing your job,' said Izzie, climbing in beside her.

'I won't,' said Esther, starting the engine, 'but I'm not in uniform and I'm not part of the case. It's just that saying I'm a WPC gets doors open.'

'Where are we going now?' asked Izzie, as the car sped towards Goring Village. Esther turned her head. 'Portsmouth, of course.'

*

Linda woke up to find a strange man leaning over her. Her head was pounding and her eye felt funny. She couldn't open it properly. She tried to sit up but she couldn't quite manage it. She shivered involuntarily.

'What the devil's been going on here?' the man barked. 'Who the hell are you and what are you doing in my caravan?' He yanked at the bedclothes and she could do nothing to stop him. With the warmth gone from her body, Linda moaned.

'Where's Izzie?' she murmured. 'I want my sister.'

She heard him gasp in shocked surprise. There was blood. Lots of blood.

'Leave her alone,' said a woman's voice behind him. 'Can't you see she's in a bad way? Call an ambulance and while you're about it, call the police. There's a dead body by the fence.'

*

When Izzie and Esther arrived in Portsmouth a police car was already waiting outside 42 Barrack Road. 'Drat and double drat,' Esther murmured, 'looks like they got here first.'

Wearily, the two girls climbed out of the car and Izzie stretched her back. It had taken them a good hour and a half to get here and as they stepped onto the pavement, a police sergeant climbed out of the police car.

The two girls walked towards them. 'Can you give me your names please?'

'Esther Jordan.'

'Isobelle Baxter.'

'What have you two young ladies been up to?' he said crossly. 'Impersonating a police officer is a criminal offence.'

'Actually, I wasn't, Sergeant,' said Esther. 'I am a WPC in London. It's just that I forgot to mention that I'm off duty at the moment.'

The sergeant scowled. 'You'd better tell me the name of

'your division,' he said. 'I shall be having a word with your superior.'

'It's my fault,' said Izzie. 'She only did it because I'm desperate to find my sister and I promise you she never said she was conducting an investigation. Mrs Sayers just assumed that.'

'And you didn't think to put her right,' said the sergeant.

Izzie looked at the floor but didn't answer.

'I don't know anything about your sister,' the sergeant went on. 'We were just asked to wait for you at this address.'

'So has Raymond Perryman been here?'

The sergeant looked blank.

'We've come here because there was a robbery in Worthing,' Esther explained. 'Raymond Perryman abducted this lady's sister as he made his getaway.'

'All I've been told is that one of you has been impersonating a police officer,' the sergeant said doggedly.

'But we haven't,' cried Esther.

'All the same, I think you'd better come down to the station with us,' said the sergeant. 'I need to get to the bottom of this.'

'Excuse me, but you are going to question Ray Perryman, aren't you?' Izzie protested.

But the sergeant wasn't listening. To her immense frustration he and the constable with him bundled them both into his car.

*

In the accident and emergency department of the Royal Haslar Hospital in Havant, the doctor frowned as he looked in the patient's notes. 'Does anyone know her name?'

The sister shook her head. 'She collapsed before anyone could get any details.'

'She looks under age,' said the doctor. 'We should get a parents' permission before we operate.'

'Frankly,' said the surgeon, 'I don't think we've got enough time for all that. She's lost a lot of blood. Still is.'

The doctor nodded. 'If I could get my hands on the blighter who did this . . .'

'You and me both, pal,' the sister muttered.

*

Bill Baxter cursed his luck.

The coppers had put him in a small bare room with only a table and four tubular steel and canvas chairs. He shivered, not with cold but with the fear that once again he would have to spend time in prison. Now they were accusing him of beating up that boy but he hadn't. He admitted to taking a swipe at him but the drunks had laid him out. It wasn't what it looked like. He hadn't jumped on top of John, the way half the people in the street were implying, he had simply fallen on top of him. His only thought had been to stop the car which was taking Linda away.

Bill put his head in his hands. He'd been a complete idiot, hadn't he. He had hoped Izzie would come to the pub last night. He'd left a note behind the glass on the front door to tell her where he was but she'd never turned up. God alone knew where Linda was. He sighed. He'd had such high hopes when he'd asked the girls to come back home all those years ago but one thing was for sure, he never was cut out to be a father. He rubbed his stubbly chin anxiously and thought of Mav . . . She'd said she didn't want any trouble. She'd said she'd had enough of prison visiting from going to see her old man before he died. He knew she wouldn't stick around if he was in trouble. What was he going to do if they locked him up? He could feel the anger building inside him again and thumped the table with his fist.

Izzie and Esther were taken into an interview room at the police station and spent several minutes explaining why they were in Portsmouth. The detective sergeant made notes and the inspector asked questions.

'We just want to know where my sister is,' Izzie explained. 'She's only just seventeen and I know she won't thank me for it, but since our mother left us, well, I've tried to look after her.'

'And you say she went off with two men?'

'Well, they're lads really. I think they might have robbed the café where I work and one of them shot the owner.'

That was the moment when everything changed. The two policemen suddenly took everything very seriously. They were asked to describe the boys in question. Esther couldn't say much but Izzie gave a fairly detailed description of Raymond and Paul. The sergeant got up and left the room abruptly.

A few minutes later, he came back into the room with another police officer. Izzie was asked yet more questions. No, she didn't know where Paul lived but she believed he used to meet her sister in a club in Worthing called The Cave. Someone there might know. She had only met him once, when Linda and the three lads came into the café for tea on the day of the robbery. She was asked to describe Paul again.

The three police officers looked from one to another. Izzie's heart began to beat a little faster. She sensed something was wrong. What on earth was going on?

'Earlier this morning,' the inspector began, 'a body was found outside a caravan site on the Portsmouth road.'

Izzie took in her breath and Esther leaned over to grab her hand.

'We believe it could be the young lad who matches the

description you've just given us,' he went on. 'He had been shot. Would you be willing to identify him?'

Izzie's eyes grew wide but she nodded. 'And my sister?'

'A young girl was taken to hospital in Havant,' he said. 'She's apparently on the operating table as we speak but we'll take you over there as soon as possible.'

*

The whole day turned out to be one traumatic experience after another. The two girls were taken to a mortuary first. Afterwards Izzie hardly remembered what it was like except that it was freezing cold in the room and she was confronted by something on a stretcher. The mortuary assistant pulled back the sheet and she gazed down at the same fair haired boy she'd seen with Linda in the Café Bellissimo. He looked as if he was asleep.

Izzie nodded. 'Yes, that's him. That's Paul, but I don't know his surname.'

That was enough for the police inspector. He nodded to someone else and Izzie was taken in a police car to the Royal Naval Hospital Haslar, with Esther following in her dad's car. They had to wait for Linda to come out of the operating theatre.

'She's lost a lot of blood,' the doctor told Izzie.

'But she will be all right?' Izzie asked anxiously.

'Yes and no,' he said. Izzie became aware that Esther had threaded her arm through hers. 'She will recover,' he went on, 'but she's had a pretty rough time of it. '

Izzie could hardly breathe. 'Oh, Esther,' she said when they were alone again, 'this is so awful.'

'But at least she's alive,' Esther said by way of comfort.

The two girls waited in the corridor until Linda came out of theatre but it was getting dark before they were able to go onto the ward to see her. Izzie had done her weeping so she

339

was able to sit by Linda's bed with an encouraging smile on her face.

When Linda finally opened her eyes, her chin started to wobble.

Linda's eyes filled with tears. 'Izzie,' she murmured.

Izzie leaned over and smiled. 'I'm here, darling.'

'Oh, Izzie,' her sister was saying. 'I thought he was going to kill me. I was so scared.'

Izzie took her hand. 'It's all over now. You're safe now.'

All at once, her sister frowned. 'Where were you? I called and called but you didn't come.'

Forty-Two

It was Thursday before Izzie could bring herself to go back to the Café Bellissimo. Linda was making good progress and she was to be transferred to Courtlands, a post-operative convalescent home in Goring-by-Sea, just outside Worthing, next week. Of course, she was still traumatised by what Raymond had done to her, but she was absolutely determined to get well. Izzie had stayed by her bedside all day on Tuesday and Esther had come to fetch her back to Worthing Wednesday evening. Linda told the Portsmouth police that Raymond had left the caravan soon after he'd raped her. 'He was so horrible,' Linda said tearfully. 'When Paul left the caravan he kept telling me it served me right and that it was all my family's fault that Gary died but I don't even know anybody called Gary.' Her voice was growing more desperate.

'I think you should wait until she's feeling stronger before you tell her Paul is dead,' the doctor told Izzie in confidence as she ended her visit.

Izzie was struggling not to break down herself. She had to stay strong for Linda's sake but it was so hard. The next day, the two of them held hands as the policewoman read her statement back to her. Afterwards, exhausted, Linda rested her head on Izzie's shoulder. Izzie had her arm around her, just like she'd done all those years ago when their mother ran away.

When she got back to Worthing, Linda was told she would have to face another interview. The Worthing police wanted to talk to her about the robbery.

'But I didn't know what they were doing,' Linda had protested.

'We know,' said the inspector, 'but the Worthing police have to conduct their own enquiry.'

'Will you come with me?' Linda asked Izzie when they were gone.

'Of course I will,' said Izzie, squeezing her hand.

Linda sank back onto her pillows and winced with pain. Her stitches felt rather tight and her bottom itched like mad. 'I know I've always said you're a bossy cow,' Linda said, 'but I am really grateful to have you here.'

Her words were like music to Izzie's ears.

When she got back home, Izzie posted a letter to her mother and she also scribbled a note for her father. When she went to push it through the letterbox of the house in Chandos Road, the note he had stuck on the inside of the glass on the front door was still there. Now that it was daylight she could read it easily.

Izzie, come to The Buckingham. I'm sorry I got annoyed. Mav and I want to talk to you and Linda. Dad.

Izzie gulped. Sorry . . . he'd actually said sorry. She could hardly believe her eyes. So why had he locked her out that night? She'd tried the doors but they were all locked. Where was her father now? It was a bit of a conundrum. She thought of going to The Buckingham straight away but decided she couldn't face it right now. She had to go to the café to see how Mr Umberto and Mr Benito were. She also wanted to find out if she still had a job to go back to.

*

As she'd expected, the cafe was closed. Izzie tapped the window and Benito let her in. Her throat tightened and she looked at him helplessly.

'I'm so sorry,' she said in a whisper. 'I only wish I could have done more.'

He gave her a gentle embrace. 'You did all you could and we are very grateful.'

Mr Umberto was there too but none of the other waitresses. As he hugged her, Izzie was suddenly overwhelmed with grief. She wept in his arms.

When Benito pushed a cup of coffee in front of her, they both did their best to comfort her, which only made her feel all the more terrible. What would they say when they found out that her sister's visit to the café was all part of the plot to rob them?

In the end she couldn't hold back any longer. With great gulping sobs she told how she had chased her sister into Bath Place and how she'd tried to help John.

'I saw them take him away in an ambulance,' she went on, 'and then I found Mr Semadini's lucky mascot in the street.' Izzie blew her nose. 'Something told me something was wrong so I came straight over to the café. The door was wide open, so I came in and that's when I found him over there, lying on the stairs.'

She sat up straight, looking for a clean handkerchief in her pockets. Bentio handed her his. 'Please,' he said gently, 'don't upset yourself anymore.'

'I could see he was horribly injured,' she continued. 'I dialled 999 and then I stuffed as many clean napkins over his wound as I could.' By now her heart was in ribbons again but she carried on telling them that the police had kept her until gone ten and how she'd got home to find herself locked out.

'Of course now I realise that I wasn't locked out at all,' she babbled on. 'My father had left a note on the door to say he was at The Buckingham but I couldn't read it by the light of the street lamp.'

'Izzie,' Mr Umberto said, 'calm now. It's all right.'

Blundering on, Izzie went on to tell them that her search for her sister had taken her to Portsmouth and that Linda had been badly injured by one of the gang (she couldn't bring herself to say *that* word). 'Linda,' she went on to tell them, 'is still in hospital but she will get better, which is why I didn't come round to the café before. I'm sorry.'

She was vaguely aware of their shocked faces and she suddenly felt embarrassed that she'd blurted it all out like that. She wiped her eyes and blew her nose a third time. 'I keep thinking that Mr Semadini's death is all my fault,' she whimpered miserably.

Mr Umberto put his hand up to stop her but Izzie cried out, 'I tried to stop the bleeding, really I did. Do you think I pressed down too hard?'

'No, no,' said Umberto putting his hand on Izzie's shoulder. 'You mustn't think that.'

'I was only trying to help,' Izzie said, wiping her eyes with Bentio's already sodden handkerchief.

'Izzie . . .' Benito began.

'But the thing is,' Izzie cried, 'I didn't know what to do. I'm really sorry. I didn't mean to kill him—'

'Izzie,' Benito interrupted more loudly, 'we are trying to tell you, Giacomo isn't dead.'

Izzie froze. 'What?'

'Giacomo isn't dead,' Mr Umberto repeated.

Izzie blinked and looked at Benito for confirmation.

'That's right,' he said. 'You saved his life.'

'The doctors tell us he wouldn't be alive if it weren't for you,' Mr Umberto chipped in.

Izzie clamped her hand over her mouth, her eyes wide. 'He's alive?'

Benito nodded. 'And what's more, he keeps asking for you.'

'But the policeman said it looked like a murder case.'

'Then he was stupid,' cried Mr Umberto.

Izzie rose to her feet. 'Can I see him now?'

Mr Umberto chuckled. 'You know what they're like in the hospital,' he said. 'Visiting is from three this afternoon.'

Izzie was trembling but she managed a small smile. 'I can hardly believe it,' she said. 'You're sure he's alive? He's really alive?'

The two men chuckled then Umberto said, 'Yes, my dear, he is really alive.'

The remaining few hours of that morning had dragged along so slowly even though they were all very busy. Izzie helped Giacomo's cousins with some clearing up and now that the shop, kitchen and the stairs were in pristine condition, Mr Umberto created a sign to put on the door. They would re-open in the morning.

The story was in the new issue of the *Herald* and so the public were obviously concerned. The whole time they had been there with the blinds down, people had rattled the letterbox and pushed get well cards through the door. It felt as if the whole town was genuinely upset that Mr Semadini was in hospital.

*

When she got to the hospital, they told her Giacomo was in a room on his own. Benito and Umberto explained that although he was still weak, he was making good progress. Miraculously, although he had lost a lot of blood, the bullet had missed all of his vital organs. He was asleep when she came into the room.

As quietly as she could, Izzie pulled up a chair to sit down. She stayed very still, watching the rise and fall of his chest. How she longed to reach out and touch him. A lump like a yawning chasm was forming in her throat and it was a struggle not to cry tears of relief. She shivered. After a few minutes he opened his eyes and when he saw her, he smiled.

'Isobelle.'

How wonderful to hear him say her name like that. Izzie swallowed hard and took a breath to control her feelings. She put the little toy bear onto the sheet near his hand. 'How are you feeling?'

He reached out and grasped the bear. 'I am so glad you are back.'

Izzie thought he was talking to the bear but then he reached for her hand. 'Oh, Isobelle. My darling, my love.'

The lump in her throat seemed to grow bigger. She was having difficulty speaking. My darling? He'd called her my darling, my love . . . She blinked in a vain hope to prevent her tears from falling.

'You saved my life,' he whispered. 'Thank you.'

'You're welcome,' she said hoarsely and with a slight shrug.

He laughed softly. 'I should have told you,' he went on. 'Dear Isobelle, I love you so much.'

'Oh, Mr Semadini,' she said, tears trickling down her cheeks.

He shifted awkwardly and painfully to come closer and comfort her. 'No, no, don't cry my darling. Please. It's all right.'

'I love you too Mr—'

'Giacomo,' he corrected.

'I love you too, Giacomo,' she said tenderly, 'but you're going to hate me when I tell you that my sister's friends were the people who robbed and shot you. I'm so sorry.'

'I could never hate you, my darling,' he said softly.

'But I feel like this is all my fault,' said Izzie.

'How can you think that?' he said gently. 'No one knew that I planned to come back early.'

'Yes, but—' she began again.

'No,' he said firmly. 'No more talk of terrible things. All that matters is that you are here.' He locked his eyes to hers. 'Isobelle . . . my darling. I want to kiss you.'

She rose to her feet and bent over him. Featherlight, he touched her cheek with his left hand as she lowered her head towards him. His kiss was so sweet and so gentle. She was left with the desire for more, but she didn't want to tire him. As she sat back down, he grasped her hand and put it hungrily to his lips.

They stayed as they were for a little while, just looking at each other and smiling. There were no words but every now and then he would caress her fingers a little more firmly. After a few minutes she could see he was struggling to keep his eyes open.

'I'm going to go now,' she said softly.

His eyes suddenly widened with an anxious look.

'You need to sleep.'

'But you will come again tomorrow?'

'Of course I will,' she said. 'Tell you what, I'll stay until you're asleep.'

'I shall fight it all the way,' he said, his eyelids closing.

Forty-Three

The judge looked over his horn rimmed glasses and frowned at Linda. 'I think even you must realise by now that you've been a very silly young woman,' he said sternly.

It was four months later and they were all in Lewes Crown Court. After a trial lasting four days, John Middleton had been found guilty of robbery, stealing a car and vandalism. The week before, Raymond Perryman had been found guilty of the armed robbery and more importantly guilty of the wilful murder of Paul Dawkins and the attempted murder of Giacomo Semadini. Ray had insisted Paul's death was an accident; that he tripped and fell as he was chasing him and the gun went off.

He had missed receiving the death penalty by a mere three days. The crime had taken place on Saturday and Raymond had turned eighteen on Monday. Had he already been eighteen when he committed the murder, he would have had to face the hangman.

The police had caught up with Ray in Southampton where he was on the lookout for a ship to make his escape. For the murder and attempted murder, he was to be detained at her Majesty's pleasure for eight years with three years hard labour. His cowardly attack on Linda was to remain on the books.

'Your sentence would have been much longer,' the judge told him soberly, 'but I have taken into account that you showed a morsel of remorse after the event. I have no doubt that you were the person who made the anonymous telephone call to the police alerting them to the plight of the young girl. Had you not done so, the person in question would almost certainly have died as a consequence of her injuries.'

Listening to all this, Izzie gritted her teeth. That Raymond wasn't even charged with the attack on Linda was a bitter pill to swallow. It seemed that there was always one rule for men and quite another for women.

Linda had faced charges of being an accessory after the fact but it didn't take long for the jury to clear her of all charges. As he discharged her, the judge told her he was going to leave her with a fatherly warning.

'I want you to go away from here and think very carefully about your decisions in life,' he continued. 'You may not think so right now, but you have been very lucky.'

Sitting in the court room, Izzie bristled. How grossly unfair that the judge thought fit to give Linda a bit of a telling off. By pointing out that because she had run away with Ray and had put herself in a precarious position, he was implying that being raped (although, of course, no one mentioned *that* word) was partly her fault! There was no doubt in anyone's mind that Raymond had violated her but the police deemed that her willingness to go with him, coupled with Raymond's assertion that it was Paul who had attacked her, which was why he had chased him, meant it would be doubly difficult to make a case. The bottom line was, it was her word against his. Furthermore, the police had advised that should the crime be made public, her reputation would be in ruins and as angry as he was, Bill didn't want Linda to suffer the humiliation of public disgrace.

Linda took what the judge was saying exactly the way Izzie would have expected. 'Oh yes, Sir,' she said in a small voice, her eyes downcast, 'and I have learned my lesson.' She raised her head and looked him straight in the eye. 'From now on I shall be a paragon of virtue.'

Izzie put her hand over her mouth to suppress a smile. The judge didn't seem to realise she was being sarcastic.

In view of her contrite attitude, the judge took out an order forbidding what he called 'scurrilous Sunday newspapers' from printing her name or hounding her for her story.

Linda glanced across the court room towards Izzie and gave her a watery smile.

As for John, he was to be detained at her Majesty's pleasure for two years. The judge took into account that although John was part of the robbery, he hadn't actually made off with any of the money. He had also confessed to another break-in but because the victim hadn't reported the crime or made a subsequent complaint, no further action was taken.

The police decided not to prosecute Bill Baxter for affray. Witness statements had been garbled and confused. As far as Izzie was concerned, now that he was firmly under Mavis' thumb, from now on he would stay on the straight and narrow. Funnily enough, in the short time she had known her, Izzie had grown to like Mavis and they got on well. She made Dad happy.

As the two boys were taken down, Linda joined her mother and sister on the benches outside the court room.

Doris squeezed her daughter's hand. In the run up to the trial, they too had reconciled. While she was still in hospital Linda had actually asked for her mother so Izzie had written to her that night. By the time Linda arrived at Courtlands, Doris and Arthur were waiting for her. Their reunion had been tearful with each trying to outdo the other with apologies, and since then, she and Linda had been frequent visitors to the Egremont Arms where Doris had taught them both the art of baking.

'I'm so glad that's over,' said Linda. 'It's a bit unfair that he got away with what he did to me but I'm glad I didn't have to stand up there in front of all those people and tell them. Did you hear what that pompous ass of a judge said to me?'

Izzie grinned.

'Try and put all this behind you,' Doris advised. 'Think of today as the first day of the rest of your life.'

They heard someone clear his throat. Bill Baxter was waiting for his turn to hug his daughter. Linda stood to her feet. As they embraced, Bill gave Doris a curt nod of the head. Izzie had persuaded him to meet Doris and Arthur and he agreed. Bill had also agreed to give her a divorce and soon there would be a series of weddings in the family. In more ways than one, 1953 promised to be a momentous year. Doris was to marry Arthur on Easter Saturday, April 4th, and Bill was to marry Mavis in May.

Later on in June, Izzie and Giacomo were to be married and it promised to be a lavish wedding. Linda was to be chief bridesmaid with Liliana and her older sister as younger brides-maids. Although Izzie hadn't told Giacomo, she planned to have the little bear incorporated into her wedding bouquet for the occasion. She understood the heartache he'd felt at losing his little boy and it was her way of telling him that although she was now his wife, Gianni and Maria would never be forgotten. When it came to the guest list, it turned out that Giacomo's cousins, Umberto and Benito, were just the tip of the iceberg when it came to his family.

'The guest list is so long,' Izzie teased, 'Café Bellissimo wouldn't be nearly big enough. Why not just invite the whole of Italy and be done with it.'

He had just smiled and crushed her to him with what he called a Latin lover's kiss.

As they left the courts in Lewes, she and Giacomo waved

goodbye to her mother and Arthur, as Arthur was anxious to get back to the Egremont to open up before six o'clock.

Linda and Mavis squeezed into the front of her father's lorry.

Left together on the pavement, Giacomo laced his fingers through hers. 'Happy?'

Izzie nodded. 'Couldn't be happier,' she whispered.

They strolled towards the Maltings where he had parked his car. As they reached an area known as the Magic Circle, Giacomo drew her closer and pointed to a park bench. 'I want to show you something.'

When they were seated, he drew some photographs out from the inside pocket of his jacket. Izzie smiled, curious. 'What's this?'

'It's a place where I think we could open a bistro.'

The snapshots were of a shop set back from the road.

'This will be the car park,' he said pointing to quite a large area in the front.

Izzie nodded. The interior needed updating but the kitchen area, much larger than the Café Bellissimo, was really good. As Giacomo began waxing lyrical about his amazing find, Izzie was quiet. 'You don't like it,' he said, disappointed.

'Is there no street parking?' she asked.

'Yes, plenty. Why?'

She paused then said, 'Why not use that area in the front for more tables? Look, if you put some sort of canvas covering over there, you could have tables as far as there. That way, it would be a real Italian bistro.'

A slow smile crept over his face. 'So you do like it.'

'I love it, darling,' she said, 'and I'm sure you'll make it the best eating house for miles around.'

'Maybe you would make your secret recipe pies for a lunch time snack?' he suggested.

'So you did like them?' she teased. When she had presented him with one of Polly's pies last week, he had been a little reserved in his judgement. At the time she was disappointed, but perhaps he was just teasing her after all.

She paused. 'Where is the restaurant?'

'Bournemouth,' he said. 'A place called Lansdowne.'

Izzie flung her arms around his neck. 'But that's wonderful,' she cried. 'I had such lovely times there with dear old Mrs Shilling and her sister lived in Lansdowne.'

'That's what gave me the idea,' he said. 'I know you like being near the sea and I happen to know that they have a very good newspaper on the lookout for women journalists.'

'Now who's busy fixing things,' she said. 'Mr and Mrs Semadini, at home by the sea.'

They kissed. 'There's something else,' he went on. 'Our honeymoon.'

'You said we couldn't afford one.'

'I know, but it seems that our families and the customers in the Café Bellissimo have all been clubbing together.'

'*Our* families?' she gasped. 'Mine as well?'

He nodded. 'Your father was particularly generous.' With that, he drew an envelope from his jacket pocket. Inside, Izzie found tickets for a coach trip. She squealed with delight. 'Venice!' she cried. 'We're going to Venice?'

'Yes, thanks to Umberto, Benito, your father, your step-father . . .' he said counting on his fingers.

Izzie was laughing and crying at the same time.

'Happy?' he asked.

She nodded vigorously, hardly able to take it all in.

He suddenly looked grave. 'And are you really sure you want to marry such an old man?'

Izzie pretended to give the matter some considerable thought. 'Well, I did have a good deal of practice looking after the elderly when I worked for Mrs Shilling,' she said. She grinned and added suggestively. 'I was very good at back rubs.'

She heard Giacomo chuckle as his lips brushed her hair. 'I can't wait for one of those,' he murmured.

Acknowledgements

I should like to thank the Avon team for all their help and guidance in writing this book. I couldn't have done it without you! I always admire the skills of the editors and copy editors whose eagle eyes pick up so many mistakes and missed out words from a manuscript I have already read a dozen times. I really do become 'word blind' at times. Thank you.

I'd also like to thank my agent Juliet Burton who is always there with an encouraging word and a friendly chat.

Thanks, too, to all my readers. Now hands up, who would like to come with me for an ice cream in the Café Bellissimo!

A comment from the author:
I am sure that some of you will be annoyed that Ray apparently 'got away with' what he did to Linda, and quite rightly so. We live in very different times now. Back then (1950) a girl's reputation was all important. I remember my mother telling me boys didn't marry girls who were 'used goods'. There seems to have been a common misconception that if a girl got raped it was somehow her fault, her dress was too flashy, she led him on, she shouldn't have been out at that time of night . . . Grossly unfair and not true of course. Personally, I don't subscribe to that view. Rape is rape and is a despicable crime but for the purposes of the story I have tried to reflect the attitudes of the day.

Read on for a short story
from Pam Weaver. . .

Pineapple Jack

The story of the beginning of Polly's pies

The chilly late afternoon mist from the River Thames swirled around her ankles making Polly Patterson shiver. Behind her back, the bright lights of the Twopenny Hop cast eerie shadows onto the street. Heavily made-up girls in gaudy dresses and scrubbed up men with flashy neckerchiefs were already crowded around the doorway, anxious to get in. After a hard day's work they were ready to enjoy themselves through the night. Polly could hear the sound of laughter and the clay hornpipes. The dancing was about to begin.

Pushing back a stray curl, Polly stood on tiptoe, straining her eyes down the street for a glimpse of Pineapple Jack. He would be head and shoulders above the rest if he was there, but although she searched and searched, she couldn't see him. He wasn't coming. Suppressing a sudden pang of disappointment she chewed the side of her cheek anxiously. He was a bit late, that was all. She trusted him. They'd made a promise together and he wasn't the sort to let you down.

Her mother had raised her eyebrows when Polly told her what she'd done.

'And you've trusted him with a shilling?'

'Of course.'

'A whole shilling?'

'It was my share of the bargain, Mother,' she'd said indignantly.

'Then that's the last you'll see of him or your shilling,' her mother trumpeted.

Polly stepped out into the thoroughfare and looked up and down the street once again. He will come, she told herself firmly, he will.

'Yoo-hoo.'

Polly turned to see Edith, her best friend, coming up behind her. Quick as a flash she put the hand holding the bunch of snowdrops she'd just bought from old Rosie the flower lady behind her back. She wished now that she hadn't bought them. Probably they were a step too far but they'd looked so pretty and poor old Rosie looked half frozen.

'Nearly time to go home,' she'd said as Rosie had handed her the snowdrops.

'Can't go yet, lovey,' Rosie said. 'Nobody's buying.' And Polly's heart had gone out to her. The life of a humble street seller in Victorian London was hard.

Edith was waving. Polly waved back and smiled to herself. Edith was wearing her dancing gown and she looked really nice. It was only a faded hand-me-down but it was Edith's pride and joy. Polly had been with her when she'd bought it off the rag and bone man in London Road.

'Belonged to a great lady, did that,' he told them, smiling through his black teeth. 'Wore it to a great ball, so she did.'

There was no doubt that it was a very pretty gown, or it had been once upon a time, but Polly didn't believe a word of the yarn he was spinning. Still, her friend had parted with her hard earned pennies and Polly had helped her mend the tears, putting scraps of fine lace over the most damaged parts.

'Don't you look a picture,' said Polly as Edith drew near. 'Go on, give me a twirl.'

Edith spun around. 'You look pretty good yourself,' she said when she stopped. 'I've never seen that dress before.'

Polly smoothed the front of her gown with her hand and inclined her head as she bobbed a curtsey. 'Why thank you kindly, Mam,' she teased but she didn't tell her friend why she was wearing it.

Edith was arm-in-arm with Paddy Riley. A good-looking man, he worked in the docks and his flame coloured hair, currently tucked rakishly under a cloth cap, was as striking as his temper.

Edith smiled up at him. 'Doesn't she look lovely, Paddy?'

'Almost as good as one of them pies she bakes,' Paddy joked.

Edith gave him a hefty nudge. 'You comin' in to the dance, Poll?'

'Nope,' Polly answered crisply. 'I'm waitin' fer Jack.'

Paddy laughed out loud. 'Ah, begorra, then you'll be there for the night,' he said. 'I heard he'd come in to some money. They say he's gone over the river.' He smiled maliciously. 'Maybe to a gambling joint?'

Polly felt her cheeks flame. For a split second she felt a slither of panic but then she tossed her head proudly and said, 'He'll be back soon enough.'

Edith frowned, puzzled. 'What are you up to Polly Patterson? Come on, out with it.'

'Well, if you must know, he's gone to look fer a Parson,' said Polly.

'Why would ye be wantin' one of them?' Paddy said incredulously.

'To arrange me weddin' day.'

Paddy threw back his head and laughed. 'Wedding day?' he boomed. 'What, you and Pineapple Jack?'

'What's wrong with that?' Polly retorted indignantly.

'Oh, Polly,' Edith cooed, 'why didn't you tell me?'

361

'She's gone off her head, Edie.'

Polly turned away.

'Getting wed?' Paddy scoffed. 'Nobody round 'ere gets married.'

'You might laugh, Paddy Riley,' Polly said indignantly. 'But Jack knows what I wants. I told him I wants to be a wife with a 'ome of me own and that's what he've promised.'

'Then more fool him.' He slipped his arm around Edith's waist. 'You should do the same as me and Edie. We're happy enough without no wedding, ain't we girl.'

'You won't find me being anybody's helpmate,' Polly said stoutly. 'I've seen too many women left high and dry with a chance child to bring up on their own to go down that road.'

Edith's face flushed as her hand went to her gently rounded belly but Polly was unrepentant. 'I'll be wed proper before I give myself to Pineapple Jack.'

'Well then good luck to you Poll,' said Edith. She leaned forward and gave her friend a kiss on the cheek. 'I just wish you'd told me, that's all. I would have come with you to wish you well.'

Suddenly sober and serious, Paddy gave Edith an anxious glance. 'You got ideas way above your station, Polly Patterson,' he retorted, 'and that's a fact.' Then, grabbing Edith by the arm, he thrust her through the door.

Polly smiled sadly to herself. Her friend had been living with him for about six months. They had a dingy room in a large house with many other families and even though Edith was pregnant, it was obvious Paddy didn't want her getting any ideas about marriage. He wasn't the type to stick around either.

As Paddy and Edith walked in, a blast of warm air from inside the dance hall drifted into the street, teasing her cold limbs and making Polly realise just how cold she was. She shivered. There was no doubt that Polly was tempted to go inside just to warm up, but she was resolute. She stamped her freezing feet defiantly as she looked up and down the street again. Where was he? Oh Jack, I hope you're not going to let me down. You promised. You promised.

*

'But you promised,' her mother had cried helplessly.

A lot had happened in the five years since her father's death. Back then, Polly was only eleven years old but she would never forget the moment the doctor had shaken his head and said to her mother, 'I'm sorry, Alice. There's nothing more we can do.'

'You said if I brought him to the hospital, he'd get well.'

Alice had wept. They were standing in the middle of an overcrowded ward full of sick people. Some coughed, some were vomiting into enamel bowls and others was calling the over stretched nurses for privy-pots. The smell, even in this scrubbed and disinfected place, was indescribable.

'I'm afraid I'm not God,' said the doctor.

Alice Patterson wiped her eyes and stiffened. Polly reached for her mother's hand. She was right. This wasn't what they'd expected to hear.

It was almost unheard of for a doctor to come out for the likes of them but Doctor Mayhew had a good deal of respect for her father. They had met on the docks and were both trying to improve the working conditions of the dockers. It was an uphill struggle against employers who would sooner sack a man than make life easier for him. After Henry had missed an appointment with Doctor Mayhew, he had turned up at the door to see what had happened. When the doctor had seen the state her father was in, he had insisted that they take him to the infirmary.

Only three days before Henry had been as fit as a fiddle, but then he had come home with a bad headache. A ship had come into port with a load of Irish workers bound for London from Liverpool. Refugees from poverty and with few resources of their own, they had been kept below decks in unsanitary conditions. The weather had been stormy, the ship delayed, and when the hatches were finally lifted, the men were very poorly. Henry Patterson had been one of those who had helped the sick men onto the dockside where they were dispatched either to the infirmary or to the mortuary.

'I ain't seen noffin' like it,' he told his wife when he came home that night. 'They was eaten alive by the lice and fleas; chucking up all over the place and no time to get to a privy-pot.'

Over the next day or so, Henry's symptoms had worsened until he had not only a high temperature, diarrhoea and a dry cough, but also a spotty rash all over his chest. It came as no real surprise when Doctor Mayhew gave his diagnosis; typhus fever.

'This is a highly contagious condition,' Doctor Mayhew told her mother as he held a handkerchief over his own nose. 'If your husband stays at home there is no doubt that he will die. This sickness will rampage through this building like wild fire and I cannot allow that to happen.'

'I can look after him,' Alice had pleaded. 'Just tell me what to do.'

Doctor Mayhew shook his head. 'If you won't allow him to come willingly,' the doctor told her, 'I shall have to inform the authorities and they will take him forcibly.'

Polly and her mother were alarmed. The thought of her dear father being dragged off against his will was too awful to think about.

'I am sure that once he's in hospital his condition will improve,' the doctor had assured her mother.

Their neighbours had been more sceptical. 'For the love of

God, Alice, don't send him to the infirmary,' Betty Cummings had said. 'Nobody comes out of that place alive, you mark my words.'

Her mother had been torn. Should she nurse Henry at home and risk the rest of the family getting the fever and incur the disapproval of the authorities or do as she was bidden? Nobody liked the idea of hospitals. Betty wasn't alone in her assumption that anyone who went to the infirmary was doomed to die. 'If your time is up,' Betty had insisted, 'better to be with your family than in a room full of strangers.'

The whole of her life, Polly had been surrounded by poverty, squalor and misery but her home was better than most in the area. She had grown up in three rooms on the first floor of the building with her parents and siblings. To begin with, there had been six of them but now there was only Polly and her younger brother Walter. Their mother, Alice, kept a clean house. Everything shone, the floors were spotless, the walls had been recently papered and the main room boasted two comfortable chairs and several stools. The cramped bedroom had two beds pushed together, one larger than the other, and both beds were covered with a multi-coloured patchwork quilt, all hand stitched by Alice herself. Their clothes were stored in a large chest of drawers. The third room was a small kitchen where Alice did all of her cooking and the washing. Polly's father had worked on the docks all of his life and was now well respected gaffer, which made it seem all the more ironic that he should succumb to a disease associated with dirt and vermin.

'Keep his privy-pot separate from the rest of the family,' Alice had told Polly when Henry first began to have the runs. 'And wash yer hands after you've cleaned him up.'

Her mother cleaned the surgery rooms for the doctor so she'd been schooled in how to keep things clean. Polly did as she was bidden religiously but now, despite all of their best efforts, here was Doctor Mayhew telling them that her father was going to die.

*

They buried Henry a few days later and with his passing, their fortunes took a nose-dive. They would have to give up their rooms on the first floor as the rent was more than they could afford. Alice went into a deep depression, which was hardly surprising. Polly's mother had not only lost her husband but two of her children; Agnes, aged three, had died of diphtheria before Polly was born, and when she was four, ten-month-old baby Silas had choked to death on a piece of bread. To add to her sorrow, Polly's brother, Matthew, who should have taken on the role of head of the family, had landed himself in serious trouble and had been arrested. Now he languished in Newgate jail.

'It's a mercy,' Alice told her daughter, 'that he wasn't transported to the other side of the world.'

Her mother was still scarred by the memory of her brother Dicken, who many years before had been one of the last British prisoners to be transported to New South Wales. Alice had been just six years old and because Dicken couldn't read or write, she had never heard from him again.

With the head of the household gone and her mother in no fit state to make decisions, it fell to Polly to look for somewhere to live. In the end, she found a more affordable basement room not far from Bethnal Green. It was a lot smaller than they were used to but with only the three of them – Polly, her mother and her younger brother Walter – it wouldn't be too cramped. Polly could see the disappointment on her mother's face. 'Don't worry,' she assured her. 'Once I've cleaned it up, it'll be grand.'

Polly's eldest brother, Sid, who had a family of his own over in Shoreditch, was a costermonger. He bought fruit and vegetables wholesale and sold it on in the markets. The life of a costermonger wasn't easy but he did alright, so when their father died, he gave Polly work. By the time she was twelve, Polly was well used to being up at four in the morning in the summer and six o'clock in the winter. She wasn't afraid of hard work either and she began by selling oranges in the summer and apples in the winter.

All day long she would call, 'Fine Kent apples. Oranges two a penny,' until her voice was gone.

The life of a costermonger was short and the women, especially those who, by the time they were twenty, already had several children, were old before their time. Unusually for a girl of Polly's age, she was ambitious. She began people watching, observing the habits of travellers, especially in the better part of town. What she was looking for was some sort of need; something which perhaps even the people themselves didn't know they wanted and she planned to be the first to provide it.

Once she had pulled herself together after her husband's death, Alice took in washing. Polly's younger brother Walter, who was seven at the time their father died, walked with Sid's donkey cart and took his turn to shout out their wares when Sid had lost his voice. Thus, on a good week, between the three of them they brought in as much as fifteen shillings. Polly was confident that Sid would always look after their mother but Polly knew that if she herself didn't hitch up with someone, she would be on her own. But with no capital and no good ideas, what could she do to better her position?

By the time she had turned thirteen, Polly decided the life of a street-seller wasn't for her. She was tired of the early mornings, the haggling, the lousy weather on market days and having to stay out all day in the open until the market was lit by naphtha flares and tallow candles.

'It's all very well saying you're fed up with it,' her mother complained. 'What else can you do?'

*

One day, Polly got home early and found that Sid had called in to see their mother. They were sitting at the kitchen table drinking tea.

'How d'you get on?' asked Sid.

'All sold out,' said Polly. 'Some soldiers came marching by and when the sergeant told them to fall out, they pounced on my oranges and had the lot.'

Sid chuckled. 'We could do with more days like that, girl.'

He looked hot and tired but he'd had a good day as well. Walter sat at the table with his head on his arms struggling to keep his eyes open.

'How do you fancy going hop-picking in the country?'

Sid's question took Polly by surprise. Of course she'd heard tell of hop-picking in Kent but it all sounded so far away you might as well have asked her to go to the far side of the moon. She'd never stepped outside of London. What exactly was hop-picking? How would she get there?

'Cat got yer tongue?' Sid teased. 'We're all going. I'm taking Walter and me missus suggested you and Ma might like to come too.'

'But how . . .' Polly began.

'You let me worry about that,' said Sid. 'Just say you'll come.'

Alice took a little persuading. 'What about me customers?' she cried. 'Who'll do their washing?'

'Let 'em do it themselves for a change,' said Sid. 'They'll appreciate you all the more when you gets back.'

'How long will we be gone?'

Sid shrugged. 'Five, six weeks.'

'Five weeks!' Alice cried. She looked unconvinced.

'It'll be like a little holiday for you, Ma.'

And when Sid went on to say that they only wanted her to look after her grandchildren and cook a meal for everybody in the evening, she wavered. 'Fresh air and only the birds for company,' he went on. 'It'll do you the power of good. You'll love it, Ma.' Sid turned to Polly. 'Hop-picking is hard work,' her brother told her, 'but it pays well and you'll be able to breathe in the fresh Kent country air all day long, Poll, so what do you say?'

*

They set off together a week later. They travelled by train, another experience Polly had never had before. Their ticket was third class and the carriages were very crowded, but once she got used to the movement of the train and trusted that it wouldn't fall over, Polly enjoyed the ride. The price of her ticket had eaten a fair sized hole into her savings but Sid had been very persuasive as to the benefits.

They were well loaded because they had had to take all but the kitchen sink. Because she knew that when they got there it would take a while to settle, Alice had made them a pie each to tide them over until she could prepare an evening meal.

When they arrived at the station, several horses and wagons waited outside. Everybody piled on board and they set off for the hop fields. People were very friendly and those who had been before caught up with old friends. Polly was over-awed by it all. She'd never seen a cow in a field before and the wide open spaces and the green of the countryside almost took her breath away. When they passed through a village or by a small cottage, everyone would wave and the people waved back. Little kids ran after the wagons until they grew tired. Polly envied their freedom.

Polly's family were billeted along with a couple of other families in a big barn. It was clean and airy with pallets for beds. Their mattresses were stuffed with hay and smelled so fresh and sweet. At one end of the barn there was a pile of faggots which were used to light a fire for the cooking. A large skillet and a cooking pot had been provided under a covered roof outside the barn. It was here that Alice and a couple of other women were to do their cooking. To keep the food safe from the mice, it was locked in large boxes and stored inside an old shepherd's hut. Everyone was given their own personal key.

The next day, Polly and the other hop-pickers met by the field. She and Sid were given a 'bin', a very large sack held open by a framework of poles at each end. They had to start at the bottom of the row and work their way along, picking as they went. When the bin was full, they had to call for the Tally man who would keep a record of how many basketfuls they had gathered. They were paid according to the weight of hops they had picked. The seasoned pickers worked very quickly and Polly and Sid soon got the hang of it. It was repetitive and hard work but the day sped by. They picked from Monday to Friday but Saturday and Sunday was their own. In the evening, they came back to the barn for their meal and while the children played, the older people would gather around the camp fire, swapping stories and singing songs.

It wasn't long before Polly had some colour in her cheeks and Alice was back to her old self. Walter worked steadily and enjoyed mucking about with the other young lads in the evening.

'Haven't seen you here before?'

Polly was strolling along the hedgerow looking for blackberries when a young man drew alongside her. He was slightly taller than her with a mop of dark hair and striking brown eyes. Only a few years older than her, he had a ready smile and a gentle voice.

'My first time,' said Polly. She reached up for a particularly juicy looking blackberry and put it in her bowl. The man stretched above her and pulled down the whole branch for her to pick the rest of the berries. 'Thank you.' She smiled.

'Are you here with your family?' he asked.

Polly nodded. 'In the barn. And you?'

'I have a tent in the field on my own,' he said matter-of-factly. 'This is my first time too.'

She carried on picking and they chatted about nothing in particular.

'What's yer name?'

'Polly. What's yours?'

'Jack,' he said, his bright eyes dancing with laughter. 'They calls me Pineapple Jack.'

Polly gave him a puzzled look until he went on to explain that he'd been among the first to see the potential of the strange and exotic fruits from the Bahamas that gave him his name.

'Messrs Keeting and Hunt buy them directly from the shipping wharf at four pence each,' he explained. 'To start with, I had the over ripe fruit they didn't want at a better price and I sold them at a shilling each or tuppence a slice.' He grinned. 'I done well, but the trick is to keep one step ahead of the competition.'

She found out that he worked as a costermonger way over in Spitalfields. 'I keep to that,' he explained, 'because it's not such a big market. There's a lot less competition than Covent Garden or Billingsgate. Now I'm looking for an opening nobody else has found.'

Polly chuckled. 'You and me both.'

'Got any good ideas then?'

'Plenty,' she teased, 'but I'm not telling you.'

They'd been on the hop farm three weeks when everybody decided to have a dance. The weather was good so they cleared an area outside the barn and several pickers turned up with their musical instruments. They had managed to pull together a couple of clay pipes, a fiddle and a drum. Rehearsals were a bit of an endurance but nobody minded much. The singers usually drowned out the worst of it and everyone had a laugh anyway.

Polly had only brought a couple of dresses but she and the other girls pampered each other by doing each other's hair and making daisy chain halos, and Polly put wild flowers in her hair. She and Alice baked a few pies for the celebration and by the time everyone had finished, the plank suspended over two hay bales positively groaned with food. Some of the men had walked into the nearest village to buy beer and by six o'clock they were ready.

By far, the most handsome man there was Pineapple Jack. The other lads were neat and tidy but he looked dashing and Polly was the envy of every girl on the farm when he danced with her.

*

Back home in Bethnal Green, it was a bit of a struggle to get used to the foul air of the city once again. Soon, the autumn would give way to winter and people would be lighting fires. Polly quickly lost the summer tan she had gained in the hop fields and she did her best to settle back into normal life again. Only now she had another interest. Pies.

'I've got myself a job in Jacob Shulman's bakery.'

Her mother put her hand to her cheeks in horror. 'You must

be mad, my girl,' she said. 'From what I hear, he's a hard task-master.'

'You know I'm not a-feared of hard work, Mother,' said Polly, 'and he pays a fair wage. One day I'm going to open a pie shop.'

Her mother had snorted. 'Don't be daft, girl,' she said. 'You need money and a good business head for that.'

Polly didn't argue. She knew that but if she was going to better herself, what better way than to learn from the grass roots up?

It was hard work, hot and tiring, but Polly was doing more than baking pastry. She was watching every aspect of the business. Before her father died, her mother had taught her to cook, something which had been rekindled in Kent, but to cook on a more commercial scale was another skill altogether. She had noticed when they were on the train on their way to the hop fields, that a lot of people were hungry. Some of the children cried for want of something to eat. Polly and her family had no such problem because her mother had baked them a pie each for the journey. The same thing had happened on the return journey. Polly thought about this long and hard. Jacob Shulman's pie men sold large family-size pies but Polly was sure there might be demand for a small individual pie, just a few mouthfuls of which could take the edge off a hunger. And where would she sell them? Outside the railway station.

She stayed in the pie factory until she had saved enough to buy ingredients and a pie tray. Apparently there was a shop near the market where they sold ready-made trays at a reasonable price. For a few pennies more she could get her name written on the side of the tray. 'Polly's Pies.' It had a nice ring to it and when she collected it, she saw that the sign writer had even drawn a couple of steaming pies next to the words. Now she was ready to take her chance.

Getting up in the wee small hours, Polly baked as many pies

as she could before it was light. To keep them warm she covered them with a fleece. Then, from early morning, she was outside the railway station with her tray.

It wasn't long before her pies were the most popular in London.

'I dunno what it is about your pies,' her customers would say, 'but they're second to none. What d'you put in them?'

Polly would smile and say, 'Ah, that'll be my secret ingredient.' But even though they pressed her, and some – probably spies from Jacob Shulman's pie shop – even tempted her with money, she wouldn't divulge what that secret was. Her costermonger skills came in useful because she knew where to get the best bargains for the ingredients she needed. She began by making her pies for a penny and selling them for tuppence, but as her fame grew, so did her prices. Eventually she was doing so well, Alice was able to stop taking in washing and do what she enjoyed doing most, baking more pies.

'If we carry on like this,' Polly told her mother, 'it won't be long before we should be able to employ Walter as well.'

Polly soon progressed from a tray to a hand cart when her customers came to buy a pie. The pies were kept inside a hay box on the cart. That was a tip she'd gleaned from the night of the dance in Kent. The hay box kept hot food warm. She had bought the cart from the same place as she'd bought the pie tray and once again the sign writer had done a grand job. Polly wished she could tell him how much she appreciated him but he was never there.

Competition was tougher now. The pie men were offering smaller pies themselves, and Jacob Shulman was doing his best to lure her customers away, but there was something very special about Polly's pies.

It was soon after that when Polly met Jack again.

'Well if it isn't the blackberry girl,' cried Jack. 'Remember me?'

374

Polly pulled a face as if she was having a hard job but she remembered him only too well. It was lovely to see him and they struck up a friendship once again.

Jack was different from all the other costermongers. He wasn't interested in the penny gaff where the singing and dancing girls entertained. When he took her out, she noticed that he shunned the beer shops and gambling houses as well. He wasn't mean but, like her, he was careful with his money. He was friendly and he was popular. When she asked around, people told her Jack was a man with ambition. He had a reputation for hard work and he was keen to be his own boss.

'I'm goin' to get on, Poll,' he told her. 'I know they laughed and called me Pineapple Jack when I started on me own but the pineapples helped me get started, see?'

He had once brought a pineapple with him and he had asked her if he could use the corner of her cart to cut it up. Polly had been amazed to see just how many slices he could get from one pineapple. His slices were very thin but he was always honest and the customer knew what he was getting.

'But you can't sell pineapples all year round,' she said, 'so what do you sell now?'

He grinned. 'Don't yer know?'

Polly shook her head.

He pointed to her hand cart.

'You?' She gasped.

He nodded. 'It turns out that I'm quite good working with wood,' he said, 'and my old neighbour taught me sign writing, so I looked around the market and saw just how many people wanted something decent to display their wares.'

'And from trays you progressed to hand carts,' she said.

'That's about the size of it, Poll,' he said.

*

Their friendship had stretched for several months when he came to her with an offer she couldn't refuse.

'Remember that old shepherd's hut, Poll?' he said. 'Well, I've bought one.'

'Whatever for?'

'Tea,' he said with a grin. He pointed towards a shepherd's wooden hut on wheels that was parked further along the street. A man was serving a mug of tea through a specially prepared hatch on the side. 'Cold day like today, the traveller welcomes a warm drink.'

Polly shook her head in respect. She smiled. 'Good idea,' she said.

'If you fancy just cooking your pies,' he went on, 'I'll take all you got on offer and sell them through my hatch.'

Polly held her breath. No more standing for hours in the cold? It was very tempting and if anyone would succeed in selling the same number of pies she did, Jack could do it.

'I reckon your pie, a refreshing slice of my pineapple for afters and a cup of the old Rosie Lee would go down a treat together, watcher think, Poll?'

'I think you're a very clever man, Jack.'

A deal was struck with a trial period of three months and to seal it, they each spat on their own palms and shook hands.

Polly sold more pies than ever and employed Walter as runner to keep the hut in stock. Pineapple Jack added coffee and chocolate to his tea wagon and did so well he began a new location with another wagon outside King's Cross station. There were even plans afoot to have a third outside Paddington.

'The best thing would be to rent a shop on the concourse,' he told Polly. 'WHSmith's have got an agreement to put their newsagent inside. We should do the same.'

Polly was impressed by his understanding of the needs of the British public but she wondered how the 'powers that be' would react to a humble tea wagon owner setting up on the platform of their station. One thing was for sure, Pineapple Jack was certainly not put off by the challenge.

Before long, Polly had fallen in love with him. She knew she was an attractive girl and she was also aware that she turned many a head on the street. But she made it clear from the start that she wasn't available to just anybody, not even the toffs who offered her a 'good time' for as much as two guineas. The same rule applied to Jack, even though she knew he would never dream of offering her money for her favours.

Her friend Edith chided her for resisting his advances. 'You must be mad,' Edith used to tell her. 'You love him, don't you?'

'To the moon and back,' she'd say with a smile, 'but I know what I really want.'

Polly knew Jack didn't love her. He simply knew a good deal when he saw one. He was always kind and gentle and if she played her cards right, he could give her what she wanted more than anything else – respectability and a home of her own. That was why she played the waiting game. And whenever she longed for just one word of tenderness from Jack's lips, she would pull herself together and tell herself that she was a fool. There was more at stake than silly romantic nonsense. If Pineapple Jack asked her to wed, it would be because she was doing well with the pies and they could make a good living together.

'He'll grow tired of waiting,' Edith warned her. 'He'll find someone else to love.'

'What's love got to do with it?' Polly said stoutly. 'Love comes only to the chosen few. What Jack wants is a good worker.'

*

But it wasn't her ability to work wonders with a bit of scrag-end, that impressed Jack. It was her ambition. That's why a week

377

ago, when they were both down the market looking for good fruit and vegetables, he finally took the plunge.

'Whatcher fink, Poll,' he said. 'We both wants to get on. We could get a good living together. You ain't afraid of 'ard work and I'll look after you.'

Polly guessed that was about as romantic as Jack could be. She looked up into his earnest eyes. 'I'll go with you Jack,' she said, 'but I ain't just going to live with you. I wants to be a wife.'

His jaw dropped. 'A wife!'

Without blinking, Polly went on. 'And I wants a proper wedding, one with a parson and prayers and all.'

At first, he was completely struck dumb. In all of his nineteen years, Pineapple Jack had never once set foot inside a church. But one look at her determined face told him she'd have it no other way. Every part of him wanted her and with her help, he knew they could both make it out of the slums and move up in the world. If they got more shepherd's huts and did well, they could even move into a decent area. With Polly Patterson and her pies, the world and its oyster was just around the corner.

Jack took a deep breath. 'Right you are then, Poll. If you'll still have me, you shall have your weddin'.'

He'd set off with high hopes but it wasn't so easy to find a vicar in a church who would do it. It was the same old story. The rich were always suspicious of the poor.

*

The clergyman at St Saviour's was shocked when Jack turned up on his doorstep, and shooed him away with a wave of his podgy hand. 'Out of the question!' he cried when Jack told him what he wanted. 'I'll wager you've never been baptised, neither of you live in my parish and besides, the banns have to be called for three weeks before a wedding!'

The priest from Our Lady and the Angels wasn't much better. 'Are you a Catholic?' When Jack said no, he was convinced Jack was a thief. 'Be off with you, you scoundrel, or I'll call the constable. There's nothing worth stealing here.'

The London City Missioners listened sympathetically and would have helped but their mission hall didn't look much like a church. Polly had made it quite clear she wanted a proper wedding in a proper church with candles and prayers.

There was nothing for it but to cross the river. On the Surrey side of the Thames at New Cut, the press of the crowds on market days made the place more like a country fair. Hundreds of stalls, lit with dim tallow candles or the red smoky flame of grease lamps, littered the streets. The pavements were crowded with traders and buyers alike. Why hadn't he been here before? The place was ideal for his huts. He could just see it now. Pineapple slices and Polly's pies.

The thought of all those sales made his errand all the more urgent. Jack hurried from street to street looking for a place of worship but without success. He was almost to the point of despair, when he happened to bump into One-eyed Tom and a drinking companion. Over a mug of ale, Jack told Tom about Polly.

'You couldn't do better than Polly,' said Tom. 'If I were twenty years younger, I'd take her for a helpmate meself.'

'That's just it,' Jack sighed. 'My Poll wants a proper weddin', with a vicar and all.'

Tom put his mug of beer down. 'Parson here used to be a cleric,' he said, pointing to his companion.

'Used to be?' said Jack, puzzled.

'De-frocked, dear boy,' said the parson, looking up at him through rheumy red-rimmed eyes.

Jack blinked in surprise. 'Why?'

The parson lifted his almost empty mug of ale. 'This was my downfall, dear boy.' He sighed. 'Beware of the devil's brew.'

Jack thought for a minute. 'Do you remember all the words?'

'Of the marriage ceremony?' said the parson. 'Of course. I've done hundreds of them in my time.'

Jack placed two shillings onto the table in front of him, one was Polly's and the other his own. The parson reached for them, but Jack covered the coins with his hand. 'Here's the bargain,' he said, 'if I finds a church, will you wed Polly and me this evening?'

The parson stared at the back of Jack's hand and licked his lips thirstily but he shook his head. 'I'm sorry, dear boy. I would if I could but no church will allow me within its doors.'

The three men looked down dejectedly.

'There's old St Dunstans,' One-eyed Tom piped up. 'They're going to pull it down soon.'

'Pull it down?'

'To make way for the new railway station.'

'Ah, Charing Cross,' the parson added.

'Polly wants the real thing.' Jack sighed. 'I promised her.'

'I'll help you make it look good.' Tom's face shone with excitement. He poked the parson in the ribs. 'Then all you have to do is wed them.'

The parson was still staring at the back of Jack's hand. 'Ahh, but would it be legal?'

Jack began drawing the coins back. 'It's got to be a proper weddin',' he said, shaking his head. 'Polly wants it done in the sight of God.'

The parson grabbed Jack's wrist. 'I can certainly do that for you, dear boy,' he said. 'Everything we do is done in the sight of God!'

They both looked at Jack eagerly.

'Well?' asked One-eyed Tom.

'That's good enough for me!' cried Jack.

*

Polly was frozen to the marrow. She was still waiting on the street even though it must be a good half an hour after the time he'd told her to meet him. Tears of disappointment were biting the backs of her eyes when old Rosie the flower lady hurried by.

'All the best, Polly,' she said cheerfully.

Polly frowned. Why did she say that? She and Pineapple Jack had told no-one of their plans. 'You've finished early today,' she called after Rosie.

'Sold every last flower in me basket, didn't I,' she called back, and as she turned the corner Polly heard her cackling laughter.

Polly turned back and there he was, hurrying down the street towards her. Pulling her shawl more tightly around her shoulders, she shivered and took a deep breath.

'Sorry I'm late, Poll,' he called. 'I hope yer not froze to death.'

She smiled and shook her head. 'I'm fine,' she lied.

'It's all arranged, Poll,' he said, coming up to her.

When she turned her face to him, his heart skipped a beat. She looked as pretty as a picture. Funny how he'd never noticed what a beautiful shade of violet her eyes were before. She was clutching a sprig of snowdrops in one hand and he admired the pretty print dress she was wearing. Her hair shone even more than usual and she'd caught it up to the top of her head in a little circle of curls. It looked very attractive.

At his invitation, she slipped her arm through his and they walked back towards the river together. Jack couldn't help but stick his chest out. He felt that proud. That's how she made him feel, with her on his arm.

381

When, at last, he and Polly stood outside St Dunstan's, he could see she was shocked. It did look a mess from the outside. The windows were all boarded up and there were no lights. His heart sank. He shouldn't have done it. She'd be angry with him. He should never have tried to fool Polly.

'Ain't nobody there, Jack,' she wailed. 'Parson's gone home.'

'No, no,' he cried. 'He said he'd be waiting inside.'

He pushed open the heavy oak door, hoping and praying that the parson hadn't found someone else to buy him a drink since he'd left him only slightly tiddly inside the church.

The church was derelict but not yet denuded of furniture and fittings. Here and there a pew remained undamaged and the altar, though quite bare, was still intact. He had expected it to smell, but not the way it did. The scent of hundreds of flowers filled the air; Lily of the valley, primrose, hyacinth, and lilac. They were scattered all the way from the door up to the altar rail. Polly gasped. Jack opened his mouth to explain and apologise.

'Oh, Jack, it's so beautiful . . .'

It was then that he noticed the candles. They lit the way towards the front of the church where, on the steps leading to the altar, a great wooden eagle, with wings outstretched, held an empty flower basket. Jack heaved a sigh of relief to see the parson and One-eyed Tom standing one on either side. They each held a candle and the parson, swaying ever so slightly, smiled as Pineapple Jack stepped forward, taking Polly's hand.

Polly took in a breath. 'Oh Jack, listen,' she said, her eyes bright with excitement.

'What?'

She paused. 'Oh nothing . . . It's silly, but I thought I heard the rustle of angel wings.'

It was the daftest thing she'd ever said to him and had it been anyone else, he might have been tempted to laugh, but taking her lead, he cocked his ears and just for a moment he thought he could hear something too . . .

He looked back at her. Even though this run down dump of a place was so awful, she looked so happy, so beautiful. All at once, he felt a sudden pang of guilt and shame. This wasn't right. He'd have to tell her. He'd done his best; bought a whole basket of flowers from old Rosie and cleared away as much of the rubbish as he could in the time scale allowed but he couldn't let her go on believing a lie. All she'd wanted was a proper wedding.

'They're going to pull this place down soon, Poll,' he explained, the pain of her pending disappointment etched into his expression. 'Parson's a real parson but he don't have no church. He's a drunk, see? But I couldn't find no other.'

She looked into his eyes. 'I don't understand. Does that mean we can't be wed?'

Jack chewed his bottom lip. 'Parson says when he says the words for your shilling and mine, it will done be in the sight of God . . . but it ain't a proper weddin'.'

She hesitated for a second. 'I want to be your wife, Jack.'

'And I wants you to be my wife too, Poll,' he said, surprising even himself with his earnestness. He paused. 'You can walk away if you wants, Poll, but I promise I won't touch you until you are my wife.'

She said nothing and he was desperate now. 'London City Missioners tell me they can wed us but it'll have to be in their hall.'

'Then why didn't we go there?' she asked.

''Cos you said you wanted a proper church, Poll.'

'Oh, Jack . . .' She reached out and touched his face. Her cold fingers caressed him, featherlight. Jack closed his eyes, savouring the moment.

Pineapple Jack wasn't given to romantic gestures but as she

took her hand back, he grabbed it and kissed her palm. 'I'm sorry Poll.'

She smiled. 'Let's do both, Jack.'

He nodded and she slipped her arm in his.

Walking up the aisle, Polly didn't seem aware of the dust, destruction and damage all around her. A rat darted across the end of one of the pews and Jack held his breath, glancing anxiously at her face, afraid she might see.

'Are they going to build another church here, Jack?'

'The trains are coming, Poll,' said Jack. 'One day Charing Cross will be the railway capital of London.'

'Perhaps the passengers would like some of your pineapple pieces?' Polly said casually.

'And your pies,' he said.

All at once he stopped.

'What?' she said quietly. 'What is it, Jack?'

'Refreshments for railway passengers . . .' He was thinking aloud. 'I got some money saved. If we can't get a place on the station itself, we'll rent a place nearby. I can get some good stuff from the market. You could bake and when the passengers come—' He stopped mid-sentence, suddenly embarrassed by his own enthusiasm.

Polly threw back her head and laughed. 'Why wait for the railway passengers?' she said. 'The gangers who are going to build the station will need pies and pineapples too. We could set up another hut for them.'

He smiled slowly, his head whirling with plans. 'You're good for me Poll. You got a level head under them pretty curls.'

They continued their walk up the aisle.

'Are you ready, Jack?' said the parson and they reached the rail.

Oh, yes, thought Jack. Marrying Polly was the best idea he'd ever had . . . apart from selling those pineapples . . . He was on his way up in the world and she'd be just the right gal for him. A lifelong commitment. The idea had always scared him before, but not with Poll. 'Ready?' he said, looking directly at her.

'Oh yes, I'm ready.'

Polly made all of her promises looking directly into his eyes.

'For richer, for poorer, in sickness and in health, 'till death us do part . . .'

And as he returned her gaze, Pineapple Jack could feel his pulse quicken. She was lovely . . . so lovely. . .

'You may kiss the bride,' said the parson.

When Pineapple Jack reached out his hand and tenderly lifted her wayward curl to kiss her cheek, something wonderful surged in his heart.

'Poll,' he whispered for her ears only. 'I . . . I just want you to know, gal, that I'll always do my best by you.'

'Thank you, Jack.'

'And . . .'

'And?'

'And, I love you.'

Polly smiled up at him with tears in her eyes. 'Then I have everything I have ever wished for, Jack.'

When the ceremony was over, he paid the parson and gave One-eyed Tom enough to buy a drink. Then the two of them walked from St Dunstan's onto the street.

'I'll get on to the London City Missioners straight away, Poll,' he said.

'Promise?'

'I promise,' he said earnestly.

'Tomorrow?'

'First thing tomorrow.'

She lifted her face and he bent to kiss her. At first it was slow and tender, but as his kisses grew in intensity she did nothing to stop him.

After, they walked to his place and she went willingly inside. 'Oh Poll,' he groaned as she snuggled into his arms.

'We're together now Jack,' she said. 'Everything in common, share and share alike. I belong body and soul to you now.'

He regarded her for a second. 'But you said . . .' he began.

'I said a lot of things,' she admitted, 'but that was before you told me you loved me. I trust you, Jack. You're a man who keeps his promises.'

He kissed her again and after a while he lifted her onto his bed.

'Share and share alike,' he said, a smile tugging at the corners of his mouth.

She nodded. 'That's right, Jack.'

'Then what's the secret ingredient in your pies, Poll?'

She cuffed his shoulder playfully then surrendered herself to the man she loved.

Can love find a way
to overcome hate?

An unexpected letter will change her life forever. . .

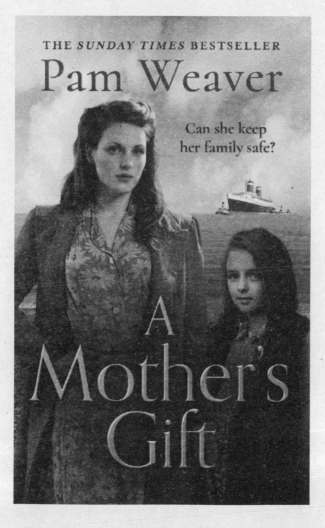

THE *SUNDAY TIMES* BESTSELLER

Pam Weaver

Can she keep
her family safe?

A
Mother's
Gift

Available in paperback, ebook and audiobook now.